Chapter One

Katie Sutherland ached to slam her foot against the gas pedal and get this night over with. Instead, she was forced to inch along, captive in the endless procession of traffic, while the Colorado sky dumped a whole season's worth of snow onto the freeway.

Her nerves were worsening by the moment. She was already dreading the torturous questions she would face at the wedding—the major downfall to being a guest and not the bride. Those same stupid questions... "Why aren't you married yet?" and, of course, "How come you don't have a boyfriend?" Katie felt certain these questions were meant to be malicious. After all, what would they expect her to say? *"My genital warts keep flaring up and I just can't keep from scratching—until the swelling goes down, I've had to give up dating."*

That would give those biddies from the old neighborhood a nice, juicy piece of gossip to salivate over. At least the talk would be different from the usual *"Hasn't Katie Sutherland turned out to be quite a beauty? I swear, with that gorgeous long hair and those green eyes, she is the spitting image of her mother. By the way, has anyone heard anything from Karen?"* Of course, no one would have heard from Katie's mother, and since that subject had been exploited ad nauseam over the years, they would keep their focus on Katie.

"Can you believe she isn't married yet? For goodness sake, even poor Penny Harwood, the hunchback—too bad her family was never able to get that fixed—was able to catch herself a nice husband—despite her underactive thyroid."

"You don't suppose she's one of those lesbians, do you?"

1

"She's too pretty to be a lesbian. I think she's just irresponsible. Girls that close to thirty have no business being single...unless they have some kind of deformity."

"Didn't you just hear me about Penny Harwood?"

Katie shook her head, trying to clear out the phantom conversations. She'd be hearing them for real soon enough. There was no way to avoid the condescension of these Barbara Bush look-alikes. Two things she knew about gossiping old maids: 1) They thrived on weddings and funerals, and 2) they were the source of her longtime trepidation of both. *I hate blue hairs, I hate blue hairs, yes I do, I do, I do...* Katie chanted the mantra to the tune of Neil Young's "Heart of Gold" as she beat her thumbs in time against the steering wheel.

For Christopher Evans—aka Mom, her surrogate brother—she would endure. And for Heather, though she hadn't met her yet, unless about a million phone conversations in preparation for this wedding counted. Why Heather had agreed to get married in Christopher's hometown was beyond Katie, but it proved Heather's affection for him was genuine. Not many women would abandon friends and family to move to their husband's hometown. Her devotion to Christopher's happiness automatically won Katie's allegiance.

An aggravating testament to Christopher's affable personality, the parking lot was already overflowing with vehicles by the time Katie maneuvered her charcoal Jeep Liberty—Rhett Butler, as she liked to call it—into one of the few remaining stalls. Placing a hand over her abdomen, she felt dread the size of a blue ribbon pomegranate settle in the pit of her stomach. She drew in one long, confidence-building breath before wrestling a cumbersome present out of the Jeep, then blazed a trail to the rear of the building.

The ornate door was much heavier than Katie imagined. When she pulled, it teased her by cracking open just a couple of inches. Shifting the present to her hip, she gave a hard, determined tug. At that exact moment, someone pushed it open from the inside. Propelled backward, Katie let out a surprised yelp and toppled over and down the bank built up from a winter's worth of snow-blowing. The heavy gift landed with an excruciating thud on her abdomen before sliding off to the side.

Upside down and fighting to catch the wind that had been knocked out of her, she heard footsteps hustling through the snow toward her. Blinking to restore her vision, she felt something, either snot or blood, dribble from her nose.

"Katie, are you all right? I'm so sorry." Sliding down to his knees beside her, mindless of his tuxedo, Christopher began digging her from her snow crater.

Minutes crept by before she could gather enough breath to respond.

"What the hell?" She dabbed the annoying drip under her nose with the back of her hand. She analyzed the smear—blood. She must have smacked herself in the face during her tumble. Not that she was in pain. Other than her throbbing gut, she just felt the nip of the zinging cold.

Christopher stifled a smile and offered her a hand, yanking her to her feet. As she brushed the snow from her body and pulled brown sugar-colored strands of hair from her eyes, she briefly noticed Christopher's friend, hovering as if he would like to help but didn't know how.

Christopher bent down to retrieve the mangled gift-wrapped package. "Criminy, Katie, what have you got in here?"

She tried not to show how pleased she was with herself. "Let's just say, after this disaster, nobody is ever getting his-and-hers bowling balls from me again."

"Really?" He snatched her off her feet into a big bear hug. "You're the best!"

Considering she was still trying to get him to take up the sport, she couldn't have asked for a better reaction.

"Well, what are friends for?"

He didn't answer, and Katie feared he might view the silence as an opportunity to get all wedding sentimental on her.

"There's snow melting in my boots." She cut through the snow back to her car.

"Sure there is." Christopher grinned. "Kate, this is my buddy, Jared Stone." He gestured to his companion as they followed in her tracks. "We were roommates in college one of the years you were playing abroad."

"Studying," she corrected.

He rolled his eyes. "Whatever. Jared's my best man."

"Duh. I know that. Who helped you plan your part of the wedding? Um, pretty sure that was me."

She stopped on the pavement and offered her hand to Jared. Then she took notice of him. The man was pure beefcake!

"It's nice to have a face to put with your name. Chris has told me so many stories about you." Jared held an almost too-tight grip on her hand as he flashed a perfect Colgate smile.

Certain that these "stories" couldn't have been flattering depictions, she shot Christopher the evil eye. He shrugged, giving her a sheepish smile. Next to his vertically inferior friend, Christopher looked like a floppy-haired beanpole.

"Nice to meet you, too." She gave Jared another once-over. He might be attractive in a Vin Diesel sort of way, but his shaved head couldn't camouflage the faint band of his receding hairline. And he might not have been as short as he seemed, but his ripped muscles created the optical illusion of being almost as wide as he was tall.

"Kate, I'm so glad you're not late," Christopher said. Before she could launch her defense, he added, "I didn't mean it like that. I mean that my mom is being—"

"She's being your *mother,*" Katie grimaced.

"Yes, and Heather doesn't quite know how to deal with her."

Does anybody? "Got it. I'll come help as soon as I change my socks and get a tissue." She wiped another smear of blood across the back of her finger.

Christopher breathed a sigh of relief. "I'm glad you're here."

Katie felt the deeper meaning in his words. Checking the emotion rising in her throat, she nodded, unable to meet his eyes.

"I mean it, Kate. It's really important to me that you're a part of this day." He took a step closer. "Even though I'm getting married, nothing's going to change—you know that, right?"

Katie gave him a tight smile. "Yeah, I know." She wanted nothing more than for him to be right, but she knew he wasn't. How could things *not* change?

As if he could read her mind, because he usually could, Christopher put his hands on her shoulders, forcing her to look up at

5

him. "I'm sorry you and Heather haven't been able to meet in person before today. But trust me—the two of you are going to be great friends."

She was confident Christopher really meant that, but she wasn't confident he was right. "I'm sure we will. Heather seems really great."

He pulled her into a satisfied hug, then released her. "So, you happy to be here?" His grin stretched from one ear to the other.

"Of course I am." Her smile hadn't relaxed any. "I wouldn't miss your wedding for anything." She fidgeted beneath the pressure of his cockeyed stare-down before he broke into a laugh. Jared gaped at him as if he were not only rude, but also insane. But Katie took it all in stride.

"What? I am, I promise."

"You've always been a crappy liar." Christopher chuckled the rest of the way to the car.

Katie flipped open Rhett Butler's tailgate and a heap of clothes fell out onto Jared's foot. Pushing aside another mound of wardrobe, she hoisted herself backward into the cargo area and rummaged through an open brown duffle bag that resembled an overstuffed baked potato. Retrieving a packet of wet wipes, she cleaned her hands and nose then found a dry pair of socks.

"Kate, what is all this?" Christopher sorted through the pile of bikini tops, board shorts, long thermal underwear, and an ultra-thick neoprene farmer john wetsuit Jared had retrieved from the snow and replaced inside the vehicle.

"I'm going scuba diving tonight—in that thermal lake past Pagosa Springs." Katie snatched the bikini top that dangled from

Christopher's forefinger. "I wasn't sure what to wear scuba diving in a thermal lake in the middle of the winter—bathing suit or wet suit."

"But you have four seasons' worth of clothing back here."

"At least I'll be prepared."

"It's too dangerous to dive so late at night. That's a long drive from here."

Katie rolled her eyes. "Relax. I'm just leaving tonight and we don't dive until first light."

"Who are you going with?"

Mother Hen finally makes his appearance! Draping her damp socks over the backseat, she put her boots back on and hopped out of the car. "Listen, Mom, don't you have enough to worry about tonight? She slammed the tailgate shut. "Just because you've decided to move back home doesn't mean you get to have input in my life."

"Someone has to guide you. You don't have parents anymore."

Katie could almost feel her confidence deflate into an uncomfortable wad at the pit of her stomach.

Jared cast her a sympathetic look. "I'm sorry for your loss," he spoke in a solemn tone that seemed more practiced than sincere.

Katie laughed out loud. "Who are you, FBI?"

He beamed. "Not yet. Soon, I hope."

"Katie's parents aren't dead, Jared," Christopher explained. "They've just retired from parenting."

"Oh brother," she sighed. "I don't need parenting—I'm old enough to take care of myself, thank you very much."

"Yeah, but they retired when you were in the seventh grade," Christopher snorted. "And I hate to break it to you, Kate, but you'll never be old enough to take care of yourself."

7

"Whatever." Turning to Jared, she wondered exactly how much Christopher had told him. "I guess Christopher's told you my story?"

Jared squirmed as if he had an itch he couldn't scratch. "Sort of."

"Well, let me fill in the rest of the details." Why not? Obviously Christopher didn't have a problem sharing Katie's personal life with people who didn't know her—so why should she withhold? "I was an accidental baby, born eleven years after the younger of my two brothers. By the time I was thirteen, both my brothers had already finished college, and, unlike Christopher, didn't bring their wives back home to live. Instead, they moved to different corners of the country to build their lives. With the two boys raised and gone, my mother decided it was time to take a break from child rearing. So, she sent me down the street to live with Christopher's family while she and my father spent six weeks in Australia. They loved it so much, they cashed in some of their investments and bought a townhome on the Gold Coast." She flipped a strand of hair behind her shoulder. "Anyway, they're not big fans of the snow, so they spend the winters in Australia and sometimes come back to Colorado for the summers."

Jared looked impressed. "So, I guess you've spent a lot of Christmases in Australia? What was that like—not having snow at Christmas?"

What is he, an ask-it basket? Katie pelted Christopher with the evil eye. "Well," she began once she'd acquired an apologetic look from Christopher, "I wouldn't know. I've only been there a couple times, and never for Christmas. I mean, with the school breaks being so short, it was better to just spend the holidays at home with the Evans'."

8

She gave Christopher a playful but not gentle punch in the shoulder. "Why are we out here discussing my dysfunctional parents when yours are inside, unsupervised and alone with the soon-to-be in-laws?"

The rosy color drained from Christopher's face. Without another word, he placed a death grip around Katie's wrist and took off, towing her at warp speed, leaving Jared to close up the car and bring in the precarious, soggy box of bowling balls.

Katie took a moment to enjoy the warmth of the wedding hall. Then, she took in the calm—it was *too* calm. That's when she heard Sheila stalking from the room. She recognized the threat of Sheila Evans' clipped steps to stomp over anyone foolish enough to stand in her way. Katie remembered the sound of that determined gait from long ago, when she and Christopher were still in high school. They had returned home just in time to witness Sheila slap divorce papers on the kitchen table and march out the front door in pursuit of her Hollywood career.

Katie shook herself free of the memory in order to concentrate on Heather's well-being. Upon further survey of the room, she spotted Heather, sitting alone on the steps of an old wooden staircase, the centerpiece of what seemed a giant satin bundt cake. A tight pucker in her forehead revealed that she was straining to keep her eyes open far too wide. It was the face of a woman trying her hardest not to cry.

Katie looked to Christopher for direction. Mouth open, mouth closed, mouth open, mouth closed was all Christopher offered. Typical. She had to do something. Sheila was carrying a full head of steam, Heather was looking like Shell-Shocked Barbie, and Christopher was suffering a case of paralysis by cowardice. Katie made a quick triage of the situation. Where had Sheila gone? *She would have to be found and contained.* Christopher was useless. *He was just going to have to grow a pair.* Nothing she could do to help there. So, she went to work on the most critical problem.

As a woman who couldn't apply foundation to save her life, Katie noticed Heather's exquisite makeup. To have a face that perfect would have cost a fortune or taken hours to apply. Either way, tears would be a catastrophe. Katie pried the twisted wedding program from Heather's hands and fanned the bride's face. She spoke in confident, reassuring tones.

"Hi Heather, it's nice to meet you at last. I'm Katie."

Heather nodded, inhaling an unnatural, long breath. "That outfit. Did you see what she was wearing?" she whimpered.

Katie took hold of Heather's cold, trembling hand. "Listen, I know you think your soon-to-be mother-in-law is a crazy shrew…and you're right—she is."

"Katie!" Christopher found his voice. "You're not helping!"

"Shhh!" Katie demanded. "Let me finish. She's about to take the biggest step of her life. She deserves to understand her mother-in-law is a diva."

The wary bride seemed to be studying Katie. "Thank you." Squeezing Katie's hand for support, she turned to Christopher with imploring eyes. "Is it too late to elope? She's evil."

His eyes glistened and his words still failed him.

Katie felt a surge of panic as she pictured Heather bolting out the door and Christopher giving her the silent treatment for the next forty years. "She's not evil—far from it," she counseled with much more calmness than she felt. "The woman took me in and raised me like a daughter. That's not evil. Sheila's become a whack-job, sure, but you will grow to love her. Once you get past her Hollywood-induced eccentricities, you'll find she's still a very lovable person."

Heather gave an unbecoming snort.

"Okay, well, you're going to *like* her—eventually. Until then, take comfort in the fact that if Christopher's mother played a significant role in his life, you would have been exposed to her bitchy tendencies long before today."

Heather nodded as if Katie's logic made sense.

Katie pressed on. "Listen, let me handle things with Sheila. I was raised by Crazy—before she turned crazy—and I'm sure that's just an extended mid-life crisis. Anyway, I'm used to dealing with her." *I don't know how to manage her, but I am used to dealing with her.*

Biting her lip, Heather finally broke out into a welcome, though unexpected, laugh. "You're on. If you can keep her under control tonight, I think I'll worship you even more than Christopher does."

Heather's acknowledgment was as artless as if it came from a friend, not an angry Bridezilla. Katie chuckled. "I'll take on that challenge. You and Christopher enjoy your special day—I'll do my part to clear away the obstacles."

"Thanks, Katie. And not just for running interference—I couldn't have planned this long-distance wedding without you." Heather's smile was truly sweet. She could see Christopher being happy with a woman who smiled like that.

"My pleasure." Katie was happy to find she actually meant that.

Christopher squared his shoulders and took a step toward Heather. "So, what has my mother done?"

"If she didn't like the dresses I chose for the mothers to wear, she should have told me before today. Instead, she insists on wearing something way different. More than inappropriate—it's hideous!" Heather zeroed in on Katie with expectant eyes.

Damn. She's really going to hold me to this. "All right, I'll go talk to her. Where is she?"

"She's in the groom's room, with Jim."

Katie spun around to Christopher and met his bug-eyes.

"What? What's the matter?" Heather demanded.

Christopher dashed down the corridor toward the groom's dressing room.

"We try not to leave Christopher parents alone together," Katie informed her. "They still have a lot of unresolved issues. Sometimes it turns into a screaming match and Sheila storms off, crying. The next time we see her, she's three sheets to the wind and reeking like a booze tanker."

***

Sheila's voice, shrill and hysterical, pierced through the crack beneath the door. Katie didn't have to listen to the words to know she was harping on Jim for some shortcoming or another. She brushed past Jared, who stood gaping, frozen in mid-knock, and gave a sharp rap at the door before pushing into the room without an invitation.

"Katie-Bug!" Sheila clacked her death-defying stilettos across the hardwood floor, extending her arms. Katie cringed in anticipation of what was to come: a hollow hug that would leave enough space between them to harbor a St. Bernard, two lipsticky *mwah-mwahs* on

12

both cheeks, and—worst of all—held at a distance for inspection while Sheila pinched around at the jiggly backs of her arms just above the elbows.

"How's your mother, darling? I haven't seen her in ages."

Katie saw the hurt flash behind Sheila's eyes at being neglected by her friend. *Big surprise!* she wanted to scream. *And stop touching my back-arm flab!* "She's good. I haven't spoken with her for a few weeks…they're still on the Coast, but I know they wanted to be here." Katie forced a smile around the lie she knew nobody believed.

"Of course, darling, we know nothing can tempt Bill and Karen away from their warm, beautiful beach before they're ready."

Not my sixteenth, seventeenth, or eighteenth birthday…or the Junior Prom, the SATs, or the car accident that put me in the hospital for three days.

"There's my favorite girl!" Jim Evans intervened, giving Katie a quick kiss on the cheek. "How have you been doing, Katie-Bug? I haven't heard from you in a while."

Katie didn't answer but latched him into an affectionate hug, comforted by his familiar Irish Spring scent.

Christopher moved behind his mother and waved Heather and Jared in from the doorway. "All right, Mom, time for you to get ready. The ceremony will be starting soon."

"But darling, I am ready." Sheila turned to face her son and ran a hand down the length of her body, as if he had missed the sight of her.

Katie flexed her triceps a few times, vowing, as she always did after a Sheila encounter, to begin toning. She didn't need to see Sheila's face to know her lips were contorted into a thin, forced smile,

13

her expression serene, each slow blink exaggerated. Any Sheila novice would mistake this look for that of a reasonable person, but if Christopher pushed the issue, her mascara-caked lashes would gain rapid momentum, enough to launch a full-blown tirade.

"Mother, you're not wearing that dress to my wedding," Christopher insisted.

Katie was so used to Sheila's eccentric style she hadn't noticed the long, glamorous toga she was wearing. The golden gown, open in front and plunging in the back, stopped mid-right thigh before flowing down the left leg to the floor. Her hair was pulled high so that the bouquet of wild blonde curls spouting from the top of her head made her look like a soap opera star on Emmy night. She was, no doubt, ecstatic by this achievement. Sheila had spent the last twelve seasons as the leading villainous vixen on *Love's Lionesses*—but this was not Emmy night.

Katie noticed Heather gaping in horror at the six-inch golden stilettos and understood why she would want the outfit banned from her wedding line.

"Where is the dress Heather had made for you?" Christopher demanded.

"Oh, that. I gave it to Goodwill. It made me look too much like a mother and it was so…so *plain*. And black."

Christopher bit his lip. "That was the point. Simple and black, like everyone else—except the bride. And I hate to break it to you, but you *are* a mother—*my* mother."

"Yes, of course, darling. But honestly, if the tabloids got hold of pictures of me in that dress…it would be career suicide!"

14

"Mother, this is my wedding. Please, for once, don't be the center of attention."

Whether Shelia was acting or truly offended, Katie couldn't tell, but Sheila's back went ramrod straight, which meant Christopher had clearly struck a nerve.

"But I tried so hard...." Sheila's eyelids fluttered—her method of producing tears.

Christopher stood his ground. "Mother, I will throw you out before I let you attend my wedding in that dress."

Sheila's fluttering eyelids froze mid-blink.

Yay, Christopher! You grew that pair just in time! Katie noticed she wasn't the only one rooting for Christopher. Jim was beaming at his son, and Heather radiated adoration.

"You wouldn't!" Sheila exclaimed.

"I would."

Sheila seemed to consider her options for just a moment, and then a reluctant look of contrition seeped into her face. Maybe even a real one—not the overdramatized kind that veiled a truly sinister plan and could be seen worn by Eve St. Sebastian, her character on *Love's Lionesses,* every Monday through Friday afternoon.

"I don't have anything black to wear."

Christopher looked again at his watch. "Well, Mother, we'll have to put our heads together, and quickly, and try to figure something out."

Sheila scavenged the room with her eyes. The stunning but devious Eve St. Sebastian smile emerged as she spotted Katie. "Katie-Bug! I looove your top! Darling, who's the designer?"

"Ummm..." Katie knew there was no safe answer.

Every eye in the room darted to the smoke-colored teardrop beads that shimmied and taunted from her black blouse. She took two instinctive paces backward.

"Oh, no! No, no, no waaay. Don't think for one second I would consider putting even one foot in that thing—that dress."

Sheila's eyes narrowed with ferocity. "This happens to be a Vera Wang original!"

Katie cowered behind the protection of Jared's wide, ripped shoulders.

"I agree with Katie." Jim stepped demonstratively over an imaginary line that separated Katie and Jared from the rest. "Sheila, you can't expect someone to bail you out every time you indulge in one of your whims."

Sheila responded as she did whenever he tried to get principled on her—by pretending he'd said nothing at all. Instead, she waited for Katie to peep her head out from behind Jared's back and gripped her with a pleading gaze.

"Sheila, I can't. Don't ask me…please," Katie begged. Reacting to the wariness in her voice, Jared reached back and rubbed her arm.

"Katie-Bug, remember when the other kids teased you about your boobies?" She feigned sympathetic eyes. "Who took you shopping for your first bra? Remember how scared you were when you started your period? Who held a slumber party to celebrate your womanhood and taught you the secret of tampons?"

"You did," Katie reluctantly conceded.

"Exactly. Katie, you never would have made it through puberty without me. Now, all I'm asking is one tiny favor so I can be a part of my only son's wedding."

Katie hung her head with the proper mixture of guilt and mortification, and gaped at the strappy golden spikes laced across the actress's feet.

"I can't…those shoes! And your feet are a size bigger than mine."

"That's absurd!" Sheila flinched at the accusation.

"Come on, Sheila, this isn't fair," Jim rose to Katie's defense. "She'll break her neck trying to walk in those ridiculous shoes."

"These are not ridiculous shoes! These are $900 Manolos!"

"Don't you have something else shoved in the back of your car that you could wear?" Christopher suggested to Katie.

"Why would I bring dress clothes to go scuba diving?"

"I don't know…maybe for the same reason you're bringing a guitar you don't remember how to play."

"I thought I might have time to practice between dives." Katie tipped her chin, challenging him to disbelieve.

He made a sound that wasn't quite a laugh and turned his attention back to the argument ensuing between his parents over the unnecessary extravagance of $900 shoes.

"Okay, here's what's going to happen," Christopher's uncharacteristic sternness quieted the room. "Jared is going to keep Katie from injuring herself. You wouldn't mind lending Katie your arm for the evening, would you, buddy?"

"Of course not," Jared agreed with a little too much enthusiasm for Katie's liking.

"What about me?" Katie demanded. "Maybe I don't want to stumble around all evening looking like a drunken, gold-dipped Aphrodite!" She forced herself to look her assailants in the eyes and noticed Heather nodding in absolute agreement. Katie felt a pang of responsibility. After all, Heather did brave a Colorado wedding and Hurricane Sheila for Christopher's sake. And Katie did promise to keep things right.

"Never mind, I'll do it."

Chapter Two

Were it possible to die of mortification, Katie would have croaked right there in the chapel. Sheila's iconic Hollywood gown clung to Katie's curves tighter than Saran Wrap, giving her the appearance of a six-foot-tall Academy Award. If that weren't humiliating enough, the across-the-front halter left a gaping cleavage-hole that had Katie feeling way too exposed. She feared that one misstep in her oversized Manolos was all it would take to jiggle a boob right out of the opening.

She gripped Jared's bicep so tightly that her knuckles turned white as she advanced past the almost two hundred seated people to take her place in the second row. They hadn't even made it halfway down the aisle when the old lady whispers of Janice and Beverly Martin began to ricochet through the chapel.

"I'm surprised to see little Katie Sutherland in such a provocative outfit."

"She's not so little anymore. She's got to be close to thirty now."

"Still, it's not like her to be so inappropriately dressed…though doesn't she look glamorous?"

"For the life of me, I can't figure that girl out. She should be married with a couple of babies by now. With those curves, it's clear the good Lord intended her to be rearing children, not parading around like some high-dollar prostitute."

Her step faltered and Jared wrapped a boa constrictor hold around her waist, supporting her so she had almost no weight on her precarious legs. She gave him a weak smile, trying not to notice the ghosts of high school past and the strangers present gawking at her. As the cesspool of gossip gurgled up around them, she had to force herself not to flounder in it as she finished her trek down the aisle.

"What in the world are you wearing?" an astonished whisper from the row behind warmed her ear.

Katie turned her head toward the familiar mocking voice. "Don't ask." Her heart was racing too fast to attempt conversation with Anna, her ultra-pregnant best friend.

"Don't worry about the old lady Martins." Rob, Anna's husband, warmed her other ear. "Like they have room to talk. They're ancient spinsters. We don't care if you look like a prostitute—we think you look hot."

Katie turned in his direction and noticed a few other loyal friends, including her dear pal Dylan, all nodding in agreement.

"I can't believe you would think to wear something like this to Christopher's wedding!" Anna said. "You've got major *cajones.*"

Katie snapped her head back toward her. "I wouldn't be wearing this dress if it weren't for Christopher." She guarded her abdomen with crossed arms. "I hate it—it shows my Little Buddha."

"Believe me, no one is looking at your belly. Who's the dude?" Anna flicked her chin toward Jared, taking his place next to Christopher at the front of the chapel.

"That's Christopher's college buddy—Jared Stone."

Anna sported her favorite menacing grin and offered one of her annoying *hmmms,* which were always laced with many layers of meaning.

The organ roared to life, announcing the bride's grand entrance. Katie couldn't help but feel proud for Christopher. Heather was an ethereal beauty who seemed to float toward him, her excited pace telling the world she couldn't float fast enough. She stopped for an infinitesimal moment to honor Katie with a warm smile. It was a bull's-eye to the heart. Katie's smile sprung to life on its own volition and was as heartfelt as if she were smiling at a sister.

As Katie listened to Christopher and Heather exchange vows, she felt certain she wasn't losing her Christopher, but adding Heather to her patchwork family. Despite gaining that comfort, Katie couldn't shake the curious feeling of emptiness that filled her chest.

After the chapel had almost cleared, Katie and Anna were still seated, sniffing and dabbing their eyes.

"Well, Dylan, I guess we should get these two crybabies to the dining room," Rob suggested. Bringing his arms in front of him in a long, exaggerated stretch, he gave Katie a playful shove. "I'm starving, and the sooner everyone gets seated, the sooner we eat. You take lumpy here," he smiled down at his pregnant wife, then glanced at Katie. "And I'll take C-3PO."

"No way! You take the Round One," Dylan joked.

"Ow!" they both cried as Anna bit one, then the other on the arm—a defense she'd been using since the third grade. Katie rubbed her arm, thinking how much less it hurt back then when Anna was missing most of her front teeth.

"Come on, man, it's always been my boyhood dream to have a life-size *Star Wars* action figure." Rob picked up both of Katie's arms and began to work them in violent punching motions, making the accompanying sound effects.

"And I've always wanted to be seen with a high-dollar prostitute," Dylan replied.

Katie wanted to laugh, but she couldn't, not with Jared standing at the front of the chapel boring his gaze into her.

Anna stood and grabbed Katie's arm, dragging her into the aisle, "Let's go. These two can stay here and play out their sick fantasies."

"This couldn't get any more perfect! It's like Christmas morning!" Rob howled with delight. "Tell me they don't look like C-3PO and R2-D2 standing there together." Tossing the little point-and-shoot camera he kept in his jacket pocket to Dylan, he shimmied in between the two women. "Dyl, get a picture of me with the two droids, will ya?"

Dylan obliged, extracting a promise from Rob to return the favor.

No sooner had Rob and Dylan swapped places than a tense arm curled around Katie's waist, pulling her away from the others.

"Come on, Katie, I'll help you to your table," Jared plowed into the moment.

"Um…uh…okay," Katie mumbled, distracted by her friends' conspicuous glances.

"See you at dinner, 3PO." Rob saluted, making no attempt to hide his smile.

Maybe if Jared displayed some conversational skills, Katie wouldn't have felt her breasts beginning to sag with age. But he didn't. He just wore a dopey grin, and Katie couldn't shake the feeling she'd squandered years instead of seconds in his company.

"Thanks." Katie forced a smile at Jared as he insisted on helping her into her seat.

Jared nodded. "You're welcome."

He's not leaving? Why isn't he leaving? He lingered statue-still and silent by her side—very Secret Service-like—until the lights dimmed and he was obligated to take his place among the bridesmaids and other groomsmen.

Anna put her hands to her mouth as if she were talking into a radio. "Pshhttt, Captain, it looks like the golden nugget has encountered a Klingon."

Laughter exploded from the table. Seated two tables in front, Heather's sister shot them angry glares and shushes. Her directorial debut, *The Life and Times of Christopher and Heather,* was about to start, and she was bent on having a captive audience for the soul-sucking slideshow. But Anna's attention span was gobbled up before Christopher had reached puberty. "So, I learned through the grapevine that your Klingon friend is a cop," she whispered.

"That explains a lot," Katie murmured.

"He's kind of hot, don't you think?" Anna studied the tablecloth, pretending to be casual.

"Not hot enough to hold this conversation." Katie was not oblivious to the eavesdroppers around the table and hoped to rip all speculations out by the roots. However, Anna bulldozed right over the "case closed" vibe.

"What's wrong with this one?"

"Nothing, he's just not my type."

"Oh jeez." Anna rolled her eyes. "Your type only exists in your imagination."

Katie pretended to be enthralled by the slideshow.

"So what makes this one *not* your type?" Dylan joined in.

23

Katie threw a scowl at him and hissed, "Nothing—he just isn't, okay?"

"Maybe she's worried he'll be a Mr. Cheapskate," Rob scoffed.

For the benefit of those who weren't laughing, Anna explained the inside joke. "Katie made the unfortunate mistake of accepting a date with the ultimate cheapskate."

"I'm pretty sure Rob's mother guilted me into going on a blind date with him," Katie corrected.

"Anyway, he insisted they go to a country-themed restaurant—the kind frequented by senior citizens." Having laughed over it a million times, Anna knew this story as if it were her own. "He announced—not just to Katie, but the entire restaurant—that he didn't have much money, so they would have to share a platter of nachos. So Katie offers to pay, right? And Mr. Cheapskate gets super pissed and reminds her that he's a 'gentleman.'"

"Anna, nobody wants to hear this story," Katie interrupted, trying to head off another game inspired by her dating disasters.

Encouraged by everyone else's goading, Anna charged on. "I don't think he'd ever read any sort of manual on gentlemanliness, because when the nachos came, he just dug right in without even offering her any. Every time he took a chip, he held it up high, hunched down, and chased the tail of cheese with his mouth, letting his tongue wag in the air until the food made contact." She made a demonstration of the movements. "Then, he'd wrestle the nacho into his mouth with his tongue, chew twice, and swallow."

Katie pictured the scene as if she were again reliving the moment and shuddered.

"The most disgusting part," Anna howled, "is that he cleaned his fingers by poking each one into his mouth."

Katie could feel the pressure of at least ten different pairs of eyes studying her. She forced a lighthearted laugh. "Okay, enough."

"I'm not done!"

"Did you guys ever hear about Mr. Sweatpants?" Rob asked, eager to keep the table laughter going.

"He was a nice guy," Anna said. "You should have given him a chance."

"He shouldn't have worn sweatpants on a first date," Katie said.

"Tell the one about the Bounty Hunter," Dylan hooted.

"My favorite is the Sex-Crazed Security Guard," Rob howled.

"That is still the most disturbing blind-date memory I have." Katie shuddered. "And we're not sharing it."

"Oh, come on, Katie," Dylan pleaded. "It's hilarious."

"No."

Though her friends respected her wishes on that story, they had no regard for the ones about the Mullet Man, the Stalking Stock Broker, or the ever-popular Gangsta Julian.

When the lights finally flicked back on after the slideshow, lolling heads around the room bolted upright as if they'd been wide awake and one hundred percent captivated. There was a collective sigh of gratitude, but no one felt the relief more than Katie. The others may have been enjoying a good laugh at her expense, but all she saw were flashbacks of a decade of failed relationships.

"Hallelujah!" Anna rejoiced. "Just in case this is only an intermission, Rob and I are making a run for it." She shot up, tugging at Rob's arm. "Bye everyone. Sorry, Dyls, we didn't get to chat more, but I'd rather eat this baby's placenta then sit another minute. Talk to you tomorrow, Katie."

Though it wasn't just an intermission, the rest of the group followed Anna's example and peeled away from the table couple by couple, leaving just Katie and Dylan. She scooted over a couple of seats and edged up to him, grateful to have a one-on-one, as opposed to a dozen-against-one, conversation.

"Finally, I have you all to myself," Katie said. "We need to do some serious catching up."

His face contorted into a guilty frown. "I don't have that long. I've got to get a taxi to the airport. I'm taking the redeye back to D.C. tonight."

Her eyebrows sprung up in mock admiration. "My, when did you get to be so important, Mr. Political Advisor to the Morally Defunct? Are you seeing anyone yet?"

Dylan, though straight, was more effeminate than Katie and Anna put together. Perfect red circles now flared at the top of his pale fleshy cheeks. "No, I've told you a thousand times, I don't have time for women. I need to focus on my career—Senator Henson is a good stepping stone for me."

"Okay, okay." Katie patted his arm. Dylan's tender feelings were extra sensitive this evening. "Just remember us little people when you've become the wildly important crap cleaner-upper to all of Satan's most prominent senators."

"Just the ones who support good policies," he corrected. "And Katie, I could never forget you—even if I tried."

She flashed him her grandest smile.

26

Dylan giggled at her obvious wiles, unable to resist bringing her in for a hug. "Oh, Katie, I've missed you!"

She nestled into the crook of his shoulder. Noticing he had the subtle scent of the Burberry cologne he'd worn since high school, she felt nostalgic for his company.

"Let me take you to the airport. I never get to see you anymore."

Dylan considered the offer for a moment. "I wouldn't dream of taking you away from Christopher's wedding. He'd be crushed."

"He'll be fine."

"Then your stalker will be crushed." Dylan nodded toward Jared, who was making his way toward them.

"Stop it." She choked on a laugh. "I want to take you—it's what I want to do the most tonight." Although she was being playful, she couldn't have been more sincere. He tried to speak, but she clamped her hand over his mouth. "Shut up. I'm taking you." She stared him down until he gave her an affirmative nod.

"Where are you going?" Jared asked, seeming a bit territorial.

"I'm driving Dylan to the airport."

"Oh." His eyes fell with the disappointment of a boy whose dog had just run away.

Dylan made a quick study of Jared before deciding to push away from the table. Ignoring Katie's silent plea for him not to leave, he announced, "I'm going to go make a call and check on my flight. Katie, I'll catch up with you when it's time to leave."

Before Dylan could step away, Jared was already asking Katie to dance.

"I'm not much of a dancer." She wasn't lying—she'd never be a natural on a dance floor.

"Neither am I." Jared flashed his perfect Colgate grin, which she felt generous to admit was his one endearing quality, as she didn't really consider beefcake an asset.

As U2's "With or Without You" played, his clumsy hands fumbled against her hips while he swayed her back and forth. She could almost feel the sweat from his hot palms seeping through her dress, and she knew they resembled that one prom couple where the boy is a solid four inches shorter than the girl.

Planting her feet, she wiggled out of Jared's hold and carefully removed her heels. "That's better," she sighed. Happy to once again be her comfortable, five-foot-six self, she looped her arms back around his neck.

"Tons better," he admitted. "I was starting to get a Napoleon complex."

Katie grinned up at him, thinking there was a lot more truth to that statement than Jared cared to acknowledge.

The song ended, and Jared made no indication to dismiss her to her table. He held her tightly even though a fast, jazzy waltz had intimidated the majority of the young dancers off the floor. Jared should have had enough sense to let it intimidate him as well.

"May I cut in? I'd like to have a turn with my favorite partner." Jim, the merciful angel, interrupted their dance. "Step aside, son, and let me show you how it's done."

She would have enjoyed the dance and the rare moment to catch up with Jim if she hadn't been so aware of Jared leaning against a wall, watching her with puppy dog eyes. She happened to notice

Dylan approach him, say something, then nod in her direction. Jared returned the nod, but kept his eyes trained on Katie. Her back stiffened. She did not appreciate being the topic du jour.

As soon as the dance ended, she shoved her shoes back on and clunked toward them, set on putting an end to their fraternizing. "Hey Dyls, what's going on?" She came to a wobbly stop by his side.

He put a steadying arm around her waist. "My flight has been delayed a couple of hours because of the storms."

"That's great! Now we can have more time to visit—maybe do something before you go?"

"What about your scuba diving trip?" Jared interrupted.

"I'll have plenty of time to do both." Her too-bright smile did nothing to hide the scowl festering under her brow.

"I don't think it's a good idea to be driving across the state in this weather, especially through the night," Jared said, more to Dylan than Katie.

Katie's fake smile faltered. *That strapping little pest is sabotaging my trip on purpose!*

"Katie…" Dylan began in his reprimanding tone, "if it were safe to be traveling in these conditions, I would be able to get on a plane back to Washington."

"I'll be fine. Rhett Butler has four-wheel drive and I have enough Mountain Dew to keep me up all night."

"Who's Rhett Butler?" Jared asked.

Katie looked away. *Anyone who didn't know about Rhett Butler didn't deserve to be enlightened.*

"That's the name ol' Scarlett here gave her car." Dylan jerked a thumb toward Katie. "Aptly named," he flashed quotation marks with his fingers as he gave his Katie impersonation, "for its sleek nature, rugged design, and the ability to rescue her from the monotony of daily life."

Katie folded her arms across her chest. "Ha ha. Don't forget the only one who truly appreciates my independent nature."

Jared seemed confused whether they were still talking about a car or a man, but it was clear he disliked this Rhett Butler, and changed the subject. "So, you're still planning to go?"

Katie and Dylan answered in unison: "Yes." "No."

Their glares challenged one another until a devious glint stole into Dylan's eyes and a villainous smile replaced the set line of his mouth. "You're going to have to make a choice: hang out with me until my flight leaves or go scuba diving."

"What? Are you serious?" Katie exhaled her annoyance.

"I'm very serious. I'm not going to hang out with you if you plan on driving through the night in this weather. I don't want to feel responsible if anything happens."

She gave a little chuckle. "Damn it, Dylan, why did you have to give me an ultimatum? You know that just makes me want to jump in my car and hit the road even more."

Dylan shrugged. "I know. I'm just testing your devotion."

"Dylan, I am hopelessly devoted to you." Without missing a beat, she began belting the song "Hopelessly Devoted to You" in her best Olivia Newton-John impression, using Dylan's thumb for a microphone.

Dylan clamped a hand over her mouth and giggled in her ear. "Shhh, people are staring."

Katie swiped her tongue along the inside of his palm, causing him to release her lightening fast.

"Ewww, that is so disgusting!" He scrubbed his hand down his pant leg several times. "You are so juvenile."

She grinned triumphantly. "Thank you. That's what you get for giving me an ultimatum." She offered him a sentimental smile. "Dylan, you're on my Top Five Favorite People list, and I would rather spend a little bit of time with you tonight than do anything else."

Dylan blushed at the compliment before deflecting it. "That list changes more often than the stock market."

"Maybe, but so far you've always managed to keep a place on it."

He waved his hand, changing the subject. "We should leave no later than 8:30, just in case the roads are bad. That's forty-five minutes. *Forty-five minutes,* got it?"

She shrugged. "Sheesh, I got it, forty-five minutes."

The whole time Christopher and Heather were cutting their cake, Katie kept wanting to check her watch—but she didn't own one. Dylan grabbed her wrist and held it down to her side. "Would you relax?"

"I'm just excited to spend some quality alone time with you. Besides, it's not going to be my fault if you're late."

A guilty smile flitted across his face. "It's fine, I remembered to calculate for Katie Standard Time."

"Katie Standard Time?"

Jared, still sticking to her like Gorilla Glue, let out a doofy laugh. "I've heard of K.S.T."

Dylan took a step away from Katie's glare, amusement spilling into his eyes. "Don't blame me—Christopher made it up." He pointed to Christopher, who, wiping cake from his cheek, came over to join his friends, with Heather in tow.

"What? What did I do?" Christopher asked, catching Katie's dagger-glare along with the tail end of the conversation.

"Katie Standard Time?" Katie accused.

"K.S.T." Heather giggled. "That's his favorite phrase."

Christopher looked impish, his face turning beet red.

It would be bad form to publicly show her irritation with the groom, so Katie turned her attention back to Dylan. "So, how much time do we have before we need to leave?" she fished, hoping to discover the discrepancy between regular time and Katie Standard Time.

"Leave?" Sheila swooped in almost in a panic. "Katie-Bug, I need your help! Heather's family has gone!"

"What?" Katie looked to either side of her as if it were a lame joke and Heather's relatives were actually standing right next to her. All Katie saw was Heather, not looking surprised or even concerned by the news that her family was MIA.

"Heather, is everything all right?" Katie asked, still uncertain why this news was so significant to Sheila and what it had to do with her.

"Everything is fine," Heather responded, staring down at her hands. "There's supposed to be another nasty set of storms coming in. Some of the interstates have already been closed. My family has a bit of a drive ahead. They were hoping to get ahead of the worst weather."

32

Dylan looked smugly at Katie. If they hadn't been surrounded by people, she'd lick his face just to get rid of that "I told you so" smirk.

Sheila sighed dramatically. "That means Jim and I are left to deal with that monster of a cake, a small mountain range of presents, not to mention whatever mess is left in the dressing rooms."

It didn't take a flash of genius to understand what Sheila was asking for. Katie racked her brain for a solution. Even if they could reach Heather's family, suggesting they get a hotel was pointless. With the amount of snow they'd been having, all the hotels for miles would be packed with ski enthusiasts. *What kind of Coloradans don't plan ahead for winter weather?*

"I had already made plans to drive Dylan to the airport." Katie gave an unconscious tug at the bodice of her clingy dress. "But I can come back after and help."

"You won't have time to do both. I'm sure Jared wouldn't mind driving Dylan," Sheila protested.

"No, Sheila." Jim had just joined the conversation in time to see Katie's crestfallen expression. "Let Katie spend time with her friend. You and I can manage just fine."

"How am I supposed to get back to L.A. tonight if I'm stuck here cleaning up all evening?"

"Katie can take Dylan to the airport and Jared can help bring everything back to the house," Christopher suggested, turning to Jared. "Would you mind?"

Before Jared could give his ready consent, Sheila interrupted. "But only Katie will know where to put everything."

"What does it matter where anyone puts things?" Christopher challenged. "That house has sat empty since you and Dad split."

There was a short uncomfortable silence, in which Katie made the mistake of stealing a glance at Heather. The bride looked sick with embarrassed distress. Before she could stop herself, Katie was saying, "That's okay. I can catch up with Dylan some other time. I don't mind helping out here."

***

"So help me, Katie Sutherland," Sheila threatened, "I love you like my own daughter, but if you get even a speck of dirt on either of those shoes or that gown, I'll ring your neck."

Katie halted just before the back door, nearly causing a Jared and Dylan pile-up. "What would you like me to do, Sheila?" Katie threw her hands above her head in frustration. "I've got to get out to my car to get a change of clothes and I'm not going out there naked."

"Give your keys to Dylan and he can bring you a change of clothes."

"No way, that won't work." She felt an overdue defiance toward Sheila. "I know exactly where everything is." Which, of course, was a lie. "And Dylan will just make a mess of everything."

Sheila contemplated the predicament for a moment.

"Do you have any other suggestions?" Katie couldn't help her own sarcasm.

The Eve St. Sebastian smirk slithering across Sheila's face was a reminder that Katie had chosen the wrong opponent. Sheila's cunning eyes sized up Katie, then her two companions. "Yes, I do." Cool as ice, Sheila gave a succinct nod that warned against argument.

The moment she was slung over Jared's shoulder like a shimmery sack of potatoes, Katie cursed herself for being so sacrificial. "Put me down! Put me down right now!" She pounded Jared in the back with her fists, but with Sheila's threats still ringing in his ears, Jared did not respond.

"I should have just said no! Why didn't I just say no?"

"Because it's not in your nature to say no." Dylan followed behind, making no attempt to hide his amusement.

"If I weren't such a damn pushover, I wouldn't even be wearing this gilded toga and these treacherous shoes in the first place! And I certainly wouldn't be being hauled across the parking lot like some caveman's booty! I would be taking you to the airport and we would be laughing outrageously, sipping overpriced hot chocolate!"

"But I am laughing outrageously."

She scowled and continued her rant until Jared deposited her on Rhett Butler's backseat. Retrieving a pair of jeans and an old hoodie from the heap of clothing in the back, she exchanged Vera Wang and Manolo for Levi Strauss and Uggs—not caring a fig for modesty. Dylan, who had been Katie's "wardrobe assistant" through most of their high school and college years, was unfazed. Jared, on the other hand, looked like his eyes were going to pop out of their sockets, his face boiling several shades of scarlet as he tried to look at everything other than the half-naked Katie.

"Well, I guess this is it." She jumped from the car with much more enthusiasm than she felt and attacked Dylan with a zealous hug that almost toppled them both into the snow.

"Poor Cinderella, I'm sorry that you're stuck here cleaning up, and I'm sorry we didn't get to hang out." His squeeze was so tight it stopped the trickle of tears that had begun trailing down her cheeks.

"Next time," she said, trying not to show her low spirits.

"I'm going to miss you, Katie."

"I'll miss you, too." She dove in for another hug.

Jared, catching a clue for the first time that evening, slogged off to warm his car.

"He likes you," Dylan began as soon as he was out of earshot.

Katie rolled her eyes. "He's a total hovercraft."

"Do you even know what a hovercraft is?"

"Yeah, it's someone who suffocates people with his omnipresence."

Dylan shook his head. "No, it's not. Do me a favor and just say yes when he asks you out?"

"When he asks me out? What encouragement have I possibly given him to ask me out?"

Dylan contemplated for a second. "Well, none, but Christopher has given him plenty. Jared has wanted to ask you out since before he met you."

Katie pitched her eyes to the heavens and cursed Christopher's name.

"Do it," he pleaded, "as a favor to me and to Christopher."

"Not for Christopher," she dug in. "I'm tired of bailing his butt out tonight."

"For me, then?"

"Why do you care so much?"

"I just don't want to see the poor guy crushed before you even give him a chance."

Katie emptied her lungs in one exaggerated exhale. "Fine," she conceded with a stamp of her boot. "But you owe me."

"Fine." He pulled her in for one last hug and planted a warm kiss on her cheek.

Chapter Three

Entrenched in her sofa, Katie stared up at her ceiling. She worried about its increasing fragility. Upstairs, her aerobics-obsessed neighbor, Stanley Speedo, was pounding his way through another session of *Sweatin' to the Oldies.*

Tha-dump-da, tha-dump-da, tha-dump-da hoomph. Tha-dump-da, tha-dump-da, tha-dump-da hoomph. Katie scrunched her eyes shut. The last thing she needed overshadowing her feelings of self-loathing was half-naked images of Stanley marching in time with Richard Simmons. There was a very good reason she'd dubbed the man Stanley Speedo—not only was she unable to wrap her tongue around his real name, but she'd never seen him in anything but a Speedo.

Just thinking about not thinking about it provoked her gag reflex. No matter how many times Katie's brain shouted *Dooonn't loook!* her eyes were always drawn like magnets to his *you-know-what.* How could they not? He was like a nappy-headed rhinoceros in Spandex.

In the two years they had been neighbors, he always greeted her with the same cheerful "Hallo Katie, pretty lady!" in a heavy Mediterranean accent. He was a nice man and a concerned neighbor, and Katie tried to not to fault him for his poor fashion sense—she'd been on the European continent enough to know he certainly wasn't the only man with a penchant for banana hammocks. But tonight, she couldn't help it.

As he rhythmically danced to bring her house down, his droopy, naked belly shaking with wild abandon, Katie realized her life had become routine. She bear-hugged a pillow to her stomach. Once—

okay, tons of times, on occasions such as this, when she felt suffocated by the monotony of daily life, she'd sketched out a life plan: her Amazing Plan. She'd spent the last hour tearing her place apart until it looked like a burglary scene, and hadn't been able to locate even one of those copies. She didn't have the will to scribble out another, so she spoke the list aloud like a well-rehearsed mantra.

1. Graduate
2. Pay off student loans (not immediately, of course)
3. Explore Eastern Europe
4. Choose a meaningful career that will not compromise a life of travel and adventure

So far, she hadn't checked off a single item of her Amazing Plan.

A snapshot of her bank statement flashed in her brain. She bent her head and stifled a scream against the pillow. It was missing a couple of zeros—thanks to the previous year's Paris extravaganza. One missing zero meant she'd have to wait a few more months to begin planning her next adventure—but two missing zeros…. She sighed and slunk deeper into the sofa. What did it matter anyway? She still had one semester to go before getting her bachelor's degree, and she was too close to actually accomplishing something to take another sabbatical.

Too discouraged to leave her sofa, Katie stretched her leg to its full extent and opened the DVD cabinet with her chipped nail-polished toe. She might as well immerse herself in the wonderful world of chick-flickdom and down a whole pint of Ben and Jerry's. If she was going to feel unfulfilled and pathetic, she might as well feel like an unfilled and pathetic cow.

She toed out a selection of classics and scooted them across the floor toward her. For no particular reason, she arranged them with her foot by favorite leading men. As soon as the discs were in order, her other foot had a temper tantrum and scattered them to hell and beyond. Weren't there any movies that didn't involve leading men—besides those snail-paced British movies where women sit around pretending to enjoy a dull life while they pine for companionship? If she were one of those British heroines, she'd hurl her sewing basket against the wall and show them how life was meant to be lived—sans leading man.

What she needed to do was get out of the house before resorting to an irrational sobfest. She glanced at the clock: six o'clock, not too late. She pushed off the couch and dashed toward her bedroom. Exchanging her purple fleece bathrobe and penguin pajama bottoms for a pair of jeans and a brown ribbed turtleneck—a boring outfit that reflected the state of her life—she gathered her hair into a loose ponytail that spilled to the middle of her back. She pinched a little extra color into her complexion, and marveled that it took less than five minutes to find her car keys. At least one thing was going right.

***

A light from the television flashed through the front window of the ivy-covered Tudor home. Katie's heart raced a little as she pulled Rhett Butler up the narrow drive. She didn't have an excuse for coming here. Not that she needed one, but she would have liked to have something prepared. She made her way up the front porch and shivered as she waited for Mr. Scott to let her in.

40

The door swung open. "Bloody hell, lass! What'cha doin' on me doorstep in this kind of weather without wearin' so much as a jumper? It's cold enough to freeze the bits off a brass monkey!" the robust widower chided, his brogue seeming thicker than usual. "Get yourself in and put wood in t'oile."

Katie was puzzled. "Put wood in the oil? Why would you put wood in oil?"

Mr. Scott stopped tightening his cardigan and rolled his eyes at her. "It's not in *theee oy-ill,* you Yank. It's in t'oile—I believe you would say 'put wood in the hole.'"

"No, I'm pretty sure I wouldn't say that—it doesn't make sense."

Mr. Scott's usual rogue curl had escaped the conventional combing of his silver hair, joggling this way and that. "For heaven's sake, impossible child, it means shut the door."

Katie stepped into the house and did as she was told. "You know, if you would have just said that in the first place, the door would have been shut five minutes ago."

His laugh was hearty, as though he had been saving it up all day long. She feared he probably had.

Her brow furrowed. "So, Mr. Scott, did you do anything exciting today?"

"Let's see now. I met a few ladies in the market and had them round for tea. Then, I invited them to lie down on their bellies so I could use their backs as canvases while I practiced me tattoo artistry. It was brilliant fun." His tone couldn't have been flatter.

"Oh, Mr. Scott, didn't you do anything today?"

41

"You know damn well I did as I always do. I read me books and did me crosswords. Now stop naggin' me. I hired you to be me realtor, not me nanny. And it's *Avery.* 'Mr. Scott' is me father, and after so many years, I'll thank you to remember that." He turned from the door and stalked off, grumbling as to why, three years ago, he'd chosen Katie to represent him in the buying and selling of some investment properties.

"Because I have a quick wit and keep you on your toes." She followed behind him, answering his mumblings. "I remind you of your British roots. That's why."

Plopping onto the plump leather sofa, he belted a laugh that echoed from the high arched doorway. "That you do, lass, that you do. Have I grown so predictable that you can read me thoughts now?"

"Well, yes." Katie's smirk pulled into a grin. "And you grumble when you're upset."

He gestured for her to take a seat. "Surely, you didn't come over just to inquire after me social life. What's on your mind, pet?"

She settled into a high-backed leather chair and took in the aroma of antiques and furniture oil. The mahogany-colored leather furniture (whether real antiques or made to look old, Katie didn't know) was surrounded by dark-stained floor-to-ceiling bookcases filled with old leather-bound hardbacks. The rich, old-world feel made this her favorite room in the whole world. She heaved a weighty sigh.

"Feelin' a bit cagey, little miss?"

"Well…yes, but how—"

"How did I know? I see the look in your eyes. I've had it before in me own eyes. You're as restless as a pride of lion cubs. We both know you can't be sittin' still too much longer."

"But the reality is—"

"Reality is what the dim-witted hide behind because they're too afraid to make their own destiny. I've never known you to be that type."

He was the one person who truly understood her. She tried to fight the tears clouding her eyes, but she knew crying would be unavoidable. Crying was always unavoidable. Every emotion she possessed seemed to be hardwired to her tear ducts. She wiped a few rebellious tears with the back of her hand and hurried to rub the moisture onto her pant leg.

"Oh, don't cry, pet. We'll get it sussed out."

"I wasn't crying."

"Were you not now? I can see the splotches on your trousers where you weren't cryin'."

Her hand went to her jeans and felt the dampness left from her tears.

"Now where's the Old Katie I know? What brought on all this melancholy? Do you think I've not noticed how miserable you've become these past few weeks? You've done a reverse metamorphose from a vibrant, whimsical butterfly into a dreary old moth."

She picked the edge of her pinky nail into the threads of the chair. "I don't know…I was just thinking about my Amazing Plan and how I haven't done anything with it yet."

"Ah yes, your Amazing Plan." He steepled his fingers to his forehead as if in deep concentration. "Maybe what you need is a Pre-Amazing Plan, just until your original has a chance to kick in."

She only needed a moment to consider his suggestion. "You're right, that's exactly what I need!" She felt better already.

"And I'll bet a good old-fashioned romance wouldn't hurt in turning that frown around."

"Oh no you don't. I'm not looking for a man, I'm looking for inspiration."

His eyes sparkled as he rubbed his hands together. "If it's 'inspiration' you're after, I could introduce you to me godson, Andrew, who's about your own age. He was raised by his granddad—one of the best men I ever knew, God rest his soul. Andrew lives with me sister when he's not faffing about in London. Poor lad seems to have lost his way since his granddad's passing. You might do him some good. And, of course, you could do a lot worse than a Yorkshire man."

"Is that where you're from—Yorkshire? You're from England? I always thought you were Scottish."

The proud man puffed out his chest. "Scottish! Indeed! Sometimes, lass, I think your head is stuffed with fluff."

She knitted her eyebrows and held up her hand to interrupt his rant. "You know what, Mr. Scott, I think you're on to something.

"About me godson?"

"No, about going to England."

"I didn't say anything about going to England."

"Sure you did, and I think it's a great idea."

"But I..." He shook his head in defeat, and she thought saw a bit of sadness settle into his baggy eyes. "England, you say? When would you be going?"

"Umm...I'm not sure yet."

"What part of England would you be visitin', lass?"

"Well...I...uh...."

"And tell me, for how long do you plan on bein' gone?"

44

"It's hard to say. My plans are still a bit vague at the present." She straightened her shoulders and shot him a challenging glare.

He gave her a placating smile. "Now, don't worry, love. Seein' as how you don't know when you're goin', there will be plenty of time to figure out what you'll be doin' when you get there."

"Okay, so I don't have all the particulars. This was your idea, remember?" She had to fight the tug of a smile at the corners of her lips.

He held his hands up in surrender. "Fair enough. 'Tis an excitin' Almost Plan. I'll be glad to lend a hand. And if you happen to find your Mr. Right along the way, you wouldn't object now, would you?"

"What is it with you and romance tonight? And why does everyone think I need a man to make my life complete?" She balled her fists tightly inside the crack between the chair and its cushion.

He looked at her as if she were daft. "Because, lass, nobody can be complete without ever having known true love."

Chapter Four

"Miss Sutherland, I need to speak with you!" Professor Bell's voice boomed across the room as the students were packing up to leave.

Katie felt like a puppy that had been caught by the scruff of its neck. She gazed up at the towering professor, with his dark arms folded loosely across his broad chest as he stared down the wide bridge of his nose at her. He could win first prize at the Samuel L. Jackson look-alike contest.

"Miss Sutherland." He came to loom over her desk before she could pack up her laptop and escape. "I hope that you took note of my subtle reminder about internships."

His insistence that she make a decision about her internship was tiring. For just a moment, she considered changing her major—again. She'd flitted in and out of at least a dozen courses of study since high school: literature, art history, communications, marketing…. Unintentionally, she'd earned a minor in French, but abandoned the program when the lectures turned to phenomenology and existentialism. She'd already ditched one philosophy degree; she didn't want to pursue another—in a foreign language.

"Yes, Professor, your subtle reminder has been noted." Despite his constant pressure, she actually enjoyed her tourism major and had no real intention of abandoning it—especially since she was so close to finishing. "You've been hounding me on the subject every week for the past two months."

He sighed. "Katie, you need to come up with some ideas and start working on them. Internships are not easy to put together, especially if you plan on leaving the state. Do you have any clue at all what you want to do?"

She shook her head on a long exhale. "I don't know" was what she meant to say, but instead, "I'm going to England" trickled from her lips. The idea was so perfect, she was surprised she hadn't thought of it on purpose.

Then the strangest thing happened. Professor Bell smiled. "Good girl. Have your proposal on my desk next week."

Katie nodded, trying to match his smile. All she had to do now was find a job—in England.

***

"It's all settled," Katie announced, plonking herself down in Mr. Scott's leather chair.

"What's settled, pet?" Mr. Scott didn't bother looking up from his crossword puzzle.

"My going to England—it's all set."

Now he looked up. There was something in his eyes she'd never seen before. Something that killed the euphoria she was feeling. She took a moment to consider how much she would miss him, and she could tell her expression was matching his.

"Is it now? So quickly? It's only been three days!" He shook his head like an Etch-a-Sketch, erasing the sadness. "You waste no time, restless child. Tell me, how's it all been set about?"

"I'm going to do my internship there."

He looked perplexed. "Sorry? Did you say your internment?"

"My what?" she gasped. "I'm dying to go to England, but I'm not literally going to die to get there! Jeez! I'm going to do my *in-tern-ship*. You know, for school, for my work experience—to graduate."

47

"I see. I don't believe we use that word in England. But then it's been so long since I did me studies...." His words trailed off and for a few moments he seemed to be someplace else. She wondered where he went when he did that, what memories he was drudging up, but she never asked. Mr. Scott was always warm and open with her, but never about his past. That was a door that had always remained locked tight.

His thoughts returned as quickly as they had wandered. "And tell me, lass, where'll you be workin' in England?"

She felt confused by the marked amusement in his tone. "I'm not quite sure yet."

"Ah, and where will you be livin'?"

"Um, well...." She caught the teasing gleam in his eye, and it dawned on her they'd had this conversation before. "Fine. Maybe it's not *all* set, if we're going to argue semantics, but at least I have a direction now." Then she added, "Now, you old coot, stop teasing me and help me come up with the next step."

He laughed. "'Old coot,' am I? I suppose I am that. Now, come over here, pet, and let us put pen to paper and suss you out a plan." Patting the space next to him, he motioned her over to the plump leather sofa.

Chapter Five

Katie nestled deeper into her pillow as George Michael sang in her ear. Normally she wouldn't mind having him so up close and personal, but she didn't appreciate his song choice. "Wake Me Up Before You Go-Go"—or "Jitterbug" (still, in over two decades, she had no idea which one was the real title)—was one of her favorite songs, but way too upbeat for this early in the morning.

After a few seconds of cognizance, she realized it wasn't the real George Michael singing in her ear, but the ringtone of her cell phone. She wondered if her phone had the ability to differentiate ringtones by the time of day. She'd never know—the instructions went out with the box the very first day she got it.

"Hello," she croaked, looking at her clock.

"Hello pet!" Mr. Scott chirped. "Did I wake you, love?"

"No, of course not. I'm always awake at 5:13 on Sunday mornings."

"Bless me heart, quick as whip even whilst asleep."

"Not whilst asleep, because I'm actually awake now. Mr. Scott, what's going on? You do know that *nobody* wakes up this early on the weekends, don't you?

"Aye lass, that could be, and it's *Avery,* if I haven't already told you a million times. However, in England it's already the lunch hour."

Katie rubbed her face and rolled over.

"And they are thrilled you'll soon be joinin' them."

Katie sat straight up in bed.

"*Who's* pleased that I'll be joining them?" She rubbed the bottom of her palm against her temple, trying to clear the cobwebs from her mind.

"Me family, of course! I've phoned them and have arranged for you to stay with me sister while you do your internment with me nephew, Lucas."

"Internship."

"Oh yes, of course, that's the word. Well, anyway, Lucas owns a travel company of sorts and has agreed to have you help him with some of the office details." He paused for a breath, but not long enough to allow Katie to respond.

"He'll soon be gettin' married and what with all the weddin' plannin'…'tis goin' to be a grand affair, I understand. Quite a blueblood he'll be marryin'. Tsk-tsk. Not that there's anythin' wrong with marryin' a fine lady, mind. Just we Yorkshire men tend to have a wild spirit about us…doesn't suit us to be always caterin' to society folk. I hope the lad is sure of what he's doin'. He's the apple of me eye, he is…." He trailed off nostalgically. Catching himself, he returned his attention to Katie. "As I was sayin', what with the weddin' details, he's happy to have an extra pair of capable hands—of course, that's only if you want to, pet?"

"Are you kidding? Mr. Scott—Avery," she corrected, feeling his scowl through the phone, "this is the best news I've heard all morning!" She felt she might jump out of her skin with excitement. "Are you sure it's okay? I mean, I don't want to impose on your family."

"Aye lass, don't you worry on that account. They are dyin' to have you. In fact, me sister Lottie is lookin' forward to having a bonny lass about."

"I don't know what to say! I can hardly believe it! Thank you."

"No need for thanks. Now, I'll be lettin' you get back to your dreams. Can you come round this afternoon to discuss the particulars?"

"Of course, I can. Thank you, Mr. Scott, thank you so much!"

Falling back into the pillows, she conjured drowsy images of the family Mr. Scott never mentioned. She imagined Lottie to be the spitting, feminine image of her brother: short, conservative, neatly curled hair, soft hands, and kind words. She pictured Lucas: probably mid-forties, scrawny, short like the rest of the family, a no-nonsense businessman.

"AAAHHHHHH! Are you ready to *sweat*?!"

Katie shot up, ready to inflict damage on the effeminate screamer who'd somehow snuck into her bed. Then came the familiar loud *thump* followed by the heavy *tha-dump-da, tha-dump-da, tha-dump-da hoomphs.*

Ah crap. Richard Simmons again. She dropped face-first into her pillow. At least he wasn't really in her bed. Afraid her quirky REM cycle would brandish unpleasant Stanley Speedo scenarios into her brain, she forced herself up, comforter bound tightly around her, and waddled into the kitchen.

Desperate for a distraction from the sounds upstairs, she reached for her laptop, still sitting open on the table. No sooner had she logged onto the Internet when she heard the familiar *zzzwwwwiiish* of Skype coming to life. The clock at the bottom corner of her screen glowed with a time that no one should ever have to see on weekend mornings. *Hallelujah for friends on the East Coast,* she cheered silently before pushing the little green phone icon to call Dylan, who appeared to be online.

She saw his image—wrapped in an old flannel robe, hovering over a cup of coffee—before she heard his voice. She loved video calling. "Katie, is everything okay?"

"Sure, why wouldn't it be?"

"Because it's Sunday morning and you're up before ten. Of course, judging by that lovely bedspread you're wearing, you're not exactly up."

"Stanley Speedo is off to an early start this morning. Plus, I have some exciting news to tell you."

Dylan listened, nodding his head, as she told him all about her internship plans and her most recent conversation with Mr. Scott. "Not that I'm not happy for you, but have you thought about how you're going to afford living in England?"

Of course this would be Dylan's reaction. "No, not really," she admitted. "I have a little bit of savings."

"Not enough. Plus, you'll need your savings when you return home. It'll take some time to get back on your feet."

"Why do you always have to put a realistic damper on everything?" She laughed, too excited to be discouraged.

He grinned at her impetuosity.

"Fine, I guess it won't kill me to do some financial planning."

"Would you like me to help?"

"Yay! Thanks Dylan, you're the best."

"No problem. Call me back once you've got your money situation figured out and I'll come up with a realistic budget for you."

52

Katie's stomach hit the floor at the word. "Budget?"

Her financial situation, which resembled more of a loose-leaf folder than a portfolio, was not as promising as Katie would have hoped. With the closing of two properties she had under contract, she would be able to support herself in England if, and only if, she adhered to the terms of Dylan's Great Depression-inspired budget. She groaned, feeling almost ill. Effective immediately, she would have to lease out her darling little condo and move into Jim and Sheila's vacant home.

***

"You'll be living with me sister, Charlotte, and her husband, Charles," Mr. Scott told Katie. "Also, me godson, Andrew, lives with them sometimes, so he'll be able to help look after you as well."

"I'm glad I'll have a big support group, but I don't need to be looked after."

Mr. Scott chortled, gave her a condescending pat on the head, and continued to update her on the arrangements. She would be working for his nephew, Lucas Hayden, who was a sole proprietor of a travel business. For a hefty fee, he not only organized people's vacations, but traveled just ahead of his clients, smoothing the way of any holiday hassles. Though Lucas was based in London, Charlotte, his mother, helped him with the clerical side of the business from her home in Yorkshire. She would be the one taking responsibility for Katie's internship.

"Mr. Scott, do you think that's too much…too much Katie-ness for Charlotte…living and working with me? Maybe I should just find my own place."

"Don't be daft, and it's *Avery.* I assure you, me sister—call her Lottie—and you are two screwy peas in a pod. You'll get on smashingly."

***

Dusk was just settling in when Katie pulled into her parking space.

"Hallo Katie, pretty lady!" Stanley Speedo called his usual accented greeting as he waved at her from his balcony. Standing in the frigid temperature had shriveled him enough to significantly reduce to the scary bulge in his briefs. Katie didn't feel the usual urgency to escape his company. Knowing she wouldn't be his neighbor for much longer, she felt a surge of affection for the jovial, half-naked hairball.

"Hi Stanley! It looks like I'll be moving soon. Why don't you put on a few more layers of clothes and come on down for some hot chocolate?"

Flaunting an adorable smile he couldn't refuse, she ascended the staircase to her apartment.

Chapter Six

"Ow! Crap!" Katie winced as her knuckles collided against the cottage cheese ceiling. An hour before the date, wearing nothing but her skivvies, she leaped along the length of the Evans' seventies-style basement as if she were a company member of the Russian Ballet. As clumps of sparkly asbestos rained down on her, she slumped to the floor and sucked her scratched knuckles.

Who was she kidding? Her stomach wasn't getting any flatter and she leaped with the grace of a water buffalo. Between trying to get her internship approved and moving back home, she was lucky she hadn't had a nervous breakdown; she certainly couldn't have been bothered to lose a few pre-date pounds. But with Dylan's promise looming over her, she didn't want to give everybody any reason to think that when things didn't work out with Jared, she hadn't made every effort. She glanced longingly at the haphazard pile of size-six pants she kept tucked away at the top of her closet and accepted they would not be seeing the light of day anytime soon.

Since Jared was already forty minutes late, Katie had plenty of time to contemplate the fact she was twenty-eight and living—worse, dating—out of her childhood home. Another twelve minutes ticked by in which she chanted an impromptu mantra: *Achieving Amazing Plans entails endurance through a temporarily abject existence.* She chanted until she was thoroughly tongue-tied. After thirty-seven more minutes, she ended a twelve-year leave of absence and seated herself at the living-room piano, declared "Strike one, Jared," and plunked out a few notes.

Two hours later, she was blinded by the headlights of his Land Rover shining through the living room curtains. She snuck toward the window to spy as he approached the front porch. He was just as beefcakey, and his head was just as shaved and seemingly incapable of growing hair as she remembered. His hands were jammed so far into his jeans pockets he could have been tickling the underside of China. He wore a tattered denim jacket and plain white T-shirt that clung to his muscular chest. *This* was the man for whom she'd leapt until she had rug burns on the bottoms of her feet.

"This is a great car," she said, eager to break the awkward silence that followed them all the way down the driveway. He grinned and hoisted himself inside. Katie stood staring at the closed passenger door. After a few moments, when Jared made no motion to even reach across and open it from the inside, she yanked herself into the car and mumbled, "Strike two."

"Sorry, I'm late," Jared explained once they were on the road. "I got hung up at work and couldn't call."

Katie dipped her head to convey understanding. "You're a cop, right?"

"SWAT. But I'm going through the interview process with the FBI."

"Oh!" Her eyebrows shot up in surprise. She had misjudged him by assuming he was only playing a cop to fulfill some schoolboy fantasy. She hadn't given him credit for having a successful career. "Wow, that's really great." She felt a little contrite for underestimating him.

He shone like a proud little schoolboy at her praise. She squirmed in her seat, bothered her opinion could have such a visible effect on him.

During dinner he managed to avoid all the major pitfalls and say all the right things, which had Katie suspecting he'd received some prior instruction from someone. Anna? Christopher? Dylan?

No doubt he was counseled that the way to her heart was a *Lonely Planet* and nineteen hours in coach class because he always maneuvered the conversation toward the subject of travel. He probed until he found her hot spot: Thailand. Then he massaged the subject until he had reeled her in, and they were calculating frequent flyer miles and routing flights to Bangkok.

***

With the help of some great coaching from Christopher, Jared hadn't earned his third strike—yet. And so, in keeping with her promise to Dylan, Katie felt she had no choice but to continue accepting Jared's invitations for dinner—always dinner, and if he didn't have an early start the next morning, perhaps a testosterone-packed action movie. They had already been on nine dates in just under three weeks.

"Soooo, how are things going with Jared?" Anna, who was hanging onto her sanity by a very fragile thread, drawled, eager to discuss anything that would make her forget about the two toddlers and the thirty-year-old teenager she'd left at home. She'd called an emergency retail therapy session with Katie and Heather after threatening to dismember her family piece by piece if she didn't get out of the house.

"You've been seeing a lot of each other," Heather chimed in.

"Fine, I guess." Katie didn't bother to muster any fake enthusiasm.

"That's it? 'Fine'? All I get is 'Fine'?" Anna huffed, massaging her fist into the small of her back as she waddled across the parking garage.

Katie shrugged. "There's not much more to say. We don't have that much in common— nothing in common, actually. The only reason I keep seeing him is that everyone insists on it."

"Not everyone!" Heather argued. "I've been against this setup from the start."

Anna craned her neck to scowl at her. "Why?"

Heather dropped back a couple of steps in response to Anna's foul temper. She backpedaled. "He just doesn't seem like Katie's type."

"You mean he doesn't ride a big white horse and live in a castle?" Anna directed her condescending snort toward Katie. "Katie needs to just forget about Prince Charming, because that ain't gonna happen."

Katie was warmed to see that Heather looked crestfallen on her behalf.

"Have you guys even kissed?" Anna asked. "Of course, Little Miss Don't Touch Me Unless You're Perfect or Gerard Butler, I know you haven't. I don't know what you're waiting for."

"Oh, I don't know, maybe a spark of attraction? Maybe butterflies in my stomach when I think about him?" Katie retorted.

"Maybe someone who makes me laugh or at least crack a genuine smile—"

"Oh please," Anna interrupted. Her annoyance was a stark contrast to the sympathetic nod that Heather, the lovestruck newlywed, was offering. "When do you see him again?"

"I made a stupid mistake and agreed, completely by accident, to go out with him on Singles Awareness Day." In response to her friends' confused stares, Katie clarified, "Valentine's Day."

"And that would be a problem because…?" Anna asked.

Katie looked at her as if to say "Duh!" before responding. "Because Valentine's Day is such an awkward holiday to navigate. Now I have to decipher if his asking me out on Valentine's Day means anything or if it's just a coincidence. There's the worry of whether he's presumptuous enough to get me a gift and should I be prepared with something for him just in case. Buying him a present, even an obligatory present, would be leading him on. But if he has something for me and I have nothing for him, it would make him feel stupid. So is it better to lead him on or make him feel stupid?"

"It's better not to worry so much about everything," Heather consoled. "If you lead him on, you didn't mean to. If his feelings get hurt, that would be unfortunate, but he'll get over it."

"I wish it were that simple. I'm the one that has to live with the stress diarrhea."

"Hurting someone's feelings shouldn't cause stress diarrhea," Anna stated firmly. "You have to get over that. Let people take care of their own emotions."

Katie shrugged, considering the validity of their advice.

She pondered her situation further in the small boutique's eveningwear department. "Why is it so hard to find a decent guy?" Katie spun an elegant twirl, holding a shimmery silver gown to her body that she knew she'd never wear, but had to own.

"It's only hard if you set unrealistic expectations," Anna snapped.

"I guess getting married to your boyfriend right out of high school makes you the authority," Katie sassed, annoyed that Anna was making no attempt to curb her foul mood.

"No, but watching you over the last decade has. Just because some guys happen to have receding hairlines, smell like patchouli oil, or wear sweatpants doesn't mean they're not decent guys."

"You're right. They're just not right for me."

Anna snorted. "Wearing sweatpants automatically determines if a man is right or wrong for you?"

"Of course not," Katie retorted. "It's the point in the relationship that he chooses to wear sweatpants that is crucial. I'm not wrong for having sweatpants guidelines."

"Maybe not, but why do you get to have sweatpants guidelines?"

"Because I've been in the game long enough now to know what sweatpants mean,"

"Enlighten me, oh Wise One, on the great meaning of sweatpants."

Katie turned to Heather for backup, only to find that the escalating argument had her withdrawing several racks away.

Plowing through Anna's biting sarcasm, Katie attempted to enlighten her friend. "If a man shows up for a date wearing sweats, it means two things: One, I will be subjected to watching him rearrange himself all evening because, for some reason, men can't seem to keep a handle on their junk when they're wearing sweats. And two, he is going to take me back to his place to watch movies. Where, as soon as the lights are off, he'll make the predictable move of trying to get into my pants."

"Ah, yes, the elusive secret garden to which no one, save Prince Charming, shall be granted the key," Anna said in her most snooty literary voice.

"Exactly," Katie agreed, choosing not to get riled. "There's nothing wrong with being particular."

The last of her impatient straws broke, causing Anna to let out a long, eerie sigh. The unnatural sound disarmed Katie's defenses long enough to notice how exhausted and worn—well beyond her twenty-eight years—her friend looked.

"There's a fine line between particular and unrealistic," Anna stated. "And you have crossed it. I'm done watching you throw aside suitable guys so you can chase fairytales."

Anna's narrowed eyes and icy tone announced an end to the debate, leaving Katie to wonder if she should feel mad about Anna's lack of confidence in her or cry for the hopeless spinster she was destined to be.

"You think I should settle?"

"I think you should compromise." Anna looked like she wanted to scratch the tears out of Katie's eyes.

Katie took a step back. Normally she wasn't intimidated by Anna. But this wasn't the normal Anna: This was a big, pregnant, sleep-deprived, and hormonal Anna.

"Jared Stone is a nice man with ambition and a good job, and he adores you. Most women would be ecstatic to find someone so eligible. What is it that makes Katie Sutherland so entitled she can turn her nose up at every decent man who shows interest? Nothing—that's what." Anna pried the impractical gown from Katie's unyielding clutch, returned it to the rack, then spun on her heels and stalked away.

Katie watched Anna's retreating back, and then cast another wistful look over the beautiful garment before deciding it was in her best interest to go after her friend.

On the silent drive home, Katie felt a million tiny pinpricks of shame jabbing at her conscience. She wondered if she felt an undeserved sense of entitlement. Was she wrong for dismissing guys who automatically pressed her puke button?

Pulling into Anna's driveway, she finally found her voice. "So this is an opinion you all share?"

"We're just concerned," Anna snapped. "We're just afraid that—" she broke off as if searching for a delicate way of expressing herself. Since she didn't possess the art of delicacy, she blurted, "Have you not considered you are all alone in this world? Pull your head out, Katie, before it's too late and you end up being alone for the rest of your life."

If Anna had struck her across the face, it couldn't have hurt more.

Katie opened her mouth to speak, but all that came out was a strangled, high-pitched, "I'm—not—I—." Even as she was formulating her defense, she thought about Christopher, blissfully married to Heather, who sat stone silent in the backseat; Dylan in D.C.;

62

and her parents on the Gold Coast. She rarely spoke to her brothers, and Jim and Sheila were now scattered across the country.

Anna and Heather got out of the car. Anna began waddling up the driveway as Heather leaned over to Katie's window.

"Don't worry—Christopher told me she always gets mean when she's pregnant!" Heather called as Katie backed out of Anna's driveway. "I'm sure she didn't mean it!"

Katie blinked back tears. With the exception of Anna, who was now pulling the rug out from under her, and Mr. Scott, Katie felt—for the first time in her life—she really *was* alone.

Chapter Seven

Since their conversation, Katie thought obsessively about Anna's words, about not chasing after fairytales. She went to bed most evenings with swollen eyes and tear-stained cheeks and woke up with a renewed determination to overlook all of Jared's faults and embrace his good attributes, superstitious that if she didn't, the fates would intervene and destine her to a life of eternal spinsterhood. Much like Sisyphus—whom she remembered from her stint as a Greco-Roman Studies major, condemned for eternity to repeat the same meaningless task of pushing a rock up a mountain, only to see it roll down again—Katie would be sentenced to a lifetime of helping loser men realize their potential, only to have them leave her for someone thinner.

It was time to stop dreaming and start facing reality. Time to get practical.

By the time Valentine's Day rolled around and Jared pulled into her driveway and honked, she'd armed herself with a new attitude and a new mantra: *Practicality prohibits princes, presents, and perfection.*

She cast a doubtful look in the mirror and considered changing into a more substantial sweater. She reminded herself Jared said they'd be indoors all evening. Giving her reflection an encouraging smile, she sashayed to the car in her favorite sweater, an intricately crocheted number that cost her a small fortune and which Dylan insisted on calling "The Doily."

Jared gave her the once-over and smiled. "You look hot."

Katie kind of suspected that she did, but she had the good manners to feign humility.

Not that looking hot in a thin sweater did her one bit of good when her surprise Valentine's destination was the ice hockey rink. She forced herself not to be annoyed that sitting by herself and cheering for Jared and his team was his idea of a good date. Or that upon seeing her flimsy sweater, he didn't think to instruct her to bring a coat. She reminded herself those issues were small potatoes to the new, realistic Katie, and remembered to see him as something other than an imbecile. Taking Anna's advice, she focused on the fact he was a decent guy who truly cared for her.

After two hours of the icy air breathing through her doily and the rhythmic *skoosh, skoosh* of skates racing back and forth across the ice, she had fallen into a sort of hypothermic trance. She didn't even notice when the sharp clacking of hockey sticks being whacked together ceased to echo through the nearly empty arena.

"Hey! Earth to Katie!" Jared nudged her in the ribs with his hockey stick. "I was asking you what you thought of our big win? You okay?"

Katie willed her knees to hinge, some of her color returning as she stood.

"Yeah, jjjust, just, fffreezing, that's all." She shivered. "I dddefinitely picked the wrong outfit tonight."

"I don't think you picked the wrong outfit at all." His eyes smoldered as they roved all over her figure.

He had changed from his uniform into baggy jeans and a thin white T-shirt that hugged his pectorals. *Whoa!* Her eyes nearly bulged at his ripped physique, which she had never seen so thinly veiled. In one purposeful movement, he wrapped his arms around her in a warming embrace. Still hot from all the exercise, he felt like a sauna.

65

As Katie let her body thaw into his, he tensed. His hands that were vigorously rubbing life back into her body became slow and deliberate, kneading a seductive course down her back.

Her breath caught. Her panic mode, which had always kept her at a safe distance, was still frozen. She had blundered and left herself vulnerable, but for some reason, this time she didn't want to avert her face. In fact, she was kind of excited when Jared dove in to claim his first kiss.

"So far, this evening is going even better than I had hoped!" Jared announced once they were back in the car with the heat vents on Katie's side, blasting welcomed hot air.

Katie had no response. Her mind was racing with the knowledge and fear that with one kiss, the course of this relationship had been irrevocably altered.

"I have something for you." He fumbled in his jacket pocket. Katie gulped. The dreaded Valentine conundrum was at hand. Retrieving a folded envelope, he slid it across the seat to Katie.

"What's this?" She stared at the L-shaped piece of paper as if it might bite.

"Open it," he directed, unable to conceal his cocky smirk.

Sliding the tip of her fingernail underneath the seal and pulling back the flap, she drew out two oversize tickets and read the neat lettering.

"They're airline vouchers," he stated what she had already ascertained for herself.

Bewildered into silence, she nodded, waiting for him to expound on the part that was not obvious: Why he had given her airline vouchers? But he didn't expound.

Catching the contagious, kid-at-Christmas excitement in his eyes, she wrapped her confusion into an enthusiastic response. "Is one of these really for me? Are you serious? Thank you! … But why?"

"I thought maybe we should do more than just talk about going to Thailand." Jared was grinning so widely his eyes had disappeared behind big laugh crinkles.

Katie nearly leapt out of her seat with shock more than excitement. Travel opportunities with a willing and able partner never came this easily.

"Thank you, thank you, thank you!" she gushed. "When are we going?"

"Whenever you want. Just say the word and I'll be ready."

"How long will we be gone?" she probed.

"As long as you want. I want to spend as much time with you as you'll give me."

She flashed a luminescent smile that gave him courage.

"Katie, I want you to officially be my girlfriend."

Chapter Eight

In anticipation of Katie's arrival, the door to Professor Bell's office had been left ajar.

"You haven't returned my messages," Professor Bell, leaning on the window ledge, stated upon hearing Katie's approach.

Katie cast a dismayed glance over his unoccupied desk. She longed to have the barrier of the tidy desktop keeping them at a cool, formal distance. Obeying his gesture to take a seat in the university-issued office chair that faced him, she noted he was towing a very fine line between annoyance and anger.

"And I noticed that you have been absent from my classes this week." He waited for a response.

Her reply was not immediate. She took the time to ponder the best way to explain her avoidance without having him suspect it had been deliberate. Which, of course, he did, and which it was.

"It's been a really crazy week for me," she declared at last, offering no further rationalization.

Raising his eyebrows in a way that conveyed he was clearly unimpressed with her answer, he sat straighter into the boxed window casing, folded his arms tightly across his chest, and bore his gaze directly into her face. Katie shifted in the chair designed to make students feel as uncomfortable as possible and tried not to notice how his biceps swelled over the cuffs of his short sleeves.

"As I told you in the several unreturned messages I left," his controlled, even tones were more severe than any angry rant, "your internship has, with no little effort on both our parts, been reluctantly approved by the Dean."

Neither one looked pleased by the news of this hard-earned victory.

"I need to have all student internship files submitted by the end of the week and yours is still missing a work summary."

He heaved a long sympathetic, or maybe impatient, sigh— Katie couldn't really tell.

"Katie, this is a simple, twenty-minute assignment. Why are you dragging your feet? Is there something going on I should know about? You haven't changed your mind, have you?"

"No, of course not." That was mostly true; she hadn't changed her mind about going to England, she just hadn't thought any more about it.

Her quick reply earned a skeptical look from the professor. "Then you won't mind staying here in my office a while longer until you've completed the assignment?" This was more a command than a question. "I have stuck my neck out too far on this for you to not follow through."

Katie flinched, not at the rising anger in his voice, but at the realization he had more than she understood riding on her internship.

"For your own benefit," he continued, "I feel compelled to remind you that without this simple assignment your file will be incomplete, which means you won't have an internship, you won't pass this class, and you won't be able to graduate by the end of the summer."

The guilt Katie had been feeling was instantly usurped by fear and a desperate longing to have achieved a piece of her Amazing Plan—to have a neatly framed degree hanging on her wall boasting of her one and only accomplishment.

69

Spurred on by that vision and the desire to make Professor Bell proud of her again, she pulled out her laptop, whipped out her summary, and went one bold step further: She booked a flight to London for the day after her last final.

Professor Bell's reaction when she slapped the assignment along with a copy of her flight itinerary down on his desk was that extra boost of reassurance she needed to know she had gotten back on the right track. He was so relieved that in his elated state, he dropped the paper he was grading, practically hurdled his desk, and captured her in a tight military-caliber bear hug.

**

"Oh, my!" exclaimed Mr. Scott as he opened his front door to Katie. "It's been a mighty while since I've seen you wearin' a smile as big as that."

"Is Heather here yet?" Katie asked excitedly. She removed one shoe and then other before entering his home, which was always kept British-grade pristine.

Katie had a mission to bring her two friends together, hoping they would eventually fuse their own friendship. It would be nice for Heather to have another friend in town, and Mr. Scott, even if he didn't agree, needed someone other than Katie to encourage him out of the house once in a while.

"We've been visitin' in the front room. Such a pleasant lass," he said. "Mind, she's not a harebrain like you—she's a sensible sort of girl—but very pleasant nonetheless."

His words couldn't have pleased her more. Not only had she made a successful match, but in Mr. Scott's eyes, Katie was the capricious girl she hadn't been in far too long.

70

"Now, what's so bleedin' important that you've had to call this emergency get-together?"

"I've had an epiphany."

"An epiphany!"

She nodded an emphatic affirmation.

"Lands, child, the things you say! I'm forever on pins and needles wonderin' what you'll come up with next. Well, come on then, let's join Heather in the next room so we can get on with it, shall we?" He made an exaggerated sweeping gesture with his arm for her to lead the way.

"I've been wearing the wrong skin," Katie blurted as soon as she had Heather and Mr. Scott seated on the sofa. She had begun pacing the length of the sofa in front of them and therefore didn't notice the confused, uneasy look on Heather's face.

When Katie turned her back to pace in the opposite direction, Heather leaned into Mr. Scott and asked in a panicky whisper, "I'm not sure I understand…is she turning *Silence of Lambs* on us?"

Mr. Scott patted Heather's hand reassuringly. "Just give her another minute—she usually comes around to makin' sense."

Just as Mr. Scott prophesied, Katie rambled a few minutes more about her nonconforming skin before coming to the point. "Everybody wants me to be this compliant, practical, uninspired person that is just not me."

Seeing Mr. Scott's mouth open and shut several times in silent, guppy-like protest, she amended her statement. "I mean, except for you two. Mr. Scott—Avery—for what it's worth, you're absolutely right— I'm much better as the Old Katie." She flashed him an uncertain Old Katie smile.

He crossed his arms, shifted in his seat, and harrumphed, indicating he would not be placated so easily.

"I turned in the last of my internship papers," she continued, "and I leave for England right after my final exams!" She fished her flight confirmation out of her pocket and, with both hands, proudly displayed it out in front of her.

A reverent look stole into Mr. Scott's eyes and a slow smile spread across his face. Then, he did something that Katie, despite having rehearsed this conversation in the car, could never have imagined: He turned his gaze heavenward and began to pray. Words of thanks and gratitude poured almost inaudibly from his lips.

Feeling a little shaken by Mr. Scott's moment of spontaneous spirituality, she cut her gaze over to Heather. Heather bounded from the sofa, grabbed both of Katie's hands, and began dancing in place like a crazy person, all the while squealing like an excited pig.

"This is so great! You're going to England!" Heather squealed. "I've never been out of the country! Promise you will call and tell me about everything! At least once a week. I want to live vicariously through your adventures."

"I'm only going to England, and I'll be working. It won't be very adventurous." Katie chuckled at Heather's naiveté.

Heather looked disappointed for a moment and then was overcome with a fresh wave of excitement. "This is so great!" She danced around with such gusto that Katie thought her arms would yank off. "What can we do to help you get out of here?"

"We need to track down a dress that I'll never wear," Katie responded without thinking, grateful to Heather for giving her the perfect segue into reason number two for calling the spontaneous meeting.

Heather and Mr. Scott looked at her in mystified silence.

"Just before I let myself be convinced I needed to change my personality, I was about to try on that absolutely amazing and utterly impractical silver dress," she recalled, retracing her past as if unlocking the clues to an important mystery. "Remember, Heather? When you and Anna and I went shopping a few months ago? That dress was the last impulse I had as the old me, before I became the new me, which is now the old me, making the first old me the new, new me again."

Heather's face was blank.

"What in the name of Angela Lansbury's tea kettle are you running on about?" Mr. Scott snapped.

"I need that dress!" Katie replied as if they were dense. "Don't you get it? It symbolizes who I was—who I am?"

Mr. Scott shook his head, thinking that Katie had lost her mind, and grinned. "Indeed, I believe she really is back to her old self."

"I get it!" Heather responded, to Katie's immense relief. "Let's go!"

"Slow down, lasses." Mr. Scott's voice of reason cut through the urgency. "It's been months since you saw that dress. It's probably long gone by now."

"That's why we don't have another minute to lose," Katie chastised. "Now stop being such an Eeyore and get your coat."

"Me?" he blurted in protest. "Go to the ladies' shops with the two of you? I'd rather have Lady Gaga sing at me funeral."

"Which is going to be a lot sooner than you think if you don't get that ornery British butt of yours into the car," Katie threatened.

73

Heather's giggles were out of control. "How does he know about Lady Gaga?"

"He watches the E! Channel religiously." Katie cast him a sidelong glance, letting him know she knew his dirty little secret.

Mr. Scott puffed up. "No one's ever caught me watchin' that tripe!"

"Just because no one has caught you doesn't mean it isn't so," Katie sniffed self-righteously as she pushed him and the laughing Heather out the door.

Chapter Nine

One boutique, two charity stores, three consignment shops, and one fabulous silver dress later, Katie used the spare key to let herself in to Jared's apartment. She shuddered, instantly feeling the raging furniture tension. An unmistakable battle warred between Asian Minimalistic East and All-American Bachelor West for reigning control of the great room.

Before she could step inside, Queen Sheba, Jared's vicious Chi-poo—a Chihuahua/poodle mix puppy—growled at her from behind the protection of two potent pooey landmines she had deposited in front of the door. Katie offered her hand out for the sniffing, and cooed in sweet soothing tones, "That's a gooood Sheba. What a good little Chi-poo. You're the best little Chi-Chi-poo-poo in the whole world. Aren't you, you hateful little doggie? Who's the nasty little Chi-Chi-poo? You are, yes you are."

Sheba dipped her head, indicating she was still not pleased by Katie's presence, but was willing to allow her safe passage beyond the poo hills.

"I've never met a dog I didn't like...until you," Katie grumbled under her breath, making a beeline for the roll of paper towels on the kitchen counter.

Sheba watched her curiously as she rolled a fat, cushy pair of paper towel mittens around her hands.

"What?" she asked defensively in response to the dog's questioning gaze. "You don't think I'm going pick those up with my bare hands, do you?" She gestured one of her padded hands toward the poop piles.

The dog made no reply.

"Great, I'm talking to a dog. And not just any dog—a dog I probably wouldn't speak to if it were the last human on Earth."

With her makeshift pooper scoopers snugly secured around her hands, she put on her brave face and went to work on disaster cleanup.

When Jared opened the door, Katie was kneeling in the entryway, her shirt collar pulled over her nose, cell phone pressed against her ear in conversation with Anna, batting a hunk of poo between her two pillowed hands.

"What's going on?" He maneuvered his way into the apartment, trying not to hit Katie in the back with the door.

Startled by his appearance, Katie dropped her phone on the floor. "I didn't expect you so soon," she admitted through the fabric of her shirt.

"I'm a half hour late," he grumbled in annoyance.

"Oh." Multitasking certainly made the time fly. "I've been trying clean up this —"

"For shit's sake Katie," he scolded before filling his chest with an impatient breath, which he blew slowly out his nostrils.

Despite his uncharacteristic, terse reaction, she couldn't refrain from snorting a giggle at the unintended pun.

He shot her a slow-motion glare that made her skin crawl. "It's only dog crap—it's not that hard to clean up."

"That's because I already cleaned up the squishy one." She didn't like being put on the defensive.

Without bothering to acknowledge her statement, he stalked into the kitchen for a paper towel.

"You used a whole roll of paper towels on a couple of dog turds?" he barked upon reentering the room, waving the empty cardboard roll.

"Not the whole roll." Sniffing, she tugged the paper towel mittens off her hands. "Part of it was already used."

He snatched the two wads of towels from her hands and pushed past her. In one swift motion he bent down and retrieved the remaining dog poo.

Katie took a deep breath to stave off the stupid tears. "What's going on with you? Why are you being so mean?"

"It's not *mean,* Katie, it's *stress.* This is what I'm like after a bad day at work. Get used to it."

Umm. I don't think so.

"Why do you always make everything so complicated?" He chucked the poo into garbage can, overflowing with several other pairs of Katie's previously discarded mittens. "What a waste!" Still griping, he yanked the plastic bag from the bin and vigorously tied off the top. "You wanted to talk to me about something? What is it?"

Katie hesitated. "Should we sit down?"

"Don't make a production out of this, Katie, just tell me what you have to say."

"Okay, then. I met with Professor Bell today—"

"Who's Professor Bell?"

"Professor Bell! My internship advisor. Anyway, he called me into his office because I was missing an assignment and—"

She was distracted by his upheld hand and the circling motion he was making with it—"wrap it up" in layman's sign language.

"Katie, I don't need all the details, just get to the point."

A spark of overdue anger ignited inside her, but before she could express herself, a shuffling noise at the door stole her attention. Katie stared slack-jawed at a woman with sleek black hair and tortoise-shell-framed glasses standing in the threshold.

"Katie, this is Natalie. She just got hired with the FBI and is helping me prepare for my interviews." Jared gave a perfunctory introduction.

She made a quick survey of the woman: five-foot-two, shapely, solid muscle, and small breasts. Not that Katie was looking, but it was hard not to notice since Natalie's neckline plunged to the middle of her sternum, revealing an intricately lacy black bra that didn't leave much to the imagination.

"Hi, nice to meet you," Katie offered meekly, never one to forget her manners, even in the face of crisis.

Natalie dipped her head in trivial recognition.

"Finish what you have to say," Jared instructed, "so Natalie and I can get started."

"What? Oh yeah," Katie replied, still stupefied by Jared's behavior and Natalie's eavesdropping presence. "Um…I had to finalize my internship today. So I'll be leaving for England sooner than I expected."

"Oh, okay" was his indifferent response.

"Okay, then…I'll talk to you later?" was the only response she could muster.

"Yeah, okay. Take the trash with you on your way out, will you?"

Feeling the sting of those damn tears behind her eyes and the flames of humiliation burning up her neck, she grabbed the top of the trash bag before stooping down to retrieve her cell phone, and made a beeline, shuddering as she brushed past Natalie, out the door.

Chapter Ten

"What a dick!"

Katie heard the muffled exclamation as she took the stairs leading away from Jared's apartment two at a time. She put her phone to her ear. "Hello?"

"Tell me you didn't take out that jerk's garbage," the voice demanded.

"Anna, you're still there? Have you been listening the whole time?"

"Yes, I heard everything! I am so sorry I pushed you into dating that jackass!"

***

"Where in the hell have you been?" Dylan strode out of Jim and Sheila's house and scolded from the porch the moment Katie stepped from her vehicle. "It's late and Christopher is fit to be tied. We've called you at least fifty times. He's been worried sick about you."

She squinted into the dark and could make out Christopher's lanky silhouette towering over Dylan's shoulder.

"Tell Mom I went for a drive and turned my phone off," she said shrugging off Christopher's motherly concern.

"For four hours?" he pressed

"Yes, for four hours. I needed time to think." She then looked at Dylan for the first time, blinked her tired eyes a few times, and did a double take.

"What are you doing here?" she squealed, running up the porch and flinging herself into his arms.

He collected her into a tight embrace and replied, "I came to see how you were doing."

She pulled back and eyed him suspiciously. "All the way from D.C.? Why?" Although she already knew she had the Anna Broadcasting Network to thank for his presence.

"Actually, I was at a conference in Phoenix and I wanted to make sure you weren't dying of a broken heart."

"Ppphhhshhh, broken heart? Me?"

He looked at her doubtfully.

"It's true. My heart is fine. It's the rest of me that's confused. I feel like the world's biggest schmuck. I didn't even stick up for myself. Instead, I took out his trash while *Natalie* and her cleavage smirked at me." She turned her face from Dylan. Picking at a crusty tear track on her check, she practically whispered, "How did I ever let myself become a doormat for some guy to walk all over?"

Alerted by the throbbing vein at his temple that he was angry, Katie broke free of Dylan and squared off in front of Christopher, unwilling to endure one of his chastisements. Meeting her challenging gaze, he disarmed her with a sympathetic smile and pulled her into a big-brother hug. "You didn't let yourself become a doormat—we bullied you into becoming one. I'm sorry, so very sorry."

Katie smiled into his watery eyes and let herself fall apart in his hold.

Anna appeared on the porch. Though she made it no secret she hated giving hugs, receiving hugs, and watching people give and receive hugs, she pushed her way in and smothered Katie with a big, clingy embrace.

"That was weird," Anna said. As soon as she released Katie, she took a giant step back and brushed hug remnants from her body.

"Yeah, it was," Katie agreed. "That was creepy."

"It seemed like the thing to do—must be the hormones." Anna patted her enormous belly. "They make me do the damnedest things these days."

With that, she grabbed Katie's hand and led her into the house. Two fat suitcases and a backpack on the verge of exploding waited conspicuously next to the sofa.

"What's this?" Katie asked, whirling around to the rest of her friends, who were stalking like shadows behind them.

Each wore a proud grin, but it was Heather who couldn't keep the surprise any longer.

"We're sending you to England!" she screeched.

Katie looked at her, puzzled. "But I'm already *going* to England."

"We're sending you the day after tomorrow," Rob beamed, happy to be a part of any scheme. "All it took was Christopher's credit card, Dylan's frequent flyer miles, and Anna's tenacity to change your ticket to first class—leaving Thursday."

"And don't worry about repacking," Anna added. "Heather managed to put your entire wardrobe into those suitcases."

"Not everything," defended Heather. "I left her one outfit and a pair of pajamas."

"But I can't," Katie argued. "I still have—"

"Finals?" Dylan finished her sentence. "You can take them early. I'm going to be here to help you study."

"Heather and Mr. Scott are going to take you to the airport," Christopher explained. "Dylan leaves a few hours earlier, so Rob or I will take him on our way to work."

"I have a doctor's appointment," Anna patted her belly apologetically.

The plan was already set in motion. There was nothing that Katie could do—besides accept. "Thank you everyone. But why? I don't understand."

"Because we finally realize we've been holding you back," Christopher said softly. "You've got bigger dreams than Jared Stone. We understand that now, and we want to make sure you don't waste another day not pursuing your heart's desires."

Katie put her hand on her heart in a silent thank you, too choked up to speak.

As if on cue, the doorbell rang. Anna ran to the peephole and hissed, "It's him!"

A hush fell over the room and a few uncertain seconds ticked by. Then, as if there were a telepathic meeting of the minds, Dylan locked arms with Katie and dragged her downstairs to her bedroom.

When the front door clicked open, they could hear Christopher's muffled voice. "This isn't a good time," he said tersely.

"Why not?" Jared asked, clueless.

Christopher pulled the door shut behind him to hold a private discussion with Jared outside.

Downstairs, Dylan pushed Katie toward her window just off center and below porch level, and twisted the blinds to get a better view of Christopher and Jared. The sound of racing footsteps hammered across the living room floor and down the stairs until Rob, followed by Heather, joined them at the window to spy on the confrontation.

Katie had never seen Christopher cut an intimidating figure, but his towering stance, arms tightly folded across his chest, made Jared's strapping frame seem insignificant.

"Dude, what's going on?" Jared asked.

Before Christopher could answer, the door flew open again and Anna charged onto the porch. "What's going on, you jackass, is that we don't approve of the way you treated Katie today!" She poked a finger into Jared's sternum as she spoke until Christopher pulled her back.

"What? Why? What did she tell you?"

"She didn't tell us anything. I was on the phone. I heard everything," Anna seethed, storming back into the house.

"Just let me talk to Katie," Jared demanded, attempting to follow her inside.

Christopher slid in front of the doorway, blocking his path. "Not now. Go home, Jared. Give things time to settle down."

Before Jared could respond, Anna came flying out the front door, screaming like a banshee, her arms burdened with a Costco-size bundle of paper towels.

"Here, if you're so worried about your damn paper towels!" She heaved the awkward super-size pack above her to hurl it at Jared's head. "Here are some paper towels! And don't ever speak to my friend again!" Realizing she couldn't produce enough strength to heave it effectively, she dropped the package to the ground with a loud groan.

Jared stood frozen, staring at the madwoman, while Anna tore into the cellophane like a she-cat and begun chucking individual rolls at him with all her might, littering the front lawn with sheets of white as she chased him off the porch.

The crowd peeping from the basement window fell into hysterics as Jared ran to his car, scooped a roll up under his arm, and took off.

Despite the extremely long day she'd had, Katie continued to laugh with her friends into the early hours of the morning, feeling almost guilty for having such a good time on the evening of her breakup with Jared. Such a good time that when someone declared it was time to go, she felt a pang of sadness, knowing it would be a long while before they would all be together again.

"Come on, let's go to bed. I'll even take the trundle bed tonight." Dylan comforted when the door had been shut behind the last of their friends.

***

"Katie, wake up…do you hear something?" Dylan had vacated the trundle beneath Katie's little girl daybed and was now kneeling over her, trying to shake her awake. "Come on, Katie, wake up! I think there's someone in the house."

A few moments later, the door creaked open. Dylan squealed like a teenage scream queen and dove in behind her on the tiny mattress.

"What the…? What's going on?" the intruder barked as he jumped back in fright, landing against Katie's dresser, knocking picture frames, books, and a bunch of paraphernalia to the floor with a loud clatter.

Katie shot up. That bark was now forever burned into her brain. "Jared?"

The lights flew on, catching Katie, with Dylan burrowing for dear life against her back, in a deer-in-the-headlights moment.

"What the hell is going on?" Jared demanded.

Katie scrambled away from her clinging bed partner. "Nothing's going on. What are you doing here?"

"I wanted to talk to you, but I had to wait for Anna to leave. She's nuts!"

"And then you broke into my house? Why didn't you just ring the doorbell?"

"What's he doing here?" Jared jerked his head toward Dylan.

"Dylan came to help me get ready to leave for England."

A range of unreadable emotions played across Jared's face. "When are you leaving?"   "Day after tomorrow." She straightened her back against the headboard. "It was going to be next week—which I tried to tell you, but you were either too angry or too preoccupied to care." She couldn't resist that last zing.

For a smart man, Jared had the clueless role down pat. "But Natalie and me are going shooting that day—I came to see if you wanted to come."

Natalie and I! Natalie and I are going shooting! Now that she was leaving, she no longer had to overlook his grammatical mistakes. He had a master's degree, for crying out loud! Even if it was in criminal justice, that was no excuse for not having mastered his native tongue.

"You're asking *me* to go shooting? With *Natalie*?"

"Well, yeah, we'll be spending a lot of time together while she coaches me through this interview process. I would like my two best girls to get to know each other."

Knowing as soon as Dylan could scramble to his cell phone it would become an iconic phrase in Katie dating history, she chose to ignore the bit about his "two best girls."

"What do you shoot?" she couldn't help asking. Envisioning Natalie's gloating smirk, she added silently, *Little children? Grandmothers?*

"Just rabbits and squirrels."

"You're inviting me to drive for hours, tromp through sagebrush, run the risk of having ticks bore into my armpits—or worse, my crotch—potentially causing me to come down with yellow fever, in order to terrorize furry little creatures?"

He shifted uncomfortably at the tenor of her reply. "We could shoot cans or targets instead."

"I don't think so. You and Sarah Palin will have to go without me. I have a flight to catch anyway."

Jared ran his hand along his head stubble, looking like he would trade his favorite AK-47 for the right thing to say. "Can I see you before you leave?"

"Why, so you can treat me like crap again?"

"I'm sorry about that, Katie. I shouldn't have reacted that way—I had a stressful day."

Katie shrugged, letting him know that wasn't an acceptable response.

"Don't you think we should probably talk?"

Katie considered the question a moment. "Yeah, I guess we probably should."

"Cool. I work all day tomorrow and then I'm getting together with Natalie. After that, maybe?"

"Sure." Katie already knew that even if she were clipping her toenails when he called, she'd still be too busy to talk to him.

Too busy thinking about her new life that wouldn't include him.

Chapter Eleven

She could only imagine what a sight they were, running down the frenzied airport corridors—she and Heather each lugging an overstuffed suitcase and Mr. Scott drilling her with instructions for her arrival in the United Kingdom.

"Bless me soul! Never in me life have I met a lass with such a knack for bein' tardy as you, miss." He wheezed as they began to slow their pace.

"A girl's got to be good at something," Katie teased. "Well, I guess this is it." She sighed and stopped before the check-in line. "I'm going to miss you guys." Her eyes welled up with tears.

Heather released the suitcase and flung her arms around Katie's neck. "Remember, you promised to call me once a week. And send me lots of pictures. I want visuals of everything and everyone in your new life."

"I will," Katie sniffed. Whispering into Heather's hair, she added, "And you'll look after Mr. Scott? Make sure he gets out of the house?"

"You can count on it. Now that you're leaving, he's the best friend I have here."

"All right, you two, this lass has a plane to catch," Mr. Scott impatiently broke in. "Lottie will ring my ever-lovin' neck if you're not on that airplane."

Katie sniffed again and wiped her eyes with the back of her sleeve. "Mr. Scott, do you think you could come and visit?"

"Bless me child! I don't believe so. And it's *Avery,* for the last time. No, pet, me home is here now and I don't much think I'll be leavin' it before I die." His eyes spoke a deep sadness that pained Katie to see.

"Mr. Sco—Avery, you're always giving me advice. Now it's my turn to leave you with some: Home, if not left from time to time, can become a cage." She held a staid expression, hoping to adopt a wise, Confucius-like manner.

A flicker of a smile flashed across his face as he contemplated her words, but there was no amusement in his tone. "That is very sage advice indeed. I will mull it over in me head."

"Please do. I'm wiser than you give me credit."

"Don't I know it," he chuckled. "Now, Little Miss Tardy, you've no time for dillyin' about. You remember your instructions for when you get to London?"

Katie nodded.

"Good. I wrote them down for you as well." He handed her a folded piece of stationery. "I couldn't decide if you'd be more likely to forget them or lose them."

She tried to look offended.

"Now don't you go scowlin' at me, pet. You're as clever as I've ever met, but you're also…what's the word? Aye…a *dingbat.* You're as dingbatty as they come."

She giggled at his description of her. "Thank you Avery…for everything. I'm going to miss you, you ornery old coot." She gave him a hug that nearly knocked him off his feet, and took in his faint scent of aftershave and books one last time. He returned her embrace and wiped a rogue tear away before sending her off.

"Be careful, lass. I'll phone me sister and let her know that I've sent you off. Someone will be at the airport to meet you!" he called out as he and Heather watched Katie make her way through security.

And just like that, she was gone.

Chapter Twelve

Katie spun a couple times trying to steady herself after being jostled off-balance by a mob of restless travelers. She didn't mind. She actually enjoyed the frantic pace of the Gatwick Airport. Her heart had felt leaden when she boarded the plane in Colorado, but now, in London, it skipped with anticipation.

Her first matter of business was to fit herself and all her luggage into the cramped toilet stall. It was an arduous chore that required gymnastic maneuvering to get properly straddled over the toilet seat, but she eventually managed. Just as she was about to relax and let nature take its course, her cell phone rang. She considered letting the call go to voicemail, but she worried it might be Mr. Scott calling with a change of plans. She dug through her backpack, sitting thankfully at squat level atop her suitcases, and located her phone.

"Hello?"

"It's Jared. We need to talk." An almost desperate plea lurked within the command.

"Um…can I call you back?" She clenched tightly against her body's urge to start peeing. "This really isn't the best time."

"No, Katie, we need to talk now. I can't stand the way we've left things—I love you."

Katie stopped breathing.

He continued without her reply. "I'm sorry if I was short with you, I really am, but after only one fight, you can't turn your back on what we had—have."

She focused on the sounds of flushing, flatulence, and peeing ricocheting down both corridors of the busy bathroom, which were much more welcome to her than Jared's pronouncement.

"Katie, did you hear me? I love you," he repeated. "Please tell me this isn't over."

Something about his pathetic plea, his exposed vulnerability, caused her gut to wrench. His proud, SWAT man dignity was hanging by a thread—and she felt compelled to save it.

"No, Jared, this doesn't have to be over. How about when I get back, we take our trip to Thailand and just see how things go?"

He must have been holding his breath because his response rode in on a rush of air. "So you'll still be my girlfriend?"

She let a moment of silence pass. She'd commit to just about anything to not be squished in this uncomfortable position any longer, having this uncomfortable conversation.

"Yes, Jared, I'll still be your girlfriend." She sounded more like an impatient mother than a girlfriend, but Jared didn't seem to notice.

***

Katie's right calf ached from the incessant tapping of her foot. She'd been waiting in the designated meeting spot for more than an hour with nothing to do but consider how she was goaded into committing herself to Jared. *New rule of thumb: Never make a promise with your pants down.* When she couldn't bear to rehash the degrading scene one more time, she picked up her cell phone and dialed Mr. Scott.

"Hi, Mr. Sco—Avery," she corrected in response to the billy goat rumble at the back of his throat. "This is Katie. You know, Katie

93

of the United Kingdom," she chirped, overcompensating for her grumpy disposition.

"Aye Katie, love…I believe I do remember. So you made it all right then?"

"To be sure I did, flower." She gave a poor impersonation of his accent.

"Ah, so I see, you're already a right British lass," he chortled. "Tell me now, who is it that came to greet you at the airport? Was it our Charlotte?" The excitement in his voice made Katie's heart dip.

"Actually, I was sans greeting party." She tried for an airy reply that would keep him from being alarmed.

"Are you meanin' to tell me you're there all alone?"

She was dismayed but not surprised that her casual reply hadn't worked. "Well, technically, yes, I am by myself. But the beautiful thing is you're never alone when you have people who love you."

"Don't you go makin' light of a serious matter, lass. Now, just you stay put and I'll have someone there in two shakes to fetch you."

"Don't worry about it, Mr. Scott. It's not worth putting anybody out. I can find my own way."

"I *will* worry about it! And it'll not be puttin' anybody out. I've still got me a few friends left in London who would be chompin' at their own limbs to spend time with a bonny lass."

Not exactly eager to meet anyone who'd own up to such a description, and less willing to spend another minute in the airport, she tried to reassure him.

"Mr. Scott, that's why I love you. If only everyone had as much chivalry! But no one does…meaning I have been abandoned in foreign countries before. Seeing as how I'm familiar with London and I speak fluent English, I think I can handle being on my own."

"You speak fluent *American*—don't confuse that with English, pet."

"Listen, I'll die if I have to spend one more minute in this airport. Even though I'm a savvy traveler and can take care of myself—" She ignored his argumentative *humph*. "I know you'll worry anyway. So here's my compromise: I'll go to one of those kiosks in the airport and book a hotel room, catch the train into the city, drop my luggage off in the room, then go have a look around. I'll call you when I know where I'm staying and will keep my phone on so you can pester—I mean, check up—on me all you want."

"Ahhh, go on with ya, pet, and have a good time." He was throwing his arms up in frustrated defeat, Katie could tell. "But mark me words, someone will be callin' for ya before nightfall."

Hauling herself and her six months' worth of packing onto the airport shuttle train, then on and off the tube before the doors and the commuters threatened to chop her into pieces, was grueling. However, the significance of just how much Heather had crammed into those suitcases didn't set in until Katie dragged them along Buckingham Palace Road, over six blocks to her shabby yet pricey hotel, then to her room, located up four and a half flights of stairs.

Goaded by her still-thrumming heart, Katie ignored the fatigue scratching behind her eyes and set out again. Driven by a mission, she hustled back down Buckingham Palace Road, not slowing her pace until she was behind a throng of other tourists at the Big Bus Tour stop.

She didn't care if the Big Bus Tour was nerdy. She loved it. She could ride the same routes all day long. Every time the bus rattled past a row of perfect Mary Poppins homes, she strained her eyes through mini binoculars to read every blue plaque that boasted of prominent historical figures who once lived inside. The Big Bus was a magical place where she could lose herself in a world where the romance of the past mingled with the excitement of the present.

A few hours of taking in fast-paced London from her slow-moving bus was all Katie could endure before succumbing to her jet lag. She didn't know what felt heavier: her eyes or her step. She stared longingly for a moment at a park bench, and for a brief moment considered sitting down to rest her eyes. Then she thought about the small fortune she'd paid for her mildewy room and lumpy mattress, and decided to persevere. As all her senses honed in on the need for sleep, the last few yards to the hotel and the stair climb to her room were all a blur.

Without bothering to untie her shoes, she kicked them off in front of the bed and crawled beneath the covers. Within seconds of closing her eyes, she was comatose.

***

Not knowing how long she had been zonked, she reluctantly surrendered her slumber to the uneasy feeling pricking her awake. Her mind was so bleary, it was difficult to recall where she was. And who the devil were the strange men standing above her?

Chapter Thirteen

Moments ticked by before Katie realized she was in her hotel room in London, and she couldn't place any of the three figures peering down at her. When full realization of that last bit settled in, she shot up. She tried to scream, but her bloody-murder screech was ensconced in a groggy croak. Instinctively she pulled the covers to her chin. Then, struck with another fear, she held the duvet back just far enough for her eyes—and her eyes only—to ascertain what she was (or was not) wearing.

"Phew." Her sigh was louder than she intended. Neither she nor the strange men had removed her clothes. *This is nothing to worry about,* her intuition said. *I'm going to be just fine.* She wanted to trust that sentiment, but parts of her that had been burned from relying on her intuition in the past told her to start screaming and run like hell. She shifted, ready to heed to those skeptical parts.

"Don't be nervous, pet." An older, white-headed stranger stepped forward. "We're here to help you, not hurt you." There was something welcoming in his kind face and she felt her apprehensions ease—a little.

Then the tallest and youngest of the men approached. She liked what she saw. He was rugged, like a man who had just stepped out of the pages of an REI catalogue, but polished as if he rubbed shoulders with the Prime Minister. It figured. The one time a man captured her interest, he was way out of her league—and possibly a murderer.

She looked between Mr. Ruggedly Polished and Mr. White Hair. If they were murderers, wouldn't she feel more nervous? Some sixth sense would kick in and scream at her to start clawing her way out of the room, right? These two men were too fashionable be murderers. Then again, British killers always sounded more eloquent than American ones (or so she would imagine, never actually having a run-in with killers of either nationality), so it could be assumed they dressed better, too.

Mr. Ruggedly Polished seemed to have sensed her deliberation. Kneeling down to her level, he reached out a comforting hand and patted her just above the knee. At least she assumed he meant to be comforting, but his touch—or maybe it was his delicious smile—emitted an electric sensation that blazed through her core. She should have jumped away. She should have screamed, "Don't touch me, Sexy Stranger!" But she didn't. Instead, she flashed him her most engaging smile.

His mocha eyes danced in response, and she felt oddly at ease by the fact they weren't flashing with murder and bloodshed. His shaggy brown hair that curled up at the ends made him seem gentle. Or maybe she just wanted him to seem that way because her arm itched to reach out and rub a lock between her fingers.

Just as he opened his mouth to speak, the door burst open and another man, about Katie's age, sauntered in as if there were no doubt of his being welcome. He was striking—gorgeous with a swoop of black hair jutting across his forehead, Zac Efron-style, circa *High School Musical.* He jumped back, surprised by the presence of the first three visitors, who seemed equally astonished at his presence.

Mr. Ruggedly Polished recoiled and bolted away from Katie, leaving behind the electric current that still thrummed along her spine.

An unsettling silence hovered over the room. Katie took advantage of the long moment to study the scene. Mr. Ruggedly

Polished and Mr. White Hair seemed confident and in control of the situation, while the third man—a dull-looking character whose greasy complexion and ginger stubble spoke of a desperate need for a shower—shifted as if he didn't know whether to stay or turn tail and run. No wonder—his faded black slacks, dingy white shirt, and name badge marked him as an employee of the hotel, clearly the culprit who'd let them inside her room.

Biting her bottom lip in contemplation, her eyes lingered again on Mr. Ruggedly Polished. She guessed him to be in his early thirties. His trousers and Burberry polo tried to camouflage his muscular physique. With his height and distinguished air, he could have cut an intimidating figure—except everything about him seemed so uncontrived and offhandedly natural. But the kindness in his eyes had now been replaced by fury. He bore the full of that emotion into Naughty Zac Efron's soul with his intense stare.

Mr. White Hair was the first to break the silence. Katie noticed now that his accent was similar to Mr. Scott's, though more refined.

"I must say, I am quite astonished to see you here," he said to Naughty Zac while laying a calming hand on Mr. Ruggedly Polished's shoulder.

Katie liked the older man, in part because he seemed caring, and also because she liked looking at the wavy lines in his thinning, perfectly combed hair.

"I could say the same thing about you, old codger," Naughty Zac said snidely in a very un-*High School Musical*-like reply.

Katie saw the hurt settle in the older man's eyes and was incensed. One thing she could not tolerate was cruelty to seniors. Without leaving her station on the bed, she rounded on Naughty Zac.

"Just who do you think you are?" she demanded. "You have no right to barge into my room like you're…you're…God's gift to…to…hotels! And you don't have the right to speak to this gentleman with anything less than the utmost respect. I'm sure he's earned his place in this world. I doubt you've done anything to earn yours."

She noticed Mr. Ruggedly Polished and Mr. White Hair exchange impressed glances, and was encouraged to continue. "Let me give you one piece of advice before I have one of these gentlemen throw you from my room. There are plenty of cocky, ill-mannered, disrespectful, and immature jackasses in this world—I suggest you try for something a little more unique."

"Blimey, who knew she'd be a bloody duchess on a massive high horse?" Naughty Zac crooned in a delicious British accent that caught her off guard. Though he acted unruffled by her reproof, he crept lower into his button-down collar. He glanced at Mr. Ruggedly Polished, who seemed ready to honor Katie's request to throw him out. Naughty Zac hesitated, then, without another word, strode out door.

Katie's mouth dropped open. She couldn't believe she'd just had an outburst. She hadn't entirely ruled out the three remaining men as serial killers, but still she turned to them, a concerned frown pulling at the corners or her eyes. "Do you think I hurt his feelings?"

The two distinguished men burst out laughing.

Mr. Ruggedly Polished again directed his attention to Katie. "Don't worry. I doubt he has feelings. You said exactly what he needed to hear. Maybe it will do him some good." Turning to his elderly companion, he added, "Sid, would you care to make the introductions?"

Mr. White Hair nodded. "Please accept our apologies for intruding and not introducing ourselves directly. I'm Sidney Ainsworth. Avery Scott is my dearest friend. Not long ago I received a call from him ranting how he'd lost a bonny lass in London."

A noisy commotion outside the door thwarted the rest of his explanation. Another uninvited man barged into her room—a stocky police officer, dragging Naughty Zac behind him by the armpit. Katie scoured the room with her eyes, looking for the hidden prank cameras. Naughty Zac was a good four inches taller than the officer, who was oblivious that he wasn't really in control, but merely being placated. Katie giggled quietly at the ridiculous sight.

All the men turned their gaze on her. Apparently, her giggle was not as soft as she had thought.

"Found this one skulking outside your door, miss," the officer announced, his words revealing a hint of Cockney. "One of the guests got concerned when she saw one of the employees lettin' a couple of men into yer room—thought ya might be in some danger."

Katie assumed this was more of a question than a statement. "That was sweet of her, but as you can see, I'm fine."

The officer, unconvinced, seemed to be acting on a deeper suspicion—or hope. "If you're certain you're fine, miss, then ya won't mind tellin' me who these men are. See, we've had quite of lot of burglaries in these cheap hotels and I just want to be sure."

His trigger-happy demeanor made its presence known at the base of Katie's nerves. Other than knowing Mr. Scott was the reason for her visitors' appearance, she still hadn't a clue who these men were.

She disguised her anxiety with the pretense of being affronted. "If you were paying in American dollars, you wouldn't be calling this a cheap hotel." As an afterthought, she added, "Sir."

"Aye miss, I didn't mean ya no offense. I'm just looking out for the safety of our tourists." He gave her the fisheye and patted his baton. "Now, if yer not goin' to tell me how these men came to be in yer room, I'll have to bring 'em in for questionin'. You, too."

Katie wasn't sure if he had grounds to do that, but one thing she'd learned from her travels was not to argue with foreign law enforcement. She didn't know if England really counted as "foreign," but she wasn't going to take the chance.

Mr. Ruggedly Polished took a step toward the officer. "I can clear up this misunderstanding. My name is—"

"Don't ya move!" the officer cut him off. One hand on his baton, he crouched into a defensive stance, looking like Kung Fu Panda. "The only person I want to hear from is the lady."

The image of the stubby officer holding Naughty Zac in one hand and beating the living tar out of the rest of them with the other was too much for Katie's inconvenient sense of humor. She laughed outright.

The officer stiffened. "Ya think this is funny, do ya?" An aggravated sneer snaked across his lips.

Laughing so hard she could barely breathe, she nodded her head.

"Maybe you'll think it's funny when I arrest ya for insubordination."

The thought of being thrown in jail for breaking the "Laughing Law" made her laugh even harder. Sidney and Mr. Ruggedly Polished looked as if they wanted nothing more than to laugh along with her. She noticed the officer turning various shades of angry, and forced herself to be serious.

"This whole situation is funny because…" She wiped a tear from her cheek. "My uh…grandfather…" She knew she had to choose her words carefully to pacify him. "He had made arrangements for somebody to pick me up at the airport this morning. When I arrived, nobody was there to meet me. So, I took a train into town and reserved this room. Knowing that my grandfather would be sending someone for me, I asked—" She glanced at the hotel employee's badge. "— Heath here to let them in, just in case I was out. The funny part is, when they came, I was so sound asleep I didn't hear the knock."

The officer wasn't willing to be appeased. "You still haven't told me who these men are."

Katie gestured to Sidney. "This is my…um…my uncle, Sidney Ainsworth. And this…" She waved her hand toward Mr. Ruggedly Polished. "This is…ah…"

Sidney cut in. "I'm sorry, sir, for your inconvenience. As the lass said, I'm Sidney Ainsworth, and this young man is Lucas Hay—"

The officer cut him off. "I said I'm only hearing from the lady!"

Sidney had supplied just enough information for Katie to connect the dots. Given the disposition of the officer, she felt he wouldn't accept anything less than a familial relationship. "This, officer, is my…uh…my…cousin?"

The office cocked his eyebrow. "You're askin' me a question?"

She turned her full lips down into a slight pout, which seemed to enlarge her green eyes to saucer size. "I'm sorry. This is an awkward situation for me. It's the first I've seen my English family since…since ever." She wanted to keep the lies to a minimum. "I hesitated before, because Lucas Hayden is going to be my new employer. I didn't know if it would be appropriate to introduce him as my cousin. I don't want to take advantage of the family connection. I hope you understand…sir."

To her relief, the officer seemed to cave. "Aye miss, I do understand. As a matter of fact, I happen to work under me own father-in-law."

The officer began to take his leave, then realized he was still clutching Naughty Zac.

"What about this one?" He gave the handsome devil another good shake.

She racked her brain for an explanation and decided to keep to her code of not telling more lies than necessary. "That one, I don't know."

A near panic flooded Naughty Zac's face while the officer looked perplexed.

Lucas stepped forward, stifling a laugh. "This is another family member, Andrew." His amused tone turned reprimanding and his eyes again blazed severe displeasure. More than just disapproval sparked behind his eyes, but Katie couldn't quite put her finger on it. "Andrew was meant to pick Katie up from the airport and failed to do so." It clearly took great effort for the heated Lucas to say no more on the subject.

The officer released Andrew. "Well, lad, I'll leave ya here with yer family…though I think you'd be safer coming with me. I hope they give ya what ya deserve. You should be ashamed, leaving a smart-looking woman by herself in the big city. If you was my family, I'd give ya a wallopin' you'd never forget."

Giving Lucas an encouraging nod, the officer left the room. Heath, the nervous hotel employee, gave him a few seconds' head start, then bolted in the opposite direction down the hall.

The absurdity of the moment caught up with them, and they all burst out laughing—all except Andrew.

Katie was the first to speak. "What I don't understand is why didn't Mr. Scott just call me and tell me someone was coming?"

Sidney and Lucas exchanged confused looks.

"When he called me," Sidney explained, "he said he had been ringing your mobile for an hour. He was worried something had happened and insisted I come fetch you."

"I got the same call." Lucas said. I've never seen Uncle Avery in such a huff."

She felt a gush of guilt swirl inside her. "I didn't realize I had been a source of such concern. I'm really sorry. I didn't mean to be a bother."

Lucas took a seat next to her on the bed. "Katie, you've been no bother at all." It tickled her spine to hear him caress her name with his velvety accent.

"I was careful to keep my phone with me all the time because I knew Mr. Scott was so worried—*unnecessarily,* I would like to add on my behalf. I wonder why I didn't get his calls."

"Listen, do you hear something?" Sidney interrupted her contemplations.

They all listened—and heard the muffled sounds of George Michael singing.

"Isn't that…Wham?" Lucas asked. "Where is it coming from?"

Katie's face began to burn various shades of red as her bum vibrated "Wake Me Up Before You Go-Go (Jitterbug)." Lifting up one cheek, she pulled her cell phone out from underneath her, the tone growing louder. Suddenly her body was flaming hot. She wanted to die. These men, two of them scathingly handsome, had just watched what looked like the act of her pulling something out of her butt.

She answered the call, but before she could manage a hello, Mr. Scott was bellowing loudly enough for them all to hear.

"What the bloody hell is going on over there? Here I am worryin' meself sick, and nobody will answer their soddin' mobiles!" Katie could imagine Mr. Scott in his brown cardigan, pacing the hallway, mussing up what was left of his silver hair.

"Hi. I'm sorry I worried you. I guess I couldn't hear my phone," she replied, giving Lucas and Sidney a sheepish smile.

Mr. Scott bellowed a few more phrases that were gobbledygook to Katie, but gave Sidney and Lucas cause to chuckle. She looked up and shrugged at the two men, confused.

Lucas smiled as he took the phone from her.   "Hiya Uncle, no need to worry. Sidney and I are both here with Katie."

Katie found herself enthralled with Lucas's polished English voice.

106

"No, no, everything is fine," Lucas continued. "I bumped into Sidney at the hotel reception... No, she's just fine... There was no problem at all, found her in her room... No, fine... Really, nothing wrong at all... Well, it turns out that my new *cousin* is a massively deep sleeper—that's all." Lucas cast Katie a playful wink. She reddened, hearing Mr. Scott howling with laughter all the way from the United States.

Lucas resumed, "Had a bit of a run-in with one of the police. Thought something dodgy was going on with so many blokes entering Katie's room... Dead set on taking us all in, too... Yeah, yeah, Sidney, the hotel attendant, me, Andrew—"

At the mention of Andrew's name Mr. Scott was again ranting loudly enough for the room to hear. "I'd like to have a few words with that lad! One thing we ask the lad to do—one thing—and he won't even follow through with that!"

Andrew shifted from one foot to the other as Mr. Scott charged on.

"...Leavin' our Katie to fend for herself in a new country! I regret that—"

Lucas cut him off. "Now Uncle, Katie is just fine, so don't waste your energy on what could have been."

The act was subtle, but Katie understood Lucas had intentionally stopped his uncle from speaking what would be damaging for both the subject and speaker. It was a small gesture of thoughtfulness, but enough for her to realize he was more than just hot body with a head for business.

Lucas added, "I was dead impressed with Katie's quick thinking. She handled the officer brilliantly... Aye Uncle, I can see how she could be a handful." He flashed her a teasing smile.

Despite the awkwardness of being the topic of conversation, she secretly relished Lucas's approval.

Finishing the conversation with a promise to call the next day, Lucas faced Katie with a broad smile. "Well, that was an adventure!"

"Well then, now that everything's sorted, I'll take the Duchess back to Yorkshire." Andrew strode forward, his cocky attitude fully intact. His eyes skimmed her body, lingering over her chest, before glancing at the two men. "And you two can get back to...whatever it is that you two do."

There wasn't time for Katie to decide if she would go with the awful Andrew before Lucas stepped between them. "What do you say we take Katie out for a bit of London nightlife? How about it, Sidney? I think we owe it to my new cousin to give her a better welcome than we've shown her thus far."

Katie, awed by his use of the word "thus," readily agreed. She was eager to know more about her new boss and Sidney Ainsworth. Andrew, on the other hand, she wasn't so excited about and felt a stab of disappointment when she heard Lucas invite him along.

Andrew was not as gracious toward Lucas. "Thank you, no. I can think of more enjoyable things to do than spend the evening with two old sods and a pain-in-the-arse duchess." His gaze brushed over Katie again before he turned and walked out.

"So, Sid?" Lucas urged, shaking off Andrew's rejection. "Are you up for taking my new cousin out tonight?"

"You know, I think I would fancy a night out for a change. But first, we have to get the lass out of this hotel and settled somewhere more suitable. I'll bring her round to my place, if that's all right with you. Mrs. Albright will enjoy having someone new to make a fuss over."

After obtaining Lucas's permission as though Katie were his charge, Sidney turned to her and asked if she would mind being his guest for the evening.

"Of course I'd love to, as long as nobody fusses over me," Katie said. "I don't want to be an inconvenience."

"An inconvenience?" Sidney exclaimed. "Goodness no, child! My home is so dull these days. It would be a welcome pleasure to have a bit of your liveliness about the place."

Lucas gave her a reassuring nod, indicating Sidney was not just being polite.

"Right then. Lucas, we'll see you round my place in about an hour," Sidney directed. He turned to Katie. "I'll have Geoffrey pull the car around while you get your things together. And welcome to London, my dear!"

Chapter Fourteen

Katie felt her heart flop wildly in her chest when he led her out to the "car," which was not a taxi, but a vintage Rolls-Royce.

"Ah, and you must be Katie. Lovely to meet you. I'm Geoffrey," said the man, obviously a personal employee, standing next to the vehicle.

She stopped short at Geoffrey's cordial address. His chipper Irish brogue didn't correspond with his appearance: a middle-aged Barney Rubble on steroids. Except where Barney Rubble seemed friendly and easygoing, Geoffrey's stoic expression radiated a definite "back off" vibe.

"Thanks, nice to meet you, too!" she replied brightly, trying to decipher which was the more accurate read—his tone or his face.

He eyed her proffered hand before clamping it in his own. Shaking hands was part of Katie's business as a realtor, and she'd been commended more than once on her strong grip. But for some reason, she felt the need to significantly increase the pressure with Geoffrey. He made a long assessment of her, and though she wanted to let go and run and hide behind Sidney, she flexed her jaw and kept a vice-like hold on his hand. Slowly the tension in his face melted and the suspicion dropped from his eyes. He gave a quick nod, which Katie did not mistake as acceptance, merely a chance at it.

"Lucas, lad, let me help with that." This time Geoffrey's expression matched his warm tone. He dashed toward Lucas, who lumbered outside trying to negotiate all of Katie's luggage.

Sidney wrapped his arm around Katie's shoulder, giving her a side hug. "Don't mind Geoffrey," he whispered. "He's just overprotective. He'll warm up once he gets to know you."

She could only offer Sidney a weak smile—she had her doubts. But she didn't have the capacity to think about Geoffrey now, not when she was about to ride in this stellar vehicle.

Lucas wandered over to Sidney's other side. Katie's thoughts about the Rolls must have been obvious, because Lucas grinned and said, "Ol' Sid here is quite an eccentric." He put an arm around the man's shoulder and touched his head against Sidney's. A small gesture, but it was obvious by the way Sidney beamed that it meant everything.

For the second time in the crazy hour she'd known Lucas, she was impressed with his thoughtfulness. He seemed to have all the manners of an old-world English gentleman, but he was modern-day hot.

After helping Sidney and then Katie into the succulent vehicle, Lucas leaned in, one long arm resting on top of the car, the other on top of the partially opened door. "You two have a lovely drive." He winked at Katie, giving her a sexy smirk that probably wasn't meant to be sexy. "I'll meet you on the hill in about an hour."

"That's a fine boy, that one." Sidney sighed as Geoffrey pulled away from the curb. "Known him from a wee bairn. He and his Uncle Avery, birds of a feather those two, up until…" He seemed to be debating whether he was saying too much. "Let's just say that our Lucas and his Uncle Avery are the apple of each other's eye—just about broke the boy's heart when Avery went off to America."

111

Katie couldn't resist this golden opportunity to finally know more about Mr. Scott. "Mr. Ainsworth—"

Sidney's hearty chuckle was stolen straight from Santa Claus himself. "Ho, ho, ho! Bless me! 'Mr. Ainsworth' is me father, God rest his soul. Just call me Sidney."

"Okay, Sidney...will you tell me about Mr. Scott?" She looked up just in time to notice Geoffrey shoot a wary glare at Sidney from the rearview mirror.

Sidney appeared not to notice. Instead, he seemed to be concentrating on Katie. His sigh was weighty. "Our Avery keeps so much locked inside. Has he not told you anything about himself?"

Katie looked away only for an instant, but it was answer enough.

"I see." His countenance was unreadable. It took a moment for him to process her request, but just as she'd hoped, he said, "Then I'll tell you what it is Avery Scott keeps bottled up...poor bugger."

Geoffrey hurled another severe look at Sidney.

Sidney shrugged him off and took Katie on a walk down Memory Lane. "Avery and I met as young men during our service in the Royal Navy. We quickly, along with Andrew's granddad, God rest his soul, became like brothers. After our tour in the Navy, we all three moved to London. Oh Lordy! Three Northern boys loose in the big city! What a smashing time we made of it!" Sidney chortled at the reminiscence.

"On one of his weekend rambles through Hyde Park, he met Jane. My, if she wasn't a bonny lass! She had traveled all the way from America to do her studies at Oxford. Mind you, in those days, we Northern boys didn't socialize much with scholars or Americans—

112

wealthy ones at that. Our Avery was completely smitten and set about to impress her. He did everything possible to get into university just to win her over. Practically moved mountains, and dragged me along with him the whole way. Wasn't anything Avery couldn't do when he was determined." Sidney shook his head and sighed. "A man born to hold the whole world in his pocket, he was. In all me years, I've never met one soul who was immune to his persuasions." He laughed at some unspoken memory.

"They did, in time, marry, splitting their time between Yorkshire and London. However, dear Jane began to suffer from such homesickness that they ended up spending more and more time in America. She once told me late wife, Helen, she felt as if she were split right in two. One half of her always in England, where she gained a wonderful new family and so many friends, and the other in America with her own relatives.

"When Jane's mother was diagnosed with terminal cancer, they bought a home in the States and remained there until she died. Afterward, Avery would fly back to England for short visits, but Jane, not wanting to leave her father alone, never did join him. It was on one of his visits home that Jane fell suddenly ill. Avery rushed back to America to be by her side, but she had passed just moments before he arrived."

Sidney's eyes met Geoffrey's in the rearview mirror. They watched Katie in silence as she absorbed this new information. At first her head was bowed and they could not see her reaction. When she did lift her head, a path of tears trickled down both cheeks.

Sidney rubbed a consoling hand across her shoulder blades and returned to the story.

113

"Poor Avery's heart broke then and there. That was not quite thirteen years ago." He stayed on in the States to take care of Jane's father, who passed away a few years back. And hasn't returned home since. Never has forgiven himself for leaving his beloved bride."

"How did she die?" Katie wiped a fresh crop of tears from her eyes.

"That's even more the tragedy. You see, Avery and Jane had been trying to have children all their married life. After a number of miscarriages, Avery gave up hope, but Jane never did. Even in her later years when most people would have thought it impossible, Jane gave her life still trying."

Putting the pieces together, Katie confirmed, "You mean she was pregnant?"

Sidney nodded. "Aye. Avery never knew. She probably kept it to herself, not wanting to break poor Avery's heart again if it didn't happen—or afraid he would try to keep her from going through with the pregnancy."

Katie's saddened face took on a look of strain.

Sidney watched her brow furrow, becoming concerned when she squeezed her temples between her fingers. "Good heavens pet! What's the matter?"

Katie looked at him. "Nothing, I'm trying to do the math— that's all."

His lips twitched, but he pushed aside his amusement to solve the puzzle for her. "Jane died at forty-three. Avery was six years her senior."

The strain overtook her face again. This time he let her work it out on her own. "That means Mr. Scott is only sixty-two? He's younger than my parents. I'd always assumed he was way older." She took in Mr. Scott's age progression with a fresh wave of sorrow. How much must he have suffered—still suffer—to be so aged beyond his years?

Sidney sighed. "I'm afraid Avery has not taken the grief well. He's turned into an old man waiting for time to pass."

After a moment's silent contemplation, he wiped the remaining moisture from his eyes. "Here we are! Home at last!" he chimed as if they'd been swapping amusing anecdotes all along.

Katie's jaw dropped as her attention turned toward her whereabouts. She reached over and grabbed Sidney's bony wrist. "Sidney, how many families live here?"

Sidney chuckled at her naiveté. "Just mine, if you can call it a family. There's meself; Mrs. Albright, our beloved housekeeper; and Geoffrey." He motioned to Geoffrey, who was already pulling Katie's luggage from the trunk. "Lucas often joins us for dinner when he's in town…and occasionally he brings his lady."

Katie felt a little stab in her chest. She wondered who Lucas's "lady" was. And was there a note of contempt in Sidney's voice?

She returned her attention to the house. "It's the most spectacular home I've ever seen." She gazed up at the steep A-line rooftops, several of which were adorned with a substantial growth of ivy. The home was a formidable red brick of Elizabethan architecture. Forty yards in front, protectively concealing the stately manor, were perfectly manicured hedges that stood at least twenty-five feet tall and ran the perimeter of the estate.

"It's a monstrosity, that's what it is," Sidney rejoined. "It's the estate that me late wife's family left her. Proud descendants of British

115

aristocracy. No doubt they're turning over in their graves knowing it's been passed on to their common son-in-law from the North." He made no attempt to stifle a snigger. "But we'll discuss them once you're comfortably settled in. No need putting a damper on a lovely evening." He offered Katie his arm and escorted her to the door.

Inside, Katie was introduced to Mrs. Albright, a portly, copper-haired woman who quickly revealed her innate drive to zealously care for others.

"We are so happy you've come to visit us, dear. I'm afraid we can be a rather dull lot," Mrs. Albright chirped. "Well now, let's have a look at you." She grabbed Katie's hands warmly and pulled her arms out from her sides. "My, aren't you a gorgeous one! And aren't your teeth just lovely!" Squishing Katie's cheeks together with one hand, Mrs. Albright admired the American teeth. "What I wouldn't give for a nice, shiny set like you've got!"

"There, there, give the lass room to breathe," interrupted Sidney. "Mrs. Albright, would you mind showing Katie her room and giving her a quick tour of the place bit before Lucas arrives?"

Mrs. Albright clapped her hands. "Of course, I'd love to!" Turning to Katie, she whispered, "I'm looking forward to seeing our Lucas. What a handsome man he's become." She gave Katie a light nudge with her elbow.

Katie reddened a little and sought another subject. "This is such a lovely home, Mrs. Albright. I've never seen anything more beautiful."

Mrs. Albright beamed and launched into her favorite topic of conversation. "Isn't it, love? Let me tell you all about it as I show you around. We're in quite a historical area, as you must know."

116

Which Katie didn't, but she smiled and nodded, hoping to conceal her ignorance.

"We're located on a private road on the sought-after Pinner Hill. This substantial six-bedroom home offers a roof terrace with brilliant views over Pinner and London," she began, as if she were an estate agent trying to sell the property. Motioning for Katie to follow, she ascended a wide, elegant staircase. "The property comprises two light and spacious reception rooms; a well-equipped, modernized kitchen; and—"

Katie felt a tug on her arm keeping her back. She looked back to find Sidney in the midst of a wholehearted chortle. "I think you've made a friend for life. She prepared this speech for the historical society and hasn't had a chance to recite it since." He released her arm, still chuckling, and turned back down the stairs.

She easily caught back up to Mrs. Albright, who was oblivious to her short absence.

"…Separate utility room, plus an additional first-floor kitchen. As I said, there are six beautifully presented bedrooms, all with en-suite bathrooms, dressing rooms, and access to the roof terrace."

At the top of the staircase, she turned to Katie, expecting her to express her admiration, which Katie did, right on cue.

"…Two contemporary shower rooms, guest cloakroom, cellar." She stopped inside a living room that was enormous and lavishly decorated in a way that only the British can pull off. Mrs. Albright pulled the curtains to reveal the back garden. Katie gasped. She had never seen anything so amazing in someone's private home. This garden rivaled that of some of the finest castles in France. The lush green lawn sprawled for over an acre and was expertly decorated with at least a dozen different types of gardens. King Louis—any one of them—would have been impressed.

Fencing in the outer edges of the lawn were those magnificent, larger-than-life hedges. There was a small opening just at the back of the lawn that led into a dense forested area. Katie could only make out the tops of the enormous trees from her vantage point at the window, but her sense of adventure had her longing to explore those woods.

Despite the manor's extravagance, it was still homey. She was surprised how at ease she felt there. She mulled this over while absentmindedly admiring the rest of the house that Mrs. Albright was describing in painstaking detail. The last room on the tour was Sidney's library, bright and airy with white walls and white furniture. The room gave Katie instant trepidation. She couldn't wear a white top without getting it filthy; she was afraid of what she could do to a whole room.

"The property is located within an easy distance of a wonderful range of shops, cafes, and bars, whilst being moments from the peaceful open spaces of Pinner Hill," Mrs. Albright's speech finally came to a close.

"Bravo! Brilliantly done, Mrs. Albright," Sidney cheered, surprising them with his applause.

Mrs. Albright and Katie turned around to see Sidney with Lucas and Geoffrey beside him.

"Yes, Mrs. Albright, well done. Lovely to see you again." Lucas gave Mrs. Albright a light kiss on the cheek. The woman blushed so furiously, her face almost matched the color of her hair.

Lucas offered a slight bow of recognition toward Katie. She took a startled step backward. "Holy crap! Did you just *bow*? You didn't just bow at me? Who does that anymore?"

She made a quick grasping motion in front of her lips, as if to catch the errant thoughts escaping from her mouth. When it was apparent every last syllable had not only escaped, but had been clearly heard by all, she clasped a hand over her mouth to silence any more rogue thoughts.

"Sorry?" Lucas's eyebrows were raised as if he were questioning her sanity.

She couldn't tell through the ringing in her ears—the kind that follows just after one has made a complete ass of oneself—but she had the distinct feeling he was laughing at her. A quick look around the room confirmed that *everyone* was laughing at her...even Geoffrey. She didn't think he was capable of mustering a sense of humor.

With effort, she pried her hands from her mouth and felt some of the heat escape her cheeks. "I'm not used to such chivalry back home." She forced herself to match the joviality of her companions. "Apparently, I was grossly unprepared to stumble into Prince Regency himself." Her smile was triumphant as she flourished a curtsey toward Lucas.

"Prince Regency. Hmmm," Lucas mused, casting a broad smile that played her spinal cord like a harp.

"Ho, ho, ho," Sidney chimed with his contagious laughter, "there's never going to be a dull moment with this lass around, I can tell."

Glancing at his watch, Lucas changed his tone and the subject. "Sidney, if we're going to go out tonight, we'd best hurry—it's nearly quarter of six."

Catching something in Lucas's tenor that hadn't been there before, Sidney asked suspiciously, "And what is it that you have in mind, lad?"

Lucas squirmed. "I completely forgot about this charity do going on tonight...and...well, Olivia is really hot with me about it...and I thought...maybe we all could go?" He managed a desperate grin.

Katie tried to hide her disappointment. Olivia, she gathered, must be Lucas's *fine lady*. Strangely, the mere mention of her name seemed to chase away the cheerful demeanor in the room.

"I thought Olivia wasn't due back until next week. What happened to Hong Kong?" Sidney inquired.

Lucas shifted again. "Hong Kong wasn't quite what she expected." Sidney's reproachful stare forced a further explanation. "She said it was a big, ugly, manky, stinky city...I'm pretty sure that's how she described it." Lucas's look of distress matched Sidney's, and Katie wondered what the big deal was—it seemed like a fair description.

Attempting to restore some of the former high spirits, Lucas turned to Katie with forced cheerfulness. "What do you say, Duchess? I promised you the royal treatment tonight. Would you like to go to a ball this evening?"

Oozing playful sarcasm, she responded, "It's difficult to pass up such a cheesy invitation—really. But alas, attending a ball tonight would be way too cliché." In a more serious tone, she added, "Thank you, though. You should go and enjoy the evening with your girlfriend."

"Fiancée," Sidney corrected.

So it's official. He's engaged. It figures, Katie thought, suddenly feeling deflated.

Lucas shot Sidney a pleading glance that was answered by a slow but definitive shake of the head. Elbows on knees, a defeated Lucas dropped his head into his hands and sat silent for a moment, running his fingers through his shaggy brown hair in frustration. Katie watched the soft pieces of tousled hair fall back into place and for a split second she wanted to crouch down next him and run her own fingers through his lush tresses. She immediately thought of Jared and his bald head, and lamented having agreed earlier to continue on as his girlfriend.

Scolding herself for lusting after another man's head of hair, Katie turned her attention back to the present moment. Lucas was now contemplating the ceiling. He heaved a frustrated sigh and motioned for Katie to sit on the sofa. Sidney took a seat next to her.

Mrs. Albright and Geoffrey took their cue. Proclaiming to have duties to do, they turned to walk away.

"Please stay," Lucas said sincerely. "You two are part of the family."

The two employees glowed with pride.

"I have to do some groveling to Uncle Sid," Lucas began. "He gave me some sound advice that I foolishly ignored and now I'm pretty well buggered."

Sidney reached out and grabbed Lucas's hand and gave it a reassuring pat. His warm display wrenched a feeble smile from Lucas.

121

Focusing on Katie, Lucas continued his explanation. "I was commissioned by Lord and Lady Waverly to plan their holiday."

The names meant nothing to her, but the mention of Lord and Lady Waverly created an excited buzz between Geoffrey and Mrs. Albright.

"They were a contact that came through Olivia's family," Lucas said. "Naturally, Olivia wanted to be a part of it."

He was interrupted by a loud "humph" from Mrs. Albright—which he pretended not to notice, still directing his tale toward Katie. "I wasn't very keen on the idea. I didn't feel Olivia was cut out for the job. But she was eager to prove herself, and knowing that I couldn't turn away such a promising client, she insisted I allow her to plan the whole thing or she would sever our connection with the Waverlys."

He turned from Katie and began pacing in front of the sofa, hands clasped behind his back. "We had quite a row over it, but in the end she convinced me. Sidney warned me it would be a bloody bad idea to give her the reins." He turned to Sidney. "I thank you, Sid, for your spot-on advice. I wish I had taken it." Then, to no one in particular, he said, "What a stupid sod I am. I wanted to believe she could manage it. Against my better judgment—and Sid's—I let myself be manipulated, romanticizing we could have so much fun scouting holidays together as a couple. Now, I'm buggered!"

Katie let herself get caught up in the idea of making a living by gallivanting across the world with one's true love. Hearing Lucas give up on that dream was far more distressing to her than anything else he had told her so far.

"Lucas, it's a beautiful dream. How could you not give it a chance? You shouldn't give up on it."

He gave her a look that was part wistful and part something else that made her heart beat erratically. "You know, I think you're the first person I've met who truly understands the magic of the concept." For a moment, they shared an intense connection—until he broke their gaze. "It is a wonderful dream, Katie, but I'm afraid it gets more complicated. The Waverlys know Olivia went to Hong Kong to arrange their holiday, so when they see her tonight, they'll be expecting an exquisite itinerary. Olivia intends to tell them Hong Kong is a horrible place and they should change their travel plans." He scratched his hands through his hair again. "She thinks she knows what the Waverlys want. What she refuses to comprehend, despite my many explanations, is that Lady Waverly is set on Hong Kong—it's some sentimental journey she's determined to have."

"Surely Olivia doesn't have to see them tonight?" Sidney exclaimed.

Lucas shook his head in dismay. "The Waverlys are helping to sponsor the charity ball. Olivia insists on going tonight—to recommend they change their plans."

Katie fought not to make a negative judgment about Olivia, but it was becoming a losing battle.

Lucas pulled up the desk chair and sat down to face Katie. He leaned in and took her hand in both of his. "Katie, Lord and Lady Waverly carry a lot of influence. I would have been much better off not to have attracted their attention. They set the standard for society's elite. Disappointing them would be career suicide. One negative word from the Waverlys can—*has*—ruined many a business. But if I can stay in their good graces, I could have every social climber in the country begging me to arrange their holiday. I *need* to get to that ball before Olivia does. Please, will you help me?"

He was so close that she could breathe in his subtle scent of manliness and laundry soap. Having him so near, making her his confidante, sent tingles skipping down the back of her neck.

"Help you...do what?" Katie responded.

He gave her hand a light squeeze, which made the tingles blaze into a hot current. Turning to include Sidney in the conversation, Lucas said, "The best help I can have right now, besides moral support, is a couple of quick thinkers at my side."

Sidney cast a sidelong glance at Katie and shrugged. Katie returned his gesture. She was game if he was.

Sidney offered a sympathetic smile and shook his head at Lucas. "All right lad, we'll go."

Lucas punched the air victoriously. "Thank you. I will make up this evening to both of you, I promise. And I'm sorry to rush you, but we haven't got much time."

"I suppose you take me for the sort of girl who keeps an emergency ball gown in her suitcase?" Katie teased.

Lucas's countenance fell and he shot a panicked glance at Sidney, who threw up his hands to express he wasn't in the business of carrying emergency ball gowns either. Lucas's head dropped in defeat.

"I guess it's lucky for you that I *am* just that sort of girl." She giggled, flashing the room a victorious smile.

Thank goodness Katie had dragged Heather and Mr. Scott all over town in search of the dress she knew symbolized her destiny! She and Dylan had later christened the dress "Greta the Magical Gown," due to its wondrous ability to vanish her Little Buddha without the assistance of oversized super-elastic underwear. When she paired it with equally miraculous strappy shoes that enhanced the muscle tone in her calves and added leggy inches to her stature, she possessed the most exquisite ensemble, one that even *Queer Eye* Dylan couldn't find fault with.

"It will take me twenty minutes to find my room, but I can be ready in ten. Will that fit into your schedule, Mr. Hayden?" she asked.

***

Locating Greta the Magical Gown in her luggage took a few minutes. Already living up to its magical moniker, Greta was wrinkle-free and ready to wear. With the help of Mrs. Albright's skilled hands at creating elegant updos, Katie was ready and looking regal in less than twenty minutes.

"Oh, just look at you, love! You're gorgeous!" Mrs. Albright gushed, circling Katie. "I wish I could see the look on Olivia's face when you come walking in with her man."

"Mrs. Albright, is she really as bad as she sounds?"

"Worse," Mrs. Albright stated matter-of-factly. "She never shows her true colors around Lucas—he thinks she's lovely. But the rest of us have seen the demon that hides behind her pretty face."

"Surely, if she were so bad, Lucas would notice," Katie said.

"If that's what you want to think—but you be careful around her. If I know Olivia, she's not going to like having you in the picture. For the sake of our Lucas, don't let her chase you off."

When Katie reappeared in the library, she found Lucas, Sidney, and Geoffrey engrossed in conversation. Sidney looked dashing, decked out in his Royal Navy best. For a fleeting moment

Katie caught a glimpse of a young Sidney—gallant, handsome, and full of life—and she felt a flurry of pride for him.

One look at Katie in her long, silvery, off-the-shoulder gown stopped Lucas mid-sentence. In fact, he did a double take—which was not lost on Katie or anyone else in the room. She ducked her head to hide her rising blush while Sidney and Mrs. Albright flashed each other optimistic, "dare we hope?" smiles.

"Wow, Cousin Katie, you look amazing! Like a true duchess!" Lucas lingered on the word "cousin," almost as if he were trying to let that point sink in. He began to look very uncomfortable, then quickly pried his gaze away from her. As if he needed something to busy himself, he patted around his breast pocket and pulled out the tickets for the evening's event, finding great fascination in the fancy embossed lettering.

"We're going to have our work cut out for us tonight trying to keep a protective eye on this beauty," Sidney guffawed.

"Thank you for your compliments, but I have to give credit where credit is due. This is all the work of Mrs. Albright and Greta," Katie said.

They looked at her with confusion. "Greta?" the men questioned in unison.

Crimson crept into her complexion. "Greta's my dress."

Sidney bellowed his "ho, ho, hos." "Bless me! Whoever heard of such a thing?"

A slow, delicious smile rolled across Lucas's face and amusement sparked his eyes. "Of course, and we appreciate Greta *very* much—and Mrs. Albright—however, some credit has to be given to the wearer of such a gown."

She returned his grand smile and issued him a dramatic curtsey. "Well then, Greta and I both thank you."

Lucas took an exaggerated bow in her direction before adding, "I don't suppose you're the type of girl to keep an emergency tiara in her luggage, are you?"

Without missing a beat, Katie countered, "What do you take me for, ostentatious?"

Lucas smiled. "Of course not. It's just that I forgot to read the fine print on the tickets. Women are required to wear tiaras."

"Are you joking?"

"I'm afraid not."

Katie shot a look at Sidney, who shrugged.

"Well then, we'll just have to pop into the tiara shop on our way to the ball, won't we?" she sassed. "What kind of event requires a tiara anyway?"

"A very pretentious one," Lucas pointed out.

Katie felt her insides begin to tremble. She hadn't the time to think much about this shindig, but she had the sinking feeling it was going to be exponentially more snobbish than any of the country club events Jim and Sheila had dragged her to.

"Now that I think about it, I'm not so sure I'm cut out for this sort of thing. I've never actually worn a tiara before...probably only professional tiara wearers are welcome there, right?" she backpedaled. "In fact, do I have to dance at this ball? Because I don't dance. I only dance with Jim because he lets me stand on top of his feet."

Lucas took a step toward her. "Jim?"

His close proximity increased her nervous babble. "Jim's my...well, he's Christopher dad. He pretty much raised me—Jim, not

127

Christopher. Christopher's my best friend, more like a brother, really, but I call him 'Mom' because he acts more like a mom to me—"

Lucas put his hands on her bare shoulders, and his thumbs caressed her naked neck for an instant. "Relax. You'll be fine. I have the feeling you're a natural tiara wearer."

His touch, meant to be reassuring, only succeeded in breeding more butterflies in her stomach.

"Well, one has to *have* a tiara to know if she's a natural," she pointed out. "So, I'll just go back upstairs and change into something more 'me,' like an old potato sack or something."

"That won't be necessary. I believe I can help," Sidney spoke up. "Mrs. Albright, would you mind fetching one of Mrs. Ainsworth's tiaras from the safe, and a choker to match?"

Both Lucas and Katie protested at the suggestion.

"Nonsense, pet," Sidney interrupted. "Helen wouldn't have had it any other way." Then turning to Lucas, he added, "I can think of no better honor than to have Katie wear Helen's jewelry back out into society. She's a special lass and deserves to be presented in nothing but the finest adornments. I'm certain Helen would have agreed." He finished with a definitive nod that indicated the subject was closed.

Mrs. Albright returned with a shimmering diamond and sapphire tiara and a matching necklace that carried a large diamond pendant. Katie put her hand against her heart to keep it from popping out of her chest. That diamond had to be at least a bazillion carats! Mrs. Albright secured the tiara into Katie's thick hair, letting a few wispy tendrils escape and fall alongside her face while Sidney fastened the necklace.

"See there, lass, Lucas was right—you are a natural," Sidney reassured.

"It's hard to believe I'm a natural when this entire day has been wholly unnatural. I don't know how things work in the U.K., but in the States, strange men just don't break into a girl's hotel room, take her home, bejewel her in diamonds and sapphires, then whoosh her off to a ball. It just doesn't happen," Katie pointed out.

Everyone laughed, though Katie hadn't meant to be funny.

Sidney bellowed. "No, I suppose that doesn't happen much in the U.K., either. But with this lot, anything can happen! We met you only a few hours ago, but already you're part of the family, lass, like it or not."

Lucas nodded in affirmation.

"Thank you for making me feel so welcome," Katie replied in earnest, before adding sarcastically, "and for throwing me into the clutches of high society, for which I am grossly ill-prepared and will, no doubt, embarrass us all. I'm looking forward to it—really."

With a chortle, Sidney announced, "Well, let's get on with it, shall we? Lucas, why don't you drive on ahead and get yourself ready. Katie and I will go with Geoffrey and swing by for you."

Before Katie could leave, Mrs. Albright insisted on wrapping her in a tender embrace. "You look radiant, love. Go on and have a wonderful time, and do whatever it takes to help our Lucas."

"I will," Katie promised.

129

Chapter Fifteen

Katie took in the sight of the other attendees as Geoffrey pulled the Rolls-Royce in front of the grand entrance of the Dorchester. They were all draped head to toe in elegance. Katie felt her limbs begin to tremble. After sliding from the vehicle, Sidney reached back inside to offer a helping hand to Katie. Instinctively, she slid across the seat and clung to the handle of the opposite door.

While Sidney tried to coax her out with encouraging words, Lucas walked around and tugged her door open. Katie didn't even have time to scream before she tumbled out of the car and into Lucas's arms. She was still trying to make sense of what had just happened when he set her on her feet and pushed her toward the building.

"I don't know if I can do this," she whispered, taking in the plush carpeting and ornate chandeliers that greeted her.

"Nonsense, pet, of course you can," Sidney reassured, offering his arm for support. As soon as Katie took it, he laid his other hand over hers, trapping it against his forearm with a forceful amount of pressure. So much for subtle messages. Bolting was apparently not an option.

Lucas stopped and turned to them before they entered the ballroom. "Thank you both for agreeing to go to this sodding carnival—especially you, Katie. I know you don't feel comfortable here—which shows good judgment on your part." Taking hold of her other hand—the one to which the circulation wasn't being cut off by Sidney's death grip—Lucas massaged it gently as if his gratitude were a soothing lotion.

Katie issued him a weak smile. It was the best she could do under the circumstances. His tender caresses had her concentrating on not drooling down her neck.

He leaned in closer and whispered, "Don't worry. I wouldn't have begged you to come if I didn't believe you wouldn't be a brilliant success."

She held her breath to steady herself against the dizzying effects of his breathy accent against her ear. What she needed was an encouraging mantra. But a quick rummage through her mind brought zero results. Her nerves were squeezing her lungs like two overripe lemons. The urge to drop to the floor and hug herself into the fetal position was powerful, but she remembered she was on a mission to help Lucas, and somehow managed to straighten her shoulders and will her legs forward. *All right Greta, let's do this.*

Before she knew it, she was inside the ball, with elegant people swirling all around her.

"Lord and Lady Waverly, may I introduce you to my friends, Katie Sutherland and Sidney Ainsworth?" Lucas presented them as they approached their dining table.

Katie pried her gaze away from the floor and hoped her knees wouldn't give out on her.

Lord and Lady Waverly were nodding and smiling like well-trained bluebloods. They were a regal-looking couple, but something about them put Katie at ease. They almost seemed as if they could be parents of some of her friends. Lady Waverly was willowy and petite with a kind aura and a natural beauty that gracefully embraced her middle age. Lord Waverly was of average height and generously proportioned with glowing skin that told of a lifetime of pampering.

131

"It is certainly a pleasure to make your acquaintance, my Lord, my Lady," Sidney purred like an expert hobnobber.

Katie was surprised to hear his accent had changed. His words were velvety and bore no trace of his usual Northern drawl.

"I am also very pleased to meet you," Katie chirped, happy her voice hadn't betrayed her frazzled state.

The Waverlys accepted both of their new acquaintances graciously and invited them to have a seat at their table.

Lord Waverly spoke with a deep, loud voice. "Katie, is that an American accent I hear? What brings you to London?"

Lucas intercepted. "Katie has come to help me out with the business."

"Oh, that's wonderful!" Lady Waverly exclaimed. "I look forward to knowing you better. Will you be involved in putting our holiday together?"

Katie looked over at Lucas, who gave her an encouraging but unhelpful nod. She couldn't make head or tail of it.

"I'm not sure what Lucas has planned for me," she answered. "I only arrived today. I understand Olivia has been working on your holiday. I haven't even met her yet."

Lady Waverly shot a concerned look in Lucas's direction, then smiled at Katie. "I do hope you'll be involved. I have always wanted to travel to Hong Kong—since I was a young girl. Have you been there?"

"Yes, I have—a couple times, but not in several years. It has changed quite a bit since the Chinese took over again, but there is still a lot of charm, especially if you know where to go."

Katie stole a sidelong glance at Lucas, who stared at her in astonishment, then Sidney, who seemed about to laugh.

Lady Waverly's eyes lit up as she clapped her delicate hands with childlike enthusiasm. "I can't tell you how excited I am to hear it. Olivia had me so worried you wouldn't be able to manage this holiday." She spoke as much to Lucas as to Katie.

"Olivia? Have you seen her yet this evening?" Lucas asked with an ill-concealed tone of uneasiness. "I wasn't expecting her for a little while yet."

"No, I don't believe she's arrived," Lady Waverly answered. "She left a message this afternoon informing me her journey hadn't gone as planned. I was quite troubled. You know I have my heart set on this holiday."

She was interrupted by the approach of an acquaintance, and Lucas took advantage of the moment. "Katie, how about I...er... introduce you to some friends of mine?" He raised an eyebrow at her, then leaned into Sidney. "Sidney, would you excuse us?"

Sidney, who had engrossed himself in conversation with a fellow navy man, waved his approval.

Putting a hand on the small of Katie's back, Lucas escorted her through the hubbub of minglers and out of the ballroom.

"Why didn't you tell me you'd been to Hong Kong?" he questioned once they were safely out of earshot.

"You didn't ask."

His lips spread into a broad smile. "It seems you are full of surprises."

"I'm afraid Olivia is going to be mad. I feel like I've undermined her project."

"What you've done is help me to retain some rather influential clients. Katie, just your short interaction with Lady Waverly has been more beneficial to me than a whole summer's worth of clerical work."

"Good, so my job here is finished? I'm ready to go back to the States now?"

"Not a chance," he chuckled. "We only have a few weeks before the Waverlys are scheduled to leave on holiday. I'm counting on you to help me save face."

"A few weeks?" she gasped. "What do you have planned so far? Where are they staying?"

The worry in his blank expression was her answer.

"Wow! Nothing, huh? You're so screwed."

"I know."

"Do you have a budget?"

He shook his head. "Just so long as everything is perfect."

Katie's brow puckered as she lost herself in thought for a few moments. "May I see your phone?"

Lucas pulled his BlackBerry from his breast pocket and handed it to her. He followed her as she wandered down the corridor, tapping away on the Internet.

"Got it!" she finally announced, triumphant, as she began to dial a number.

"Got what?"

"The Peninsula Hotel in Hong Kong." She pulled the phone to her ear. "There's not a snowball's chance in hell we'll get a room, but we have to at least try. Maybe we can get on a waiting lis— Yes, hello. I'm hoping that you can help me." Her tone was instantly poised and professional. "I need to see if you have any suites available for—" She turned to Lucas. "What are the dates?" she mouthed.

He held the numbers up with his fingers.

"Yes, I know it's very short notice, and I do realize the hotel books out months, even years, in advance." Her voice changed slightly in pitch; she sounded sweeter and hapless, which she used to her advantage when talking to men—only as an absolute necessity. "The thing is, I just got my big break with these high-profile clients, but I only have a few weeks to pull off a miracle. So, I was hoping maybe you had a cancellation or could put me on a wait list? I'm sure it's way too much to hope for the Peninsula Suite—but I'm a dreamer. Please, I'm desperate…is there anything you can do to help me?" Biting her lower lip, she listened to the tapping on the keyboard as the reservationist spent what seemed like a century checking his reservations.

"Really? You can get me a suite?" She held her fists up to her shoulders, giving Lucas a silent "Yay!" "You are a lifesaver! Which suite is it?... The Marco Polo? That's great!" Not that she was an expert on the hotel's rooms, but even a basic suite at the Peninsula was nothing to turn your nose up at—at least her nose, anyway. She wouldn't see the inside of the Peninsula in three lifetimes. "I can't thank you enough… Of course, I'm happy to hold."

She did a spastic celebratory dance, forgetting she wasn't a natural in heels. Fortunately, Lucas caught her by the elbow just as her ankles toppled.

"Yes, I'm still here." Her voice, competing with her embarrassment, rasped as the reservationist's sudden return caught her by surprise. "You're joking?... You're not joking? Holy crap!"

She tapped Lucas on the arm and mouthed, "Credit card! Credit card!"

He fumbled through his wallet.

"Okay, I'm ready to hold the reservation," Katie went on. "I don't want anybody snatching up this room." She gave all the necessary information to secure the suite. "Thank you so much! Now, one last thing—can I reserve a car and driver now, or do I need to wait until they check-in?... Absolutely, I'd love to have a driver meet them at the airport... Perfect, I'll call you in a few days with the flight information. Thanks again, I'll talk to you soon!" She ended the call and turned to face Lucas.

"We got it! The Peninsula Suite!" she squealed. "The most prestigious room in the whole city!"

A crooked smile lapped across his face. He ran his hand over his hair, disheveling it to perfection. "Do I dare ask how you know so much about Hong Kong?"

"Many tuition dollars spent on a quality American education," she teased proudly.

"Really?" He sounded astonished. "They really teach you that sort of stuff at a proper university?"

She nodded. "Of course. I considered a lot of degrees before choosing a practical course of study—like hotel rooms in China..." she flashed a playful smile, "as opposed to...anthropology at Oxford?" She cocked her head, venturing a guess at his education.

He shook his head, laughing, encouraging her to make another attempt.

"Literature at Cambridge?"

"Business at Durham," he supplied on the heels of a chuckle.

"Yeah, I wouldn't have guessed that."

"Much to Olivia's chagrin," he mused.

"Why to her chagrin? I thought Durham was a really good school."

"It is. It's just that Olivia is a blueblooded Londoner. She doesn't really approve of anything associated with the North."

"*You* come from the North."

"Yes. It's a bit ironic. She doesn't like me to speak of it," he grinned. "So, of course I mention it often. I'm proud of my roots. Sid and I like to put on our thickest accents and tease her with our favorite Yorkshire sayings. She hates it!" he laughed.

"Like what?"

"Oh, I don't know…something like…." He turned his face up to the friezed ceiling. "Better to fettle an shaht abaht it nor nivver to fettle a t'all."

"I have no idea what you just said." Her giggles pealed into laughter.

"Exactly. Speaking of Olivia—we should be getting back. She'll be arriving any time now. "Cheers for getting the hotel sorted. You were brilliant."

Lucas escorted her back to the table before making his way to the main entrance to meet Olivia. Katie felt all her earlier apprehensions return. She hadn't noticed before how big their dining table actually was. Now that most of the occupants were seated, she realized there were close to twenty other diners at her table. Before she could swallow the lump in her throat and embrace the prospect of having to make appropriate conversation with so many exquisite people, Sidney drew everyone's attention to her.

137

"Ah, here she is." He announced her presence as if she were of significant importance. "Allow me to present to you all Ms. Kathryn Sutherland."

Katie flushed at the undeserved attention as a wave of polite salutations greeted her. She plastered on a grand smile and gave an uncertain wave to her new acquaintances. Something about Sidney's use of her full name stirred her to stiffen her posture even more—if that were possible. She didn't know it, but the ensuing effect was arresting. Neither Katie nor Greta, clinging loyally to her figure, had ever looked more radiant.

She was pretty sure she was doing a decent job of showing just the right amount of charisma while keeping up her share of small talk around the table, but she couldn't help notice that a few women were eyeing her. She felt the dread of public humiliation creeping up on her. They probably sensed she was not a natural in a tiara, and were therefore ready to have her branded as an imposter and heaved out onto the street. She caught the sympathetic eye of Lady Waverly, who issued her a supportive smile.

After what seemed like many unnerving minutes, one of the gawkers, a flashy middle-aged woman who reminded Katie of the "Unsinkable" Molly Brown, addressed her. "Kathryn, dear, please don't think me impertinent, but I must know…are you wearing part of the Chatworth collection?"

Her question was not loud, but carried a weighty tone that caused a halt in the conversation around the table. All eyes were focused on Katie. A surge of panic whooshed over her. She racked her brain to think of what a Chatworth could possibly be. She was pretty sure Greta didn't belong to any sort of special collection.

She glanced at Sidney for some help and noticed he was wearing an aggravated expression. He quickly rearranged his countenance to something more pleasant and spoke in Katie's stead.

"As a matter of fact, I believe those are part of the Chatworth pieces." His tone was sardonic as he laid a meaningful gaze upon Katie. "Dear girl, how did you get your hands on such extraordinary jewelry?' he queried, eyebrows knitted together.

Instinctively, she laid a hand over the magnificent diamond pendant Sidney had loaned her. Fortunately, she was spared from having to give an answer.

"Oh Lordy, would you look who's coming? Esther and Gordon's daughter…thinks she's the bloody Queen herself," one woman announced to her partner in a voice above a whisper.

And there they were: Lucas and Olivia.

"Good evening, everyone." Lucas gallantly nodded to the crowd and introduced himself to the few people not of his acquaintance. "I believe you all know my fiancée, Olivia Denby."

There were a few curt acknowledgments.

"Olivia, I would like you to meet Katie."

Katie stood to greet Olivia, who looked her up and down with evident surprise, then disdain. "I'm so happy to meet you, Olivia. I've heard so much about you." *None of it good.*

Olivia made no reply.

Katie was not unaware that Olivia was a good three inches taller and two sizes—okay, maybe three—smaller than herself. Besides these advantages, she was beautiful: silky blonde hair (that was probably natural), Caribbean blue eyes, and a perfect set of perky boobs (that also appeared to be natural).

Under Olivia's intense scrutiny, Katie could feel every eye at the table watching her. Before she could crumble under the pressure, Lucas curtailed the tension.

"I'm sure you and Katie will become good friends," he said to Olivia as he pulled her chair out for her. Though he spoke lightheartedly, there was a note of reprimand in his voice.

"Fat chance," Olivia uttered.

Humiliation burning her cheeks, Katie slunk into her seat with as much poise as possible. Sidney gave her hand a reassuring squeeze under the table, which didn't do much to restore her composure. Though Olivia seemed unbothered, Katie could not ignore the fact that they were still the center of attention.

Lord Waverly threw some compassion in her direction and broke the uncomfortable silence.

"Katie, we never did finish our conversation—I'm still intrigued by your American accent. What part of the States do you call home?"

Katie looked up at the Waverlys, who were both wearing kindly smiles. "I live in Colorado—not far from Aspen."

"That's a lovely area. Do you ski, then?" another gentleman replied.

"Actually, I'm not much of a skier," she confessed.

"How can it be possible to live in such a place and not ski?" inquired another.

"Well, usually when I go skiing, it's with my guy friends— Christopher, Dylan, and Rob—who are much more advanced than I am and have more testosterone than I do." Except for Dylan—but she didn't say that out loud. "Inevitably, I'd get talked into taking a trail

140

that was far beyond my skill level, and I'd spend the rest of the day tumbling down it—by myself." Pulling a chagrined grimace, she added, "I've learned that it's better for my health *and* my friendships to stick to water sports."

Her explanation won a round of chuckles from the table, and a few people broke into a conversation about skiing anecdotes. Thankful to have the attention off of her, Katie caught the eye of the Waverlys and mouthed a grateful "Thank you."

Despite the menacing scowls Olivia fired off in her direction, Katie relaxed a little when dinner went off without incident. However, during dessert, the Unsinkable Molly Brown, who had been hawk-eyeing Katie all evening, seized another opportunity to question her.

"You never did tell us, dear, how you came to be in possession of those Chatworths?"

Olivia's eyes bulged. She reared her head toward Katie to gain confirmation of what she thought she heard, but Katie wouldn't look at her.

"Where did she get those?" Olivia hissed at Lucas. Her eyes, spitting ferocity, locked on the pendant resting against Katie's throat.

Pretending not to hear Olivia, Katie responded with diplomacy. "A very good friend loaned them to me for the evening. I'm sure you'll understand if I don't disclose the name. I don't think my friend is aware of the significance of these pieces—I know I wasn't."

"Please be sure to explain to your friend the enormous value of the pieces she's holding. They would fetch a brilliant price on loan in an exhibit. Do you know…does your friend own more Chatworth?"

141

Katie squirmed uncomfortably as Olivia seethed, "Friend? She doesn't have *friends* in town. I'll just bet I know who loaned them to her."

Molly Brown perched on the edge of her seat, eager for Olivia to let the name drop.

"That's enough, Olivia," Lucas spat tersely under his breath. The sound was so unnatural for him that it made everyone within earshot straighten up like scolded children.

Turning to Molly Brown, Katie replied, "I'm sorry, I don't know what other pieces my friend owns. But I will be sure to pass on the importance of their value."

Another miffed reply came from Olivia, this time louder and directed toward Sidney. "I can't imagine who this 'friend' of hers is, can you, Sidney?"

Sidney's jaw clenched, and Katie felt panged by the range of emotions dashing across his face. Impressively, he wrangled them and offered a smooth reply. "I cannot guess, Olivia, only that it must indeed be a very loyal friend." He shot a look at Katie.

Lucas's face was braided with anger and embarrassment, and his eyes pleaded for Katie's forgiveness. Something about the pained expression in his chocolate eyes broke Katie's endurance. Maybe it was the jet lag or perhaps it was because she had never been treated so abominably—especially in fancy-pants public. Whatever the reason, Katie, for the second time that day, was riled enough to speak her mind. With more willpower than she knew she possessed, she was able to keep an even voice.

"I don't think you have any right to suppose so much about my personal life—especially since I've just met you. Believe it or not, I do have friends in London. Two of them are sitting at this table, and your ridiculous behavior is making them uncomfortable. You have singlehandedly turned the term 'polite society' into an oxymoron."

This extracted a few sniggers and even a "Here, here!" from a fellow diner.

"Now, if you will excuse me, I'll leave so you won't feel compelled to cause me or my *friends* any more embarrassment."

As Katie pushed herself from the table, she noted with some satisfaction that Olivia was staring at her speechless, mouth gaping.

"If you will excuse me everyone." Katie politely nodded, setting her napkin on the plush chair and making her exit with impressive poise—in high heels, no less.

Once out of the ballroom, indignation began to burn her cheeks. Fighting the blindness of angry tears, she shot out of the first exit into the courtyard and wove her way through a maze of low hedges, where she plopped herself down on an elaborately carved marble bench and let the tears flow.

"Well done," soothed a wispy voice above her. Katie looked up to meet the kind face of Lady Waverly.

"May I?" Lady Waverly gestured to the bench.

"Of course," Katie squeaked, scooting over. "I'm so sorry I made a spectacle."

"Nonsense. I assure you that those who heard—and really, it wasn't so many—are applauding you."

"Lady Waverly, I don't belong here. Olivia has made that clear."

Lady Waverly sighed. "Olivia is spoiled, selfish, and adolescent. And I am so glad someone has finally stood up to her."

Katie looked confused, so Lady Waverly continued. "Olivia's father is a very prominent MP. Most people of our rank can't afford offending Olivia for fear of landing on the wrong side of her father."

"MP? He's Military Police?"

"Member of Parliament," she gently corrected, stifling a giggle.

"But she's planning your vacation," Katie persisted.

"No, she nearly ruined it. We had heard such good things about Lucas and had inquired after him with Olivia's father. Next thing I knew, much to my disappointment, Olivia was involved. I can't tell you how grateful I am that you showed up to be of assistance."

"Lady Waverly?"

"Please call me Chelsea. I hope we will become close enough friends to make it appropriate."

"Thank you," Katie gushed, recognizing the privilege offered her. She suddenly realized what she needed to do—and though she couldn't explain why, she felt the urge to be completely honest with this gracious woman.

"I'm going to turn down my position with Lucas," Katie said. "Even if he doesn't fire me for speaking to his fiancée like I did, I could never work closely with her. I've made a mess of things…Lucas will be furious."

"You don't give him enough credit. And please—call me Chelsea." She reached out and put a soft hand on Katie's cheek.

Katie smiled, grateful to have a new friend. *See, Olivia, you anorexic cow, I do have friends here!* she thought, barely feeling the twinge of guilt from having resorted to name-calling.

"Chelsea?" The name sounded out of place to Katie's ears. "I know I have no right to ask, but...I did promise Lucas I'd do what I could to help...I should at least try to keep my promise before I quit. Will you allow him another chance to put your holiday together?"

"Of course we will. We chose Lucas on his merits, not for his connections with Olivia's family."

Katie doubted this was true, but she was not going to argue.

Lady Waverly hesitated for a moment. "Would you mind doing me a favor? Would you meet with me soon and tell me all about Hong Kong?"

"I'd love to," Katie said. "I can't believe you've never been there. I assumed you've traveled all over the world!"

Lady Waverly sighed deeply. "When I was a little girl, my father was stationed in Hong Kong. He would fill my head with brilliant stories about his time there. I was always so enthralled with what it must be like. Of course, I know it's changed—modernized drastically since then—but I want to believe there still must be pieces left of those same novelties he shared with me. I want to find them."

"I'm sure there are!"

"We travel quite a bit, you know, usually for social or business engagements. I've been to chateaux and elite social clubs and resorts all over the world...but I'm tired of all that. I want to have an adventure! I want to feel and live the culture...not be trapped behind the gates of an exclusive resort." She stopped and checked the passion rising in her voice. "Do I sound horribly ungrateful?"

"Not at all," Katie replied. "One time I was invited to Puerto Rico with some acquaintances who booked us rooms at the Ritz-Carlton. Their idea of a vacation was to lounge by the pool and play on the private beach. As their guest, I felt obligated to stay with them, but I was dying to get out and explore the area. I spent a lot of time looking out the window, but other than that, I never did get to experience more of Puerto Rico than the confines of the Ritz-Carlton. But how can I say spending a week at the Ritz-Carlton was awful without sounding like an ingrate?"

Suddenly embarrassed, like maybe she had said too much and was coming across as one of those "vulgar Americans," she quickly added, "I'm sorry, that was a stupid story. I talk way too much."

"No, I'm glad you shared that story. You know exactly how I feel whenever I go someplace."

A silent moment passed while each woman collected her thoughts. Then, catching each other's eye, they burst into inexplicable, spontaneous laughter.

"Oh my, I can't remember the last time I've laughed so hard," Lady Waverly proclaimed, smoothing a dainty hand over her blonde chignon.

***

Katie made quite a spectacle as she reentered the ballroom arm in arm with Lady Waverly. She felt self-conscious—but untouchable. So it was easy to ignore the snippets of whispered speculations that floated within earshot:

"…Chatworth diamond…"

"…wealthy American…"

"…lovely girl…rather witty, I'm told…"

"…came with Lucas Hayden, Olivia Denby's fiancé…she's in a right froth over it…"

"…heard they're cousins…"

"...quite a favorite of the Waverlys...."

Katie colored at some of the gossip, but it was hard to be offended with Lady Waverly next to her sputtering soft giggles and patting her hand knowingly.

Sidney and Lucas looked relieved to have Katie returned to them, and then astonished—as was the rest of the table—by the friendliness she shared with the revered Lady. Olivia's face contorted into an angry scowl that bore right into Katie's soul. Involuntarily, Katie shivered and rubbed down the goose bumps that shot up and down her arms.

"Are you cold?" Lucas was already taking off his jacket to put around her shoulders.

Olivia's eyes shot Katie with even more death daggers before she turned to Lucas. "What about me, darling—what if I'm cold, too?"

Lucas looked uncomfortable. "Uh, I apologize, you didn't seem cold." He rubbed her arm tenderly to give her warmth, which only made her bristle.

Katie shrugged off the jacket and gave it back to Lucas. "I'm fine. Thank you, though."

"You sure?" Lucas asked.

"Positive."

He started to put the jacket on Olivia, who turned and pushed it away.

"Actually, I'm warm now." Her tone was as cold as ice.

"Sidney, I'm getting tired," Katie said. "Would you mind if I had Geoffrey take me home?"

"Not at all. In fact, I'll take my leave as well." Sidney seemed a little too eager to quit the table.

147

"Goodbye everyone. It was a pleasure meeting you all." Katie spoke to the room as loudly as she could while still being polite. "Thank you for the delightful evening. Lord and Lady Waverly, thank you especially."

"Leaving so soon?" Olivia asked triumphantly. "Before the dancing? You *do* know this is a *ball*. Perhaps you've finally realized that you don't fit in here."

Katie took a deep, steadying breath and forced herself to take the high road—or as close to the high road as she could muster. "You're absolutely right, Olivia. I don't fit in with *you,* but thankfully, I haven't come across many people who do. You are definitely one of a kind." Flaunting her most dazzling smile, she added, "It was lovely to meet you."

As Katie and Sidney walked away, she heard Lucas snap, "Well, Olivia, it looks like you've been outclassed."

There was a low murmur of consent around the table as Olivia silently watched Katie exit.

Chapter Sixteen

"What a bitch!" Katie spat when she and Sidney were tucked away in the car. Remembering her manners, she added, "Sorry."

"Aye pet, that she is. I should have known," Sidney apologized, his Northern accent miraculously reappearing.

"Geoffrey, wait!" Lucas called as he came trotting out a minute behind them.

Katie stiffened as he slid onto the seat next to her. Away from the social pressure, she could feel her fury mounting, and there was plenty of it to divide equally between Olivia and Lucas.

He put his hand on her arm. "Katie, I'm really sorry. There is no excuse for—"

She jerked her arm out from under his touch. "Please don't talk to me," she whispered.

"Katie, I—"

"Please," she insisted even more quietly.

She sat erect, staring straight ahead out the windshield, allowing Sidney to gingerly pat her hand. Like clockwork, the tears were building behind her eyes. It was all she could do to hold them back.

As if he could feel her determination not to cry, Lucas eased the attention from her by speaking to Sidney—or maybe just himself. "I feel sick with guilt for subjecting Katie to...to what? Olivia? I've never seen this mean-spirited side of her before. Have I? I'm beginning to understand the sour expressions and cryptic remarks made at the mention of her name."

The sound of his cell phone ringing, much too loudly for the confined space, interrupted his reflections. He fidgeted awkwardly, trying his best not to touch Katie as he wriggled his phone from his pocket.

"Bollocks," he muttered under his breath, glancing at the number, then answered it. "Yeah, hello Mum... I'm sorry. I didn't think... We went to the Waverlys' charity ball... You're where?... Of course, of course you are," he said with a sarcastic note. "Listen Mum, it's not a good time right now. We're in the car on our way back and we'll be at Sidney's soon. Can you wait until then to bite my head off?... Yeah, love you, too."

He hung up and looked at Sidney. "Looks like there's been a change of plans. Mum's come into town. She's already settled herself at your place."

Sidney chortled. "You didn't tell her you were keeping our Katie, did you lad?"

Lucas shook his head. "She's in a right snit—took the first train from Yorkshire as soon as Andrew returned alone."

"Well, Katie, love, this day just gets more and more eventful for you," Sidney sniggered.

Katie's eyes softened and she responded with a feeble smile.

Seeing that her mood had lightened, Lucas took her hand, which she instantaneously recoiled and tucked away under her folded arms. She resumed her intent stare out the front window and stayed in her brooding position for the remainder of the ride.

***

"Whoa, Avery didn't tell us he'd sent a bloomin' princess!" Lottie Hayden threw a demonstrative hug around Katie. "Hello Miss Katie, I'm Lottie."

Katie took in the short, fashionable woman and smiled, allowing Lottie's enthusiasm to thaw her anger.

"Sounds like you've had quite a day," Lottie noted.

She turned her slender, nearly five-foot frame on Sidney and Lucas and gave them a lighthearted reprimand. "She was supposed to be *my* new playmate. Avery promised *me* a niece to dress up and show off. And you two already beat me to it! That wasn't a very nice thing to do to your Mum." She sashayed over to Lucas and caught him up in a tight embrace, her head not quite reaching his chest. "How you doing, Chicken?"

Not waiting for a reply, most likely because her mother's intuition told her that her son was not doing well, she went to Sidney and planted a kiss on both of his cheeks.

"Hello love. Happy to see you again."

"And you," Sidney smiled.

Rounding her full attention once again on Katie, Lottie continued her inspection.

"Well, didn't these boys do a brilliant job? You look ab-so-lute-ly fabby, darling—just fabby! And would you get a load of those ivories—straight outta Hollywood, those are." Lottie perched on her tiptoes, squeezing Katie's cheeks together for a better look at her teeth.

Before Katie could say thanks, Lottie let out a screech. "Bloody hell, Sidney! These are the Chatworth diamonds!"

"So I've just learned."

151

"Why am I not surprised that after sixty-odd years of obscurity, you produce them out of your arse?"

Sidney blew out a long breath. "Upon my soul, I've never before heard of the bloody Chatworth diamonds! I assure you, I am just as astonished as everyone else."

"Lordy, I can't believe you boys sent her into London society for the first time wearing these! I'll just bet she stuck out like a dog's bollocks."

Katie shuddered, not so much from being compared to canine genitalia, but from the accuracy of the statement.

"Was it so bad, dear? Did those status-stalking arseholes eat you alive?"

"Just one," Katie retorted, casting an angry glare at Lucas.

Lottie turned an accusing scowl on her son. "What has your fiend—I mean your fiancée—done now?"

Lucas's jaw set. Ignoring the question, he crossed the room and plopped down on a chair.

Katie hoped someone would change the subject. The last thing she wanted to hear was more talk of Olivia. In the awkward silence, Sidney slid toward to the next room, beckoning Lottie to follow. Katie got the feeling Lottie wasn't following out of obedience or concern for their privacy—she seemed eager for dishy details—but she trotted after Sidney and disappeared.

"Katie, I feel horrible," Lucas began.

Katie snapped her head away from him.

"Please Katie, let me make it up to you."

"I have never been treated so hideously."

He was straining to hear her words. She hadn't turned her head back to face him; she wouldn't let him see her cry. Especially since she didn't know herself if they were angry tears or tears of humiliation.

"I know. I'm sorry." His fingers twitched.

At the thought of Olivia, she snorted. "Funny, isn't it? You asked me to help protect you from the wolves tonight, and the only wolf I saw was the one you're marrying, and it was my jugular she was after."

"It's all my fault. I had no idea Olivia could be…I didn't know she was so…I didn't know. I'm sorry. For what it's worth, thank you."

The good news was she'd found Lucas's flaw: He had horrible taste in women. She knew he couldn't be that perfect.

"I want to go to bed now, I'm tired." She sighed and started for the stairs. "Please tell your mom and Sidney goodnight for me."

Once safely in her room, Katie traded Greta for her fleecy pajamas. Wrapped in a bundle of softness, her world, though it was all going wrong, began to feel a little right. For the first time since her toilet promise, keeping Jared as her boyfriend felt like the right thing to do, and she felt an ache in her heart to have him comfort her. In her hurt and confused state, she was able to imagine a Jared who knew all the right things to say.

Her moment of self-pity was interrupted by a soft knock at the door. Pulling herself together, Katie called to her unseen visitor to enter.

Lottie cracked the door and hesitated before poking her head inside, her maroon boy-cut hair framing her tiny face.

"Katie, may I sit with you, or would you rather I just bugger off?"

"Of course not…come on in," Katie invited, glad to have friendly company.

"Is there anything I can do, flower?" Lottie took a seat on the oversized bed, the fluffy duvet swallowing her bottom half.

Katie shook her head. "No, I'm fine. I don't know why I'm so upset."

"I know why—you've met my soon-to-be dragon-in-law," Lottie smirked, patting the spot on the bed next to her as an invitation for Katie to sit.

Katie accepted. "It's not that. Well, partly that…but normally someone like Olivia wouldn't get to me. I think it's probably a mixture of PMS, jet lag, and thinking about my boyfriend."

"A dangerous combination for a woman's nerves." Lottie put an arm around Katie's shoulders and pulled her into a hug. Katie couldn't remember the last time she'd had a genuine maternal hug. She wished she could stay in Lottie's embrace forever.

"Don't think I'm letting you off the hook from telling me all about this boyfriend." Lottie winked and squeezed Katie tighter. "But right now I want to talk about something else. I don't want Olivia to drive you away. We're so excited that you've finally come to us."

Katie felt the sincerity of her words and a guilty lump rose in her throat. "Thank you, Lottie. I already love your family. But after tonight, I don't think I can work for Lucas."

A look of concern crept across Lottie's face. "I was afraid of that. I can't say I blame you. I'm not going to try to change your mind. But we can still keep the other half of the arrangement."

"What other half of the arrangement?"

"That you will stay on in me home and be me new playmate."

Katie hesitated. She didn't even want to be in the same county should Lucas and Olivia pop by for a visit.

Lottie read her mind. "Olivia wouldn't stoop so low as to be caught dead any further north than Nottingham. You'd be seeing Elton John posing for *Playgirl* before you'd find Olivia knocking on me door. Charles and I are not her kind of people."

Katie had to admit that the idea of staying with Lottie sounded more appealing than going back home with her tail between her legs. Especially since everyone had gone through so much effort to get her here.

"We'd have to find some way for me to earn my keep—*if* I were to agree. Can I sleep on it and give you an answer in the morning?"

"Of course you can, dear. I'll let you go right to sleep so you'll have plenty of time to dream about how much fun the two of us will have."

Lottie gave Katie a gentle kiss on the top of the head and pranced toward the door. Pausing before exiting, she added, "I heard what you did tonight—with the Waverlys and the hotel. Lucas is very thankful. And the rest of us are very grateful to you, too."

Katie gave her a puzzled look.

"Because of you, he finally saw her for what she really is. We've been trying to get him to open his eyes to that ogre for years."

"But I didn't do anything," Katie protested. "I was just there to be a warm body."

"Sometimes that's all it takes."

Lottie winked and closed the door behind her.

Chapter Seventeen

Before Katie could turn out the lights, a heavy sleep blanketed her. Not until the next morning, when she was awakened by a timid rap at her door, did she budge. Unable to pry her eyes open, she was reluctant to croak a groggy "Come in." She rolled onto her side and fell back to sleep.

"Katie, I need you to wake up, please." Someone was shaking her lightly.

Only semiconscious, she moaned and wiggled onto her other side. She felt the mattress bounce a little as her awakener took a seat on the bed.

"Katie...Kaatie...Kaaaatie." The shaking became a little more vigorous.

"Hmm?" She moaned, enjoying the way her name sounded in British English.

"Wake up," the voice demanded.

"Mmm...no thanks," she muttered, determined to defy the human alarm clock, and flopped again, turning against the voice.

A firm hand tugged at her shoulder until she dropped onto her back. Only when she felt herself the subject of intense scrutiny did she force her eyelids halfway open. She was confused by the scrumptious chocolate eyes staring back at her. Then she caught sight of Greta in the background, folded over the foot of the bed frame, and remembered her surreal first day in London. She zeroed in again on Lucas's eyes above her and let the ugly memories of the night before trample over her.

"Ugh, go away. Didn't you get the memo that I quit?" She pulled the duvet over her head and squinched up into a tight ball, scooting as far away from Lucas as the bed would allow.

"Yes, I did receive that memo—twice actually—from my mother and Lady Waverly." He was laughing at her.

Lady Waverly? When had he had a chance to speak to her, and what did they say? She didn't know which she found more annoying—the fact that he was laughing at her or that he was trying to bait her with curiosity. Refusing to bite, she pushed her interest aside and focused on being annoyed.

"Then why are you bothering me?" Her voice was muffled by the covers.

"I need you to work today."

"I don't work for you anymore, Mr. Hayden. It was lovely while it lasted, now goodnight." Her desire for him to go away was excruciating—her breathing was making it extra hot underneath the heavy bundle of bedding and she was dying for some fresh, non-morning-breath air.

"Isn't it customary to give two weeks' notice?" His voice was teasing.

"The two weeks' notice principle becomes null and void when one has reason to fear certain dismemberment from one's employer's fiancée."

"Is that so?" He made no attempt to hide his humor.

"Look it up."

He let out an exaggerated sigh. "I was hoping it wouldn't come to this, but you're forcing me to play dirty."

She made no reply.

158

"This morning I've been having a nice long chat with your Professor Bell." His voice was taunting and smug.

Uh-oh. It took all the self-control she possessed not to react. She lay perfectly still.

He let her marinate in silence until she couldn't take it anymore. She threw the covers back and kicked them off.

"What do you want, and why did you call my professor?" She sat up to receive his explanation.

"I want to make a compromise." He chortled again, smoothing down the wild static in her hair.

She inched out from underneath his jovial petting and glared at him.

"After you went to bed, Mum was really cheesed off with me," Lucas said. "She accused me of being a total bum-sucker—among other, much less flattering insults. She informed me of your decision to quit, and insists on taking you to Yorkshire with her. I've been banished from your presence until further notice."

This time Katie was the one to laugh. "Good!"

He leaned in and nudged her with his shoulder. "Knowing my mum will carry out her threats, I needed to gain the upper hand. So I called your professor and informed him that my mother has been laid off from her position as your supervisor."

Katie gasped. "You can't lay off your own mother!"

"I can and I have, but only from the duties where you're concerned." He was already getting a good laugh envisioning his mother's miffed reaction.

"Well, that's an impressive way to get one up on your mom, but it doesn't affect me—I still quit."

159

"But you haven't heard the compromise yet."

She turned her head away from him in defiance.

Undaunted by her dismissal, he said, "Maybe you've forgotten that you can't graduate until I sign off on this internship."

She whipped her head back to stare at him dumbfounded. "What are you saying? This sounds more like blackmail than a compromise."

"The compromise is this: Help me get through the Waverlys' holiday, and if you still want to leave, I'll sign off early on all your internship papers."

"What about Olivia? She's going to be livid."

A pained smile scribbled across his face. "I'll handle Olivia."

"And if you don't?" she pressed. "What if she tries to scratch my eyes out or something?"

"If you hear so much as a cross word from Olivia, I promise to sign your papers and let you quit on the spot." He sighed. "So do we have a deal?"

"It doesn't seem like I have much of a choice." She shook his hand, accepting her defeat.

In a sudden burst of energy, he jumped from the bed and yanked her up alongside him. "Brilliant! We've got to get moving then." He pushed her toward the en suite bathroom. "I need you ready in fifteen minutes."

"Ready? Where are we going?"

It was at that moment she realized the moon was still shining through her window.

"Hold on a second." She planted her feet firmly, refusing to be rushed around. "What time is it?"

He reminded her of a rascally little boy with his hangdog expression and the way he shuffled from one foot to the other. "It's nearly five."

"Nearly *five*?" she questioned with a mother's skeptical tone. "A.M.?"

"Maybe closer to four-thirty."

"Four-thirty!" She made a beeline back to her bed.

"Wait!" Lucas grabbed her arm, pulling her back toward the bathroom. "Lady Waverly called me late last night inviting us to brunch at their estate in Suffolk."

Katie locked her eyes on his face expecting him to expound, but he didn't.

"What? Are we brunching at the crack of dawn?"

"No, Miss Sassy Pants, I'm sneaking you out of the house before my mum wakes up, for one. Two, Suffolk is nearly a ninety-minute drive from London. We still have to get to my place so I can change clothes and get my car."

Katie hadn't realized he was wearing the same clothes from the ball, minus the jacket and bow tie. Now that she was focusing on his looks, she was beginning to soften a little. He looked tired; he couldn't have had much sleep. She'd only caught three or four hours and she hadn't stayed up talking to Lottie or Lady Waverly...or Professor Bell.

"Okay, you win," she sighed in resignation—actually sighing because it was adorable how he called her Miss Sassy Pants. "I'll get ready."

Pushing past him, she went to her bags, tossing them to the foot of the bed, and began pulling out her shampoo and conditioner.

161

"Sorry Duchess, we don't have time for you to shower. Plus, the way the plumbing works in this old place, the running water would wake up the whole household." He rummaged through the pile of toiletries she was stacking on the bed.

"Lucas, I have to take a shower. I'm still grimy from my layover in Newark."

Without showing an ounce of sympathy, he thrust a washcloth at her. "Here then, wash up with this."

She glowered at him, grabbed the cloth and her hairbrush, stomped into the bathroom, and huffed under her breath, "Obviously you've never been to Newark if you think this little rag will do the trick."

"Do you mind if I help to speed things up a bit by finding you something to wear?" he whispered into the wood of the bathroom door.

The thought of a man other than Dylan choosing her attire was disconcerting, but she chose not to dwell on it because she had no clue how one was supposed to dress when brunching at a Suffolk estate. She cracked the door and whispered back, "Um, sure go ahead, but doesn't that seem kind of weird?"

"Not at all. It's the least I can do for my cousin—especially when I know she's going to take more time than we have finding an outfit."

She couldn't resist sneaking in one last jab before closing the bathroom door. "I think that goes above and beyond the call of 'cousinly duty.' It almost borders on 'creepy cousin snooping through my underwear territory.'"

Lucas rifled through two of her three suitcases, never imagining it could be so difficult to put an outfit together. He couldn't

162

help but chuckle at the contrast between Katie's and Olivia's wardrobes. For every haute couture item of Dolce and Gabbana, Prada, Kate Spade, and Gucci Olivia owned, Katie possessed an equal number of Patagonia, Kuhl, North Face, and Prana. He decided on a pair of Silver brand blue jeans and a heather grey Hollister cashmere V-neck. As he unfolded the jeans from the top of a stack, a small piece of colored paper flittered to the floor.

He tried not to read its message as he scooped it from the carpet, but he couldn't help himself.

Katie,

We just know at some point along your journey you're going to need this reminder:

Jared is—

A scribble scratched across the page, indicating the paper had been torn away from the first writer. There was a change in the handwriting and ink color.

...a grade A, son-of-a-bitch jackass with a short man's complex who is too imbecilic to treasure a woman who's way too good for him! He doesn't deserve you!!

Another scribble ran across the paper and the original ink and penmanship returned.

We love you!
Anna, Scott, Christopher, Heather & Dylan

Lucas cracked a smile, finding humor in the note, but not at it implications. Was this "Jared" her boyfriend? And why didn't he deserve her?

The soft squeak of the faucet turning off alerted him that she was close to being ready. He hurried and tucked the note between the folds of some pajamas at the top of her suitcase, where she would be sure to see it soon.

***

"I guess summer doesn't mean much in England," she noted conversationally through chattering teeth as they made their way to the tube station down the hill from Sidney's home. The air was soggy and threatening rain in the predawn chill.

"We might see summer for a few hours today." He half grinned, helping her into his tuxedo jacket, which he'd been carrying over his arm.

As they came up the stairs from the tube station, Katie was pleased to notice that despite the spongy clouds, the sun was attempting to rise. The streets were speckled with only a few haggard-looking people making their way home from their Friday night pub crawl. Walking among them, Katie didn't feel too self-conscious about the appearance of Lucas and her sharing his tuxedo at dawn.

"It's just a few houses up this street," Lucas informed her.

Now that she was more alert, his feathery accent tickled every nerve down her spine. Her eyes honed in on her whereabouts and she was surprised to find that she recognized this street. She hadn't paid attention last night when they'd picked him up because it was dark and she was too engrossed in conversation with Sidney, but she definitely knew this street—she'd passed it many times on the Big Bus Tours.

"You live here?" She failed at sounding unimpressed as he led her to the end of a row of fancy three-story white brick buildings.

Lucas opened the iron gate that permitted access to his building. Katie made a little skip toward the perfect Mary Poppins home, but stopped as she heard a strange clinking noise. She turned just as a burly man dressed in dark jeans, a sweatshirt, and a ball cap leapt out from behind a tree, snapping pictures of the two of them. Katie knew she should bolt inside, but she was frozen in place, like a deer in the headlights, while the photographer had his way with her image.

Lucas shouted a few expletives at the photographer before jumping protectively in front of her. Holding out a large hand toward the lens he hustled her into the building.

"Wh...What was that?" Katie heaved shakily when they were behind the safety of Lucas's door.

He shook his head. "I don't know."

"Oh well...I guess strange things happen in big cities," she chirped, happy to let the incident go.

"Yeah, guess so." But he didn't seem so certain. "Well, make yourself at home."

His home felt oddly familiar and welcoming, and without ceremony she fell back into the plump leather sofa. She studied the lacquered antique moldings and bookcases of dark wood with familiarity, and then the brown sofa she was sitting upon. The room was almost identical to Mr. Scott's library, but instead of hundreds of books in the cases, Lucas had removed some shelves to accommodate

165

his giant television and stereo system, and where Katie's favorite tall leather-backed chair should have been were a couple of red leather space-age pod chairs. Katie's eyes rested on the funky chairs that wouldn't have dared to even think about setting foot—rather, pedestal—in Mr. Scott's home.

"They were a gift from Mum," Lucas clarified, amused at Katie's gawking. "She's been trying to encourage me to modernize my flat."

"Why? I like it this way. It's almost exactly like Mr. Scott's home."

He pressed his lips into a smile that she couldn't decipher. "That's because it *is* his home. Actually, Uncle Avery owns the building. I'm sort of managing the property for him."

Katie's eyes widened and her mouth formed a silent "Oh" as she tried to catalogue this bit of information.

"Which reminds me…" He was suddenly off on another track. "I promised I would call Uncle today and let him know how you're doing." He dashed into his bedroom, his words trailing behind him. "We'll have to call him from the car."

Ten minutes later, he returned wearing loose-fitting jeans, an untucked designer button-up, and a delicious smile that gave Katie the urge to lick her lips. Her eyes narrowed as she discerned certain wisps of his shaggy hair curled from dampness. Reaching out her hand, she stepped toward him and squeezed a tuft at the back of his neck. "No fair! You showered!"

***

"Hello Katie, lovely to see you again." Lady Waverly's small voice was warm and as silky as her flaxen hair. She clasped both of her

166

smooth, powdery hands over Katie's. "Welcome to Pellyn Hall. I'm so pleased you've come."

Katie gave her most brilliant smile and tried not to notice how her hands looked like man-hands inside Lady Waverly's dainty clasp.

"Thank you for inviting me," Katie replied with the proper amount of gratitude and politeness.

Dropping the formality, Lady Waverly turned to Lucas. "So, how did you manage to get her here?"

His grin was sinister. "Blackmail."

"Brilliant!" Lady Waverly's tinkling laugh rang through the grand foyer.

Katie savored every detail of her surroundings as Lady Waverly escorted them through the main rooms on the ground level before leading them into the garden through a set of heavy French doors. She wasn't fanciful enough to believe brunching in a noble's country estate was anything more than a once-in-a-lifetime opportunity. Katie noted with admiration how Lady Waverly seemed to float rather than walk. She wore a notably expensive ivory-colored ensemble which no doubt had been custom tailored to fit her petite frame. An ivory silk scarf wrapped her shoulders and flirted airily with the breeze behind her. Katie thought she looked like a graceful fairy and tried envisioning herself in the same outfit. The result was disheartening. For the remainder of the day, she could not erase from her mind the image of herself looking like a posh, lumpy sofa.

"Denny should be here shortly," Lady Waverly told them after they were seated in a freestanding glass conservatory. "He's just making sure the meeting room is ready. He's hosting some Members of Parliament today to discuss whether we're going to allow the government to lease some holdings we have in Bosnia."

"That could be a real heated argument, I imagine," Lucas commented.

"Yes, I imagine it will be," Lady Waverly agreed.

Katie recrossed her legs, sat a little straighter, and nodded, hoping she looked as though she were up on current events.

"What are your views on Bosnia, Katie?" Lady Waverly asked. "It would be interesting to get an American perspective."

Katie's nodding came to a halt. She swallowed hard to keep her heart from jumping out of her throat. "What do *I* think?" she repeated, trying to buy time for an epiphany. "I think…" *Crappity crap craaaap!* "Well, I think that…"

Lucas and Lady Waverly pinned her with expectant stares, as if they were waiting for her to say something profound.

Katie shifted in her seat, noticing how the soft cushion did little to make her feel comfortable. "That is to say, my stance on the subject is…hell, I have no idea what you're talking about." Her heart leapt from her throat and tried escaping through her ear. She could feel it pounding against her brain.

A crooked smile meandered across Lucas's face. He beamed at her as if she were a favorite toy.

Katie watched Lady Waverly's reaction apprehensively. The lady's face strained as if she were holding something back. Then her body twitched, followed by her lips. She no longer looked like a fairy. She gave one tinkling giggle, then opened her mouth and broke into a full-blown belly laugh.

Katie was so absorbed in gaping at Lady Waverly that she didn't notice Lord Waverly's arrival.

"Good gracious! What have I missed?" he boomed.

Katie squeezed her eyes shut, hoping to make herself invisible. She did not want to explain she was the reason for his wife's unladylike cackling. She slunk deep into her shoulders and turned to face him. If Lord Waverly was going to grab her by the back of the neck and throw her out, she didn't want to make it easy.

His face wore an odd expression, as if he were trying to recall something. He looked perplexed, but not angry.

Like an enthusiastic child, Lady Waverly leapt from her seat to seize her husband's hand and led him to the chair next to her. An inkling of a smile crossed his face as his gaze floated from his wife to Lucas, then to Katie, and back to his wife. As Lord Waverly's confusion seemed to give way to affection for his wife, Katie felt herself relax a little. She had the distinct feeling he was trying remember the last time he had seen his wife have a genuine laugh, let alone a sidesplitting fit.

Lord Waverly turned to his guests. "Hello Katie, Lucas. Thank you for coming. We need to have you over more often—you do my wife good." His smile was now complete and his words were genuine.

Katie breathed for what seemed like the first time since their arrival.

"We were just filling Katie in on the newest conflict in Bosnia," Lady Waverly explained, still fighting the giggles.

Her husband nodded; a practiced air of conversation overtook him. "Right, right, such a mess, with no easy solution—what do you

169

think, Lucas? Do you think the British government should get involved?"

"I really don't see any way around it." Lucas sighed, his demeanor now very serious. "No, I don't want Britain to get involved, but if we don't, I imagine Bosnia will have another war on its hands."

Lord Waverly nodded. "I agree with you, but just for argument's sake, why shouldn't we just let them battle it out among themselves?"

"We saw what happened in the nineties—we have a moral obligation to help protect innocent people from being slaughtered. Second, we should consider our economic situation. We can't afford to support many more people seeking asylum in this country. We're already bursting at the seams with refugees and struggling to provide adequately for our own countrymen. We'd be fools to think we won't have our own uprising if we foot the bill for thousands more coming in from Bosnia."

Katie basked in the cadence of his accent, trying to absorb everything he was saying. The mental checklist she made on him already consisted of *gorgeous, tall, witty, luscious hair, sensitive, owns a tuxedo.* Now, she was compelled to add *intellectual, holds his own with England's most influential.* It was hard not to compare that list against Jared's: *short, balding, wouldn't pick up a book if his life depended on it, likes to shoot furry creatures with Other Best Girl.*

"Well said!" Lord Waverly's enthusiastic approval broke into her thoughts. "That's almost the exact stance I plan to take at the summit this afternoon."

At that moment the breakfast trays were brought in.

"You know, Lucas, if you ever decide to give up the travel business, I think we could use you in parliament," his Lordship suggested cordially.

"Thank you, I'll keep that in mind," Lucas replied with a modest but uninterested smile.

"So, where do things stand with our holiday?" Lady Waverly was anxious to get down to business.

"Thanks to Katie, we're right on track. How she was able to do it is beyond me, but she has arranged for you to have the Peninsula Suite overlooking Victoria Harbor at the Peninsula Hotel." Lucas's eyes sparkled approval of his new employee.

"Brilliant!" Lady Waverly clasped her hands together. "Everything is going to be just brilliant. I have every confidence Katie understands exactly what this journey means to me." She gave Katie a conspiratorial smile.

"I'm sorry to have to eat and run," Lord Waverly pushed away from the table, "but my guests will be arriving soon and I should be prepared to greet them. Lucas, are you sure you wouldn't like to stay for the meeting? I'd be very interested to hear more of what you have to say."

"Thank you, but I'm afraid I'll have to decline. I have put the day aside to show Katie around the countryside. I was thinking about taking her around to Framlingham Castle."

"That sounds lovely," Lady Waverly gushed. "You should take her to the coast near Aldeburgh and Thorpeness."

"I was reading in the paper there are quite a number of markets being held in the area this weekend. Maybe Katie would fancy seeing some local crafts," suggested Lord Waverly.

"What a brilliant idea! It's been ages since I've been to a market!" Lady Waverly exclaimed.

"Well, Katie, what would you like to do? It looks like you're spoiled for choice." Lucas turned to her expectantly.

Katie considered her options, then exploded, "I want to do it all!"

She paused abruptly, seeing in Lucas's eyes that "doing it all" wouldn't be an option. "I know, let's pick a direction and choose the roads as we go! It'll be a completely spontaneous adventure!"

"How exciting!" Lady Waverly commented.

"Lady Waverly—" Katie began.

"Chelsea," she reminded.

"Chelsea, why don't you come and hang out with us?"

Lady Waverly's eyes bulged and her hand flew to her chest. "Oh, Katie, if I could bottle a little of your spirit. I don't think I know how to 'hang out' anymore."

Katie saw the surprise on Lady Waverly's face, then noticed the others also seemed shocked by the invitation. She bit her bottom lip and worried she'd crossed a line of propriety. Still, the damage was already done, and she could see the contemplation behind the woman's eyes.

"Come on, it'll be fun," Katie urged.

"Thank you. It would be wonderful, but we're having guests and it's always such an ordeal to go out." Lady Waverly's protest was unconvincing.

"Yes! Why not go?" Lord Waverly belted, catching the wave of Katie's enthusiasm. "We'll be in meetings all day…you won't be expected until dinner. Why not go and have some fun?"

"Do you really think so?" she asked her husband hesitantly. "What about the photographers? Katie, you don't want to go with me—we'll have photographers chasing us the whole time. You won't have any fun at all."

"What if we dress you up—or down—to look like an average person? We'll be in Lucas's car; the press may never know you've left the property. If it doesn't work, we'll make a game of trying to lose them."

"It does sound like an amusing challenge," Lady Waverly agreed. "Would you mind, Lucas, if I joined your party?"

Lucas quickly recovered from his shock. "Not at all. I think it's a brilliant idea."

With an excitement she hadn't displayed in years and with Katie in tow, Lady Waverly darted off to find something to make her look "average."

Lord Waverly heaved a happy sigh and together he and Lucas set off at a leisurely pace through the gardens.

"I'm absolutely delighted Lady Waverly has taken a shine to Katie. It's been ages since my wife has taken on a new friend. I don't think I've seen her so lighthearted in years."

"Katie is hard not to like," Lucas agreed.

"I can't tell you how happy it makes me to see my wife smile. I'm afraid life in the spotlight takes its toll on her," Lord Waverly confided.

***

Lucas had his Volkswagen Touareg waiting by the side entrance where the ladies could get in without being noticed. Lady Waverly looked uncomfortable wearing a pair of crisp jeans that were

173

found folded in the depths of her wardrobe and a snug baby doll tee borrowed from one of the maids. She insisted on lying down in the back seat as they rolled out of the drive. Katie felt a rush of exhilaration as she pushed on her large round sunglasses and gave a pert wave to the reporters waiting outside the gate hoping to catch a glimpse of the attendees of the summit meeting.

"It looks like we haven't attracted any interest," Lucas announced, making one last check in his mirrors.

Lady Waverly shot up and cheered, suddenly losing her inhibitions. Katie smiled to herself, thinking the Lady had missed her calling as a Dallas Cowboys cheerleader.

At their first stop, Katie bought enough car snacks and beverages to last a week, a navy blue ball cap that had "England" embroidered in cursive across the front, and an enormous pair of diva-type sunglasses. Handing the disguise to Lady Waverly, she ripped into a package of licorice and joked, "There, now you'll just be mistaken for Britney Spears."

They had been traveling in comfortable silence, watching the scenery roll by, when Lady Waverly shrieked, "Turn it up!"

Katie nearly shot through the roof at the unexpected squeal, and Lucas almost jerked the car off the road.

Lady Waverly was undaunted. "Hurry, turn up the radio! It's Blondie!"

Katie did as she was told and watched in wide-eyed amusement as the refined Lady Waverly made a microphone of her half-chewed licorice rope and used the whole backseat as a dance studio, crooning shamelessly to "The Tide Is High."

Katie cranked up the volume even more and grabbed a bottled-water microphone, eager to join in. Soon, all three were slaying the contagious melody at the top of their lungs.

Chapter Eighteen

"Yes Mum, I'm sorry, but you left me no other choice."

Katie nestled into the leather seat and giggled as Lucas argued with his mother. She and Lucas were almost back to London and Lottie had been berating him for nearly half an hour.

"That's right, Mother, you're off the job. You're no longer Katie's boss—I am. That gives me the right to take her wherever I please." His grin stretched from one lobe to the other. He rumbled a deep, throaty laugh. "You can't ground me from my own employee."

Katie couldn't make out the words, but she could hear Lottie trilling her response. From the look on Lucas's face, it must have been a good one.

"Okay Mum," he sighed. "Listen, I don't care which bits of mine you're threatening to cut off, I'm taking Katie out for a celebratory dinner... Bye Mum—love you."

She was still nagging when he shut the phone down.

***

"Of all the restaurants in London, you choose *this* place?" Despite his words, Lucas couldn't have seemed happier when they tucked into their table at an obscure but cozy little pub.

"If you don't like it, it's your own fault. I told you I hate having to choose restaurants."

"On the contrary, I like your choice. I'm just surprised. I was expecting you to pick something more...I don't know...posh." Lucas's eyes searched Katie with curiosity.

Throwing her hands up, she shrugged. "Considering I haven't showered and have had less than ten hours of sleep since leaving the

176

States, which was technically three days ago, this is preferable to 'posh.'"

"Point well taken." Lucas shook his head theatrically. "I can't help feeling somewhat responsible. Can I make it up to you by buying you a drink?"

"You are totally responsible, and I'll just start with a Coke, please."

He leered at her, the corners of his mouth fighting a grin. "Surely you want something a bit stronger than a Coke—after what I've put you through the last two days?"

"The only thing strong enough to counteract what you've put me through is a bludgeon to the head. I'll just have the Coke."

He arched an inquisitively sexy eyebrow at her.

A giggle rippled through her words. "Just a Coke, really. I don't drink."

"You don't drink?" He searched her face for any signs of a joke. "I've never met anyone who doesn't drink at least a little."

"Now you have," she said smugly.

"Never?"

"Not since Anna's seventeenth birthday party when Christopher had to call his parents to pick us up because I had broken out in hives and was throwing up and he was too drunk to drive. Holy crap, did we ever get in trouble that night! Even the tiniest bit makes me super sick. I learned that the hard way when I had a glass of champagne at my brother's wedding."

"Right then, two Cokes it is!" He gave a definitive nod.

"Don't pass up a beer on my account—I don't mind."

"I'm not. I don't touch the stuff either."

She glared at him suspiciously. "I don't believe you."

"It's true. My granddad was a massive alcoholic. It's not a condition I'm keen to inherit."

The last thing Katie wanted was to cloud their day with drunken granddad stories. Lucas obviously thought the same and quickly changed the subject. "Right! Now that we've found something in common, can we be friends?"

She swung her ponytail over her shoulder and declared, "Maybe. We'll have to see how dinner goes."

As they ate, Katie tried not to notice Lucas kept staring at her, until she couldn't endure it another moment longer. "What? Do I have something on my face?"

He had the decency to look embarrassed. "Nothing. It's just you look the quintessential American stereotype—with your Coke, hamburger and fries, ponytail, and blue jeans. You remind me of a Skipper doll, and it's triggering all the boyhood fantasies I'd gleaned from watching American sitcoms.

If she wouldn't have been so flabbergasted, she might have given him a response, though she wouldn't have known what to say.

"What would you like to do now?" he asked, focusing on tidying up the discarded plates as if he hadn't just thrown her with his random and confusing comment.

Of course he didn't mean anything by it. He's your boss—super hot, sexy, out of your league, engaged boss. She looked at the plates with disdain and put an arm over her stomach. "I think I need to walk off about eight thousand calories."

178

"All right, *Cousin* Kate." He put much more emphasis on the word cousin than was necessary. "We can walk to Oxford and back if you'd like."

"Sure. Is that very far from here?"

His whole body shook from unrestrained laughter. "You're very agreeable. It's only fifty-odd miles. Perhaps we'll save that for another day. How about we head toward Hyde Park?"

"That sounds perfect."

***

Katie would have preferred the fifty-mile walk to the sound of Olivia's voice.

"Lucas, darling, there you are!" The pitch was just a note below hysteria.

Katie froze in her tracks. The piercing sound was worse than fingernails on a chalkboard. "Well, it *was* a nice walk," she muttered under her breath as an opal-colored Jaguar slowly rolled past them.

"Andrew, pull over!" Olivia demanded of the driver.

The vehicle nosed its way into a nonexistent parking space, the rest of the body jutting diagonally into traffic. The passenger door flung open and Olivia's stick figure flew out and pranced over to them as quickly as her Prada heels would allow.

"Darling, where have you been? I haven't heard from you all day!" Olivia shot a murderous glare at Katie just before she planted Lucas with a territorial kiss. Katie took a deep breath to steady the crushing feeling that bore down on her chest.

Lucas drew back from Olivia's affection. "We've spent the day in Suffolk. Lady Waverly requested I bring Katie to Pellyn Hall for a visit."

Olivia's eyes blazed fire, and Katie took a step back to keep from getting singed. Olivia opened her tightly pursed lips—no doubt to speak something horrible—when Katie let out a startled yelp as she felt a loud swat on her backside.

"Hello Duchess. Lovely to see you again," Andrew crooned.

Lucas drew himself to full stature. An angry muscle spasmed at the back of his jaw line.

"Darling, look who I bumped into! I was hoping we could all go for dinner tonight, and I thought it would be so much more enjoyable for Katie if she had a partner, so I invited Andrew to join us." Olivia's face radiated so angelically that Katie could almost believe she cared.

"We've already eaten," Lucas replied. "We were just walking off our dinners."

Morphing from angel to demon in less than half a second, Olivia cast her narrowed eyes over Katie. "Lovely idea, darling. Katie could stand to walk off a few dinners."

Katie knew her mouth was hanging wide open, but she was powerless to draw it closed.

"Olivia!" Lucas spat, the harshness of the word causing everyone to flinch. He took a few moments to gain his composure. "Perhaps we should pop inside there." He jerked his head toward the pub across the street. "I'd like to have a few words." There was a stern patriarchal set about him that no one dared refuse.

Once they'd found a table, Katie quickly excused herself to find the restroom. Olivia's insult was haunting her. She subconsciously rubbed her Little Buddha, wishing for a dark, inconspicuous hole to

180

crawl into and spend the rest of the night—the rest of her life, even—so she wouldn't have to face Olivia after Lucas had his "few words."

At the very least, she planned to stay gone until she could be sure Andrew had enough time to return from parking the car. A hopeless groan escaped her as she realized the flaws in her plan: She was relying on Andrew to help make the evening bearable, and worse, if she stayed in hiding that long, Lucas might assume she was having a difficult bowel movement. She stared at her defeated self in the mirror for another moment before deciding to trudge back to the table.

"There you are!" Lucas looked relieved.

Olivia offered Katie a warm and seemingly welcoming smile. She couldn't be certain, but she thought Olivia's eyes looked as though she had been crying. It tweaked Katie's heart a little. She hadn't thought Olivia had enough sensitivity to cry. And crying must mean she's sorry, right? A sucker for another person's tears, Katie decided to dismiss every horrible insult chucked at her and allow the poor woman a clean slate.

"We ordered you a drink," Olivia offered with some humility as she scooted a glass of something colorful and fruity toward her.

Katie couldn't stop the color from rising to her cheeks; she hated to turn down Olivia's peace offering.

"It's okay, there's no alcohol," Olivia smiled. "Lucas informed me about your allergy."

Olivia must have read her mind. Katie accepted it graciously and took a long sip, savoring the medley of sweet citrus flavors.

Considering the painful start, Katie felt the visit was going surprisingly well. Somehow they had all managed to put bygones aside and enjoy the effortless conversations rolling out over a round of drinks. She was surprised by the few glimpses she caught of the genuinely good guy that lurked beneath Andrew's angry, bad-boy persona. By the time she'd reached the bottom of her drink, Katie was convinced they could all be best friends.

"Katie...you all right?" Lucas stopped everyone in mid-conversation. "You don't look well."

She wiped a bead of sweat from her forehead. "Yeah, I'll be fine. It just got really hot in here." She rested her head against the window, finding comfort against the cool pane of glass. Her stomach began to churn loudly enough for the whole table to hear.

"Poor dear, let me get you a cold Coke—a little bit of fizz might settle your stomach." Olivia dashed out of her seat and headed for the bar.

Katie tried to protest. "But I don't have an upset stoma—" She snapped her mouth shut as her gut made another vigorous lurch.

"Here you are sweetie, drink up. This will help." Olivia was back in a flash, thrusting an icy glass at her.

Katie sucked down a desperate gulp, praying that it would hold back the vomit long enough for her to get to a toilet. Pulling a contorted face, she pushed the drink away.

"There's something wrong with this Coke."

Olivia encouraged her to take another drink. "Perhaps the syrup has gone out of the machine. It's the fizz you want anyway—go on, take another sip."

Katie did as she was told and pulled the same face. "No, it's not that...it's gone bad," she insisted, now sweating profusely.

With morbid curiosity, Andrew picked up her glass and took a sip.

182

"My God, Olivia! You must have called in a slew of favors with that bartender! There's enough Captain Morgan in here to take down a sailor," Andrew chuckled, ignorant of the murderous glare Olivia was giving him.

Katie groaned and doubled over.

"Olivia, you didn't!" Lucas snarled.

"I'm sure there was some sort of mistake," Olivia protested, growing nervous as crimson splotches started to speckle Katie's skin.

Lucas picked up what was left of Katie's fruity drink and took a swallow. Disgust colored his face. "And this one happened to be a mistake, too?"

Olivia was silent.

"Good God, Duchess, you're turning scarlet!" Andrew exclaimed.

Katie looked befuddled at the pattern of red splotches starting from the back of her hands and running the entire length of her arms.

She looked helplessly at Lucas, unable to speak for fear of barfing at the table. Her body was an inferno that melted every muscle to the point where she could barely hold her head up. Lucas understood her look and in an instant was by her side, half carrying her out of the building. Andrew and Olivia followed closely behind.

"I didn't know...I didn't know she would get sick," Olivia sobbed.

"Of course you knew. I told you," Lucas growled. "You just didn't realize she would get *this* sick!"

"What can I do? What can I do?" Olivia continued to sob as Katie's color turned to an eerie ash.

Lucas turned a deaf ear and focused on Katie, who was struggling to stand up straight.

Andrew stared at Olivia in shock. "You did this on purpose?" he gasped. "You forced that rum and Coke on her—after she was already feeling sick?" He reeled backward, away from Olivia. "You're on your own. I never agreed to help you poison anyone." A nervous trill replaced the arrogant calm of his voice.

"Shut up, Andrew," Olivia hissed. "Just shut up!" She ran over to Katie and resumed her sobbing. "Katie, I'm so sorry. What can I do? What can I do?"

For some reason, Katie felt the need to comfort Olivia. With what strength she could muster, she stood to face the hysterical woman, ignoring the violent complaints of her macraméd intestines. She opened her mouth to say something consoling just as the breeze picked up, carrying the scent of a nearby curry restaurant, and she vomited a deluge of burger and fries all over Olivia's Chanel top.

Chapter Nineteen

Sunlight streamed across Katie's face as the sound of a chainsaw snarled around her.

Katie peeked one eye open, swiped a look around her unfamiliar surroundings, and groaned, exhausted by the effort, into the pillows. She groaned again as flashbacks from the night before tumbled through her mind.

Olivia's shrieks at being plastered in vomit still pierced Katie's brain. She remembered Lucas holding her hair as she puke-graffitied half the streets in London, and his soothing accent as he sat on the edge of the tub consoling her while she writhed in agony on his bathroom floor. Vaguely, she remembered it was sunrise when he moved her to the couch, laid her head in his lap, and wiped her tears with his thumb as she continued to spew bile into a bucket. Beyond that, she didn't remember.

She knew she wasn't dead because she felt too rotten to be dead. The pain of being alive tormented her entire body. And if someone didn't put a stop to the relentless wail of that chainsaw, her brain was going to explode. Lucas must have been jarred awake by the sound, too, and came barreling down the hall—hopefully to make it stop.

He paused at the bookshelf next to the bed and picked something up. *Strange to keep a chainsaw on the bookshelf,* she thought, peeking at him through her one conscious eye. He looked like a rumpled little boy in his flannel pajama bottoms, baggy T-shirt, and half a dozen rooster tails sticking up in his hair.

"Hello," he said to the chainsaw, his voice hoarse and sleepy.

185

The chainsaw must have asked for her because he said, "Yeah, this is Katie's phone, but she's sleeping. Can I have her ring you later?"

There was silence while the chainsaw replied.

Lucas pulled the chainsaw away from his ear so he could scowl at it face to face. "This is Lucas Hayden, Katie's employer. No, we aren't sleeping in the same bed—I'm sorry, who is this?"

He must not have liked the chainsaw's name because he looked like he was going to slam it against the wall.

"You're where?... Here? Here in London?"

Silence again.

"Are you in town for long? It's just that she's been sick through the night and has only just gone to sleep." He nodded his head, answering, "Right… right… uh-huh… yeah, no, right… uh-huh… yeah" to whatever the chainsaw had to say.

"Listen," he said, "I'm certain Katie won't be up for a meal— like I said, she's been sick all night. You're more than welcome to come visit her here. I'll wake her up and let her know you're on your way. Will that work for you?"

He looked seriously annoyed as the chainsaw replied, then he said, "Right, once you get off the tube at Holland Park, ring back and I'll give you directions to the house."

"I'm not getting up," Katie mumbled after he'd said goodbye. "Tell the chainsaw I'm busy and can't meet today."

He gave her a "poor baby" look. "What chainsaw?"

"The one you were just talking to."

"You mean Jared?"

"Jared…?"

186

He gave a self-satisfied chuckle. "From what he tells me, he's your boyfriend."

Katie rubbed her forehead. "Oh yeah, I guess...kind of." Making a cohesive sentence out of her thoughts was too difficult.

He chuckled again. "He'll be here in about twenty minutes."

"Okay." She was just about to tumble back over the edge where sleep was waiting to reclaim her, but the news registered before she could take the plunge.

"Wait! What? He's *here*?" She shot up, regretting the action immediately; her head seemed full of both lead and helium, and she tweaked a muscle in her neck trying to negotiate its awkward weight.

"He says he has something important to tell you."

"I don't care! That's what phones are for—not airplanes!"

"It must really be important if he came all the way to London to tell you." She noticed the muscle at the back of his jaw clench.

She lugged herself out of bed and wobbled around on legs made of Jell-O. "I need to find my shoulder bag? Where's my bag?" She looked down at her bare legs and feet and changed her line of questioning. "Better yet, where are my pants?" The oversize T-shirt she wore hung off one shoulder, *Flashdance*-style, and was a little too short for comfort.

"You mean your trousers? 'Pants,' in England, means your underpants—and you kicked them off."

"I kicked my pants off? Why?"

"No, you kicked your trousers off; you are still wearing your pants. Please don't get those confused—especially in front of my mum."

He waited for her to express her understanding before he would continue. "You kicked your trousers off because they had vomit on them—your top, too. They're in the washing machine. I'll get you something of mine to wear."

She shrugged with resigned acceptance and went back to looking for her handbag, which she found by the side of the sofa, and made good use of the emergency comb and toothbrush she kept inside. Her face was still red and swollen from excessive puking, then crying—then puking and crying some more—and her skin was still marked with faint pink blotches, but there was nothing she could do about that.

"How are you feeling?" Lucas asked, handing her a pair of grey sweatpants.

Sweatpants! Aha! Lucas's second flaw!

"Like I've been used for a med school cadaver."

"Are you still feeling nauseated?"

"Not bad." She shook her head gingerly.

"Good. I'm going to make you some tea and toast and see if that doesn't help you feel better."

"Ewww, no tea," she said almost urgently. "I mean—no thanks."

"You don't like tea?" He cocked an inquisitive eyebrow.

"It tastes like a stinky, crusty, dishrag that's been left sitting in the sink too long."

He smiled at her vivid description. "Well, you're in England now, you'd better get used to it. We drink loads of tea. See if you can't manage a few sips. I think it will make you feel better."

"Oh, all right," she muttered.

She tightened the drawstring of the sweatpants—karma really was a whore—as much as it would go, then rolled the waistband down twice to keep them from falling off. Even then, the cuffs fell completely over her feet and dragged along the floor as she slogged behind Lucas to the kitchen.

***

"Wow, you look like crap," Jared greeted Katie when Lucas opened the door and stepped aside.

She gave him a "no shit, Sherlock" smile. "Yeah, I've been sick. What are you doing here?" She was in no mood for banal small talk.

Jared grinned his Cheshire cat grin. "I've got some really big news to tell you."

"And you came all the way to London to tell me?"

"Yeah—well, kind of. We're heading to Thailand anyway, so I just arranged the flights so we'd have a stop in London. I know it's not really on the way, but I thought, what the hell! That way I get to see you, right?"

She examined him skeptically. "Right."

"I just felt funny about the way we left things. I've been pretty pissed about catching you in bed with Dylan."

Lucas gave Katie an intrigued look that made her blush to the roots of her hair.

"Even after we talked on the phone the other day, things still didn't seem right," Jared continued. "I really wanted to see you in person to clear the air—let you know that I'm not mad anymore."

"You did not catch me in bed with Dylan!" she snapped. "Okay, maybe you did—kind of—but Dylan is one of my closest

189

friends—we don't do that. Anyway, that's what you get for breaking into my house."

"Relax. It took me a few days to work it out, but I get it now—Dylan is your gay friend."

"He is not gay!" She struck back in his defense. "Wait, back it up a minute—did you just say 'we're' going to Thailand?"

He bobbed his head excitedly. "Yeah, Natalie and me are going."

Natalie and I! Natalie and I! she hissed in her head before the information could really seep in.

She thought she must have misunderstood, but sure enough, when she peered around the doorframe, Natalie was standing at the bottom of the stairs. Adding insult to injury, Jared's annoying little Chi-poo, Queen Sheba, lounged inside Natalie's shoulder bag. *As if anyone besides Paris Hilton could pull off the rat-dog fashion without looking completely ridiculous,* Katie thought, *and even then.... I wonder what strings they had to pull to bring that nasty dog into the country? It'd serve them all right if some Thai family indulges on a Queen Sheba shish kabob.*

"But I planned that trip. Planning that trip was the basis of our first three dates," Katie protested quietly so Natalie wouldn't hear. "You gave me that trip for Valentine's Day. You can't just give another woman my Valentine's present." *Half the reason I agreed to remain your girlfriend was so things wouldn't be awkward when we went to Thailand!* Katie thought.

Jared furrowed his brow as if she were speaking crazy-nese. "What do you mean?"

190

With a defeated shake of the head, she tried to dismiss having been dealt the sucker punch of the century. "Nothing—forget it."

Lucas's jaw muscle was working overtime. "Come in, I'm Lucas Hayden, Katie's employer."

Jared and Natalie stepped inside and followed Lucas to the front room. Lagging behind to shut the door, Katie took a moment to clear her head. Her brain rummaged to find her Jared mantra. *Practicality prohibits princes, presents, and perfection. Practicality prohibits princes.... piss on it!* She was in England now, and nobody was pressuring her to be practical anymore.

"I did it! I got the job with the FBI!" Jared boasted the second Katie entered the room.

"That's great!" she said with forced enthusiasm, accompanied by Natalie's clapping and Lucas's polite words of congratulations.

Jared motioned her over to have a seat next to him on the sofa.

"Katie..." He wrapped his arms around her and placed a sweaty hand over hers, casting an anxious look at the two bystanders in the room. She had never seen him this nervous.

Panic struck her heart. She felt suddenly claustrophobic—penned in by the hold of his strong arms.

His trembling hand moved to her cheek, hoping to soften her stony face.

"Katie, I love you, and I want you to come with me."

"Go with you...where?"

"Virginia, to start. Then, after I finish my training—who knows, we'll have to wait and see."

191

Katie made a quick assessment of the room. Jared looked like an eager little puppy waiting for a treat, Natalie made no attempt to hide the sneer on her face, and Lucas...*was that worry on his face?*

"I've still got the kettle on," Lucas said. "Natalie, why don't you and I go into the kitchen and make some tea—give these two a little privacy?" He pelted Katie with a cautionary look before leading Natalie away.

Katie began to swelter in Jared's close proximity, but his arms kept her belted so tightly against him that she could only wiggle an inch or so away from his body.

"Ooohhh-kaaay," she drawled, feeling like she'd swallowed a sauna. "I wasn't expecting that." Again, she struggled against his closeness before giving up and declaring, "I don't want to move to Virginia."

A hurt expression skimmed Jared's eyes. "Don't you want to *think* about it?"

"Jared, if someone hands me a turd sandwich, I don't need to think about it to know I don't want to eat it."

"What's that supposed to mean?"

"It means I don't belong in Virginia."

"You belong with me."

Her eyes bulged from their sockets like two baseballs that had just been whacked out of their leather covers, and it felt like the heat on her internal sauna had been jacked up another hundred and eighty degrees. A tepid trickle of sweat crept down her back.

"Why don't we discuss this over food? I'm totally craving fettuccini Alfredo. I bet you'll feel better once you've put something in your stomach," Jared suggested.

The phantom aroma of fettuccini Alfredo played around her nostrils, making her stomach roil. She struggled once more for breathing room, but his grip, like his insufferable confidence, was unbreakable.

"Aren't you going to say anything?" he prodded when she remained silent.

She began to speak, but instead of a protest, hot, stinky, dishrag-tasting tea and toast spewed from her mouth.

Jared finally released his grip. "Son of a bitch!" he snarled, pushing Katie, who, with one hand covering her mouth, was relying on the other to help her wriggle off the sofa.

His shove knocked her off balance and sent her sprawling face first across the carpet. The vision of fettuccini caught in her brain, her stomach gave another lurch and more vomit squirted out between the seal of her hand and between her fingers.

At the sound of her master's bark, Queen Sheba leapt out of the shoulder bag, issuing a tiny yip, and ran out of the kitchen, making a beeline for Katie.

"Oh jeez! Don't eat it! Bad puppy! Bad Sheba!" Jared's voice bellowed.

Lucas and Natalie trotted out of the kitchen after the puppy, arriving just in time to see Katie scrambling to her feet, puke dripping from her chin and fingers, running to the bathroom.

Tears pouring down her face, she tossed tea, toast, and imaginary fettuccini into the toilet. Lucas seated himself on the edge of the tub and gathered her long, tangled hair away from her face, twisting it into one long cord down her back. She cringed, not because she didn't appreciate his help, but because they now had their own puking modus operandi.

"Do you want me to get rid of them?" he asked.

She nodded and put her cheek against the toilet seat, long past the point of caring that its primary purpose was to accommodate butts, not faces.

"I'll be right back," he promised, giving her shoulder a light rub.

From her vantage point, slumped over the toilet, she watched his calves disappear down the hallway.

"She's been sick like this all night," Lucas explained to Jared and Natalie apologetically. "Why don't the two of you go see some sights? I'll have Katie call you when she's feeling better."

"That's a good idea. Damn, that was nasty," Jared replied with an exaggerated whole-body shudder. "Actually, I kind of want to shower now. Maybe we'll just check into a hotel. I don't want to risk catching whatever she's got."

"I don't blame you. In fact, why don't you throw your bags in the boot of my car? I'll change my clothes and drive you to a decent hotel." Lucas was willing to do whatever it took to not have them back again. He found his key fob and pointed it toward the street until he heard the *bleep bleep* that unlocked the car door. "There you go, the car's just there—outside the gate," he called, already halfway to his bedroom.

***

When Lucas came downstairs, Natalie was already sitting in the backseat next to a pile of luggage, but Jared was waiting at the front gate to catch a word in private.

194

"Lucas, I need to ask you a favor. Will you give this to Katie for me?" Not giving him a chance to respond, Jared shoved a little black ring box into Lucas hands.

The note he found in Katie's suitcase flashed through Lucas's mind. He recalled all the adjectives used to describe Jared and thought they were too kind. "This isn't something I feel comfortable with. You should give it to her yourself."

"Nah, the timing's not right; she needs a few days to feel better and have some time to think. Listen, if you won't give it to her, will you at least pass it off to someone who will, or hide it someplace where she'll be able to find it later?"

"I guess I can do that," Lucas agreed reluctantly.

Lucas pulled his car to the curb just outside Soho and sent Jared and Natalie off in pursuit of their hotel. Once they were out of sight, he pulled out the delicate box that had been burning a hole in his pocket and his brain ever since Jared had burdened him with it. "Stupid git," he mumbled to himself, and opened the lid. A hurriedly scribbled note was tucked inside that read:

Katie,
We belong together. Please don't say no.
I love you.
Jared

Pinching the ring between his thumb and forefinger, Lucas held it out for inspection. Engraved inside the band was the word "promised." He eyed the ring with disgust. He hadn't known Katie long, but it only took him one look through her wardrobe to know that she would hate that ring. The too-shiny, yellow gold band was twisted ornately into a pair of sideways hearts that were joined together by a small, round diamond set in a gaudy bed of braided golden loops.

An uncomfortable emotion edged through his veins, which he convinced himself was concern. Concern that she deserved better than this man who didn't appreciate her enough not to comfort her when sick, to not take another woman on her holiday, didn't understand her well enough to know she didn't like tacky gold jewelry, or care that she'd be burdened with guilt if she refused it. Lucas barely knew her, and already he understood that much about her.

Chapter Twenty

Lucas didn't get to keep his promise to be right back. Before he returned, his mother had come and snatched what she felt was rightfully hers—Katie—claiming in the snarky message she left him that he was unable to give Katie the proper care she needed. To some degree, Katie had to agree that was true. Though he was attentive and kind, she was embarrassed by his attention to her, and his skills couldn't compete with the quality of pampering and coddling she received from Lottie and Mrs. Albright. Under their maternal watch, her stomach was eventually set at ease, and she was cosseted into a deep, all-consuming sleep.

***

"Holy shit!" Anna exclaimed after hearing Katie describe her last several days in full detail.

"I know, right?" Heather agreed.

"What should I do?" Katie asked her conference call attendees. Locating the remote control on the bedside table, she turned down the volume on the television Mrs. Albright had considerately unearthed from behind the doors of the sturdy armoire.

Dylan spoke up. "Which one takes priority: trying to one-up Jared—because, let me tell you, you are NOT going to mope around while he's treating some G-woman to your vacation—or getting out of there before the psycho fiancée succeeds the next time she tries to kill you?"

"G-woman! Is that…something *sexual*?" Katie asked, alarmed by the very real possibility. She remembered Natalie's low-cut shirt the first time they'd met, and the glimpse she'd caught of her seductive black bra.

"No, doofus, 'G-man' is gangster slang for an FBI agent," Dylan informed her. "Obviously Jared's head over heels for you—"

"I'm not one for petty games," Anna chimed in, ignoring the simultaneous "Yeah, right" from Dylan and Katie. "But Dylan's got a point—you've got to do something that will really get under Jared's skin."

"And do something about that Olivia monster," Heather contributed. "Now that you're not dead, she's going to keep ambushing you."

"Maybe you could sleep with your hot boss," Dylan suggested.

"Get real. Lucas is like a cousin," Katie argued.

This time the "Yeah, rights" chorused from Anna, Dylan, and Heather.

Drawn in by the television program humming in the background, Katie was spared from having to further contemplate her options. She heard the soft voice of the narrator: "...looking at the pristine beaches and the throngs of Western European tourists, it's no wonder why so many refugees of the former Yugoslavia have found Croatia to be their safe haven...." The camera panned across an enticing coastline before cutting to a majestic waterfall, then followed a sparkling river as it highlighted all of the country's bounties.

Safe haven.

"Don't worry, I've got an idea," Katie announced.

"What do you mean?" Alarm bells rang through Anna's voice. "Are you thinking of doing something stupid?"

198

When Katie didn't respond, Dylan reported, "She's lost in thought. Which means she's going to do something stupid."

He was right on one point. Katie's thoughts had evolved too far to issue a response.

"Okay, whatever, just keep us posted," Anna said, and all four friends sounded their goodbyes.

A hot shower was just what Katie needed to glean perspective. With intense focus, she scrutinized the soapy bubbles, believing they were carrying with them down the drain all the blemished events since her last shower, all the way back in her parents' basement. She felt a sort of renaissance imagining vomit, airport, Jared, Natalie, and Olivia germs swirling into oblivion. Cleansing the residue of those memories from her body left her feeling as though she could do exactly as she pleased. And right now, she pleased not to let Jared and Natalie hijacking her dream vacation make her miserable. She also pleased to never have to see Olivia again.

By the time she was ready to leave her room, she felt as though she'd had a second round through the birthing canal. She was a brand-new person, tired and weak but smelling fresh and ready to make her mark on the world.

Lottie and Sidney were in the library chatting and having tea, with the television on low volume, when Katie made her appearance.

"Well, bugger me, if it isn't Sleeping Beauty!" Lottie exclaimed.

"Lottie, if you don't watch your language the lass will think she's woken up in the gutter," Sidney lightly reprimanded.

"Oh sod off, Sidney, I'll speak as I bloody well please," Lottie returned lightheartedly. Then, speaking to Katie what she clearly meant

199

for Sidney, she added, "The old fossil still thinks he can treat me like his baby sister."

"That, my dear woman, will never change so long as you continue to act like an adolescent." He betrayed just a hint of a smile.

"Oh piss off," Lottie uttered under her breath.

Delighting in their playful banter, Katie slid onto the sofa next to Sidney and waited for the right moment to tell them her decision.

"Well?" Lottie prodded, "I can see that you've got something to say…go on with it then."

Katie giggled at Lottie's no-nonsense approach, since everything about the woman was so nonsensical.

"Sidney, thank you so much," Katie enthused. "I feel so honored that you allowed me to borrow these." She pressed and held the priceless diamonds she wore to the ball into his palm. "I hope I haven't caused you too much trouble by wearing them."

"Nonsense, love. I sincerely hope we'll have the opportunity to see you wear them again." He gave her hand a light squeeze.

"I hope so, too," she agreed, then fell silent.

Feeling Lottie staring down the bridge of her thin nose at her, Kate wrung her hands together as she struggled for the right words. So much had taken place; it was hard to remember she had only met these people a few days ago.

"I've decided to go to Croatia." Katie made the announcement with the speed of a cattle auctioneer, then squeezed her eyes shut in anticipation of their reaction.

The tiny woman clapped her hands, her eyes bulging from their sockets. "Oooh fabby! Can I go with you?"

"Croatia?" Sidney's response was closer to what she'd anticipated. "Apart from Olivia, have we done something to drive you away? Dear girl, have we upset you?" Beyond the puzzlement, he looked hurt.

"No, Sidney, not at all," she gushed, distressed to have caused him pain. "You've been wonderful—you all have. But after two encounters with Olivia, I'm starting to get an inkling she doesn't like me much." She tried to lighten the mood with a playful wink. "It doesn't feel right working for Lucas, seeing how his fiancée tried to poison me last night. I think it was last night...crap, I don't even know what day it is."

"I can certainly understand that. But why would you leave *us*?"

She was surprised Sidney even asked; she would have thought the answer was obvious.

"Because you're Lucas's family, soon to be Olivia's. This is their home more than mine. I shouldn't be here."

"Oh bollocks," Sidney retorted. "Now you listen very carefully." His voice was stern. "I'm forgiving you this once because you've just arrived. But let me set you straight, young miss. You have been part of this oddball family from the moment we clapped eyes on you."

Katie tried to make a point, but Sidney shot her a look that warned her to hold her tongue.

"Not because our Avery sent you here, but because you're a beautiful, kindhearted, outlandish wit of a lass. You're as ridiculous as our Lottie here." His jaw softened as Lottie punched her tongue out at him. "Once you're a part of this family, you don't turn your back on it."

"He makes us sound like the bloody Godfather," Lottie mumbled under her breath so Sidney couldn't hear.

Katie had to force herself not to laugh as Sidney's solemn reprimand was still raging forward.

"I hope, pet, you don't find us so fickle as to expect you to leave because of Olivia's actions."

"Of course not," Katie lied, though she wouldn't call it fickle. She did think a choice needed to be made before she ended up in the hospital. She, a stranger, would certainly be trumped by a fiancée—even if said fiancée was a malicious vampire in a siren's body.

As if reading her thoughts, Sidney placed his thumb under her chin, lifted her eyes to his, and said so softly that Katie could not doubt his sincerity, "In my home, Olivia will be tolerated as long as she is Lucas's choice. You will always be welcome because you are my family. Lottie isn't the only one who's excited to have a new niece."

When the weight of his sentiment sunk in, Katie flung her arms around Sidney, nearly knocking him over. A hug was the best response she could produce, but it was more than sufficient.

"Ahem," Lottie broke in, "I feel the exact same as Sidney. But if you breathe so much as a word of it to my son, I'll skin you alive and have a dress made out of ya."

The gruesome image made Katie shudder. She intentionally changed the subject before Lottie could embark on the haute couture of flesh dresses. It was time to tell a little white lie.

"Sidney, I've already purchased my ticket, and after the past couple of days, it would be nice to go away for a bit and clear my head. Would you mind—if I promise to come back?"

"No, you go, child and have a wonderful time. You can leave your spare things in the room. It's yours now."

"Thank you, Sidney."

"Uncle Sidney will do."

"What about you?" she said, turning to Lottie. "Do you want to be Aunt Charlotte?" Katie ribbed.

"I would like to be called 'Aunt Charlotte' about as much as I'd like a boil on my arse," Lottie countered. "'Lottie' will do just fine, unless you're feeling an overwhelming surge of affection—then call me 'Auntie.'"

"Auntie! La-ti-da! It sounds so dignified," Katie teased.

"Well, yes, because some of us are," Lottie said with playful snootiness.

"Until she opens her mouth," Katie whispered to Sidney.

"Ooh, isn't she a cheeky monkey—I heard that!" Lottie chided.

Returning to her serious state, Lottie began, "Now, two things I want to know. One: Can I be there when you tell Lucas? He's been moping around all day waiting to talk to you. He's just popped to the shop to buy you some chocolate bribery, as per my suggestion. I'm hoping you'll share. Sidney keeps a poor supply of sweeties on hand. And two: Can I go with you—pretty please?"

"I wouldn't dare say no." Katie stood to receive Lottie's constricting embrace.

"My! That's quite a healthy set of boobies you've got." Lottie pushed against Katie's breasts with both hands. "They nearly poked me eyes out."

Lottie's eyes darted mischievously to the doorway where Lucas loitered, looking like a dream in denim jeans and a long sleeve T-shirt. His eyes sparkled and his face wore an apologetic smirk for his mother that almost made Katie's knees buckle.

"Wicked woman!" Katie hissed under her breath, perceiving that Lottie found vast amusement in watching her turn ten different shades of red.

"I imagine your boyfriend's quite ecstatic with that rack of yours," Lottie quipped again.

Lucas's smirk faltered, which he quickly regained, but the sparkle had vanished from his eyes. He strode over to his mother, handing her a box of decadently wrapped Thornton's chocolates.

Kissing her sweetly on the cheek, he said, "Here you go, Mum. Had a sneaking suspicion you'd enjoy these. Where is it that you're so excited to be going?" He turned to Katie and bestowed her with an even bigger box of chocolates. "For whenever you feel up to eating them."

Lottie and Katie exchanged glances; one set of eyes nervous, the other full of mischief. He fixed a fierce stare on Katie. "Where are you going?" he repeated.

It took all her willpower to meet his gaze. His look of contrition ran through her like a dagger, causing her to stagger over her decision. She couldn't deny she felt residual anger toward him, and she felt some satisfaction he was bothered by her leaving, but her resolve was crumbling under the intensity of his mocha-dreamy eyes. Before she caved, she straightened her shoulders and reminded herself her anger was justified. She made a quick mental list of his crimes: subjecting her to Olivia—twice, being engaged to Olivia, waking her up at four-thirty in the morning so she could have breakfast with noble people (*hmmm, that one didn't seem so bad when you put it in perspective*), refusing to let her shower before breakfasting with said nobles (*now that was a good one*), practically forcing her to attend a ball (*where I got to wear real jewels and a dress so magical it actually vanished inches from my waistline*). She realized she was fighting a losing battle. She might also add to his list of infractions: chivalrous, handsome, and provides comfort to women reeking of vomit.

How was she supposed to stay even a tiny bit mad at him? For a moment she let herself warm to the idea of them being friends, better than friends—cousins—but even she couldn't pretend Olivia would ever allow it. Seized by the frustration and anger she'd been trying to rally against him, she delivered her answer. "I'm going to Croatia. As per our agreement, I'm exercising my right to resign."

His expression remained remorseful. "I see. When do you leave?"

"Tonight."

"Can we talk about this?"

"No."

He raked both hands through his hair. "I'm sorry. I never imagined Olivia could do anything so horrid. I had no idea she'd spike your drinks to make you ill."

"That wasn't your fault." She was gracious enough to concede at least that much to him.

"Is there something else you're angry about? I don't believe it's in your nature to hold a grudge. Please tell me."

Katie folded her arms and chewed on the inside of her cheek. Who was he anyway to assume her nature! She certainly wasn't going to tell him she was pissed he didn't have enough sense to realize he was marrying a truly awful woman. And if truth be told, which it would never be, it seemed downright wrong that horrible Olivia would get Mr. Perfect, while she had to make do with Mr. I'm Taking My Other Best Girl on Your Dream Vacation.

Lottie smirked, giving Katie the unnerving sensation the woman was reading her thoughts. "Get on with it, love. Tell him what he wants to know."

"There's no explanation I could give that wouldn't make me look and feel like a complete idiot."

With a wicked grin, Lottie settled into the armchair, snuggling her cup of tea as if preparing to watch a television drama. "I know. Now, go on, so I can have me morning's entertainment."

Challenged by Lottie's naughty sense of humor, Katie gave her own devious smile. Reaching into Lottie's opened box of chocolates, she purred, "You poor bat, it seems you need help knowing when to stuff it." She chucked a chocolate at Lottie, which the woman caught and popped into her mouth. "Now you sit there quietly and behave yourself while the grown-ups finish talking." Katie batted her eyes and smiled with perfect sweetness.

"Ho ho ho," Sidney hooted. "It's about time Lottie got some of her own back!"

Stamping down his own amusement, Lucas grabbed Katie by the wrist. "Let's talk someplace else, away from Mrs. Busybody." He gave his mother a meaningful glare before pulling Katie out of the French doors. Lottie stuck out her chocolaty tongue in response.

"Now, please explain what you were trying to tell me," Lucas insisted.

Katie found herself in the same back garden she had admired so much that first day.

"Actually, I had no intention of telling you anything," she responded coolly.

"I know you're upset, Katie. Why won't you tell me what's going on?"

She felt the heat burn in her chest before it reached her cheeks. "Nothing's going on! Everything is fine." She stalked off down one of the winding pathways leading deeper into the garden.

In one stride he surpassed her and hedged his body between hers and her intended path. Glancing toward the upper story of the house, his brow furrowed. "Shut the window, Mum! The whole lot of you have been caught!"

Katie turned just in time to see the heads of Lottie, Sidney, Mrs. Albright, and Geoffrey dart out of view from the living room window.

"They're worse than children," he chuckled, causing Katie to giggle in spite of herself.

Before she could recover her state of anger, Lucas seized his opportunity to speak earnestly. "Katie, I don't want you to leave."

She made to speak, but he held a silencing finger to her lips, which not only silenced her words, but also her breathing.

"Maybe this sounds corny, but I feel like we're already brilliant friends."

"I do, too," she admitted reluctantly. "But I'm sure Olivia won't approve of us being friends. And I'm not looking forward to another bout of alcohol poisoning." She sidestepped him and continued her exploration of the garden.

"Olivia and I are over," he announced flatly, stopping Katie in her tracks. "We broke up last night."

Katie felt a sudden chill run over her, and it wasn't from the ugly dark clouds that were beginning to gobble up the sun. She resumed her brisk walk, not sure she wanted to hear the rest.

He kept pace with her. "I can't be with someone who would deny me the close friendship of a cousin." He nudged her playfully, then looked at her in all seriousness. "Katie, you helped me see a side of Olivia I never knew. And you helped me keep the Waverlys' account. Why would I let you quit—well, other than the fact that I promised you could? You're my lucky rabbit's foot."

A slight breeze blew through the light weave of Katie's skirt and nipped at her bare legs. Feeling a panic not from the weather, but from his words, she picked up her pace. Of course she didn't want Lucas to marry Olivia, but neither did she want to be responsible for their demise.

"Lucas, just because I bring out the worst in people doesn't mean you should second-guess your engagement. Plus, the Waverlys were never going to fire you. They wanted to work with you before Olivia ever got involved. You're giving me way too much credit."

They had come to the end of the garden where the break between gargantuan hedges led into the tall wooded area. Just like the first time she noticed it, she had an overwhelming urge to discover what was beyond the forest of trees. It had to be something magical like Narnia or Hogwarts.

Fueled by her impulse, she let the conversation fall and ventured beyond the ordered protection of the hedges. At the opening of a wide shady clearing, an ornate metal bench sat at the base of a large, flowering tree that began the thick wall of forest.

"Oh, it's wonderful!" she exclaimed, walking to the back of the clearing, ready to explore further. Lucas caught her by the arm. "What are you doing?"

"I want to see what's beyond the trees."

She didn't have to wait for an answer. She could hear it whistling through the treetops with such velocity that she barely registered the panicked expression on Lucas's face before the charging white blur crashed into the side of her forehead. The force of the impact propelled her body into a helpless freefall. Everything was fuzzy except the excruciating pain. Somewhere in the back of her subconscious mind, she sensed his strong arms reach her before she hit the ground. And then she felt irritated that just then, someone cued the rain, but that was all she felt before she felt nothing.

Chapter Twenty-One

Something was wrong. Something was definitely wrong. Her head was searing with pain, and she could hear voices.

"What are we going tell Richard? This will put him off the game forever," one voice remarked.

"He'll be devastated," agreed another.

Lucas was calling her name. He sounded so far away, but she could feel his minty soft breath warming her face. Suddenly she was very aware of the taste in her own mouth. *Gross!* She had to muster up some spit and swish it around before she could pry her tongue from the roof of her mouth.

She stirred, not because she felt like moving, but because she felt like she was lying in a bed of pudding.

"It looks like she's coming to," one gentleman announced.

Pulling her eyelids back enough to give her the tiniest slit of vision was no easy feat. Her vision was blurry…but it looked like there were two older gentlemen bent over her, hands on their knees, clad in colorful plaid trousers and plaid caps. *Holy crap, I've landed in Brigadoon.*

"Katie, are you all right?" Lucas spoke, lightly stroking her cheek.

Speaking was much more difficult than she would have imagined, but somehow she managed to choke out the pressing question "Is my breath bad?"

Lucas's face was so close that if Katie hadn't already just done so, she would have fainted. He was on his knees hovering above her, shielding her from the rain with his body. He studied her for a moment, as if trying to ascertain whether she was fully cognizant. "What do you think, doctor?" He turned to one of the men, a hint of a smile hovering around his mouth.

The slight, grey-haired man he called "doctor" stooped down closer to her, adjusting his cap so it wouldn't tumble off his head—his *golf* cap. She felt nauseous with disappointment—or maybe from a concussion—that she wasn't in Brigadoon, or even Hogwarts or Narnia, for that matter. All that was through the copse of trees was a crumby old golf course.

"Miss, do you hurt anywhere?" the doctor called to her.

Duh! Her hand instinctively went to the source of agony on her temple, spreading a swipe of mud across her forehead. "It feels like someone hammered a stake into my head, then filled the bloody hole with molten lava."

"She's not too injured for dramatics," the doctor's companion chuckled.

"Did she hit the ground hard when she fell?" the doctor asked Lucas.

"No, I was able to catch her before she landed."

The doctor seemed to consider that information for a moment before thrusting his face into to Katie's, staring straight into her pupils, the brim of his corny cap pressing into her eyebrows. His hazel, owl-like eyes, growing in diameter, focused intently on hers. She heard a small squeak escape her lips, and knew she was going to have an attack of the awkward-moment giggles. She bit down on her tongue hard enough to make the situation not so funny and waited out the doctor's assessment.

After several minutes—okay, probably several seconds—the doctor straightened, took her head in both his hands, and let his fingers conduct a thorough survey of her scalp. Katie gulped for air as the pain thrashed across her forehead.

"I think she's going to be just fine. Damn lucky though, the way Richard sends them down the fairway. Imagine having a swing that can take out a woman in her own garden. It's the damnedest thing," the doctor said, shaking his head at what could have been. "I don't see any danger in moving her. Just keep an eye on her if she wants to sleep, which I'm sure she will. Would you like help getting her to the house?"

"I'll be fine, thank you. You should be returning to your game—Richard's probably starting to worry." Lucas smiled. "Thank you, doctor."

"Woods, my name's Woods." He held out a steady hand to Lucas.

"Lucas Hayden, and this is Katie Sutherland."

Katie raised a muddy hand in recognition.

The mention of Richard's name ignited a worried debate between Woods and his companion over how to tell him his wild swing took out an unsuspecting woman.

"He doesn't have to know," Katie said in a loud whisper, which was all her voice would allow. "It would only make him feel bad, and I'm fine. I won't tell if you won't." She managed a weak smile.

The two golfers exchanged questioning glances.

"She's right, you know," the other man said to Woods.

"Bless you, Katie Sutherland, that's very kind of you," Woods remarked. Deliberating over the idea, he added, "He doesn't have to know as long as you really are fine. May I come round later this afternoon to check on you?"

Katie nodded feebly, then closed her eyes while Lucas exchanged information with the doctor.

"Well," Lucas began once the golfers had gone, "let's get you in out of this rain."

Ready to comply, she began to raise herself up.

"Whoa, what do you think you're doing?" Lucas halted her just as she was consumed by dizziness and pain. He scooped her up. Holding her close to his chest, he began the trek back to the house.

"Put me down," she demanded. "I can walk." She would happily field golf balls with her head all day long before she'd have Lucas pick her up and ascertain her actual mass.

He gave her that "poor crazy person" smile and continued walking.

"I mean it, Lucas Hayden! You put me down right now!" The pain surged and her head lolled onto his shoulder, rendering her threats unimpressive.

She remained there in a lethargic state for a few minutes until a breeze kicked up and blew a fresh anxiety into her mind. She could feel the wind playing at the back of her skirt while a cool draft chilled her backside, making her instantly aware the bottom of her skirt was hanging wide open, exposing her backside. More disturbing was the fact that her cradled position was giving her a massive wedgie, and her naked rear end was squished snugly atop his forearm.

213

She tried to squirm free of his hold, but every movement caused unnecessary pain in her skull.

"I can make it from here. It's too far to carry me all the way up to the house."

"If you really want to make this easier on me, then you'll stop squirming."

"I'm not going to hold still until my bare butt is off your arm."

A look of amusement stole his expression, and he almost gave way to a laugh.

"Let's compromise," she said, defeated. "There's a bench up ahead. We could sit down and...um...readjust. I'm sure your arms could use a rest."

He paused at the bench just long enough for her to exhume her underwear and adjust his hold, this time ensuring the back of her skirt was held properly in place. The rest of their journey to the house was spent in silence. Within moments, the fuzziness in her head had engulfed her entirely and she was lulled back into semiconsciousness by the rhythm of his slow, steady pace.

Warm, vanilla-scented air from the house besieged her along with the buzz of commotion, but her body was unwilling to revive itself. In her handicapped mental state, she was still preoccupied with the fact that Lucas had lugged her cow frame across the entire length of the garden. Fragments of conversation seeped through the haze and reached her brain.

"Maybe we should get her in hospital," Sidney suggested.

"She's chilled right to the bone—we have to get her out of these wet clothes," trilled Mrs. Albright.

214

"Let me take her from you while you get your muddy shoes off," Geoffrey offered.

Katie registered being transferred from one set of arms to another.

"Hmmph," Geoffrey groaned. "She's a lot heavier than she looks."

Katie wanted to retort, but the words were too hard to produce. She would just have to remember to hold that remark against him for a long time.

"I'll go turn down her bed," volunteered Lottie.

"No!" Geoffrey wheezed. "That's too far!"

Make that a very long time.

She was jostled once again as another transfer took place.

"Oh, for the love of Pete, Geoffrey—give her back to me," Lucas huffed.

Sidney, using his military voice, commanded, "Put her on the settee in the library."

Everyone, even Katie, was startled into action by his uncharacteristic sternness.

Katie uttered a feeble protest. "Please, not the white room. I'm not allowed near white furniture."

"Nonsense," Sidney comforted her.

"Lottie...you must protect the white sofa!" she pleaded, placing her thumping head on Lucas's shoulder.

"Bloody hell," Lottie sighed, though secretly pleased to be called to a position where she could be bossy. "Sidney, Geoffrey, go fetch a couple of blankets and bring some extra chairs into the library

215

and wait for us there." She turned to Mrs. Albright. "Penny, go fetch a fresh pair of pajamas for Katie."

Once the room was cleared, she clucked her disapproval at Lucas and Katie.

"Look at the two of you! You look like two pigs that have been wrestling in the mud."

"Next time Katie gets hit in the head, we'll make sure she does it on a soft grassy bit," Lucas grumbled.

Lottie sniffed, swatted him playfully on the butt, and went back to business.

"Katie dear, are you able to stand?"

"I…I think so."

Lottie gestured for Lucas to put her down.

Hesitating, he did as he was instructed. Katie swaggered, trying to support her full weight, but was only able to manage with a supporting arm from Lucas.

"All right, both of you," Lottie demanded like a drill sergeant. "Knickers. Are you wearing any?"

Despite finding the question odd, Katie followed Lucas's lead and answered with an affirmative nod. The small motion launched shoots of agony through her cranium.

"Strip down to them," Lottie ordered.

"Mother, this is ludicrous…" Lucas argued, but Lottie halted his words with her "Mother's had it up to here" glare.

"If you think I'm going to allow a child of mine to drop even one speck of mud on Sidney's white carpets, you need your thick head examined."

She didn't need to continue her scolding—Lucas already had his jeans around his ankles and was pulling off his shirt—but she did.

"Katie here has been brain-damaged and even *she* has enough respect to consider the furniture. Now shut your eyes—I won't have you stealing peeks at our Katie in her knick-knocks." She rapped a warning on Lucas's head with her knuckles.

At this point, Katie was too dazed, too pained, and too relieved that she wasn't wearing scaggy panties to argue. Every movement made her head scream with agony, but she did as she was told. Like scolded children, they stood side by side in the mud room: dripping wet, muddy clothes discarded, Lucas's eyes squeezed shut, Katie on the verge of collapse, and Lottie scrubbing their faces with a damp cloth until a very startled Mrs. Albright returned with Katie's pajamas.

***

"Have you seen this?" Olivia screeched.

"That's complete rubbish. You shouldn't let it upset you." Lucas's fatigue wore in his voice.

"It doesn't matter if it's rubbish—it's bad for my image. This is bad press. It needs to be corrected."

"Come off it, Olivia. Neither of us is a celebrity—no one will give it a second glance. And even if they do, who cares?"

Her face contorted at Lucas's indifference to her social status. The look she gave him was fierce, as if he had accused her of being a Walmart shopper.

"*I* care!" she seethed. "Do you know what this looks like? It looks like *I*, Olivia Denby, have been dumped for *her*…for that American *nobody*!"

In the next room, Sidney, Lottie, Geoffrey, and Mrs. Albright were eavesdropping on the argument, while Katie, a captive on the white sofa, was actually trying to ignore it—but Olivia's shrill tones were making it difficult. Now, it was clear *Katie* had something to do with all of this, and all eyes in the room were on her.

She tried not to absorb Olivia's latest insult, or that the argument was about her. She had to think about something else, something that would keep her from hearing this conversation. Katie chose to concentrate on her physical pain, which was much more preferable to her than Olivia's voice. Her temple pulsated rhythmically, and she found it easy to focus on that.

She envisioned the goose egg on her head as a beacon, a mechanical monstrosity set below her hairline to protect her from unpleasantries. She even imagined its engineering: Whenever an unpleasant thought or word would enter her vicinity, Bartholomew, the noble beacon, would radiate pain, cueing a mental filter that would spring up with lightning speed to net anything that threatened her internal peace.

"Olivia, don't talk about Katie like that." Lucas's calm voice was infused with impatience. "She's my friend; we're practically cousins."

A short, maniacal laugh burst forth from Olivia. "She's no more your cousin than I am! I'll tell you exactly what she is: She's a con artist!"

Katie focused on Bartholomew the Beacon, who was vigorously carrying out his job. Her head raged with pain. Any second now, the filter would go up and block out the spiteful Olivia.

"You don't think she knows she's the strongest thread between your family and your uncle in the States? She's totally taking advantage of all of you."

Cue the filter! Where the hell is the filter? Bartholomew was zealously firing off the alarm to an unreliable filter while the militia of Olivia's words marched right through her brain. Katie's only form of relief was Kamikaze Lottie, who had flung herself at Katie's side, acting as an ineffective shield against Olivia's sound.

The assault raged on. "Lucas, she is jeopardizing our relationship. You're giving her privileges that should be mine. It should have been *me* bringing out the Chatworth diamonds—it was *my* right, as your fiancée! *This* should be *me!*"

In the next room, heads swiveled back to Katie for answers. Even the act of shrugging her innocence was painful.

"She is not jeopardizing our relationship, Olivia. We broke up. There is no relationship."

"Because of her."

"Because of *you*. Because I never realized how shallow you were—*are*. Let's make sure we have a couple of things crystal clear." His tone turned crisp and frightful. "Those diamonds belong to *Sidney*. Not me, not my family. You would have had absolutely no claim to them. They belonged to Sidney's wife, and whatever value they hold is of no importance to anyone in this family. Nobody is to know that Sidney owns these pieces. *Do I make myself clear?*"

By her nearly inaudible squeak, it was obvious that Olivia was not accustomed to being reprimanded. "I don't want us to be over. I think you should take some time to reconsider." Olivia's voice shook with panic.

"What's to reconsider?" There was a sardonic amusement in his reply. "We obviously don't know each other that well. I had no idea how manipulative, materialistic, and just plain mean you were—*are*. And I don't think you really understand my circumstances. I have no claim to any of this." He gestured to the room. "I don't own my home in London. It belongs to Uncle Avery. If you believe your own accusations, then it would one day become Katie's. All I can lay claim to is my business and what I have in the bank—and that's plenty for me."

Olivia's face must have betrayed her ignorance about his future worth, causing him to belt a cynical laugh.

"I thought you might see things a bit differently," Lucas said softly. "You can keep the ring. I don't want it."

The next thing Katie heard was the slamming of the front door, followed by a very full silence.

Chapter Twenty-Two

"Hello Chicken. Did you have a nice chat with Olivia?" Lottie cooed innocently, having just returned to her white overstuffed armchair as Lucas strode into the room.

Her innocent smile eased a bit of the trouble from his face.

"Hello Mum." Kissing the top of her child-size head, he laid the morning's paper in her lap. Since Katie had the whole sofa to herself, she pulled her legs toward her chest and offered Lucas the cushion at the other end. He took the offered seat and swept a reproachful gaze over the group, who were behaving a little too casually.

"You can drop the charade—all of you. Am I supposed to believe you lot have suddenly developed scruples against eavesdropping?"

A guilty silence hovered over the room. Now that Lucas was present, everyone pretended to respect his privacy. After what seemed like forever, but according the wall clock was only a couple of minutes, Katie wanted to scream, just to hear something other than the abnormally loud ticking of said clock, but Lottie beat her to it.

"Tina Turner and the Holy Trinity!" Lottie shouted.

Poor Mrs. Albright let out a startled yelp and almost fell over backward in her armchair. Fortunately, Geoffrey was right there to hold her hand and help calm her heart.

Lottie held out the front page of the newspaper's gossip section. Holding the prominent place was the headline:

Much More Than Scandal Unearthed at Waverlys' Annual Charity Ball

Underneath was a photo of Katie and Lucas at the ball. Despite her utter shock, Katie was relieved and flabbergasted at how pretty (and thin) she looked.

Lottie cleared her throat and read the article aloud.

Those in attendance at the eighth annual charity ball hosted by Lord and Lady Waverly couldn't help but hear the whispers about American newcomer Kathryn Sutherland.

An inconnue to most, she seemed no stranger to Lady Waverly. This young woman took center stage when she turned up on the arm of Lucas Hayden, proprietor of the reputable Hayden Travel consulting firm and fiancé of Olivia Denby, daughter of M.P. Gordon Denby, wearing diamonds recognized as part of the private Chatworth collection.

For those readers who have been keeping their heads in the sand, the Chatworth collection, which hasn't been seen in circulation for more than sixty years, is believed to include pieces that contain cuts of the Excelsior Diamond. The Excelsior, known for its bluish-white tint, was the largest diamond second to the Cullinan. In 1904, the Excelsior was cut into 21 pieces; each was sold individually. Many of the buyers remained anonymous; however, speculations about the ownership of the diamonds are always in the minds of diamond aficionados.

The mysterious Ms. Sutherland left the ball (followed by Mr. Hayden) before this reporter could attain a private interview. Sources say a heated row with Ms. Denby may have been the reason for her early exit (meow!).

I was able to ascertain, however, that Ms. Sutherland was wearing a silver shimmer, off-the-shoulder floor-length, which was overheard to be a Greta. When asked about her gown, Ms. Sutherland reportedly flashed her pearly American whites and replied that there is only one Greta.

Debuting her new designer, new man, and old jewels, Ms. Sutherland has become quite a person of intrigue.

Other notes of interest...

Lottie turned the page and gasped again, showing the group a second picture of Lucas and Katie entering his gate, with a saucer-eyed Katie wearing his tuxedo jacket, looking surprised and guilty to be caught in the predawn light.

"I'm gobsmacked. You could absolutely knock me over with a feather," Lottie proclaimed.

Katie pressed back into the arm of the couch until the she could feel the wooden frame digging into her back. For some reason she'd rather be uncomfortable than feel the numbness that was threatening to take over.

"That's good publicity, that," Geoffrey plugged.

"They've made me out to be a total skank," Katie squeaked.

"A what?" Sidney asked.

"A skank," Katie repeated.

"A slapper," Lottie said.

"A tart," Mrs. Albright supplied.

"A trollop," Geoffrey put in for good measure.

"A floozy," Lottie added.

"Okay, that'll do. I think he gets the idea." Lucas took control before his mother could continue.

"Take heart, dear, at least you're not the only one who appears to have loose morals. Lucas comes off as a fantastic lecher," Lottie taunted. "It does me heart proud: me niece a slapper and me son a rounder."

"Mother," Lucas warned reprovingly.

"At any rate, that top one is a smashing picture of the both of you," Mrs. Albright doted.

"How come I've never heard of a Greta gown? I must get one," complained Lottie.

Katie's thoughts were a blur. She couldn't tell where the effects of the golf ball ended and the shock of the article began. She tried to sort out the jumble of the last two days, carefully mulling over the tender spots. Lucas and Olivia were arguing because of her...and after that article, Olivia had even more reason to hate her. And Sidney had been so generous to let her wear his wife's jewelry...and now every wealthy citizen in London and beyond would be trying to get their polished hands on them.

As for her own interest, she couldn't help but feel a little smug. The one time in her life where she took the perfect photo—wearing a tiara, no less—it got delivered to nearly every home in the United Kingdom. And though she would never admit it out loud, it was a teeny tiny bit satisfying to have Olivia slighted so publicly; it bolstered Katie's belief in karma. But then there was that dreadful skanky photo of Katie outside of Lucas's place....

A creepy feeling invaded her thoughts. She glanced around to see everyone staring at her. *What?!?* She made a snaking movement with her head to counteract the prickling sensation at the back of her neck.

"Okay, here's the thing," she began. "I can't imagine this article is going to affect my life, but I feel horrible that it will affect yours, Sidney. The diamonds—"

"Oh pshaw," Sidney interrupted. "So what if people find out I have some expensive jewelry? I'm glad for this…otherwise I never would have known what I own. It's really quite something— unbelievable, isn't it?"

Katie could feel Lucas's eyes on her. Avoiding his stare, she said, "I'm sorry about Olivia. She has every right to be upset."

"You have nothing to be sorry for. None of this is your fault. Things turn out as they're supposed to," Lucas reassured.

"Even so, it still sucks big time."

"Eloquently put, cousin."

The arrival of Dr. Woods spared them from having to say anything more on the subject. The doctor had a different companion with him this time. Katie prayed this gentleman was not Richard. She didn't feel up to meeting her assailant just now.

"Good afternoon, Katie. How are you feeling?" Dr. Woods asked gently, his old-school British a perfect match for his classic looks. "This is my friend Ian Caldwell, a fellow doctor." He gestured toward his lanky companion. "Ian was back at the cart with Richard when we found you this afternoon."

Katie was happy to note they were not wearing their golf attire. It would be hard for her to take any doctor dressed like a leprechaun seriously. There was a polite round of greetings and introductions before the doctors turned themselves loose on Katie.

"It's quite astonishing, really. What are the odds of someone getting clonked by a golf ball in her own garden—especially with that dense barrier of forest between the fairway and the private homes?" Dr. Woods calculated.

"With my luck lately, the odds are better than average," Katie brooded.

"Looks like you've got a nasty bump there," Dr. Caldwell pointed out the obvious, giving Bartholomew the Beacon a little tweak.

Ooowee! Son of a... Now her filter flew up from out of nowhere, thwarting the myriad cuss words she was about to spew as the beacon raged in protest.

The two doctors continued their poking and prodding for not a minute less than Katie could endure. All the while, Bartholomew pounded his resentment.

At last, Dr. Woods proclaimed, "Well, young lady, I think you're going to live."

"Any instructions, doctor?" Sidney inquired, overly concerned for a man who had spent years in the military seeing wounds that would make Katie's injury look like a paper cut.

"Just keep an eye on her. If the dizziness persists, bring her round to me. She should be fine to move about as soon as she feels up to it." Dr. Woods presented Lucas and Sidney with his card.

As they all exchanged their thank-yous and goodbyes, Dr. Caldwell caught sight of the paper Lottie had placed on the floor. His prominent features sprang to life.

"May I?" he inquired of Lottie, motioning toward the paper.

"Be my guest," she replied, a touch of mischief in her voice.

Lucas and Katie exchanged apprehensive glances as Dr. Caldwell presented the article to Woods.

"I was telling you about this earlier. It's actually quite remarkable. The whereabouts of this extraordinary collection of jewels—the Chatworths, if you follow that sort of thing—have been untraceable for over half a century. Mysteriously, they turned up last night at the Waverlys' do on some American woman that nobody other than Lady Waverly has ever heard of."

Everyone watched Woods intently as he scanned the article. A look of recognition flitted across his face.

Caldwell prattled on. "It's all Alice could talk about this morning. She's quite upset that we didn't attend the ball and catch a glimpse of the jewels and the girl wearing them."

"Indeed?" Woods replied, his curious eyes searching Katie's face, which was now half hidden under the quilt that draped her body. She tried to convey an anxious plea with her eyes as she gave a very discreet shake of the head.

He gave a slight nod, followed by a reassuring smile. "No doubt Alice missed an opportunity to meet a remarkable young lady. You must do something to make it up to her."

Sidney breathed a nearly inaudible sigh of relief. Despite what Katie said, she knew he was anxious to postpone the barrage of phone calls and questions that would inevitably arise over the jewels.

"Shall we go then, and let this young lady get some rest?" Dr. Woods suggested. Shaking Lucas's hand, he requested in an overly loud tone, "Will you bring Katie around next week? I'd like to do a follow-up." Leaning in covertly, he added, "I'd also like to discuss terms for surprising my wife with a holiday—it's our forty-second wedding anniversary."

Dr. Woods turned his attention back to Katie. "Your secret is safe with me—doctor-patient confidentiality." To appease Dr. Caldwell's questioning glance, he added with a playful wink, "Richard will be none the wiser. We'll see you next week then?"

Geoffrey showed the guests out.

"Katie, you truly are good luck for me!" Lucas exploded. "Forget the foot—you're the whole rabbit!"

"Well then, Rabbit, would you mind telling us what my son is running on about?" Lottie demanded of Katie, who could only respond with her usual naïve shrug.

Lucas jumped in, excitedly repeating Dr. Woods' whispers. The news provoked an eruption of congratulatory cheers.

Katie watched intently as Lucas received pleased-as-punch hugs from his family. She couldn't help but feel a lukewarm enthusiasm as she compared this mishmash family to her own. A stab of envy slashed through her as Mrs. Albright doted over Lucas. He shared a closer relationship with Sidney's housekeeper than she had with her own mother.

The loneliness she felt under the umbrella of this family's affection made her uneasy. She had an overwhelming desire to get away, to resume the quest to plunge into her Amazing Plan, to go searching for some meaning to her dysfunctional life. This time, however, the solution was easily attainable: She still had plenty of time to make her flight to Croatia.

As Katie tried to escape from the sofa, Bartholomew raged in protest, dashing her hopes for a subtle exit. She made it to a wobbly stand and noticed Lottie studying her.

"Where are you going, Rabbit?" Lottie asked.

Katie cringed, knowing Lottie had brought two fates upon her: making her the center of attention and bestowing her with a new nickname to add to the growing list.

Debating whether to express the curses that were racing through her mind, Katie steeled herself to meet Lottie's taunting eyes. However, what she found in Lottie's countenance was unnerving. Her smile was not menacing; it was warm. Her eyes, instead of teasing sparks, were a sympathetic sea of blue. When was the last time her mother looked at her with that much concern? Before Katie could stop herself, she was already wrapped in Lottie's expecting embrace, tears flowing, sobs unchecked.

When Katie finally lifted her head, she could feel Bartholomew along with the rest of her head complaining loudly. She noticed that the others had cleared from the room and suddenly felt ashamed. Lottie held Katie's face in her soft hands, wiping the last of tears with her thumb.

"Let's get you upstairs. I'll help you pack while you get cleaned up."

***

Katie came bounding down the stairs two at a time, a large pack sitting lopsided on her back. The sob session and another shower left her feeling invigorated, despite the crushing ache in her skull and the weakness incurred by her day and a half of puking.

Lottie was not far behind, her wheeled carry-on thunking loudly against the stairs behind her. The noise created by the enthusiastic pair sounded like a parade of pachyderms on the staircase. Alarmed by the commotion, the rest of the household raced over to meet the two at the base of the stairs.

In answer to their confused stares, Lottie trilled, "Bye all, we're off to Croatia. See you when we see you."

Katie giggled at Lottie's nonchalance as the group gaped in disbelief, still trying to sort out what had taken place in the library. In an effort to avoid Lucas's catlike stare, Katie threw her arms around Sidney. The weight of her backpack threw her off balance and, missing Sidney altogether, she reeled off the landing, gaining sideways momentum. She could see Lucas's wide eyes in her peripheral vision as he braced for impact. The force of the collision left them in a tumbled pile on the floor. Lucas, on the bottom, was pinned by Katie flailing against his chest and held captive beneath the bulk of her pack.

She held her breath, anticipating Lucas's stern reaction. Instead, he bellowed a laugh. *He's laughing! Jared wouldn't have laughed.* She had to resist the urge to wrap her arms around Lucas and hug him tightly.

Where did that urge come from? Her neck and face began to burn, and it wasn't because she'd just made a fool of herself. She really needed to stop comparing Lucas to Jared, and she really needed not to be lying chest to chest with her boss. The more she tried to get up, the more she flailed, and the more everyone laughed—except her. She was forced to remain in a heap on top of Lucas until Geoffrey and Sidney could gain control of their hysterics enough to offer a hand.

"Damn you, Katie, now you've made me wet me bloody trousers!" Lottie abruptly stopped her laughing and stormed back up the stairs.

Once Katie was set right again and Lottie had returned wearing new jeans, the mood turned serious, aided by Lucas's foreboding expression. Lottie made a beeline for the Rolls-Royce, pulling Geoffrey with her. Katie hesitated at the front door before pulling a folded piece of paper from her back pocket and tucking it into one of Lucas's balled fists.

"Good luck." She couldn't meet his eyes.

"Don't go," he whispered.

Okay! That's what she wanted to say, but what she told him instead was "I have to. I've had nothing but bad luck in this country."

She headed for the car without looking back.

Chapter Twenty-Three

Lucas waited until he could no longer see the Rolls-Royce racing down the hill before he pulled the door closed and unfolded Katie's note. Sidney and Mrs. Albright watched in silence at the range of emotions that played across his face. When he'd finished reading, his jaw set with resolve and he fumbled in his pocket for his car keys. Dropping the paper on the floor, he sprinted out the door without saying a word.

"Never a dull moment," Sidney shook his head, smiling. "That boy is so much like his uncle Avery. Did you see the determination in his eyes? He'll not rest until he has exactly what he wants." He stooped down to pick up the discarded note and read its contents aloud to Mrs. Albright.

> *Lucas,*
> *Thank you for giving me the opportunity to work for you. I'm sorry it didn't work out. Despite everything, I really did enjoy my few days as your employee. I wish you every happiness in your life. I haven't known you long, but I know you deserve it.*
> *Your cousin,*
> *Katie*
>
> *PS: Remember to call the Peninsula Hotel and confirm the Peninsula Suite. The hotel also has a Rolls-Royce Phantom on hold. You need to tell them whether you want it with or without a driver. I suggest taking the driver. I also suggest having the Waverlys do the following:*

- *Hike the Dragon's Back trail to Shek O Beach. Do this on a weekday—it won't be as busy. (Don't worry about sending them on a hike. I promise it's just that touch of adventure Lady W is hoping for.)*
- *Temple of Ten Thousand Buddhas (a long walk, but worth it)*
- *Hong Kong Museum of History. Plan on a full day (Lady W will want plenty of time to experience the Hong Kong she remembers from her father's stories).*
- *Victoria Peak. Do this on a clear day and in the late afternoon so they can watch the scenery change with the dusk.*
- *Recommend they take early morning walks to the parks. They'll see people doing their morning exercise—various types of Tai Chi, including ladies with large red-cloth fans and people with swords (very old-school Hong Kong-y).*

I hope that helps! Good luck!

***

Lottie dug into her purse, trying to locate her ringing mobile. "Hello Charles, darling!" she greeted her husband enthusiastically. "You'll never guess where I am!" A look of disappointment flitted across her face. "Huh, that was quite a good guess." The line moved swiftly, and Lottie's expression seemed to become increasingly bothered. When they were next, she covered the mouthpiece of the phone with her tiny manicured fingers, and instructed Katie, "See if there's still room on the flight. I'll catch up with you at the gate."

Katie gave her a confused glance. "You sure?"

Lottie nodded and waved a few people ahead of her while she finished the call.

After a brief exchange with the ticket agent, Katie turned and gave her the "thumbs up" sign.

As soon as Katie was lost amid the sea of travelers, Lucas approached his mother. "Hiya."

"Charles, I'm going to have to call you back." Lottie disconnected the call and dropped the phone back in her purse. "Ooohh, you're a cheeky monkey!" she chided, smacking his arm. "I suppose this was your doing, having your father bribe me with a shopping spree at Harrods and first-class seats if I postpone me travels a day?"

He didn't try to hide his smirk. "I need to talk to Katie."

"It's too late, she's already through the gate—you can't stop her."

His eyes flashed with determination.

"And I'll run you through like a shish kabob if you try."

"Then I'll go with her."

"But you've not one thing packed!"

His shrug was indifferent.

Her eyes sparked as her lips spread into a thin smile. She ducked under the ropes and exchanged places with Lucas. "Why are you chasing after her?"

He hesitated. "I don't know. Lots of reasons, I suppose…Uncle Avery told me to look after her."

Lottie narrowed her eyes and folded her arms across her chest. "That's the reason then, is it?" she said flatly, unconvinced.

234

Lucas shifted on his feet. "I guess it's more than that. Olivia got me thinking—"

"Bloody hell, this ought to be interesting."

Lucas ignored his mother's quip. "Olivia was right about one thing: Katie is the strongest link we have to Uncle Avery—she's the closest thing to a cousin I have."

Lottie began to argue, but Lucas, taking a guess at her thoughts, cut her off. "Andrew doesn't count—he's no more a blood relative than Katie—and he's made it clear he wants nothing to do with me."

She sighed impatiently. "That's your only reason then?"

Lucas shrugged again, and Lottie zeroed in on him with her omniscient mother stare. He studied the toe of his shoe for a long moment, then spoke to the floor. "I guess I'm also being selfish. I enjoy her company. She makes life fun—even when it's not. Do you know what I mean?"

"Of course, Chicken, I know what you mean." Her face beamed with hopefulness. "I support you in everything you've said, except for one thing," her voice took on a hard note. "Katie is no closer to being your cousin than I am to being a Pussycat Doll."

He snapped his head up to meet her eyes, then shuddered. "Mum, please, the visual is burning my brain."

She donned her mischievous grin. "Oh, all right then, but unless you want another one," she said, gyrating her hips, "you'll stop calling that girl your cousin."

Lucas shook his head. "Let me get this straight—you call her your niece, but I'm not allowed to think of her as a cousin?"

"You are such a brilliant boy!" she patronized.

235

"Explain to me how that makes any sense."

Lottie sighed with annoyance. "I'm allowed to think of her as family because I don't want to shag the girl."

Lucas's eyes shot up at her innuendo, and much to his chagrin, his mother's voice was not quiet. He could feel the appalled stares and the heavy judgment raining over him from those nearby. "Mother!"

"Don't you 'Mother' me!" she warned. "I'm saving you from shagging a cousin and the years of therapy that follow."

Chapter Twenty-Four

One of these days I'm going to wake up and know where I am, Katie reassured herself. She waited for her eyes to focus, which seemed to take extra long on account of the dull throb at her temple. Then she heard the sound of splashing water, rhythmic and peaceful. Soon, the moon came into view, not quite full, but still bright enough to spray light through the curtains, allowing her to make out shapes and figures around the tiny room: a small television with a rabbit-ear antenna, a kitchenette, a deep armchair, and a two-person table.

She heard a man's deep, ragged breathing next to her and froze. Then she spotted Lucas sitting on the floor with his head lolled against the bed. His hand was clasped tightly around hers.

"Hey," she whispered, gently nudging his arm. "What are you doing here?"

His head bolted upright. "Katie, are you all right?"

"I'm fine. Where are we?"

"Croatia."

"How did we get here—in this room? Where's your mother?" she yawned.

"Shhhh. Go back to sleep, I'll explain in the morning." He was on his knees now, stroking her face. She was still tired, too tired to protest, but too aware to leave him sitting on the floor. She scooted over and patted the bed. "You don't have to sleep on the floor. There's plenty of room—I don't mind."

Something akin to panic flitted through his eyes. He opened his mouth to argue, but she stopped him.

"Don't be gallant. You're exhausted and I'm exhausted, and I don't need this whole bed to myself. Now get in before you piss me off."

Lucas laughed, though it seemed in spite of himself, and crawled in beside her, careful not to make body contact. Katie was asleep within seconds.

When she woke again, the sky was still dark, but with the light of the moon, she watched the ripples in the bay until her finger twitched, then her entire body. She couldn't lie still any longer. Paying careful attention not to wake Lucas, she eased herself out of bed and tiptoed to the glass doors. Opening them quietly, she stepped out onto the veranda and savored a long breath. The temperature was perfect. A warm night breeze licked at her face and she had a sudden rush to feel the wind across her entire body. She shed yesterday's clothes down to her bra and panties and stretched her limbs, enjoying every sensation.

The rhythmic lapping of the waves was like a siren call for her to dive in—also a siren call for her bladder. She crossed her legs and crouched into a squat—boy, she really had to go. As quickly as her legs could move without unflexing her bladder muscles, she padded back into the room and dashed toward the bathroom, sparing a look over her shoulder to check that Lucas hadn't stirred. Before she knew what was happening, something grabbed her ankle and then— WHOMP!

***

Lucas shot up in bed and looked around anxiously, panic filling up to his eyeballs. Then he caught sight of her disrobed figure sprawled face down across the floor, tangled in her backpack straps, and burst out laughing—loudly. He scrambled off the bed to kneel

238

beside her. His hands hovered tentatively over her bare skin, not knowing where he could touch.

"What are you doing? Are you okay?"

"No, I'm not okay," Katie huffed. "I'm all tangled up, I have to pee, and Bartholomew is raging furiously."

"Bartholomew?" His eyebrows rose.

Grabbing onto his forearm, she pulled herself to a seated position. She lifted her hand to the level of her head and poked her pointer finger toward her goose egg.

Her glare challenged him to laugh. He refrained—barely. "And your clothes?"

Even in the semidarkness, she knew he could see her turning red. She felt like Violet Beauregarde in *Charlie and the Chocolate Factory,* only instead of turning into a blueberry, she was morphing into a tomato.

"On the veranda."

"Of course."

"Would you stop teasing me and help me up!"

As soon as she was on her feet, she grabbed his arm and dragged him to the veranda.

"See how beautiful it is?" She pointed out into the bay. "Now stay here so you can't hear me pee," she ordered, and was gone before he had time to respond. She stole one backward glance and noticed him contemplating his palm. She wondered if he still felt their touch zinging his skin, like she did. *Yeah right!*

"I'm pretty sure it wants me to go play in it," she announced upon her return.

He turned, startled out of his reverie. "You're going out there alone?"

She giggled, looking dramatically to either side of her to emphasize a lack of people. She had a vague awareness of her semi-nakedness, her boldness, her impulsiveness—but she couldn't snap out of it. Was it the exhaustion? The delirium from the pain? The giddiness at being in a foreign country with a handsome man? *Um, okay.* "Yes, unless you're coming with me?"

He stepped back from her, surprised—frightened, maybe—by the invitation. Then a slow, impish grin scooted across his face and he tore off his shirt, discarding all but his boxer-briefs into a heap next to Katie's clothes.

The race to the water was exhilarating. She couldn't remember the last time she'd felt so uninhibited. Lucas plowed right into the bay at full speed with Katie following his lead, squealing as she hit the warm water.

Almost instantly, his large hand covered her mouth. "Shhhh. You'll wake the whole village."

She nodded sheepishly and didn't protest as he waded them deeper into the dark waters before releasing her. They bobbed in silence, staring at the stars for a very long time, while her mind worked overtime trying to not to think about the fact she was half-naked and fantasizing about—er, swimming with—her boss. She had to break the sizzling silence.

"I'm sorry I screwed everything up between you and Olivia."

Instead of responding, he studied her with a mysterious gaze that made her knees tremble in anticipation. Then just like that, he dropped to the sea floor, took her face in his hands, and brought her

240

deliciously close to him. "Katie, you had nothing to do with the problems between Olivia and me. The only thing you've done is help me realize I was making a huge mistake."

She swallowed hard. "Don't put too much trust in me. I'm a poor guide when it comes to relationship issues."

"Why would you say that? Aren't things going well with Jared?" He seemed a little too eager to hear the answer.

She shrugged. "Well, he's on *my* vacation with another woman."

"Does that hurt you?" he asked, though he didn't look like he really wanted to know the answer.

"It hurts my pride," she admitted. "But I probably brought it upon myself. If I'd been more accepting of him, maybe he wouldn't be in Thailand with someone else."

"Tell me about it."

To her surprise, she did. They stayed in the warm bath until he'd extracted the whole story of her relationship with Jared, right down to the details of Anna chastising her for being too unrealistic, Mr. Scott's immense dislike of him, and her frustration at having felt pressured, while on the airport toilet, to agree to stay his girlfriend.

Katie stopped, suddenly sick of hearing her own voice. "Wow, I've been talking for a long time. I'm sure you're ready to die of boredom."

"No, actually there's still more I'm dying to know."

"More? I've told you everything."

"Not everything."

"What more can there be?" She looked down at her hands. "I'm already a giant prune."

He rolled his eyes at her in mock exasperation and led the way to the beach. Choosing a place to sit in the dry sand a few yards from the water, he pulled her down with him.

"You still haven't told me if you're in love with him."

Katie wrestled with the question. "Isn't that obvious?"

He shrugged. "Maybe, but I want to hear your answer anyway."

"It's complicated—how do I answer a question like that?"

"You answer 'yes' or 'no.'"

"You make it sound so easy. It's not that simple when you're having problems." She was nettled, wrestling between telling the truth and saying what was required of a dutiful girlfriend.

He seemed to be enjoying her reaction, and exacerbated her confusion by scooting closer to her and slinging an arm around her shoulders.

"What if I asked you the same question about Olivia?" she countered.

He pondered for just a moment. "I would tell you that I thought I loved her, but I was mistaken."

"Oh."

"Now, it's your turn," he pressed.

She took a while to formulate her words, but he waited patiently—kind of. His body language was patient, but the spark in his eyes seemed anxious.

"I feel like I *should* love him…."

"So you don't love him?"

"No, I don't."

She shivered. A breeze had picked up, and a layer of goose bumps now covered her wet skin. He was so chivalrous: He moved around to shelter her with his body and rubbed her chill-bumps away. Eventually, as his rubbing turned into mindlessly scrawling designs up her arms, he encouraged her head against his chest and she relaxed into him. He wrapped his arms tightly around her. Panic began to squish her lungs. *What is he doing? Is this a pity embrace—a really, really hot pity embrace?* She tried to wiggle from his hold, but he squeezed her tighter.

"Katie, I don't know what I'm doing either. But it feels right—can't I just enjoy holding you?"

Katie didn't answer. She couldn't, not with her heart lodged in her throat.

Chapter Twenty-Five

"Katie, we should go back to the room now. The sun's about to come up and the village will be waking soon." Lucas stroked her cheek lightly.

Katie wasn't asleep, but she was as lethargic as she'd ever been. If it weren't for her stiff muscles from sitting in the same position for so long, she would be in a perfect state of heaven. She nestled her face into his touch, wishing she could come alive to his purring accent every morning. Then reality set in: This was her boss. Who was probably only being attentive to her because he needed her help getting the Waverlys through Hong Kong. She'd do well to remember this—whatever it was—wasn't real.

She groaned in her attempt to stand, coaxing her reluctant muscles to respond. "I look like a giant sugar cookie," she remarked, brushing loose sand from her body.

Before she could read Lucas's delinquent smile, he sprung toward her, pouncing like a puma, and clasped her underneath his arm like a rugby ball, running the distance into the deeper part of the water.

She came up sputtering, wiping wet hair and seawater from her face in the same quick movement, no longer groggy. "Ha, ha, I get it, no more sugar cookie—very funny." She took a swipe at the water, sending splashes his direction.

There wasn't much space between them, but he drew even closer to her, still wearing his roguish grin. He locked on her gaze and the grin vanished. For a split second, she saw two emotions countering within him: certainty and uncertainty. But despite his opposing thoughts, he wasn't retreating. His eyes were exploring her in a way that made her skin prickle with anticipation. She had lost the ability to move. She was paralyzed by…fear? Desire? *Yes.*

His actions were slow, offering her the opportunity to withdraw, but she was all the more mesmerized by his deliberate pace. With no space between them now, the warmth of his breath stopped hers altogether. His smile was timid as he held her head and gazed into her eyes. She knew he was searching for something that would call him off. He must not have found it. He traced his thumbs down her neck and out across her collarbone, gathering up long strands of hair that intersected with his path and brushed them behind her back. Moving to her shoulders, he replaced each satiny bra strap with a tender kiss as he slid them down her arms.

She couldn't quite catch her breath and had to be satisfied with shallow gasps of air. *Holy crap! Holy crap! This can't be good.*

But it was good. So good she lost control of her neck. Her head fell back against her shoulders and he took advantage of her vulnerable throat. Her knees buckled, but he drew his hands down her back as her body dipped and secured both her legs around his waist, removing her bra in the process. *He's not only good, but tricky.* As he rounded his hands over her bottom, she remembered to be thankful for the extra buoyancy the saltwater gave her.

With both arms he wrapped her body tightly to his. She almost died when her bare chest pressed against his, not because he was her boss or her pseudo cousin, but because her hormones were on fire…a serious, four-alarm fire. She felt like she was back in high school—not that Christopher would ever have allowed her to get this hot and heavy with a boy back then. *STOP THINKING ABOUT CHRISTOPHER!* Lucas laid a few more lingering kisses on her neck, her jaw, her ear, until she could barely remember her own name.

Somewhere not too far away, a fisherman chuckled something out loud. "Loov-a bird-es," it sounded like through the Slavic of his accent.

"We need to get out of here," Lucas breathed, his lips pressed to her ear.

Still grappling with her senses, she nodded.

Dropping down to set her on her feet, he pulled away. The sensation of the subtle breeze that replaced the heat of his body made her aware—*very* aware.

"Where's my bra?" she whispered. "It's gone!" She was sure the few early risers starting to speckle the beach were zeroing in on her nipples.

"It's okay, don't panic." He helped her scoop around in the water, to no avail. He brought her close against him again, protectively. "Let's just go—we're starting to make a scene." His whispered tone was calm and reassuring. Rising from the water, he clutched her against his dripping body to guard her from the curious onlookers and carried her up the beach to their room.

Once the curtains were drawn, he reluctantly set her down and moved away—but not before stealing a glance at her exposed breasts. On impulse, her arms flew up to cover herself. He looked away, embarrassed.

Idiot! she admonished herself. She was still high on pheromones and her mind was a hallucinogenic blur, but she knew she had only an instant to recover before the awkwardness became irrevocable. Pushing her confusion aside, she dropped her arms and flashed a wicked smile.

"Someone is being a naughty cousin."

He turned back to her. This time she let his eyes linger wherever they liked. His laugh tolled throughout the small room. "Only because you are very irresistible, Rabbit."

He scooped her up and tossed her onto the mattress before barreling down beside her, the bed protesting against the rough landing.

"Wait!" she squealed as his hands picked up where they had left off. "I need to brush my teeth first!"

With a soft grunt and a roll of his eyes, he acquiesced, complaining only a little when she snatched the throw blanket from the foot of the bed and wrapped it around her body before bounding from the mattress.

"I just realized...I still don't know how we got here," she said as she rummaged through her bag.

"I...I was on your flight. I followed you. I took Mum's place," he admitted sheepishly. "After we landed...you passed out in the airport." He groaned, throwing his head back against the mattress as if he were trying not to relive the ordeal. "It scared me half to death."

"What? I don't remember...." Her hand rose to touch Bartholomew, who seemed to have grown smaller during the night.

"I called Dr. Woods. He told me that you most likely had a concussion-jetlag-exhaustion combo, and the most practical thing was to keep a close eye on you and let you sleep it off. Then Mum called to make sure we'd made it all right. She was in a right snit with me that she wasn't here to take care of you." He shook her head, no doubt imagining the scolding he was going to receive.

"How humiliating! I'm so sorry...what a pain I've been! Did I cause a big scene at the airport?" She tried to thwart mortification by keeping her nose in her bag and focusing on the silent debate of whether or not to put on a fresh pair of underwear.

"No."

His answer seemed too quick to be truthful. He smiled. "And you've been nothing but sheer enjoyment, I promise, since the moment we met." He strode from the bed to the bathroom, where he exchanged his wet boxers for a dry towel. "You have no idea how much I envy you at this moment."

247

"Me? Why?" She knew he couldn't be serious; there was nothing enviable about her.

"I would give anything to have a toothbrush right now."

He had a point. A toothbrush was a desirable commodity. She snuck on the new panties, then sauntered with her toiletry bag to the bathroom, where he was drying off. "You'd give *anything*?" she said, pulling two sparkly toothbrushes from her toiletry bag. "Meet Donny and Marie." She held one in each hand triumphantly. "Which one would you like? Donny's had a bit of use, but Marie is brand new." She thrust Marie at him, guessing at his answer.

"I have to ask—why do you carry two toothbrushes?" he questioned amusedly.

She held a finger up, instructing him to wait while she rinsed her mouth. "You never know when you might drop one on the floor or in the toilet or something. I'm not going to put a mungy, germy toothbrush back in my mouth," she replied, examining her polished teeth in the mirror. "And isn't it lucky for you that I do?" She flashed him an exaggerated smile that flaunted her pearly whites and flicked her brush in his direction, misting him with the excess water, before sashaying from the room.

She left him to his grooming as she stared out the glass doors onto the beach, lost in thought. Her hair was tossed over one shoulder, and she was mindlessly rubbing it dry with a towel.

"I'd almost give your toothbrush back to know what you're thinking."

Katie jumped. "Jeez! You startled me."

Lucas stood behind her and folded his arms loosely around the base of her neck. "What's going in that head of yours?"

There was no way she was about to share what she'd been thinking, but she couldn't hide the furious burn in her cheeks. He returned her blush. *Is he actually embarrassed? Sooo cute!*

"I was totally out of line, wasn't I?" he worried.

She squirmed in his arms to meet his contrite expression and grinned up at him. "Totally."

She didn't know why she did it—yes she did: she was still tripping from her lust overdose—but she let the blanket around her body slip to the floor and reached up on her tip-toes and kissed him.

She had only a second to register his surprise before he grabbed her up in one arm and yanked the curtains closed and tore the duvet from the sheets with the other. His warm mouth worked feverishly against hers as he brought her the short distance to the bed. He was a masterful artist, using his hands and lips to resculpt her body until it contoured to his. In the back of her incoherent mind, she knew that this—that *he*—was what she had been holding out for. No mullet, no excessive jewelry, no deplorable table manners. The dream of something like *this* is what kept her from giving her full self to Jared.

Jared!

"We have to stop!"

Lucas was just unhitching his towel. He paused mid-motion, then gave a tormented groan as his body fell defeated against hers.

She shimmied out from underneath him, fully aware of his agony. "I'm so sorry…sorry…I'm sorry."

He groaned again, pulling his knees underneath him, his face smashed into the pillow.

"What can I do to make it better?" she asked in guilty desperation.

249

He turned his head just enough to roll his eyes at her and shoot her a wry smile. He didn't have to say it—the response was written all over his face. *Duh!!!*

She sucked her breath in, making a backward hissing noise. "I'm sorry, really I'm sorry…soooo sooo sorry."

He held up a silencing hand. "S'alright," he slurred into the bedding. "Jusht give me a shecond."

Needing to do something—anything—that could be helpful, she scrambled off the bed and made her way to her backpack. She threw on a pair of shorts, then seeing a pair of fleece pants, she threw them on, too—along with jeans, a T-shirt, a sweater, a parka, even a beanie hat. When she had donned herself in as many clothes as possible, she waddled back to sit by him and began patting his head.

From the way he looked at her when he pulled out from underneath her pats, Katie thought he was going to bite her arm off. She cowered away from him, but it was hard to cower when she was layered to the point of looking like the Pillsbury Doughboy. Then his eyes took in the sight of her, and he laughed.

"Two things," he said, the agony dissipating from his tone. "One, all the clothes in the world can't erase your naked image from my mind. And two, why in the bloody hell did you bring all those warm things on a beach holiday?"

Great, now he's mad that I've overpacked. "I was just trying to ease the sexual tension. And you never know when you might need a sweater."

He worked his way to a kneeling position, tightening his towel as he straightened. "A sweater, fine—but a parka? Isn't that a little overkill?"

Humph.

"If you really want to be helpful," he continued, "do you mind telling me what just happened?"

He reached over to help her shed her layers. He manhandled her like she was a bratty nine-year-old, but at least he was still willing to touch her. Once she was down to the shorts and T-shirt layer, she offered an explanation.

"I guess I…lost sight of who I am. Last night was so perfect that it seemed surreal. But then I had a reality check…."

He cocked an eyebrow at her. She repressed a shiver. If he kept being sexy, her resolve was going to crumble quicker than a dry leaf sandwich on toast.

"Does this come from Anna telling you that you need to be practical?" he asked. "Because for the record, I think that's bollocks."

He was actually listening when I told him that story? "No. Yes…maybe…I don't know." She held her head in her hands. "It has to do with the fact that we only met three days ago. And…I don't want to be your rebound thing."

He started to reply, but she put her hand over his mouth.

"Shhh, I'm still talking. And…even though I don't *love* Jared, I'm still his girlfriend. I'm not a cheater."

He nodded his understanding, but she wasn't finished.

"And I'd be mortified if your Uncle Avery ever thought I was the kind of person to sleep with his recently unengaged nephew— especially after just three days."

"Four days, but it feels like five," he corrected.

"Okay, four, but that doesn't make it much better."

251

Lucas was silent for a long while. Katie was beginning to think the conversation was over. "You're right, you're absolutely right," he said, his voice rich with penance, "except for one point. *This,*" he pointed first at himself, then at Katie, "is definitely not a rebound thing."

It took an amazing amount of self-control, but she was able to refrain from jumping on the bed and doing the Happy Dance.

"Katie, you are amazing, and I value my time with you more than you can imagine. I don't want to do anything that would spoil us from furthering our friendship. Will you forgive me?"

Friendship. Of course. "There's nothing to forgive. We both got caught up in the moment. And it's not like it was a bad moment."

His smile was lecherous. "No, it was a brilliant moment." His hand reached for her face and he stroked her cheek with his thumb. "You should get some sleep. I don't want Bartholomew acting cranky again." He laid a tender kiss atop Bartholomew and the savage beacon seemed to melt under his dreamy touch.

"So should you. I don't want you acting cranky, either."

There was an infinitesimal moment where something unspoken was communicated between them. At the moment he pulled her, she advanced until his arms had enveloped her. She nestled against his chest and he burrowed his face into the tangles of her hair. Neither one spoke until a heavy cloak of drowsiness had fallen over them.

She felt the movement of his lips against her head, though she was only vaguely aware.

"Maybe one day we'll get back to this place." His whisper was so hushed she wasn't sure if she were meant to hear it.

She had only a second to wonder if he were speaking figuratively or literally. "I hope so," she murmured, not knowing if her words were audible, before sleep vanquished her.

Chapter Twenty-Six

Lucas peeked an eye open and glanced around the room. His cell phone, still in his jeans pocket, was ringing on the veranda. Katie was still in his arms, her breaths hot against his chest.

"What am I doing?" he muttered quietly.

Katie wanted nothing more than to die. Maybe she was dead and this was Hell. She wondered how long she could get away pretending she was still asleep. A month?

She could feel him staring down at her. She forced herself not to freak out, and continued to play asleep as if she had an Academy Award depending on it.

He drew his finger down her cheek. His touch was so soft, she wondered if she'd imagined it. "You, my little rabbit, have made quite an impact." His words were even softer than his touch. It was all Katie could do to make out what he was saying. "Four days ago, my life was streamlined: I had a fiancée, I was too busy in London to have even considered leaving the country, and four days ago, I never would've imagined I'd have an adopted cousin. And I certainly would never have ended up in bed with her! You have turned my world on its ear."

His phone chimed again. He ignored the second call, then a third. When the fourth call sounded, Katie couldn't take it anymore. She was going to have to face the humiliation sooner or later. She might as well get it over with. Her mind and her body were at odds, but she managed to pry her eyelids open. Her eyes, still out of focus, ran over the contours of Lucas's upper body. Her left cheek seemed to have melted into the warmth of his skin. Slowly, like a Band-Aid, she peeled her face from his chest and prayed that she hadn't drooled on him. She sat up, attempting to rub away the sleep indentations from her face. She could still feel his gaze on her, and reluctantly snuck a peek up at his face. A slight five o'clock shadow enhanced his strong jaw line, while the untamed layers of his chestnut hair were tangled haphazardly, a few strands sweeping across his forehead. His bare torso was defined by a natural athleticism that had Katie self-consciously pulling the covers securely across her Little Buddha in a hurry. He was scathingly handsome, and he was smiling at her. *Why was he smiling? Oh crap. I had drooled on him. Or maybe farted? Please, anything but a fart!*

"You all right?" he broke the silence.

"Fine," she replied, trying to hide her face behind her hand under the pretense of feeling Bartholomew.

A worried crease wriggled across his forehead. "Katie, I...I wish that you could know I'm not a one-night-stand type of bloke. I hope in time you won't be nervous around me. Please, will you give me a chance to make it up to you?"

In his earnest request for forgiveness, he moved closer to her. Her heart squeezed at the pain in his voice. She wanted to reassure him; however, his close proximity alerted her to her morning breath. Pulling away a few inches, she pulled the collar of her T-shirt around her nose and spoke through the loose material.

"Lucas, don't be silly, I have no reason to be nervous around you. You've done nothing to apologize for."

She could tell by his shattered expression that he believed her actions rather than her words.

"It's okay to be wary. I'm supposed to be your protector, not your predator." "Lucas, I could never be wary of you."

He shook his head and supplied her with a lame courtesy smile.

Damn. Why did he have to be so thoughtful? If he could be even a little bit of a jerk, she could feel angry instead of just pathetic. She let the shirt drop from her face. "Do you know what bothers me the most?"

He shook his head, looking uncertain he wanted to know the answer.

"If I'm going to wake up next to someone, I want to be the pretty one. It sucks that I'm the ugly one in this relationship!" Her cheeks went so hot she felt her face was melting. "Not that I think we're in a *relationship* or anything…I mean, I know we're practically cousins…I'm talking about more of a *familial* type of relationship…."

His roaring laugh interrupted her sputtering. "Crikey, that bump on your head has made you mental!" Grabbing her shoulders, he forced her to look him in the eyes. "You are abso-bloody-lutely beautiful. How could you think you're not?"

"Have you taken a look at yourself?" she replied. "You're like perfection—a Michelangelo masterpiece. Next to you, I'm just…I'm a…I'm a…Andy Warhol."

His cheeks turned scarlet. His humility was even more irresistible than his unfathomable good looks. The incredulous expression he wore had her believing, if only for a second, that maybe he wouldn't prefer to chew his arm off than wake up beside her.

"If that's the case, then I've just become Andy Warhol's biggest fan." His eyes crinkled as he cracked a heart-stopping grin. "If you don't get things sorted with that boyfriend of yours, I'm going to be the first one queuing up for you."

256

Did he really mean that? Though he sounded sincere, she couldn't help but think he was speaking encouragingly—a British cliché, like when the Martin sisters insisted Katie must have to "beat the men off with the stick"—which she'd never had to do, not even once.

Just then, Wham's ever-untimely song pealed through her phone, ending their conversation.

"You'd better get that," Lucas suggested, looking chagrined. "I'm sure it's my mum checking in on you."

Katie nodded and scuttled to her phone. "Katie, is that you, love? Are you all right?" A very concerned and familiar brogue tickled her ear.

"Mr. Scott!" she cried enthusiastically. Lucas's head snapped to attention at the mention of his uncle's name. "How are you? It's so nice of you to call," she effused, her eyes glossing over with happy tears.

"Nice of me to call?! Poppycock! I'm callin' because I'm told you might be dyin' and no one's heard a word from you or Lucas all mornin'! What in the name of Maggie Thatcher are you doin' in Croatia, and where the bloody hell is my nephew who's supposed to be keepin' you out of trouble?"

Stifling a giggle, Katie handed the phone to Lucas, who no doubt could hear every word his uncle had bellowed.

"Hello Uncle." Lucas had the tone of a naughty child about to be scolded. "Everything is just fine, I assure you. Katie is perfectly well. She just needed to sleep off a nasty bump on the head, that's all."

Just the sound of Mr. Scott's voice in the room was filling Katie with the guilts. The fact that she couldn't peel her eyes away from his towel-clad nephew wasn't helping things any. She had to find something to occupy herself with or she'd rip the phone away from Lucas and confess the whole evening to Mr. Scott.

Lucas's phone rang again, saving Katie from herself.

"Do you mind grabbing that?" Lucas whispered to Katie, begging his uncle's pardon. "That'll be my mum anxious to know that you're still living."

Katie trotted off in the direction of the sound. On the veranda, she plucked the beckoning phone from the pocket of his jeans. "Hello, Lucas Hayden's phone. May I help you?"

The noise from the other end was more of a screech than a reply.

"Hello?"

"You!" the caller hissed, "You whore! You sneaky, rotten, bloody gold-digging bitch! Let me talk to Lucas!"

"Hello Olivia." The hairs on the back of Katie's neck bristled, but her tone was sticky sweet. "Lucas is busy at the moment, but I'll be sure to let him know you called. Thanks and bye now." Before she could think about what she was doing, she powered the phone down. Just then, Lucas threw his head back in a roar of laughter at something his uncle had said. *At least one of us is having a pleasant conversation,* she thought sourly.

Katie tromped back into the room carrying a wad of clothes. She had never hung up on anyone before, but she wasn't going to let it upset her equanimity. Olivia had no effect on her. She gave Lucas a tight smile, threw her pile of clothes in a heap at the foot of the bed, and began hurling them one by one with all her might into her bag. Okay, maybe Olivia affected her a little.

"…So, I see Mum hasn't left out any details. I know it doesn't look like I've been doing my job, but then I didn't realize what you'd sent me. Katie's a magnet for trouble." Lucas shot her a playful wink, then leveled a questioning gaze at her.

"Olivia called," she whispered casually—perhaps not as casually as she'd intended—and tossed—okay, chucked—his BlackBerry onto the bed next to him.

"Uh, listen Uncle, I'll have to call you back. Olivia has been trying to ring me."

The last thing Katie heard before she stalked off to the shower was Mr. Scott's hooting laughter. "I'd give me last shilling to be a fly on the wall for that conversation!"

A few minutes into her shower, Lucas tapped at the door.

"Come in."

He cleared his throat to declare his presence. "I'm sorry you had to speak to Olivia. Was she terribly nasty with you?" He closed the toilet lid and took a seat.

Katie stopped mid-soap to contemplate. "No more than could be expected when a woman you hate answers your fiancé's phone."

"Ex-fiancé," he corrected.

"The thing is," Katie continued, poking her head around the shower curtain, her hair still sudsy, "I can't be upset with her. I deserved everything she said to me…I nearly had sex with her fiancé!" She pulled her face back in, but not in time to hide the color that burned her cheeks.

"Ex-fiancé," he corrected again.

"I don't think Olivia would agree."

A groan of frustration escaped his lips. "Katie, the blame is mine. I instigated everything—"

"Not everything," she interrupted, glad he couldn't see how her face was growing still hotter. "And I didn't try to stop you."

"You stopped before we had intercourse."

"*Intercourse?*" she giggled. "Please tell me you didn't just say that. I feel like I'm back in my eighth-grade health class. Only you're slightly less masculine and much better looking than Ms. Brooks, the girls' gym coach."

"You stopped when it was important."

Katie was just about to comment on how if the tables were turned and if Jared were kissing Natalie—which she was pretty sure he wasn't—how infuriated she would be, when Lucas retracted his words.

"That's not true. It was all-important. Katie, what happened last night was brilliant—not accidental. I knew exactly what I was doing when I kissed you. God knows I've thought about it a thousand times since meeting you, but it just didn't make sense. Then, after holding you on the beach, I didn't care what the repercussions would be. I didn't need it to make sense. I was going to make my intentions clear."

Despite the warm water pouring over her, she shuddered as the thrill of his speech raced up her spine. Words evaded her, though it didn't matter. He left her no time to respond.

"It wasn't until you stopped us that I realized how unclear my intentions may seem to you. I was a selfish sod not to think about your situation."

Turning off the faucet and wiping the water from her face, she held her hand out beyond the curtain.

Lucas obediently handed her a towel. She enjoyed the ease that they felt with one another, despite the weightiness of the conversation.

"So here's the issue," he continued as she dried off behind her screen. "Nothing would make me happier than to announce to Mum, Uncle Avery, Olivia—everyone—that we're together."

Before he could finish his thought, she whipped her head out from behind the curtain and stared at him. Her emotions flickered between shock and terror.

A hearty laugh ricocheted through the bathroom. "But, as you have a boyfriend and have previously implied—which your face now confirms—you are commitment-phobic, I don't think that would be a wise idea."

He was still chortling when she stepped wobbly-legged, towel hitched around her figure, from the shower. "Where does confidence like yours come from?" she wondered aloud, finding it alarmingly sexy. But not sexy enough to make her become a relationship whore, dashing straight from one man to another. She wasn't sure she'd made the right decision committing to Jared. How could she be sure Lucas wouldn't be a mistake as well? She couldn't.

A cocky grin scribbled across his face. "Comes from following my instincts."

"Did you follow your instincts with Olivia?" she quizzed tartly, hoping to daunt his surety.

"No, I didn't. I deliberated every decision I ever made with her," he answered without hesitation. He claimed the vacated shower, throwing his towel over the rod. "Every wise decision I've ever made has been impulsive. It's when I have to really think about something that I make a bloody bad decision."

Katie silently acknowledged the truth of his statement in her own life as she cherry-picked Donny and some toothpaste from her toiletry bag.

"So, as I was saying," he said, waiting for the water temperature to adjust, "are you ready to be with me and make it known to the world?"

She didn't appreciate the comedic lilt in his voice. Her legs turned to melted marshmallows and she grabbed the porcelain sink for support, letting the toothbrush fall slack in her mouth. Out of the corner of her eye, she saw Lucas peering above the shower rod, finding too much amusement in her numb reaction.

Be cool, Katie. She finished brushing and returned blithely, "Sadly, no. And you can blame Ms. Brooks and my American education for my commitment phobia."

"Ms. Brooks the health teacher?" He gave her a goofy smile. "You know, one of the things I adore about you is your peculiar logic." He sailed over the compliment as if sharing his feelings were no big deal.

She was pretty sure that no one had ever complimented her logic before.

"I'm emotionally scarred from that class. You don't know the lasting effects that learning about the birds and bees from a macho lesbian gym teacher can have on a preteen."

"Right then, I'll just have to be patient and offer you lots of therapy. Take all the time you need, I'm in no rush...except Uncle Avery told me that my parents caught an earlier flight and should be here shortly. We'll need to find less conspicuous sleeping arrangements in a hurry if you want to keep things…er…platonic."

Katie felt her eyes nearly pop out of her head. Panic sent her into warp speed. Before Lucas could finish his shower, she had thrown her hair into a loose over-the-shoulder braid, finished packing her bag, and was basically ready to depart, barring one small conundrum: She had no bra and no baggy top to conceal her less-than-perfectly-shaped C cups.

Chapter Twenty-Seven

"Bloody hell, Katie, it's nearly ninety degrees. Would you take off that ridiculous sweater?" Lucas asked for what seemed like the twentieth time. At first he seemed amused by her outfit, but now that they'd been wandering the stone streets for what seemed like forever, looking in vain for a shop where they could each purchase their required undergarments, Katie could tell he was annoyed. Well, so was she.

"I'm fine," she muttered, "Some of us don't do commando as well as others." She was definitely having a bit of penis envy—not in the disturbingly creepy Freudian sense—over how easy it was for Lucas to forgo his damp boxers and slip into his jeans. Right now, she'd give anything to have a tuck-away-able member instead of having to play boob-wrangler all morning.

They had spent the previous hour searching along the coast for accommodations with enough luxury to satisfy Lottie—another vain attempt. It seemed this rudimentary village relied on its minimalism to draw out a visitor's appetite for passion. Eventually, Katie and Lucas gave up the quest and returned to their original lodgings, booking two extra rooms, one for Lucas and one for his parents.

"Lucas, we're on a futile mission," Katie declared, wiping a bead of sweat from her brow and billowing the alpaca sweater she had bought from an old woman in the Andes. The bursts of air felt refreshing against the perspiration soaked T-shirt she wore underneath. "This village was obviously built around romance. Why would we be successful in finding underwear in a place where the sole purpose is to get people to remove it?"

Lucas chuckled. "You're right, this town is probably too small. We'll have to go into Dubrovnik." He glanced at his watch. "I wonder when Mum and Dad will arrive."

As if on cue, his phone rang. He fished it out of his hip pocket and checked the number. "Let the scolding begin." He put the phone to his ear. "Hello Mum."

"Hello darling," Lottie trilled loudly enough for Katie to overhear. "How's our Katie?"

"She's fine. Listen, Mum, how long 'til we'll be seeing you?"

"Oh, not long, Chicken. I forgot to ring you when we left the airport—ooh, look Charles, isn't that a lovely landscape? Once we get settled, I'd like to come back and sketch it for my collection."

"Darling, what collection?" Lucas could hear his father's voice in the background. "You don't sketch."

"What's that got to do with the price of cucumbers in Madagascar?" Lottie snapped.

While his parents finished their exchange about sketching and cucumbers in Madagascar—and what in the hell did that mean anyway?—Lucas grabbed Katie's hand and led her briskly back toward the hotel.

"So, Mum," Lucas interrupted, "you'll be here soon then?"

"Chicken, that's what I rang to tell you—we're not ten minutes from the address you gave me last night. You're still there, aren't you?"

"We're not far…we've just been for a walk. Katie needed some fresh air. We'll meet you back at the hotel." He quickened their pace.

Just as Katie was running out of breath and ready to die of heatstroke, Lucas came to a screeching halt, causing her to slam into his back. He dove through the door of a shop that carried a hodgepodge of touristy items. Among them was a scant collection of swimwear.

"Here," he said turning her by the shoulders toward the rack of bathing suits. "Pick something quickly." He already had a pair of black board shorts in hand.

"But I don't need a swimsuit."

"No, but Mum and Dad are probably already at the hotel, and since you insist you need a bra..." He held out a strappy bikini top. "Unless you want to meet them wearing that ridiculous sweater and raise the suspicions of my mum, I suggest you put on one of these." He thrust the top at her and walked toward the makeshift changing room.

Katie glared at him—well, at the back of him—and almost put the bikini top back. Then she thought about meeting Lucas's father with her breasts in a state of freefall, and reconsidered.

Having something for support, even if it was a tiny something, did wonders for Katie's attitude. For added good cheer, she undid her braid and let her hair tumble over her shoulders. She breathed her first easy breath all morning. She was triple-covered—bikini, T-shirt, and hair—not even Lottie could find anything amiss.

They arrived at the hotel just as Charles was pulling the last of the luggage from the cab.

"Dad, let me help you with those," Lucas insisted.

"All right," Charles agreed, but not before grabbing his son into a heartwarming embrace.

Katie felt a knot tighten in her stomach. It had been a few years since she'd seen her parents, and she wondered if they would greet her with such affection.

"It's good to see you, my boy," he rumbled with fatherly pride. "And this must be our Katie!" He rushed over and gave her an embrace that was no less affectionate. "Welcome to the family! I'm Charles Hayden."

Katie assessed him. Despite his sleek salt-and-pepper hair, he bore a strong resemblance to his son: same chiseled features, same artless countenance. A few inches shorter and a little leaner than Lucas, Charles carried the distinguished grace and ease of having embraced the passing of middle age. When he welcomed her to the family, Katie had no doubt he truly meant it. She felt a tear slide down her cheek, and quickly wiped it away.

"Oh, for the love of Rod Stewart's mental hairdresser," Lottie belted in exasperation as she came bustling out of the hotel. "You boys get inside and put things right. They haven't got enough rooms."

"What do you mean, Mum?" asked Lucas.

"Apparently one of us is an idiot and it certainly isn't me," Lottie snapped. "I mean exactly what I said: They. Haven't. Got. Enough. Rooms." Turning on the heels of her strappy espadrilles, she marched back through the door.

Lucas picked up the remaining suitcases and exchanged shrugs with his father, and they all followed Lottie to the hotel reception area, trailing her mutterings: "...primitive hotel doesn't even have a decent lobby...think I'm going to camp out like bloody Swiss Family Robinson...got another thing coming."

"Or even Robinson Crusoe, Mum," Lucas corrected.

"Excuse me?" she halted, lips pursed and eyes fluttering at a thousand bats per second.

"Robinson Crusoe. The Swiss Family Robinson lived in a tree. Plus, they're a loose adaptation of the Robinson Crusoe story, so, in essence, we expect you to camp out like bloody Robinson Crusoe." He and his father both chuckled.

She rounded on them and smiled with the perfect sweetness of a proper British lady. "Piss off and die, the both of you! Not you, Katie, love—you're lovely."

The next instant, Katie was barraged by hugs and anxious inquiries about her health from Sidney, Geoffrey, and Mrs. Albright— as well as a stealthy boob grope from Andrew—before she even crossed the threshold into the lobby. *So that's why there weren't enough rooms,* Katie thought.

A shifty young man in his mid-twenties was at the reception desk poring over his newspaper, trying to ignore the family commotion going on in front of him.

"Excuse me." Lucas interrupted the clerk's concentration. "Do you have any more rooms available?"

The man's olive skin grew a shade darker with annoyance. Without bothering to look up from his paper, he answered, "No sir, we are full." His thick accent carried a marked difference from that of the local villagers.

"Well then," Lucas said, turning back to his family, "we have three rooms and there are…" He made a quick head count. "…Eight of us. We'll just have to make do. Sidney, Andrew, and I can share a room."

Andrew communicated his disapproval with a half snort. "I'll be buggered before I share a room with the two of you." He pulled out a hundred pound note and approached the desk. "Would you mind checking once more for a room?" he crooned smoothly, sliding the bill across the counter.

The clerk looked up enough to register the bill and Andrew with disdain. "No sir, we are full."

Andrew quickly repaired his disgruntled face and returned to the group. "That's fine," he spoke coolly. "I will be more than happy to share a room with the Duchess, then." He draped a predatory arm around Katie's neck.

The clerk's shady eyes shot up with interest at Andrew's announcement. Untangling herself from Andrew's boa constrictor arm, Katie approached the desk.

"Excuse me…" She quickly registered the name on his tag. "Mensur, would you happen to know who else might have rooms available?"

His eyes interrogated every inch of her in a way that made her pine for her alpaca sweater. "It's the weekend—all the village is full."

"I see. Thank you anyway, Mensur." Folding her arms protectively over her chest, she turned from one horndog to another, warily scrutinizing her new roommate, Andrew.

"Lady! Hey lady!" Mensur called before she could walk away. Nonchalantly, he flipped through his rooming list. "Okay, I will give to you room."

Katie caught his black eyes in hers; something she found there made her shudder. "Thank you Mensur, thank you very much."

"See her pull a room out of her arse?" Lottie scoffed. "Now that Miss Magician has got us sorted, let's get settled in. Lucas and Andrew, you two take a room. Penny and Katie, Geoffrey and Sidney, you take the others."

Almost at once, there was a ripple of complaints.

"What the bloody hell does it matter who rooms with who?" Lottie nearly shouted.

"Well," Mrs. Albright spoke timidly, "Geoffrey and I were hoping to have a room together." Her face turned pink before she had finished her sentence.

"Criminy, Penny! Are you two shagging?" Lottie belted.

"Lottie!" "Mum!" Lucas and Charles reprimanded in unison.

Sidney inched closer to Katie and nudged her covertly with his elbow. There was a mischievous glint in his eyes that poorly masked his desire to burst out laughing. She tried to keep a stoic expression, but she couldn't keep the corners of her mouth from twitching. She pretended to scowl. "Shhh. You're going to get us in trouble."

"Of course you and Geoffrey should have your own room," Lucas soothed Mrs. Albright. "I believe this one will be the most secluded." He placed his key into her plump hand.

Geoffrey puffed out his chest and patted Lucas approvingly on the back before issuing the crowd a brisk nod and trotting off arm in arm with the housekeeper.

"Well, bugger me," Lottie sighed, staring after them in disbelief. "Right, then. I guess that leaves Sidney and Andrew in one room and Lucas and Katie in the other."

Andrew scowled in protest, but Katie could see he knew better than to argue with Lottie. As she let the instructions settle around her, a

270

fresh spell of panic gripped her. She was so worried about having to fight off Andrew's tentacles, she hadn't considered the other possibility: another night alone with Lucas. She was pretty sure she wasn't woman enough—or maybe she was too much woman—to withstand another night alone with him.

"Actually, I don't mind sharing a room with Andrew," she blurted.

Everyone, including Mensur and Andrew, gawked at her in bewilderment.

Lottie threw up her arms. "Fine! Do as you bloody well please."

She stalked off to her room, mumbling under her breath, "…people shagging practically right under me nose and nobody has the decency to say a word about it."

The others grabbed their bags and followed her like a flock of lambs.

Lucas caught Katie by the elbow, pulling her out of the entourage. "Katie, what's going on?"

Katie shrugged, refusing to meet his gaze. "Nothing."

"Nothing? Katie, I think you owe me more than that. Do you feel uncomfortable around me?" His question was pointed and marinated in apprehension.

"Sort of," she admitted to the floor, tracing the wood grain patterns with her toe.

Placing his thumb under her chin, he fought against her reluctance to bring her face toward his.

Seeing the cocoa sadness in his eyes, she quickly amended her answer. "I mean—not like you think."

271

His eyebrows rose in curiosity.

"I mean, I don't feel uncomfortable around you." She exhaled deeply, knowing she was going to regret this. "But sometimes I have uncomfortable *feelings* around you."

"What? You just said the same thing."

"No I didn't."

"Please don't play games with me, Katie. I thought we really had something."

There was a tone in his voice, a tone he had never taken with her before. Anger? Annoyance?

"I'm not playing games!" She felt insulted by the accusation. "I'm trying to tell you that I get the tingly-pee feeling around you!" Her voice rose to a near shout.

"Sorry?"

Katie grunted in frustration.

"You make her horny." Mensur's thick accent cut through the lobby.

Lucas blinked a few times in response to this new bit of information, then threw his head back in laughter. Katie felt the flames of humiliation lick up her cheeks like a relentless puppy.

"Ah, thank you Mensur." Lucas laughed and gave the clerk a congenial wave.

Mensur made no other acknowledgment and went back to studying his newspaper.

Katie stamped her foot in a little pout. *This wasn't funny!* Lucas pulled her into him, holding her head snugly against his chest and whispered into her hair.

"It's okay Rabbit, you make me horny, too."

She didn't intend to, but she let her body relax against his. In a twisted sort of way, those were the nicest words she'd ever heard.

Mensur cleared his throat loudly and the two broke apart just before Lottie, dressed head to toe in creamy chiffon, reentered looking like a miniature Jackie O with a pixie cut. Despite Lottie's ostentatious figure with her huge sunglasses and gargantuan floppy hat, both Lucas and Katie stared at Mensur—their unlikely advocate.

"Oh lovely, there you are!" Lottie called. "I took one look at the water from my room and I just couldn't wait to take a walk along the beach." She made dramatic sweeping gestures with her arms, showing off the elegant draping of her wide, open sleeves.

"Your father insisted on 'testing' out the bed and now he's taking a zizz. Katie, love, are you feeling all right? You look a bit flushed. Is that knock on your head bothering you?"

With the practiced hand of a concerned mother, Lottie brushed back the swoop of hair that concealed Bartholomew's remains.

What was bothering Katie was that she had no resistance to Lucas, and they'd almost been caught. A few more seconds and they would have been kissing for sure.

"I'm fine, I'm great. I'm better than great—I'm great," she answered distractedly.

"You sure she's okay?" Lottie sidled up to Lucas and whispered, "She seems a bit crackers."

Lucas smirked. He linked his mother's arm through his and led her toward the exit. "I think we could all stand to take that walk."

On her way out, Katie detoured past Mensur. His head was buried in his paper. "Um…thank you," she whispered awkwardly to

273

the top of his head. Not one of his shiny black hairs even wiggled in response, and she continued toward the door.

As soon as she had gone, he flipped backward through his paper agitatedly, about halfway back. In the London society pages, he found it again. He ran his fingers over the photo of Lucas and Katie, as if it were telling a story by Braille. "You're most welcome, Duchess."

Chapter Twenty-Eight

"Would you look at this?" Lottie marveled, taking in the sapphire waters. "This certainly makes up for having such primitive accommodations." She swept her arms along the landscape, admiring even more how the sleeves of her fancy new top floated compliantly along with her movements.

Lucas rolled his eyes and winked at Katie, who snorted while trying to stifle a giggle at Lottie's display.

Lottie looked upon her sympathetically, as if convinced Katie was suffering from brain damage. "Did you two have a nice swim today?" she cooed slowly and loudly for Katie's benefit.

There was a slight catch in Lucas's throat. "We haven't been swimming." He took his mother's arm, resuming their leisurely pace.

Not technically, Katie amended silently, feeling the color rise to her cheeks.

"Am I to believe that you haven't jumped at the first opportunity to sneak a peek at Katie in a teeny bikini?" Lottie ribbed her son.

"Yes, mother, that's exactly what you're to believe."

"I'm just saying that after dating Miss Skin and Bones for so long, it's only natural a man would crave something with loads more meat—like our Katie." She spoke with the sweetness of pure innocence, but the naughty gleam in her eye told otherwise.

Lucas grew red-faced, either from anger or embarrassment—Katie couldn't tell. But he obviously wasn't adept at playing his mother's games.

Katie laid a calming hand over Lucas's arm and spoke to him with rivaling syrupiness. "Oh, don't let her get to you. She only wondered if you were taking advantage of fresh young meat," she said, sliding her hand demonstratively down the length of her body, "before it turns into a tough old cow." She jerked her thumb toward Lottie with pretend sneakiness, then turned to her, batting her eyelashes. "Isn't that what you meant?"

"Oooh, you cheeky little monkey!" Lottie gave Katie a playful swat on the butt, then wrapped an arm around her waist, pulling her into a hug. Effortlessly, the two women fell into step.

"Oooh, looky here, it looks like *someone* has been a naughty bunny," Lottie trilled.

Katie took one look at the waves tumbling her recently departed bra and Lucas's mother stooping over to get a closer look, and wanted to die—now.

"Hmmm…I thought you said you hadn't been for a swim?" She eyed her son with playful suspicion. The soggy, sandy undergarment dripped onto his toes as she dangled it from the tip of her finger in front of his face.

Katie felt dread as heavy as cement filling her chest cavity. Lucas was completely unruffled and looked as though he might confess the previous night's activities. He snuck a side glance at her. Her mortification must have been apparent because he quickly changed his expression into something more severe and scolded, "For God's sake, Mother, you're disgusting. Would you put that thing down— you've no idea where it's been!"

"Simmer down. I was only trying to have a little fun," Lottie sniffed. "Honestly, I don't know who taught you to be such a prude. If

I hadn't pushed you out of me own fanny, I would think you belonged to somebody else."

Katie felt her mouth drop open and almost hit the sand.

"Mum!" Lucas snapped.

"She birthed you out of her butt?" Katie couldn't help asking, trying to make sense of something she knew to be impossible.

Lottie's head spun so fast she looked as if she were possessed. "What in the name of Santa's queer elves is she talking about?"

"What are *you* talking about?" Katie shot back, unconsciously scrubbing imaginary filth from her arms.

"I never said anything about having babies out of me bum," Lottie insisted.

"You did! I heard you!" Katie argued.

They gawked at each other in bewildered silence, each looking certain the other was certifiably crazy.

"Stop!" Lucas crumpled to the ground in a fit of laughter, tears streaming down his cheeks. "Please, stop!" he gasped.

They both turned on him like hungry wolves. He looked at Katie, then Lottie, and fell apart laughing again. Then he pushed himself to stand as both women glared at him, arms tightly folded across their chests, neither one willing to give him a hand. He took his time brushing the sand from his body and composing himself. "Let this be a lesson to you, Mum, for being so crude. In America, the word 'fanny' doesn't mean the same thing as it does here. It means 'bum.'"

He seemed to be enjoying his mother's slow reaction as she absorbed this new information. Her eyelids fluttered rapidly, then slowed to a few exaggerated blinks. "Oh. Oh my!" and then she put a hand over her heart and burst into a laugh that matched her son's.

"Excuse me!" Katie stamped her foot, still completely grossed out and feeling more than a little fidgety standing next to her wayward bra. "I still don't understand what's going on."

Lucas sobered up. "In the U.K., 'fanny' is a very crude term for...for a woman's...well, for her—"

"It means 'twat,'" Lottie blurted.

"Mum!"

"Hello!" someone called out from a distance.

Holding her hand up to her eyes to shield the sun, Lottie took a few steps in the direction of the voice until Sidney was in clear view. He was making a fast approach.

"Owww!" Lucas cried as Katie stomped on his foot.

"Get it!" she muttered, pointing vigorously at her bra.

"Are you mad? She'll catch us for sure!"

"I refuse to just leave it here for everybody to gawk at—it's embarrassing!"

"Nobody knows it's yours."

"*I'll* know!" she hissed, and stalked away before he could opt out of the job. Pulling Lottie along with her, she went to greet Sidney.

***

Katie arrived back at her room to find Andrew had gone out. At last, a bit of good fortune. She took one longing glance at the bed. She'd probably be up all night fighting off Andrew's libido.

The plump pillow was cool and felt like heaven against her cheek. Her eyelids grew leaden and she snuggled into prime napping position. She snuck in a long stretch, knowing it would be her last cognizant one.

"Katie, love, are you in there?" Mrs. Albright's concerned voice was a welcome as a wet willy to the ear canal.

Katie considered ignoring her, but if she did, she'd end up feeling too guilty to sleep anyway. She pried herself out of her nest and trudged to open the door.

"I'm so glad you're here." Mrs. Albright spoke with a strange urgency. "I was hoping to get some time alone with you." Her shortness of breath indicated she had power-walked her plump frame all the way from the other end of the hotel.

The old wooden chair groaned its displeasure under Mrs. Albright's weight as she sat down at the round turquoise table. She fumbled through her handbag as she spoke. "After you got conked on the head and I went upstairs to fetch you a change of clothes, I found these folded up inside your pajamas." She pulled the ring box along with the note Katie's friends had planted in her suitcase and slid them across the table.

Katie sat down, opened the box, and stared blankly at the atrocious golden ring. She was frozen in shock.

"I'm so sorry, love, I didn't realize things were so serious with your man in America. I should never have insinuated that there could be anything between you and Lucas." She burst into tears. "Can you ever forgive me?"

Katie reached out and held Mrs. Albright's nervous hands in her own. "There's nothing to forgive. You've never said anything to offend me."

Mrs. Albright sniffed. Her copper hair, curled by the humidity, bounced as she sobbed. "The thing is…I kept the ring in my pocket on purpose. You would have found it by now if I hadn't done that." Her frame shook as she blubbered her guilty tale.

Katie supposed she should have felt angry or at least annoyed, but the only resentment she held toward Mrs. Albright was for her lost nap. She moved over to the distraught housekeeper and held her in a consoling embrace.

"Please, Mrs. Albright, don't you worry one more second about it. I wouldn't have wanted to see this ring any sooner than right now anyway."

"I didn't want you to get engaged and leave us."

Katie gave her a tight squeeze. This crazy family really did care about her. "It's going to take a lot more than a little old ring to get me to leave just yet."

"What about that scary Olivia?" The question was asked with such innocence that Katie chuckled in spite of herself.

"Well, yeah, scary Olivia did send me running…then again, the last time we met I puked on her, so I doubt she'll show up to bother me anytime soon."

Mrs. Albright offered an uncertain smile. "I hope you're right." Gathering herself up, she gave Katie one last embrace. "I'll be off and give you some time to yourself. I should start getting ready— oh, that reminds me, I'm supposed to tell you we're dressing up for dinner tonight."

"Great, thanks." Katie couldn't offer any enthusiasm to go with her weak smile.

Mrs. Albright grasped an opportunity for redemption. "Please let me make your excuses. I'll tell them that you're having a lie down and not feeling well."

"Thanks, I'd really appreciate that. I guess I do need some time to think things over."

***

Paper in one hand, ring in the other, Katie tore down the beach trying to escape the claustrophobia bearing down on her. Why did she have to get this now? Was this a sign? She knew she didn't love Jared, but maybe she was supposed to try? What if this was her last chance to ensure she wouldn't be, as Anna had reminded her, *completely alone*? Did she dare risk it? In his own clumsy way, Jared adored her—maybe she could grow to care for him in return. He, at least, was real…while Lucas, if he wasn't just rebounding from Olivia, was probably too good to last.

Scraps of conflicting conversations whirred through her mind, making it hard to breathe even under the expanse of the cloudless sky: Anna admonishing her to stop chasing fairy tales, Mr. Scott talking about true love, Lucas telling her in his dreamy accent that he would be standing first in line for her. She reminisced about the blissful memories from the night before, savoring them much longer than a girl holding another man's promise ring should. As exciting as a romance with Lucas might be, for once in her life, Katie considered making a practical decision.

When her lungs finally gave out on her, she crumpled to the ground gasping, two breaths short of a sobfest. The sun's rays created a kaleidoscope of colorful squiggles that skipped across her closed lids. She lay in the sand, allowing the abstract images to distract her from her profound confusion until the sun no longer shined. Only then did she reluctantly pull herself up to begin the long trudge back to the hotel. A new mantra was taking shape in her mind: *Kissing cousins*

281

cause catastrophic confusion and create colossal consequences. By the time she neared the front doors, she had just about convinced herself that her escapade with Lucas was just an illusion—a product of a man, a woman, and a head injury caught up in the romance of a foreign country.

Chapter Twenty-Nine

Katie entered the room to find Andrew sitting on the bed curled into a ball, his arms locked around his shins and his forehead pressed down against his kneecaps. "You look the way I feel," she observed.

He raised his head at the sound of her voice and ran his eyes over her. "That can't be a good thing…you look like shite. Do you want to talk about it?"

Katie narrowed her eyes at him.

He responded to her skepticism with a pitiful grin. "I'm not always as awful as I seem."

She detected no trace of malice or cockiness in his demeanor, only genial self-pity. She could relate to self-pity.

She shook her head. "No thanks, I don't feel much like talking. Do *you* want to talk?"

"No."

With a hefty sigh, she plopped on the bed next to him. The bounce she caused in the mattress knocked him off balance.

"Easy there, Duchess," he said, adjusting himself so he was seated next to her, his legs dangling over the edge of the bed. "What's that you're clutching?"

Without much reluctance she surrendered the ring box along with her notes.

"May I?" He nodded toward the papers that had taken the shape of the inside of her fist.

"If you want."

He was meticulous in his task of uncrumpling, first the note from her friends and then Jared's. "Hmmm. I didn't realize you were seriously involved."

He craned his neck to look her fully in the face. Her lips pulled into a taut line and she shrugged.

He muttered, "I'm surprised I didn't notice—you're positively giddy with love."

For once, she approved of his sarcasm.

Andrew opened the ring box. "Bloody hell!" He tilted the box to get a different perspective. "This is hideous! I'd say your friends hit it right on the money. Any bloke who would choose this ring is a total cabbage!"

She couldn't say exactly which part of Andrew's reaction struck her as funny—the way he stared at the ring in complete horror or the image he created of beef-cakey Jared with a big leafy cabbage head. But she held onto the humor with both hands and let her laughter flow uninhibited, releasing her glut of pent-up emotions. Soon, Andrew joined in and they both fell back onto the bed. Eventually their hysterics subsided into long gasps for air. When speaking again became a possibility, he tugged at a lock of her hair, splayed wildly across the comforter.

"Are you hungry, Duchess? What do you think about going out and gorging our sorrows?"

Yanking her hair out of his clutch, she replied, "I'll be ready in five minutes."

***

"Why don't you tell me about this man of yours?" Andrew probed, putting aside the game he was making of sliding his beer glass from one hand to the other.

Katie skewered a forkful of salad. "What do you want to know?"

"For one, why you're so conflicted. You already seem to know he's a wanker."

"I know, but it's hard not to second guess myself. What if turning him down is the wrong decision?"

"What if it isn't? Let's cut through the crap. I think you're scared to cut your wanker boyfriend loose because you're afraid of what could happen if you make yourself available."   "I don't understand." Or maybe she didn't *want* to understand.

Andrew cocked an eyebrow at her. "Come on Duchess, I can see what's happening. You and Lucas fancy each other." His voice was kind and encouraging, nothing like the cynicism she expected.

"Why do you hate him so much?" she ventured.

"I don't hate him. It's just really hard for me to like him."

Her eyebrows shot up. He was actually being truthful with her.

Andrew drew on her silence to finish his explanation. "He's the golden boy: He farts and china patterns appear."

Katie giggled at the visual. "And Sidney—why do you resent him?"

"I don't know." He traced his thumb contemplatively around the bottom of his smooth chin. "Sid and Avery...it's like they expect me to be like my grandfather."

"Is that bad?" she asked with increasing curiosity.

"Of course not, it was my granddad who raised me. He died when I was almost seventeen. He left some big shoes to fill." He dropped his chin to chest. "Perhaps I've never felt up to the task."

She laid a hand over his forearm. "I have a feeling that when you decide to get off your butt and start trying to fill those shoes, you'll do an amazing job."

"Ta. Cheers." He gave her a crooked smile before channeling his focus toward her hand.

She slid her hand off his arm and placed it in her lap. "You're welcome. I truly believe that."

His phone buzzed against the table with a text message alert. Subconsciously smoothing his sleek black hair across his forehead, Andrew read the message. Katie noticed the dejected turn of his face. Warm eyes freezing over, he threw back what was left of his beer.

"Well, I think that's enough sharing for one night. Let's go find some fun."

He threw some money down on the table, then tore out the door with Katie, setting a relentless pace. Testing the limits of her improvised bra by being dragged by the wrist faster than her flip-flops would go was not Katie's idea of fun.

"Andrew, stop!" she wheezed, trying to dig her heels into the broken stony road. Twinges of pain radiated at the base of Bartholomew's remains.

He was nearly yanked off his feet by her abrupt halt. "Oh sorry, Duchess…I guess I let my one-track mind run away with me."

She held her sides, doubled over, gasping for air. He patted her back and slid the thin spaghetti straps of her sundress back onto her shoulders.

286

"What's with the sudden urgency?" she demanded once she was able to hold herself upright.

Placing her arm over his, he began to escort her at a leisurely pace. "Just wanted to get my mind off things, I guess."

"What things?" She prodded him with compassionate eyes.

He shook his head, sighing as if she'd forced the confession out of him. Retrieving his text message, he handed over his phone.

A,

I can't make Lucas listen to reason over the phone. My flight arrives in Croatia at 11 a.m.—meet me at the airport.

Hugs,

O

Katie stared at the note incredulously. "Andrew, why are you here—to spy for Olivia?"

With a toss of his head to clear the hair that had fallen over his eye, he answered shamefacedly, "Sort of."

Her face contorted as she recalled her initial dislike for him. *Stupid, stupid, Katie!* she chastised herself.

"I can't believe I let you charm me into thinking we could actually be friends! You know what, Andrew…Andrew…I don't even know your last name! Whatever's going on between you and Lucas and Olivia, leave me out of it!" She stomped off toward the hotel.

"Wait! It's not like that." In two strides he caught up to her. "Duchess, listen to me."

She turned a deaf ear to him.

"Katie, please…" The sorrow in his voice as he spoke her name, for the first time ever, stopped her. "Believe me when I tell you that nothing about being with you tonight was contrived."

"Why should I?" She kept her head tipped away from him.

"Because," he said, jamming his fists into his pockets, "I would like to have you for a friend."

"Why?"

He couldn't seem to meet her eyes. "Because I don't have many—any real friends."   Katie didn't have an immediate response. She put her hand to her head, feeling Bartholomew. "Damn it, Andrew! I've never met anyone who ignites my temper like you do."

A proud grin stretched across his face.

"I'm not going to lie—it makes me sick that you let her manipulate you into betraying your family. What is up with you two anyway?"

Even before she comprehended Andrew's tortured expression, her intuition caught up with her.

"Holy crap, Andrew—you're in love with her!"

Chapter Thirty

"All right, all right, stop bludgeoning me with questions. I'll explain everything. Just let me get a word in." Andrew held up his hands.

Katie made a dramatic production of zipping her lips and throwing away the key.

"I've been crazy about Olivia since before she and Lucas ever met."

Cutting Katie off before she could interrupt, he added, "Yes, Olivia knows—has known for ages."

As Katie opened her mouth, he cut her off again. "No, Lucas doesn't know, and I'd like to keep it that way." He waited to extract Katie's promise before going on. "Lucas doesn't know we're acquainted beyond his introduction. I didn't know they were dating until they were already serious. Olivia never mentioned me to him, and by that time she had obviously made her choice. So I figured it was best for everyone that I keep my gob shut." He pulled a tight smile and flipped his hair with a toss of his head.

"Can I speak now?"

"You may." He granted her request with a condescending sweep of his hand.

"First of all, I want to apologize—you're not nearly as big a jackass as I thought. I can totally understand why you're so…unpleasant. But I have to ask: Why help her?"

"Because I'm a prat," he joked humorlessly, jamming his fists deeper into his pockets. "Because I'm still pathetically hopeful." A smile overtook him as he nudged her. "But thanks to you, I have reason to be more hopeful than ever. Which reminds me…let's get on to discussing this crazy love triangle of yours."

"I never said there was a love triangle," Katie defended flippantly.

An approaching silhouette of a man and a pixie rescued her from having to dish on the subject.

"Oh, hello dears, there you are," Lottie trilled as soon as she was within earshot. "Feeling any better Katie, love? Are you a promised woman?"

Katie opened her mouth to reply to the first the question, then snapped it shut upon hearing the second.

"Darling," Charles lightly reprimanded his wife. "We were supposed to keep that confidential."

"Oh pshaw," Lottie dismissed. "I'm sure Katie didn't expect to keep it from the family." Applying a thin layer of guilt, she added, "And now that it's out—not that she asked for my two bits, though I'm sure she was meaning to—if the thought of a life with this bloke makes her feel out of sorts, then I don't know what there is to consider."

"Lottie, this is none of our business," Charles reproved.

"Of course it is." She took a step toward Katie and wobbled slightly. Andrew reached out and steadied her by the arm. "Thank you, you are a dear." She stretched up and clumsily patted the middle of his face. "As I was saying, it *is* our business because Katie is our family now." She tilted her head toward Katie and shone her big calf eyes up at her. "She's trying to make a big decision, and while she's faffing about trying to make it, we have two boys here who seem to fancy her company plenty enough."

290

Andrew chuckled a "you have no idea" sort of laugh, and Katie threw him a menacing glare.

"Isn't that right, pet?" Lottie patted his face again.

"Course it is, love," Andrew humored.

"All right, that's enough of that." Charles stepped in. "Lottie dear, I'm taking you back to the room."

She clung to Andrew's arm like a disobedient child. Katie choked on her laugh, inciting a glare from the intoxicated woman.

"It's all right," Andrew grinned to Charles. "We're on our way back ourselves. I'll take her."

"You'll have to excuse my wife; she's had a little too much wine," Charles beseeched Katie as they fell into step a few feet behind Andrew and Lottie.

Letting her giggles escape, Katie said, "There's nothing to excuse. I adore her."

"I do, too!" he laughed, teeming with pride. "She's a silly, daft woman—but God, how I love her!"

Stung by his sentiment, Katie wondered: *Could I ever feel that kind of passion for Jared?* "Have you…always felt that way?"

"From the very first moment I met her." His eyes shone from the sincerity of his emotions.

Katie felt him reading into the apprehension behind her empty smile. As if he'd ascertained a vital piece of information, he gave a low, indiscernible drawl that caused her to study him with curiosity.

"Let's have a seat." He escorted her to the crumbling steps of an archaic cathedral they were passing. "In the absence of your own father, may I offer you some advice?"

She nodded, desperate to hear some paternal wisdom.

291

"As you know, I've already been informed about the decision you have before you." His voice was sensitive, but firm. "If I interpret what I know about the situation correctly, I would say you're trying to convince yourself to love someone who's not fit for you."

She was a little dumbfounded by his extensive knowledge of her private life. "How do you know if someone is fit for you?"

"You just know. Everything about you is drawn to that person. When you've met the right person, your entire soul will take flight because you know life couldn't possibly get any better and you never dreamed you could be so happy. Then, you'll be surprised to find that every stage thereafter brings you even more happiness, and you thank God every single day you held out for the right one."

Prompted by his poetic declaration, one fat tear fell from the corner of her eye and trickled slowly down her cheek.

"Do you feel like that about your man?"

Unable to deny him the truth, she shook her head.

"I thought not." He wrapped an arm around her side in a fatherly embrace, and she burrowed obligingly into him. "Don't let your head talk you into something your heart doesn't feel."

***

Katie's heart thrummed like a hummingbird on crack upon seeing Lucas. He was combing his hand agitatedly through his hair as he paced in front of the hotel doors. Charles greeted his son with a nod.

"I'll leave you here then," Charles said, kissing Katie lightly on the cheek.

She captured him in an appreciative hug. "Thanks for the talk."

Squeezing her hand, he showed her from whom Lucas had inherited his dazzling smile. "It was my pleasure. I enjoyed having a daughter, if only for a few minutes."

Lucas came to her as soon as his father had disappeared. "Where have you been? I've been searching all over for you."

"I've been hanging out with Andrew." She stared at his Adam's apple, unable to force her eyes to his. "Have you been shopping?" she asked, noticing his khaki capri pants and dusky-hued button-up, one sleeve rolled up his forearm, the other dangling open at his wrist.

He nodded, taking a step closer. Her eyes now fixed at his waist, she silently applauded him for being one of few men able to look hot in man-pris. Her stomach turned a somersault as his clean, soapy scent enveloped her.

Wordlessly, he took her face in both his hands and forced her to look at him. There was a disquieting intensity in his eyes. She struggled unsuccessfully against his firm hold to turn her head away. Her imagination ran wild as groin electrodes whizzed around, tickling her pee region into a frenzy. Her skin rippled with a deluge of sinful sensations.

Deliberate to the point of excruciating, he drew her to him and parted her lips with his. Eyes drifting closed, she melted into the minty, warm mouth massage. One arm slid down, wrapping her waist, while his other hand traced along her jawline, making its way to the top of her neck. Splaying his fingers through her hair, he supported the back of her head. Straightening to full height, he lifted her off her feet and walked to the side of the flat-fronted hotel for more privacy than the desolate street offered, his lips never leaving hers.

He clutched and released fistfuls of cascading hair, kneading her scalp to the spiking rhythm of his erratic heart as the kiss crescendoed with intensity. A low guttural moan escaped her as she surrendered herself to his passion. As if he could make them one, he pressed her body tighter against him. She shared his mutual desire to meld into the same frame, and felt the muscles of his forearms and biceps tighten against her. The groin electrodes were whirring at an unprecedented rate. When she was sure she was about to explode, his arms slackened. His hands returned to cupping her face and his mouth relinquished hers. Leaving behind three soft, warm kisses, he pulled completely away. He turned his back to her and ran his hand through his disheveled hair with a groan.

She only stared at the outline of his back, dumbfounded and unfulfilled for a second, before she had to silence the groin electrodes. She turned away, staggering a few steps before holding herself in an agonizing crouch. *Make it stop! Make it stop! Make it stop!* She bounced on both feet, then hopped from one foot to the other. Once the tingly-pee feeling had simmered down, she gathered up her pride and turned to face what she suspected in the absence of light was Lucas's curious stare.

The outline of his rugged contours aggravated that darn peeing sensation again, and she had to cross her legs in order to make her mind function. Turning an abrupt about-face, she speedily recited her latest mantra under her breath: "Kissing cousins cause catastrophic confusion and create colossal consequences."

"Sorry?" he questioned, straining to hear her words.

She stiffened at his sound. Flipping her hair casually over her shoulder, she answered, "Oh nothing." Then, gaining her composure, she said, "What the hell what was that about?"

He shrugged unabashedly. "I couldn't help myself. It might have been my last opportunity." His gaze was fixed to the ground. "Have you made a decision yet?"

"I can't believe that Mrs. Albright is such a blabbermouth! Is there *anybody* who doesn't know what's going on in my personal life?" She threw her hands up in embarrassment as much as annoyance.

"Don't—don't blame Mrs. Albright, please. She feels horrible. It was Mum who tricked it out of her."

It wasn't hard to believe that the guileless housekeeper could be duped by the artful Lottie.

"Fair enough, I can see how that could happen...but still."

A tense silence hovered over them while his eyes searched hers for an answer to his question.

"Yes, I've made my decision." Her face bore no expression. "I should go call Jared now to give him my answer."

"Which is...?"

"I'll tell you after I've made the call."

***

"What time is it in Thailand?" Katie asked Andrew as she rifled through her bag for her pajamas.

"How the shit should I know?" He was only pretending to be aloof. "Quite late, I imagine."

A single lock of hair had fallen over her eyes. Tucking it behind her ear, she tossed her pajamas onto the bed and slipped onto the veranda, cell phone in hand.

Before Andrew had time reposition himself into a non-eavesdropping, nonchalant position, she was back.

She stormed past him, scooping up her pajamas along the way. "He didn't answer." She slammed the bathroom door shut before he could reply. Fifteen seconds later, she poked her head out the door. "It's late here—it's probably later in Thailand! What could he be doing that he couldn't answer his phone?" Again she slammed the door, not allowing Andrew a response. Thirty seconds later, hair twisted into an exploding bun, toothbrush dangling from her mouth, she opened the door again. "I mean, heesh shupposed to have a girlfriend! We're practically promised! There should no reashon he wouldn't anshwer my call sho late at night." Her striped cotton pajamas hung loosely at her hips, allowing her semi-fitted tank to expose her torso as she wielded her arms about frantically. A foamy drool of toothpaste slithered down her chin, sending her back to the bathroom—slamming the door again.

Mid-spit, her phone "Jitterbugged" along the countertop. She quickly rinsed, wiped her mouth with the back of her arm, and ran out to Andrew, waving her hands in front of her as she jumped around.

"It's him, it's him! What should I do? What should I do?" she whisper-yelped as if Jared might hear her.

"Breathe," Andrew instructed, halting her with the pressure of his hands on her shoulders.

She did as she was directed, bringing a long inhale through her nostrils.

"Now, pick up the phone."

The spastic hopping commenced again. "What should I say? What should I say?" Her neck and chest were beginning to blotch with nervousness.

"Crikey Duchess, tell him whatever you planned on saying in the first place."

The phone chirped a series of chimes indicating the call had been dropped. She stared at the "one missed call" message, stupefied.

Andrew pried the phone from her clutch. "Pull yourself together," he ordered. "Whatever you're planning on telling him, remember you still only have lukewarm feelings for this bloke—that gives you the upper hand."

Katie put in to argue, then closed her mouth over her words and nodded.

He pressed the phone back into the palm of her hand and slapped her on the behind as she headed for the veranda.

"Jared, hi. Sorry, I was brushing my teeth and couldn't get to the phone in time." Her stomach churned with nerves, prompting her to push her head into the room and beckon Andrew out for moral support. He ran over to share the earpiece with her.

"Katie, what do you want? You woke Natalie up."

Woke Natalie up? Are they sleeping together?!

Katie was prodded by Andrew's annoyed scowl. "Are you and Natalie in the same bed?" She didn't want to sound like a jealous girlfriend, but she couldn't help it. She also didn't want to consider her hypocrisy. She'd shared a bed with Lucas…and would be sharing one with Andrew as well.

"Relax. We're sharing a room, but we have double beds. Is that why you called—to check up on me?" He sounded pleased.

297

Katie was losing control of the conversation. She knew it because Andrew elbowed her sharply in the ribs. "No. I…I called because I just found the ring."

"Oh yeah, about that, I wasn't thinking clear when I asked you to come with me."

Clear-ly! You weren't thinking clear-ly! She pondered his answer and suddenly felt a hundred pounds lighter. "Whew! I can't tell you how glad I am you've changed your mind."

"Huh?"

She prattled on. "It's funny how things always seem to work out, don't you think? I've been so nervous to call and break up with you. Turns out I didn't need to be—you were thinking the exact same thing!"

"Break up with me? What? I haven't changed my mind at all," Jared spluttered. "I was only going to say that while I'm in training I wouldn't be able to see you anyway, so you don't need to quit your internship early."

Andrew rolled his eyes and began making a crude gesture as he mouthed "Wanker." "Katie, I love you. I don't want to break up—I want to marry you."

Katie turned a frightening shade of puce and Andrew began massaging her shoulders encouragingly.

She managed to utter a feeble "You want to marry me?"

"Of course I do."

"What about Natalie?"

"What about Natalie? We're just friends."

"Then why did you take her on *our* trip to Thailand?"

"Because you're always telling me I need to be more spontaneous."

"Spontaneous with *me,* dummy. I didn't want you to be spontaneous with other women!"

He gave a short frustrated breath. "Well, how was I supposed to know what you wanted?"

Prodded by Andrew, who had resumed his crude gesturing as a silent description of Jared's mentality, she collected enough pluck to say what she should have said a long time ago. "I guess that's the point, Jared. You don't understand me well enough."

If she would have thought him capable, she would have given him credit for being witty when he asked, "What do you mean?"

"I mean…it's not going to work between us," she answered with an unapologetic note of finality.

And that was that.

Chapter Thirty-One

Katie took a slow, calming, deep breath. Looking at how still and peaceful the water was under the moonlight, it was hard to believe her day—no, her life—was so crazy. She glanced at her watch. She had been walking for nearly an hour, and Andrew would probably be worried about her by now. She hadn't told him where she was going, just that she had to clear her head after her breakup call with Jared.

As she walked down the hallway to her room, she saw Lucas ahead, about to knock on her door.

"Hey," she called softly.

He turned around. "Are you okay? Did you and Andrew have a row?"

Katie shook her head. "I just went for a walk."

"I got you something." He pulled a small object wrapped in pink tissue from behind his back.

"What is it?" Her fingers wiggled of their own volition to hold the package that looked so light it could float away.

"Open it and find out." His grin was mischievous.

Like an eager kid, she snatched the present from him and pulled the delicate paper back. She put her hand against her cheek in an attempt to hide the rising blush.

"Ha! You didn't!" Moving her hand over her mouth, she giggled. "You're a lifesaver! Thank you so much."

She bounced on her tiptoes a few times, then wrapped Lucas into a quick hug. Before he could return the gesture, she broke away to hold out her new bra with both hands.

In half a minute she'd freed herself of the bikini top, fastened her new bra over her tank top, wiggled out of the straps, pulled the tank down to her navel, then quickly pulled it up again over the new bra and replaced the straps—revealing not even one tiny glimpse of breast.

Lucas gawked at her, fascinated.

"So much better." She cupped her boobs admiringly. Not giving a fig for Lucas's gaping reaction, she put the new garment to the test by doing an assortment of shimmies, hops on one leg, then both legs, and jogging in place.

"Whoa! Try not to wear it out before you've had a chance to use it." He put his hands on her shoulders to stop her movement.

She opened her mouth, but instead of a retort came a loud crash from inside the room.

"Crikey, what's Andrew up to?" Lucas's eyes fixed on the closed door.

Then came a muffled *harrumph,* followed by more pounding.

"He's probably just throwing a temper tantrum," Katie speculated before throwing open the door.

She blinked, then blinked again, trying to make sense of why Andrew would be duct-taped and squirming around on the floor. Then she noticed the two men wearing dark ski masks. One was not hard to spot; he was kneeling into Andrew's back and neck, smashing his face against the floor. The other she only noticed when he tackled her to the ground.

Like a wild creature she punched and kicked for all she was worth. She knew by the broken-knuckles sensation that she'd tagged her attacker a few times. But soon her blows only cut through air and she could no longer feel his presence. She paused, realizing her eyes were clenched shut so tight they ached. She pried one eye open just in time to see Lucas throw the man across the room. The foundation seemed to shake as the man hit the wall and slid to the floor.

Lucas stooped down to check on her. "You all right?"

"Yeah, I'm fine." She took his proffered hand and was just about to pull herself up when her resilient little attacker charged across the room and barreled straight into Lucas.

"Lucas!" Katie screamed as the two men went tumbling into the hallway, nearly taking her arm with them. The sensation felt like piranhas gnawing at her shoulder. She gritted her teeth and ran into the hall, intent on clobbering the piss out of that intruder.

"I've got this. Help Andrew!" Lucas huffed between dodging and delivering blows.

Katie cast a glance toward Andrew, whose eyes were nearly bulging out of their sockets, blinking wildly as if they were trying to communicate something his duct-taped mouth could not. With no forethought whatsoever, Katie mustered all her Tae Bo training and flew like Crouching Tiger toward Andrew's attacker, landing him with a stellar fly-kick to the head—if she did say so herself.

Katie's problem with Tae Bo was that she'd never actually kicked anything but air before and was unprepared for the jarring collision. She had to have impacted at least forty vertebrae—she could tell. She cursed that man and his stupid hard head as she came to a sudden halt and fell painfully to the ground.

Lucas jumped off his opponent and ran toward the sound of Katie's screech. He was just about through the door when he was struck from behind with a sharp blow between the legs. He dropped to the ground as his opponent hurdled him. He staggered up just in time to have the door slammed in his face with such force that he was knocked over backwards.

All of a sudden Katie's mouth went dry and her world went dark. She wanted to fight, but her limbs seemed paralyzed. Some heavy breather was manhandling her into something scratchy—a sack of some kind—and she was overwhelmed by the smell of rotten produce.

"Geet up, fool!" a man screamed in a staccato accent Katie had never heard before. She bristled—was he calling her a fool? It wasn't as if she didn't deserve it. She had gotten herself stuffed into a bag, after all. "Forget heem!" the man continued. "We have Duchess."

Duchess? Oh no! Was she being hauled off to Baghdad to become a sex hostage in some high-end prostitution ring? To be tied to a flea-infested camel while some hairy man—or worse, hairy woman—fondled her with dirty, calloused hands? Other, more appalling scenarios played in her mind, each one encouraging the fear gnawing at her stomach to work its way up into her throat.

In response to the ruckus, Charles opened the door next to Katie's room. Lucas bolted through, bounding over their suitcases. "Mum, Dad, they've got Andrew and Katie! Call the police!"

"What are you runnin' on about? Who's got them?" Lottie asked, but Lucas had already run through to the veranda. Charles was right on his heels.

A graphite Volkswagen Golf was parked just up the beach from the back of Katie's room. Lucas and Charles tore onto the sand just in time to see the two shrouded men fighting a kicking laundry bag into the trunk of the vehicle. The muffled squeaks coming from the bag left no doubt Katie was inside.

Lucas ran with lightning speed, charging toward the men, sacking one of them to the ground. Charles made for the other, who dropped the bag of Katie against the bumper and onto the sand.

Katie gasped, hungry for air, but was only treated with a throat full of rancid smelling rag. *Focus! Breathe—through the nose!* Breathing through the nose when gagged and squished inside a hot smelly sack, with the wind knocked out of her, was as good as impossible. She had no choice but to do the next most reasonable thing that came to mind: flail desperately and irrationally for air in a blind panic. As if to show her she was not alone in that dark, scary bag, her special beacon, Bartholomew, plucked up his remains and tweaked at her temple, demonstrating that size doesn't matter by raging just as excruciatingly as he had on that first day.

"Someone check on Andrew!" she heard Lucas order. Katie felt a shiver run down her spine. She'd forgotten about Andrew in all the commotion. Suddenly, it didn't matter that she was suffocating; people she cared about were in danger. Then came the gruesome thud of skin and bones, compounding her fear. Lucas let out an anguished roar. Katie's heart stopped cold.

She exerted double the effort to get some air into her lungs. It seemed the more she struggled, the more critical her circumstances became. When she had no more fight left to give, she succumbed to the exhaustion and accepted that her death by bagging was imminent. She lay motionless in her cocoon, waiting for whatever came next, and let the guilt—or maybe it was just her stinky bag—scratch at her. She wished she could be out there helping, not lying there motionless.

Then she saw the light slowly creeping in from above her. Everything became hushed and still, and she felt calm at last. She squinted into the increasing intensity of the beam and slowly brought focus to the angelic face that appeared before her: Andrew. He was beautiful and iridescent. A second being came into view. He greeted her with the warmest and kindest eyes she had ever beheld. He wore a warm smile that made her want to run for comfort into his arms. His hair against the blinding light was brilliant white, and she had the distinct feeling she was meeting her Savior.

The moment she accepted her destiny, the world seemed to open up around her. She stretched her neck to enjoy the refreshing breeze that tickled her face. Her mouth was liberated from the gag and the gift of speech was once again hers. She looked into the face of her Redeemer, a little chagrined she was meeting him in her pajamas—thank goodness she was finally wearing a bra—then blinked wildly and spoke her first celestial words.

"You're not Jesus."

The man who radiated unconditional love looked upon her with laughing eyes. "Neither are you," Sidney observed.

Andrew rolled his eyes. "So dramatic." He had a cut above his lip and the beginnings of a black eye.

Katie squinted into the blinding beam of the floodlight mounted to the back of the hotel roof, and took in the sight of him. Her smile grew wider than was appropriate for the situation. "Andrew, you're not dead!"

"Course I'm not dead, you nutter."

Katie wiggled out of the laundry bag with Sidney's help. "You were a lot nicer when you were dead," she sassed, but she still couldn't wipe the smile off her face.

Andrew ruffled her hair before pulling her to her feet. "You okay?"

She nodded. It didn't matter that she hurt in more places than she had body parts. She and Andrew were both alive.

As she tried to orient herself to what was happening around her, she realized the situation was anything but under control. Lucas was in full pursuit, chasing one of the attackers but losing ground. Charles was doubled over, breathing hard: "Bloody (*pant, pant*) fast (*pant*) buggers (*pant*) if you (*pant, pant*) ask (*pant*) me (*pant, pant, pant*)." Lottie and Mrs. Albright were holding each other at a safe distance from the scene, and Geoffrey was nowhere to be seen.

"Does anyone understand what's going on?" Katie cried. "And where's Geoffrey?"

Sidney shook his head. "We don't know why this is happening, but not to worry. Geoffrey has gone to alert the authorities." He took Katie by the hand and followed Andrew toward Lottie and Mrs. Albright.

They hadn't taken two steps when Lucas, who had failed to catch one of the attackers and was drudging himself back, suddenly cried, "Katie, looooook oooouuuuuut!"

Before Katie could register the warning, a third man leapt from the backseat of the car. In one swift pounce he tackled Katie, taking Sidney to the ground with her. The man gripped the back of her head and shoved her face into the sand. Slithering his body until he was half lying on top of her, he put his mouth next to her ear and hissed, "Get in the car now or I will start killing people."

She let out a pain-filled cry as she was jerked by her hair onto her feet. She took in the miniature curved-blade machete he placed at the base of her throat, and shut up.

"Stay down!" the man ordered Sidney, striking him with an angry kick to the ribs. As he did, the knife tipped just enough for Katie to catch a glimpse of her aggressor's reflection.

She gasped. "Mensur?"

The hotel clerk froze, and through their clothing she could almost feel his blood turn to ice. He jerked the knife away and pointed it threateningly toward Sidney, keeping the other hand around Katie's throat. Forcefully, he turned Katie's face to his.

"You don't know me!" he growled, holding her off the ground by her throat.

She clawed at his wrist, but his hold would not ease. She didn't know she was crying until she tasted the tears. She hated herself for not being braver. When she had no more wheezes left, he chucked her into the back of the car, where she writhed, taking in big, hungry gasps.

Mensur shouted something in an unfamiliar language and a fourth person appeared from hiding: a timid, cherub-faced boy with olive skin—no more than eight years old. Mensur barked at the boy again. The boy hesitated before crawling into the car with Katie. With shaky little hands, he began duct-taping her hands and feet.

"Noooo! Stop! Please!" Lucas pleaded breathlessly as he ran toward them, tearing up the beach.

Mensur pushed the boy out of the way upon Lucas's approach. Without warning, Mensur sliced the side of Katie's thigh. Neither her thin pajamas nor her flesh protested against the acute sharpness of the blade. Katie wailed—more from shock than pain. A warm well of

307

blood gushed from her wound. She'd never seen so much blood—not in real life, anyway.

"Get back!" Mensur waved his knife at Lucas, flinging drops of Katie's blood across the sand.

Lucas dropped to his knees. With his head bowed, he wheezed, "Please, won't you take me instead?"

Sidney ran up alongside them. "Take me," he begged. "I'm quite wealthy if it's money you want."

Katie choked as if she were gagged all over again. More tears streamed from her eyes. But these weren't cowardly tears.

Mensur took an astonished step back. "No! It is the Duchess we want!"

Lucas and Sidney exchanged confused glances.

"Duchess? You mean Katie? She can't be—she's American! Listen to her accent," Lucas ventured.

Katie mouth dropped open. If she weren't bleeding to death, she might have laughed out loud at the notion.

Lucas's words went ignored.

The boy, who had moved to sopping Katie's blood with old blankets, suddenly grabbed a paper from the backseat and dashed off to meet up with one of the original attackers, who was returning to the scene, huffing and puffing. Mensur and the other attacker shouted a heated discussion in their own language. The other attacker thrust the paper in Mensur's face and stabbed his finger into Lucas's society page photo.

Mensur flung the paper to the ground and threw up his hands. "Okay, you can come." He jabbed his knife toward Lucas. "Janek thinks you could be useful."

"Thank you." Lucas stood and took a tentative step toward Katie.

Mensur swiped the knife through the air, inches from Lucas's face. "Tie him up!"

"Please," Lucas entreated the other man, Janek, and nodded toward Katie. "She needs help—let me have my hands."

Janek inched in Katie's direction and peered into the vehicle. His shoulders lurched and his fists clenched until his knuckles turned completely white. He gaped at the ceaseless flow of Katie's blood and her wan complexion. His pupils grew large and his arm flew up, backhanding Mensur across the cheek.

Janek turned back to Lucas. "Okay, but we don't want no trouble. You give promise for yourself not making trouble, no one get hurt." He gestured first to Katie, then Sidney, before extending his motion down the beach toward his assembled family.

Lucas nodded. "I give you my word." He ducked into the vehicle and Mensur slammed the tailgate shut, practically smashing Lucas on top of Katie.

"Why did you do that?" she demanded. "You have to get out of here!"

"Shhhh," he consoled, tracing his finger along her cheek, repositioning himself out of a pool of blood. The side doors flew open as the two men and the young boy took their places and the engine roared to life.

A nauseating moment of panic flashed through her, and she was afraid she was going to be sick. "Get out of here, Lucas!" she whispered fiercely. She pushed at him, hoping maybe she could send him through the rear window.

He trapped her flailing wrists in one of his hands. "I won't leave, so just lie still."

She shot up. "I mean it, Lucas! Get out of here before you get yourself killed!"

He pressed a wadded blanket against her wound. She yowled.

"What's the point?" he said. "As soon as Uncle Avery finds out what's happened to you, I'll be dead anyway."

"Lucas, you can't leave your family—they'll be worried sick about you."

"They'll be fine." He took one last look at the crowd of loved ones growing smaller with the increasing distance. "I'm not leaving you."

"You stubborn ass!"

He chuckled.

His untimely amusement set her already-frazzled nerves on edge. "Don't be stupid, risk your life, *and* break your family's hearts for the chance to be a hero!"

He leaned unnervingly close to her face. "I'm not. I'm going to be stupid, risk my life *and* break my family's hearts for the chance to be with you. But first I have to save you."

Chapter Thirty-Two

The tension between Mensur and Janek was palpable as the Golf wove through a maze of cobblestone streets. The young boy kneeled against the backseat and peered over the headrest, eyes glued on Katie and Lucas. Lucas held a hand against Katie's forehead while applying pressure to her wound with a clumsy wad of blankets. She wanted to wail, but the silence was so taut she didn't dare disturb it.

Every muscle ached against the urge to bolt upright, but the force of his hand kept her firmly pinned. She ground her teeth, balled her fists, and hissed. Maybe from pain, maybe from anger—she didn't know and she didn't care. She just knew that being pissed off made her less afraid. Clenching her eyes against the pain Lucas was inflicting upon her, she focused on building her rage.

A hovering presence broke her concentration. Her eyes shot open just as the boy reached over the seat and collected one of her tears on his dirty little finger. She locked eyes with the boy in a moment of mutual assessment. With his big dark eyes, he reminded her of a lost fawn. He dipped his head as scarlet began to creep into his chubby cheeks. She tried to give him a compassionate smile, but only managed to choke on a sob.

He leaned further over the seat and did what he'd seen Lucas do a hundred times already: He pushed the hair away from her face and stroked her cheek with his hot little hand. This time, she couldn't have stopped her smile even if she'd wanted to.

He melted into an adorable dimpled grin. Putting his lips against her ear, he whispered, "You are movie star?"

Her low chuckle hung in the air, at odds with the heavy atmosphere. "No, I'm not." She wanted to laugh, but his face was so serious. "What would make you think that?"

He puffed out his chest and gave her a toothy smile. "Your eyes are shiny—like green kryptonite."

For the first time, Lucas took his eyes off Katie. He grinned at the boy, "You know, I've never noticed that before. You're absolutely right."

The boy beamed, then was flung into the passenger side door as the car screamed around a corner and came to a screeching halt, depositing him on the floor between the seats. After a short bout of foreign dialect, the two front doors opened in unison. Katie's heart froze mid-beat as she heard the footsteps that brought the men to the back of the vehicle. Mensur threw open the tailgate and faltered, nearly fainting at the sight of the blood-soaked blankets and hostages.

"She needs a doctor," Lucas pleaded to Janek, a short, sturdy man in his late forties. Janek's head exploded with a thick nap of fat black and grey curls, and Katie couldn't help but notice the family of tiny buttery-looking nuggets lurking inside his ears.

He gave Lucas a noncommittal nod and produced a thick roll of duct tape.

Already chafing around the binds at her hands and feet, Katie flinched, provoking an angered reaction from Lucas.

"Remember promise," Janek warned. "We no want trouble. You help me, I help Duchess."

After a moment's contemplation, Lucas dropped his hands and submitted to being bound and taped.

"Stop! Please…" Katie raised herself up. "You don't understand! I'm American. I'm not a duchess! Don't—"

With a nasty smirk, Mensur brought the roll of tape around her entire head as he taped her mouth, then gave her the same treatment around the eyes. The ominous screeching of crisp, new tape being ripped from its roll thundered around her, making it almost impossible to hear Lucas's rising protests against her maltreatment. Eventually, she was shoved to the back of the vehicle, flinching as the tailgate slammed shut, and the Volkswagen Golf tore off down the rutted road.

***

Lady Waverly stared disinterestedly out the window into the gardens, barely hearing the conversation taking place among her brunch guests, the wives of some of the men in attendance at Lord Waverly's committee meeting.

"Nonsense Esther, Samantha Cameron is a wonderful and quite respectable figurehead."

"Honestly, if Sam-Cam is going to compete with Michelle Obama, she really needs to—" Esther Denby interrupted herself as she heard her cell phone ring. "Pardon me a moment, ladies. I must take this call." She dipped into her intricately beaded, limited-edition Fendi baguette and pulled out her bedazzled Christian Dior phone. "It's my daughter, Olivia. She's just gone to meet her fiancée in Croatia."

Lady Waverly, having been informed by Lucas of Katie's exodus to Croatia, could not imagine a worse plight for her new friend than Olivia's presence. She strained to hear Esther's voice over the clackety-clack-clack of her high heels as the woman glided to the other end of the room.

"He's been taken hostage! Lucas has been kidnapped!" Esther cried as she returned to the group, nearly toppling over as her pencil skirt refused to accommodate her long strides. "Oh dear God, this can't be happening! I'm sure they must have been after my darling Olivia—who survived the danger intact, thank the Lord."

Lady Waverly's hand flew to her mouth as the other women were set about clucking like chickens.

"Gordon! I must tell Gordon!" Esther fanned herself with both hands, as she tried to squint out a few tears.

"Of course, Esther, I'll go find him." Lady Waverly was already making the move to the meeting room.

"Have you heard from Katie?" Lord Waverly asked when his wife spoke the news into his ear.

Lady Waverly answered with a discreet shake of the head.

"You must try to contact her and find out what the devil has happened. I'll apprise Gordon of the situation."

Lady Waverly stole into her private library. Unable to make her trembling fingers work fast enough, she flipped through the pages of her address book. She punched in the numbers, praying intently Katie would answer.

***

After an entire night of questioning, the only vital clues they held were Mensur, whose identity could not be found in any background search, and the torn newspaper article retrieved from the beach. No one could say how long Lucas's family and a flummoxed, underequipped police team stared glossy-eyed around the room in a state of disbelief, muttering only half-coherent sentences.

"Where in Imelda Marcos' shoe cupboard is that noise coming from?" Lottie demanded grumpily.

Sidney perked up and Andrew flung himself toward Katie's bags as they both recognized the upbeat tune of her ringtone. They all beheld the ringing phone with apprehension, looking to their assigned investigator for instruction. He signaled for Lottie to answer the call.

***

The commotion downstairs alerted Lady Waverly that all the men and women were in knowledge of the situation and had assembled. She pressed her hand over her free ear to better hear, horrorstruck, Lottie's account of the kidnapping.

"Thank you for confiding in me, Lottie," Lady Waverly said. "Please allow Lord Waverly to represent your family to the American and British governments. You concentrate on remaining strong for your son and Katie. God bless you all. Please keep me informed— we'll be in touch soon."

Her legs wobbled, but she willed them to carry her down the grand staircase. The room fell silent as the ashen Lady Waverly made her return.

"Well?" urged her husband, racing up beside her to take hold of her trembling hand. "Do you have any news?"

"It was Katie they wanted." She spoke barely above a whisper.

"What! A common American girl?" Esther exploded. "Not my Olivia? There must be some mistake."

Lady Waverly inhaled a deep, calming breath, trying to refrain from slamming a dainty fist into Esther's brand-new nose.

"I'm sure this crime wasn't committed as an affront to Olivia," Lord Waverly declared.

315

"As I was saying," Lady Waverly continued, "the attack went awry and one of the men threatened Katie with a machete." Her throat constricted and she squeezed her husband's hand for support. "She has been injured."

A low hum of murmurs rippled across the room.

Lady Waverly added, "Lucas negotiated with the terrorists to be allowed to accompany her."

"What a noble act of chivalry!" one lady exclaimed.

"Noble, my foot!" Esther nearly shouted. "What about my darling daughter? He's abandoned my precious baby! She's over there alone, unprotected against those terrorists—those murderers! All for the sake of that American piece of trash!"

Lady Waverly held up her hands, commanding silence. "Esther, it's certainly not my place to tell you this, but as I know it will be a great comfort to you in this time of distress, I will share what I know. As I understand it, Lucas and Olivia are no longer engaged. I heard it was broken off days ago—before Lucas left for Croatia."

If Olivia had already shared this news of her breakup with her mother, Esther's face didn't show it.

"Lucas and Katie were taken between twelve-thirty and one in the morning," Lady Waverly continued. "Olivia surprised everyone with her arrival just a few hours ago. You have nothing to trouble yourself over. She was never mistreated, never in danger. She is now safely surrounded by quite a number of Lucas's family."

Esther choked out a reluctant thank you, and Lady Waverly's kind owl eyes fluttered sweetly in response.

"Now that you have been put at ease…" Lady Waverly dropped the phony civility. "You have been very ungracious regarding our Katie. She is a personal friend of mine. Those of you who met her at the ball the other evening can attest that she deserves of all the prayers, concern, and help we can offer."

Tears pricked at her eyes. Her concerned plea won a round of refined applause from nearly the entire room. Those who had not attended the ball had certainly heard about it, and the few who had not heard had such deference for Lady Waverly as to honor her wishes without question.

"Have the terrorists made any demands?" a gentleman from the back of the crowd inquired.

"Are there any speculations as to why this happened?" the Unsinkable Molly Brown lady asked. "Is it about the Chatworth diamonds?"

"Very little is known at this time," Lady Waverly explained. "We do know the terrorists are operating under the misunderstanding that she is of ranking British nobility."

A few murmurs across the room were interrupted by Esther's haughty snort.

Lady Waverly shot her an icy glare. "They continue to call her 'Duchess,' though Lucas tried explaining to them she is an American."

"But why her?" someone asked.

"I'm sure it must be for the diamonds," Unsinkable Molly Brown persisted.

"This just came by special delivery," Lord Waverly interrupted, returning from having been summoned away by one of the staff. "I've already phoned Alistair Drummond of Scotland Yard."

Escorting his wife to the settee as if she were an invalid, he seated himself by her side and spread the contents of the parcel onto the marble table in front of her.

"Ladies and gentlemen," he announced as his wife collapsed onto his shoulder. "The kidnapping has now become a matter of Parliamentary concern. We must insist on your cooperation in keeping this matter confidential."

A beautifully scripted note accompanied the article from the society pages, along with two Polaroid photos of Katie and Lucas, duct tape over their eyes and mouths, the bruising on Lucas's face seeping far beyond the edges of the tape. Both were smeared with frightening amounts of blood.

While the photos made their way around the room, Lord Waverly cleared his throat and began to read:

This is not an act of terrorism. This is an act of desperation. We know you are not unaware of our current state of oppression. Seeing these photos of your friends, you can now understand the torture we feel every day because we anguish over the fate and health and safety of our family and friends and countrymen. You can no longer pretend that our troubles do not exist. Now, we all share the same sadness. When your hearts hurt over your Duchess and her companion, think of the children of Bosnia and how they must at all times breathe this same pain. Please do not ignore the needs of our people.

The ladies dabbed at their eyes and the gentlemen hung their heads, but no one spoke.

Chapter Thirty-Three

"What have you done? Is this who you think we've become?"

The shouting match ensued as Katie was manhandled from the car. Through the winded, huffy breathing of her transporter, she strained to place the angry man's voice. Despite the now-familiar unfamiliar dialect, she had no trouble recognizing the second voice as Janek's.

"English please!" the first voice snapped. "We cannot risk for anybody to understand what you've done!"

"Please, brother, I need your help," Janek begged with desperation, shedding his role as militant terrorist.

"No! I will have no part in this! Take them away from here! I have nothing to do with you!"

"The girl! What I do with girl? She's dying!" Janek howled.

Dying? Is that true? Katie's pain was excruciating, unlike anything she'd ever experienced, but she hadn't yet considered dying as a real possibility. Would they kill Lucas once she was dead? She could feel the slow creep of panic taking root in her veins. She ached to press her hand against her chest to steady the crushing sensation.

The squeal of a stubborn door brought Katie out of her head and back into the moment. She heard her captor's footsteps scrape across a stone floor. The temperature dropped a few degrees and she was enveloped by stale air that held the strong scents of farm and dirt. She slid her tongue against the roof of her mouth, trying to scrape off the strong taste of her environment. She sensed they were in a long-forgotten barn or shed. Whoever was holding her—Mensur, she guessed from his bony frame—shifted, and she felt a blaze of terror as her body went into freefall. She hit the dank stone floor shoulder first, head second. The cracking sound reverberated in her head, momentarily stalling the pain. Something inside her snapped—and not just physically. She fought to right herself, and despite the gag strapped over her mouth, she managed to twist her lips around a series of expletives. "Mummm mmmiidd munnn mm mmiith!" she swore with every fiber of her being. She was rewarded by the slam of the creaking door and the sound of footsteps retreating from the other side.

"Mammee mm mmann mmuuu?" She heard Lucas's muffled call and the scuffling of him scooting toward her. Eventually he landed his back against hers. The pads of his restricted fingers gently danced against hers in greeting. She could not have been more grateful to feel his touch. A zing of exhilaration punched through her. She wiggled her fingers in response, contemplating how *not* close to death she felt.

As she toyed with Lucas's hands, her brain worked feverishly to remain self-possessed—and to find a way out of this…this…nightmare. She would have to remember to find a better word that encompassed the horrors of being kidnapped, beaten, and terrorized. Just then, the smoothness of the duct tape binding Lucas's wrists caught her attention—or the tiny ridge that interrupted the smoothness. She rubbed her thumb across the seam a couple of times before trying to lift the edge with her fingernail. It was a slow process, but spurred by her fervent desire to escape, and the need to concentrate on anything other than the countless worst-case scenarios she was conjuring in her mind, she was eventually able to lift the edge enough that her fingers could begin pulling at the tape in short increments.

Now free, Lucas sprung into quick action. He pulled the tape from his mouth, then his eyes, which adjusted painfully to the sunlight streaming through the dirty windows. Removing the tape from Katie's mouth proved more difficult. The adhesive had captured at least a zillion strands of hair. She reminded herself not to whine—he was doing his best not to rip her hair from her skull. When he eventually rid her of the mouth gag, he smoothed his thumb over her chapped lips and moved on to deal with the tape over her eyes, working as gingerly and patiently as his clumsy man-fingers would allow.

The door creaked and parted a few inches from its jamb. Before Lucas could gain a defensive position, the young boy ran in and flung himself into Katie's lap, placing his hot little hands on each of her cheeks. Katie's dormant nurturing instincts sprung to life, causing her arms to fly up and snuggle the boy's little body against hers.

"Is lady dying?" the boy whispered.

"I'll be okay," Katie reassured, holding him. "Just as soon as I'm able to see."

The boy hesitated a moment, then wordlessly stood over her and with extreme gentleness began removing the tape from her head as Lucas moved to check the makeshift compress on her leg.

Lucas tousled the boy's hair. "What's your name, little man?"

The boy practically melted into a blushing heap of dimples, then snapped his head toward the door in alarm. There were voices just outside.

"Please, cousin. Let us stay one night—then we go."

Leaving the tape dangling from Katie's eyes—only one critical piece left across her face preventing her from sight—the boy bolted into a dark corner of the musty old shed and hid.

"No, Mensur!" a voice boomed in response. "You will leave immediately."

322

"Then, Stanislaus, we have no choice but kill them," Mensur threatened.

The wooden structure groaned and rocked as a body slammed into the wall.

"Do not threaten me!" Stanislaus yelled. "We have troubles enough! I will not keep your hostages! I will kill you myself before I let you bring danger and ruin upon what is left of this family!"

The body fell to the ground with a loud thud.

"I will do what I can for the woman," Stanislaus continued. "Then you must leave and never return to this house!"

The door of the shed burst open. Like a starving dog protecting a fat steak, Lucas hovered in front of Katie. The round-bellied Stanislaus dropped the old-fashioned medicine satchel he was carrying and threw up his hands in a proclamation of peace.

Janek appeared in the doorway, stopped short with a girlish yelp, and hid behind the broad shoulders of his brother, Stanislaus. "I'm not understanding! They have made themselves free!" He scattered a few projectile flakes of crusty ear-cereal as he vigorously shook his head.

Upon hearing this, Mensur scuffled through the door, skinny arms raised in pugilistic posture, frightening the chubby-cheeked boy out of hiding and into a flat-out run straight back to Katie's unsuspecting arms.

"Marko!" Janek shouted.

"Marko! Come here to me immediately!" Mensur seethed, as Katie, eyes still covered and unsure who was protecting whom, held the boy tightly. Mensur's slow, fiendish drawl caused her goose-pimpled skin to try to crawl up the wall. The boy scrunched into a tiny ball and burrowed into her embrace.

Holding up a silencing hand to Mensur, Stanislaus spoke gently to Lucas. "Please, I don't want trouble. I want only to help your Duchess."

Katie cocked her head, trying to place why his voice seemed so familiar.

Lucas exhaled a low growl and squeezed his skull in frustration. "Please," he said to Stanislaus, cutting the air with his tensely clawed hands. "She is not a duchess! For the hundredth time, I'm telling you all she is a bloody damned American."

As if he could discern her nationality at a glance and put this issue to bed, Stanislaus peered around Lucas to catch a glimpse of the woman in question. He blinked his eyes, then dove in for another look.

"May I?" Stanislaus asked Lucas, gesturing toward Katie.

Lucas assented by taking one small step to the side, keeping his narrowed eyes on Mensur and Janek.

Stooping over Katie, Stanislaus gently pulled back the veil of her hair and exclaimed a shocked Slavic expletive. A genuinely pleased smile flaunted his abnormally bleached bright teeth.

"Hallo Katie, pretty lady!"

Katie jerked her blind eyes toward the sound of the familiar greeting. *Stanley Speedo?*

"Stanley? Is that you?!?"

She released Marko with one hand and yanked without hesitation at the remaining tape on her face. "Oww-eee! Son of a bi— !" Immediately conscious of the youth in her lap, she added, "bi— biscuit!"

Squinting against the prickling pain and the blazing sunlight like an unearthed mole, she searched for confirmation that the man's face matched his old neighborly greeting. A wave of calm blanketed her as she took in the sight of his clothed figure, sans Speedo.

"Stanley, it really is you!" Katie cried. A feeble smile stole from her lips to her still-smarting eyes as she admired Stanley's knee-length khaki shorts and respectable, though faded, vertical striped button-up. He took hold of her blood-encrusted hand.

Lucas, Janek, and Mensur stood gaping, wide-eyed, at the friendly reunion. Their stunned expressions in this improbable situation caused Katie to emit one of her untimely giggles.

"This is nothing to laugh about—this could be serious," Stanley admonished, already unwrapping the blood-soaked blankets wrapping her thigh.

Swooping to his side, Lucas knelt down and assisted Stanley in removing the knot of blankets. Katie's giggles were quickly halted by shoots of pain as the men poked about her leg.

"Bring me my bag," Stanley ordered Mensur as he tore open the leg of Katie's pajamas.

Katie peered into the satchel as Stanley extracted a sterile water bottle and puffy white gauze strips.

"Stanley, are you a doctor?" she asked, stunned by this revelation about her neighbor.

"Was." His face turned melancholy. "Gave it up after the wars—I could not bear to see any more brutality." He dabbed at the spurting slice in her flesh. "This was no accident." The statement was more of a question as he looked to Lucas for affirmation.

One deliberate shake of the head was the only answer needed to break Stanley's pretense of composure.

"I'll be back." Handing Lucas a gauze compress, Stanley stalked away, shuttling Mensur and Janek out the door with him. The air hung heavy with the threat of Stanley's livid tirade. Marko scurried back into hiding.

"Do I still have eyebrows?" Katie rubbed a knuckle along where her eyebrows should be.

Lucas, massaging the back of his neck with one hand and dabbing at her leg with the other, looked at her as if she'd grown horns, and shook his head. "What? Of course you still have eyebrows. Are you all right?"

"I'm fine…except I think I just tore my eyebrows off. You didn't even look—seriously, do I have any eyebrows left?"

Setting the gauze on her leg and wiping his hands on his blood-stained man-pris, he scooted toward her. Gazing into her face, he seemed to be searching for something more than just eyebrows. Unsuccessfully, she tried looking anywhere other than into his smoldering eyes—and the bruised skin and bloody gashes surrounding them.

"Thanks for coming along to protect me," she blurted.

"My pleasure." He made an exaggerated mockery of trying to find her eyebrows. "Good news," he finally announced. "It looks like the little buggers are still there."

"Are you sure?"

"Of course I'm sure. I'm staring right at them. Don't worry, they're lovely." He caressed his fingers tenderly across the war paint of dried blood traversing her cheek. "How do you know that man, Stanley?"

"He's my old neighbor from the States. I used to live in the condo below his." Her gaze focused on the dusty ground. "Lucas, you can still get out of this. You should go. Stanley won't let Mensur or Ernie Earwax hurt me."

"Ernie Earwax?"

She shrugged. "Come on, it's not like you couldn't have noticed."

He chuckled. "Rabbit, I'm not going to leave you. I…" He hesitated over his next words, then swallowed them down. "I just won't."

"Some lucky rabbit I turned out to be. I've had nothing but horrible luck since I left Colorado."

"That's not true! Who else could get grabbed by terrorists and find themselves held up in their former neighbor's shed?"

Basking in the encouraging smile that brightened his whole face, she let herself be semi-consoled.

***

"God help me, Mensur, I wish I could run that knife right through you! That girl has done nothing, not even committed the crime of being nobility!"

Mensur sniffed in disbelief. "I read the article. I heard them call her 'Duchess.'"

In a stampede of Slavic swear words, Stanley tackled Mensur to the ground like a bull pouncing on a chipmunk.

"Has our family not suffered enough? Has our country not suffered enough?" Bestowing Mensur with a spittle shower as he roared, the purple-faced Stanley persisted. "When will you learn to think with your head and not your black heart? Listen to the girl—does she sound like her British companion? No, she does not. Because she is American!"

"My grandparents and my father will have died in vain if I do nothing to stop our repression," Mensur asserted.

Stanley drooped his head as if defeated. "No, they will have died in vain if we cannot find a peaceful resolution. Are you too young to remember the brutality and terror of the past?" He stepped off of the cowering weasel and bent over, pressing a hand against his racing heart.

Mensur lifted his chin in defiance. "The sacrifice of two of their countrymen will force the British government to help bring peace and equality to this country."

Filling his barrel chest to maximum capacity, Stanley exploded. "You stupid, stubborn boy! The sacrifice of two innocent people will make us villains! Bloodshed is not the answer!"

"I will take my hostages and leave this house," Mensur declared, unmoved.

"I know that girl—she is my friend. My friend from America. Why will you not understand that? You will not cause her any more harm." Stanislaus pulled back his thick shoulders, in full force as the alpha male.

Spinning his back to his elder foe, Mensur faced his accomplice. "Janek, let's go!"

Janek shifted uncomfortably, not meeting Mensur's eyes.

"Janek!" Mensur ordered.

"Mensur…I…" Janek sputtered, glancing from Mensur to Stanley. "I cannot finish." He hung his head. "I am not too young for to remember."

Mensur gave a harsh, throaty cough and spit a chunk of green-tinged mucus on Janek's shoes. Sprinting toward the Golf, he retrieved his bloody knife and a pocket-sized pistol and stole toward the shed.

Chapter Thirty-Four

Mensur sprinted toward the shed, spite and anarchy fueling his purpose. The two stocky brothers chased after him, but could not compete with his lanky strides. Huffing like locomotives, they failed the chase midway through the field.

"Lady! Run!" Janek cupped his hands around his mouth and yelled the warning at the top volume.

"She can't run, you numbskull!" Stanley said.

Somehow the brothers found the strength to muscle through the sensations of collapsing lungs and bursting spleens and pick up their pace, forcing their squat legs to work double time.

Screaming like an angry chimp, Mensur flung open the shed door. He cut wildly through the air with his dagger, simultaneously firing off three arbitrary rounds in all directions with his pistol. After several seconds of kamikaze attack mode, he paused.

The shed was empty.

**

Taking cover behind a tall wall of hay bales, Lucas palmed the tops of Katie's and Marko's heads and shoved them face down into the tall pasture grass, blanketing them with his body as the shots were fired.

"Shhh, lie still," he commanded.

Katie marveled that Lucas was able to keep a steady voice; it was all she could do to keep her bones from shaking out of her skin. She could tell by the rough kisses he kept planting on her forehead that he wasn't completely unfazed. When he had turned from the dirty window in the shed and scooped her and Marko off the floor, she'd been frightened by the fierceness behind his eyes and his tightly clamped jaw. He'd taken off so swiftly across the field she hadn't dared ask any questions. How had he known they were still in danger? She realized she'd probably have been shot dead by now if Lucas hadn't argued his way into the back of Mensur's trunk at the hotel. The thought turned her insides cold.

"Marko!" Janek shrieked, still in running full pursuit toward the gunfire. Driven by rage, Mensur burst from the shed, leveled the pistol at Janek and fired. His cousin's upper body reeled backward, but Janek did not break his pace.

"Listen to me," Lucas commanded Katie. "Stay here, stay low, and try your best to keep Marko from hearing anything."

She stared at him doe-eyed, scared out of her wits.

"Can you do that?" He grabbed her wrists and kissed each bloody palm before covering her mouth with a quick kiss that left her feeling needy for him.

She nodded, but she knew it wasn't convincing. He gave her an encouraging smile, then positioned her hands over Marko's ears. Ruffling the boy's hair, Lucas dashed off from behind the safety of their shelter.

Katie stared after him for a few moments, paralyzed. Panic began nipping at her. Before the fear could seize her mind, she forced herself to do as she was told. Ignoring the spasming pain and spurting blood, she drew her legs underneath her, curling into the fetal position around Marko and singing into his ear the only song that came to mind: "Barbie Girl."

***

Janek, shrieking Marko's name, was just steps away from Mensur. Once again Mensur took aim at the thundering rhinoceros charging toward him. From behind the shed, Lucas picked up a baseball-size stone and hurled it with all his might and precision right into the back of Mensur's head.

Staggering sideways off balance, Mensur whirled around and fired the bullet meant for Janek.

***

Her voice quavering as she sang, Katie tried to sound psyched about Barbie going partying. Keeping Marko from dwelling on the debilitating sounds of infuriated shouts, wails of agony, and gunfire had to be her priority. Otherwise, she'd go mad trying to envision what was going on. Hovering over little Marko's shaking body, she ignored the thick haze floating through her brain and the blood that was now pulsing from her flexed leg. She cringed at the haunting sound of bodies colliding and bones cracking, and tried to concentrate on Barbie's fantastic plastic life. Another gunshot. Someone yowled, then a crisp silence—a spooky, unnerving calm.

The grass rustled with the sound of approaching footsteps. Trying to keep her whirling head steady, she squinched her eyes shut and hovered even tighter over Marko. When she looked up, Lucas was standing above them holding his side. A blood splotch, growing in diameter around his hand, stained his shirt.

Terror haunted his expression. His image zoomed in and out of her focus, his mouth wagged and his face contorted as if he were screaming, but she heard only muffled snippets of sound. She followed his horror-struck expression to the dense watermelon-size puddle of blood pooling under her leg. The thick clouds inside her head swarmed solid black. He looped his arm around her waist. She felt the blood hot and sticky from his hands smear across her neck and cheeks as he cradled her up into his arms. The wound at his side took root in the threads of her clothes and seeped her pajamas red up the entire length of her body.

***

The recipient of Lucas's stone throw and Janek's NFL-grade tackle, Mensur had landed on the wrong end of his machete. The silvery tip of the blade penetrated clean through his body just above the hip. Lying on his side, his cheek turned into the cool grass, a triumphant sneer sewed up his face as he watched a silver Peugeot creep unnoticed out of the drive and disappear down the country road.

Chapter Thirty-Five

"What I'd like to know is which one of our guests leaked this information!" Lord Waverly stormed the aisle of his private jet, strewing several stacks of newspapers that were neatly piled on the plush leather bench seat. "Every media outlet from here to America is broadcasting the details of the abduction—scant though they may be."

Lady Waverly wrung her hands, her dull, sunken eyes making her frail pallor look worse.

"I don't know how I'll bear their faces—that poor worried family. If only we didn't have the worst kind of news to deliver to them." She sobbed into her intricately embroidered handkerchief.

"We're doing everything we can, dear. You can at least assure them of that." He fixed his eyes on the handpicked forensics and investigative team sitting somberly in the back of the jet, pretending to blend into the swanky furniture, then turned back to his wife. "Try to get some rest. It won't be long till we're on the ground and I worry that this day will be overly taxing for you."

He took a seat next to her. Pulling her into his embrace, he held her for the remainder of the flight.

The cavalcade of the Waverlys' vehicles pulled in front of the Croatian hotel. A throng of media was already posted outside, vying for the newest information from the investigation taking place within. As the new investigative team ran in, Sidney ran out, picking his way through a double line of media and policemen.

"How do you do? Lovely to meet you again…Sidney Ainsworth." He greeted the Waverlys through the partially opened tinted window.

"Of course, Sidney, we couldn't forget you," said Lady Waverly. The door unlatched for him and he slid onto the spacious rear seat. "How are you all managing?" she inquired.

"Not well, I'm afraid," he admitted. "Charlotte has holed herself up in her room and has done nothing but cry for two days." His eyes glossed over. "It's like losing two children. Though we've not had Katie long, she's as much our family as anyone."

Pressing her hand firmly into his, Lady Waverly croaked, "I understand. We'll do what we can to get them back." Her voice faltered and a tear streamed down her pale cheek. "I cannot manage the cameras today. Please make my apologies to the family for our not coming in. I…" She broke off, losing her thin veil of composure.

"We have taken the liberty of renting a cottage for the family—we felt you would all be more comfortable there," Lord Waverly spoke in his wife's stead. "Has Katie's family been contacted?"

"There was a number saved under 'Mom' in her mobile. When we phoned, it went straight to voicemail for a chap named Christopher. I left a message, remembering Katie had mentioned a friend named Christopher—I hope he's one and the same. Lottie's brother, Avery, who lives in the States, has been informed. He knows how to get in touch with Katie's friends and will try to notify her family through that channel," Sidney informed like a well-trained officer.

"Well done," Lord Waverly commended. "The drivers have been instructed to bring you all to your new lodgings. We'll call in about an hour to discuss the particulars of the investigation."

Sidney shook hands with Lord Waverly and slid from the extended vehicle. After waving the fine couple goodbye, he instructed the remaining drivers to wait ten minutes, then drive around to the back of the hotel, where he'd have everyone waiting outside on their verandas—away from the prying eyes of the majority of media hounds.

***

"Shoot me down and bugger me ear! This is what they call a *cottage*?" Lottie had put her grieving aside to marvel at the beachfront mansion the Waverlys had procured for them. Showing her first signs of pluck since the incident, she skipped across the marble floor and up the expansive staircase that was situated in the center of the contemporary front room. With the excitement of a small child, she set about exploring their new accommodations. The others followed suit, scattering to lay claim to one of the nine oceanfront bedrooms.

"You see," Lottie proclaimed when they'd all gathered in the parlor with the Waverlys, "this is how I insist we holiday from here on out." She nestled into the cushions of the plump sofa and winked a red, puffy eye at Lady Waverly.

"Whatever you say, dear," Charles placated, looking pleased by the faint etch of a smile on his wife's face.

In an effort to further lift her spirits, Sidney ribbed, "From here on out she'll be swaning about like she's bloody Cleopatra."

"Too late—someone's already beat her to it," Mrs. Albright grumbled, looking up from her teacup as Olivia burst through the entrance.

"Well, *this* is more like it," she exclaimed as Andrew came tottering in behind her, wheeling her stack of Louis Vuitton luggage.

The whole group stared at her. Lord Waverly nearly choked on his tea.

"Now that we're all assembled," Lord Waverly summoned the practiced air he used to administrate difficult meetings, "we have again heard from the Bosnian rebels." His voice was so solemn it was obvious the news wasn't good.

Lottie clenched Charles' hand, Andrew dropped his head into his palms, and Mrs. Albright snuggled into Geoffrey, who rubbed her back consolingly. Olivia, ignorant of Lady Waverly's murderous glare, inspected her manicure and mumbled something about when she would get to be on television.

"No demands have been made," Lord Waverly continued, "and we fear the rebels have no intention of returning Lucas and Katie." Reaching into the inside breast pocket of his blazer, he pulled out a photo wrapped by a single sheet of paper, which read simply: *This is Bosnia.*

He hesitated before handing the photograph over to Charles. It was a *Time* magazine cover-type image of Lucas, bruised and bloody, carrying a blood-caked corpse that hung limply over his arms. Sheets of blood-soaked caramel hair cascaded from the head that lolled lifeless toward the ground, one arm dangling slack out in front.

The room went cold as the self-possessed man choked on a sob and crumbled. The photograph made its way down the line, each person experiencing an equally wretched reaction. Lottie fell half-unconscious into the consoling arms of the weeping Lady Waverly. Andrew's lips quivered, sniveling back tears as he embraced the sobbing Sidney. Geoffrey fled the room and shouted profanities from the balcony to the heavens.

"Oh vile!" Olivia gasped, staring at the photo. "Look how bloody he is! That is sooo disgusting. Is that a dead person?"

337

The air hummed with the peculiar sound of every exhausted nerve in the room snapping.

Lord Waverly cleared his throat several times, trying to communicate to Olivia her lack of decorum. "That's Katie," he answered.

Her perky little nose twitched at the mention of Katie's name and her thin lips set into a hard line. "Is she dead?" She posed the question no one dare ask.

"We can't be sure." Lord Waverly hedged.

Olivia shuddered. Holding an internal debate out loud, she mused, "She looks dead. I don't know if I can be with someone who has handled a dead person. They're soaked in each other's blood!"

It was the benign Mrs. Albright who finally had enough.

"Lucky for you he's chucked you to the curb then."

Olivia's perfectly plucked eyebrows shot up. Her face contorted with rage and her mouth opened, then shut, then opened again. Her words were restricted to something between a croak and a squeak.

"Olivia dear," Lady Waverly hastened to quell the situation. "This is a very difficult time for the family. I think it's best we put you in a car to the airport and send you home. I know your mother is dreadfully worried."

Olivia gave a sharp, angry laugh. "The *family*—indeed!" Gesturing to Mrs. Albright, she continued, "*She's* here and she's nothing but a servant!" She turned to the housekeeper. "When Lucas and I patch things up—and we *will* patch things up—I'm going to have you sacked!"

338

Sidney rose to his feet. "Penny is as much a part of Lucas's family as anyone. She's no more a servant than I am your father—thank God for that. You'll not fare very well at a reconciliation if you continue to look down your nose at everyone he loves."

"Oh for God's sake, Sidney." Lottie gathered her shredded wits. "Damn your bloody politeness!"

She confronted Olivia with all the ferocity of a mama bear. "No more!" she roared, the rough, menacing sound out of character for her tiny frame. "No more will I let you ridicule and scorn my family. For three years I've stayed silent, for my son's sake. No more! Bloody English propriety be damned! Get your delusions of superiority and your skinny arse out of my sight! And the next time you want to turn your plastic nose up at someone—just remember, it could be their vote that keeps you draped in Gucci."

Covering her nose defensively, Olivia stood, mouth gaping. She looked to Andrew to come to her rescue. He swept his bangs across his forehead, rolled his eyes, and turned his head from her. Her baby blues welling with indignant tears, she stamped her foot and made her way to the door, stumbling as she dragged her luggage. "Excuse me, I'm going home now."

"Bon voyage! It's going to be a long way back to hell!" Charles yelled in response to the slamming door.

Lottie clapped her hands approvingly. "Ducky, you've just had a major breakthrough! How does it feel to say something naughty for once?"

"It feels bloody great!" Charles replied, flushing only slightly.

Chapter Thirty-Six

Afraid to open her eyes, Katie lay on the hard surface and listened to the sounds of chaos ping-ponging around the room. She sniffed and almost wretched at the myriad foul odors her lungs were forced to intake: bodies—stinky bodies, blood, vomit, and bad breath all broiling under the sweltering heat to create a perfectly nauseating concoction.

Having to squinch one eye shut in order to peek with the other, she made a Cyclops reconnaissance of her surroundings. A large crack ran in the plaster on the ceiling and down half of the far wall of what seemed to be a makeshift triage unit. Janek, she could tell by the cheese curds in his ear, lay, possibly naked—*eeeww!*—on a table next to her, groaning. Sunlight streamed through a large broken window that had been mended back together with multiple crisscrosses of medical tape that had since begun to fade and crumble away.

She snapped her eye closed in response to someone's piercing, incoherent screams and was suddenly transported to the hospital scene in *Gone with the Wind*, where the putrescent filth and stink and helpless wails of the soldiers provoked Scarlett O'Hara to flee into the dangerous Atlanta streets. Only in this fantasy, she wasn't Scarlett. She was one of the soldiers—the one whose screams drive through Scarlett's sanity as the doctors, administering bourbon in place of anesthesia, amputate his gangrene leg.

"Noooooo! I need my leg!" Piercing the room, the stench, and multiple sets of eardrums with her shriek of terror, she jerked herself upright. Staring intently at nothing in particular, her breaths came rapid and shallow. Someone rushed to her makeshift hospital table and she slapped savagely against the hands that tried to touch her.

"Katie, it's me. Everything is all right."

She recognized that velvety accent: Lucas. She allowed his gentle touch as he pushed back a strand of sweat-plastered hair from her head. She turned her glossy gaze to him; he was bare-chested and on his side wore a bright white gauze bandage splotched red in the center. Focusing on the small patch of curls just below his collarbone, she followed the contours of his taught, smooth skin over his deliciously defined pectorals, across his gently rippling abdomen, and down to another sparse growth of hair just below his navel. Heating up another hundred degrees, she let herself be carried away into a much happier fantasy.

Stanley, dripping sweat and shirtless, but not wearing a Speedo—thank the heavens and all the glorious angels above—stood over her, shoulders hunched from exhaustion, torturing her afflicted leg.

Stab. *Oww.* Stab. *Oww.* Stab. *Oooww.* Stab. Stab. *Yeeeoooww!* She squeezed the strong hand Lucas had placed in her grip. "Why won't he let my poor persecuted leg have a moment's peace?" she whispered pathetically.

"Because poor persecuted leg needs stitches," Lucas replied as if speaking to a young child.

She flopped her head to the side and watched the shallow rise and fall of Janek's chest and played back her memories of the morning.

"What happened?" She gingerly caressed the bandage at Lucas's side before pointing her chin toward Janek.

The muscle at the back of Lucas's jaw twitched as he began grinding his teeth, shaking his head at the remembrance. "He was shot in the shoulder."

341

Katie swallowed. "Is he going to be all right?"

Lucas nodded.

"What happened to you?" She picked the edge of her fingernail into a couple tiny squares of his bandage.

"Mensur got off one last shot after Janek took him down. It just grazed my side." Craning his neck, he looked down at his wound. "I'm fine. I promise," he added in response to her worried stare.

"Marko?"

"He's fine."

"And Mensur...did he get away?"

His face turned somber and he shook his head. "He fell on his knife."

"Is he dead?" Clenching his hand tighter, she worried that she didn't want to know the answer.

He shook his head again. "He's just on the other side of Janek." He jerked his head in that direction. She strained to hear his slow, gurgled breathing. "Stanley doesn't think he'll make it."

She gulped. She didn't know why, but she felt sorry for her young, crazed captor.

Lucas wiped the tear running down her cheek and she concentrated on the slow, jerky movements of Stanley's thread as she tried to sort through her emotions. What would happen to them when the hostage taker died just two men down from her? Would they be able to go home? She didn't really even have a home...only a large, empty basement that belonged to her absentee parents. She took in the pungent stench of the room and wondered if it were the smell of death. Traumatized by the thought of death fumes entering her lungs as much as anything else, she finally broke through the wall built up over multiple frightened, sleepless nights and bawled. She tried to silence herself, but all she managed to do was choke on her sobs.

"Don't cry, Katie, pretty lady." Stanley clipped the thread. "Everything will be fine." She wanted to give him her good-little-trooper grin, but she couldn't. Instead, she flipped her head to the side, only to find the apologetic eyes of Janek staring at her. Jerking her head in the other direction, she found Lucas's troubled stare. Self-conscious under their concerned scrutiny, she felt certain she was going to combust right there on the folding-table gurney.

"I know just the thing to make you feel better," Stanley exclaimed, eyes brightening. "Would you like to take a shower? I have some nice Biolage shampoo I bought in bulk at the Walmart salon."

The corners of Katie's mouth twitched. She remembered his gusto for Walmart; he was bestowing her with a great honor. Even if she didn't want a shower—though thankfully she did, almost more than she wanted to keep her leg—she knew she couldn't refuse his offer.

Stanley was already digging through his medical bag. Retrieving a roll of waterproof medical tape, he rolled it out across her wound. "We must be careful not to get these stitches wet," he directed animatedly, obviously eager to help her wash away her troubles.

She wobbled to a stand and instantly lunged toward Lucas for support. It was as though even her good leg wanted to atrophy from the days of nonuse. With Lucas's help, she relearned to walk. Half dragging her injured leg, Katie leaned on Lucas as they followed Stanley down the corridor over the threadbare rugs that were no doubt fabulous in their prime.

Stanley flipped on the bathroom light, pointed out the fresh towels, and offered her a crisply packaged bar of soap.

"Thank you Stanley," she uttered, feeling like she might start crying again.

He flashed his Rembrandt-white teeth. "Take your time. When you're finished we can meet upstairs and discuss how we're going to get you home safely." Patting Lucas's shoulder, he trudged back to the swelter where his patients waited.

"Um…right then. Are you sure you can manage from here?" Lucas seemed reluctant to release his hold on her.

"I'll be fine. There's not much here to manage." She gestured to the fallen straps of her dirty tank and flimsy pajamas, now split up the entire length of the leg; only the thin elastic waistband remained intact.

He traced a thumb along the path on her cheek where the tears had cleansed a streak through the blood. "Right, of course, I'll leave you to it then. I'll be just outside the door."

She waited until he was gone. Pulling back the yellow daisy-clad shower curtain, she adjusted the water before gingerly removing her clothes. After a moment's hesitation, she bent over to retrieve her turquoise and yellow polka-dotted panties, and carried them into the shower with her. Spending nearly half the bar of soap, she scrubbed the panties and her body with all her might. She watched with morbid fascination at the rusty brown colors streaming off her body, and got lost in a daze waiting for the water to drain clear.

Only when her leg began to ache and the water ran tepid did she reluctantly turn off the faucet. Shimmying herself dry, she secured a towel turban to her head and spied her panties flung over the shower curtain rod—still dripping wet.

As she made her way over to her pajama bottoms, her stomach lurched into her throat. "Oh crap! Oh no, oh no!" she squealed in hushed tones. The result as she tried on her pants was just as she'd feared: The open leg left nothing about her left bottom half to the imagination.

Stripping off the pants, she flounced in place, naked, shaking her hands in front of her as if to draw inspiration. She wrung the underwear into the shower with all her strength. When no more water could be extracted, she rummaged the cupboards unsuccessfully for a blow dryer.

Lucas rapped lightly at the door. "Rabbit? Just checking to see how you're doing."

Katie balled her fist and bit down on her knuckles to silence her flustered scream.

"Everything all right?" His voice rang with concern in response to her silence.

"Umm...just a second!" She heard the panic rising in her voice. Pulling the towel off her head, she secured it around her body.

Struck with a sudden flash of genius, she hooked the underwear around her pointer finger and whirled it above her head with the skill of a Harlem Globetrotter, the fabric shedding tiny droplets of water as it gained momentum.

She was certain she was making progress with her drying technique. Then suddenly, startled by Lucas's unexpected entrance, she lost focus—and control—of her underwear. Wet polka-dotted panties propelled with helicopter speed—*shwock!*—onto his unsuspecting face. Mortified, both her hands flew up to cover her face, triggering her towel to drop and land effortlessly at her ankles.

Like an overheated thermometer, the color ran rapidly, starting from her toes, up the stem of her body, and nearly exploded out her ears.

Lucas, tugging off the underwear, struggled to avert his eyes.

"What are you doing?" she hissed vehemently, retrieving the towel and bunching it front of her naked body. "Get out!"

"I was concerned." Lucas fought to contain his laugh.

"Well, be concerned outside!"

"What on earth were you doing?" A chuckle escaped him and she scowled, provoking a medley of unrestrained laughs.

"Get out!" she ordered again, marching carefully up to him and snatching her panties from his grasp. One-handed, she pushed him toward the door.

Not even trying to check his laughter, he didn't budge. "What's the big deal? It's not like I haven't seen you...well...like...well, naked before."

"Not my cooter!" she exploded. "You've never seen my *down there* before!"

Clenching his eyes, he pressed his lips together until they began to turn white. She knew he was about to explode.

She pushed with all her aggravated might against his solid unmovable frame before punching his arm and retreating a couple of steps in defeat.

"Wait a second. I brought you something." He wiped the tears from his eyes. "I thought you could use this." He had crumpled in his hand a giant flannel nightshirt for her and the matching bottoms for

346

him. "Stanley says we can keep them," he chortled, shaking the wrinkles out of the clothes.

They did a do-si-do around each other, Katie trying to protect the sanctity of her bare bottom as he pushed his way toward the shower.

"So what's with the high-flying knickers?" he inquired jovially, stepping into the shower, pulling the curtain closed across him, and tossing his man-pris over the rod.

"I was trying to get them to dry. I didn't want to put on reasty panties, so I washed them," she sniffed, indignant.

The water discouraging further conversation, she fastened her bra and pulled Stanley's tent of a nightshirt over her head. Bidding farewell to her favorite striped pajamas, she shoved them into the wastebasket and let herself be slightly mollified as she began patting her underwear dry with Lucas's towel.

***

Katie padded timidly up the stairs behind Lucas and was surprised at the small group gathered in the large sitting room, sparse with ragged furniture. A worn-looking middle-aged woman had her short grey hair pulled into a tight ponytail as she labored over some kind of sewing project.

"This is my sister, Kata," Stanley introduced with big gestures as he welcomed the couple. He spoke something to Kata in his native language. She raised her head and gave them a weary, if not curt, nod, then returned to her task.

"Of course you know Marko, my grandnephew." The boy raced over and hugged them both around the waist, his short arms barely reaching across the combined breadth of their bodies.

Stanley escorted them across the room to meet a fragile, pale-faced girl of about twenty. She was lying under a bundle of blankets on an old, torn couch that was lopsided from a couple of missing feet. "This is my niece, Indira. She speaks only a little bit of English…her schooling has been cut short by her health." His voice dropped as he continued, tainted by a note of impatience. "And Janek, who you know."

Janek could barely look at them.

"Please, please have a seat." Stanley gestured to the floor. "I'm sorry, but we haven't got much furniture," he admitted with embarrassment. "I'm not the same Stanley you knew in America. Here I have nothing fancy, except this television." His eyes beamed at the fifty-two-inch flat-screen. "It's our one indulgence." He smiled and winked tenderly at Indira, who was self-consciously adjusting the scarf around her bald head.

"The floor will do just fine," Lucas assured.

The girl spoke something in a feeble whisper to Stanley, causing her pasty cheeks to burn red.

"Indira would like to know if you would allow her to comb your hair," Stanley asked Katie.

"I would like that very much," Katie responded, giving the young woman her warmest smile.

Indira fussed over Katie's hair with a reverence that made Katie's heart ache. She untangled the ratty strands, making long gentle strokes with a comb, stretching the hair out to its fullest lengths. Braiding and unbraiding, twisting, knotting, and ponytailing, Indira was absorbed with an energy that obviously pleased her uncle Stanley. Lucas sat next to Katie, lightly running a tickle-rub combination with the pads of his fingers over her bare leg, as Marko nestled into her lap. Janek lounged, favoring his injured shoulder in a broken recliner, Kata was intent on her sewing, and Stanley channel-surfed through the stations of his one remaining material possession.

From hostage to houseguest in just a short time, Katie felt the situation was a little too cozy after all she had experienced.

The unperturbed atmosphere only lasted a few minutes before Stanley's channel surfing landed on the BBC news, causing everyone in the room to gawk, horror-struck, at the broadcast. Plastering the screen in high definition was a color photo of a haggard and bloody Lucas carrying a lifeless and bloody Katie from behind the hay bales in Stanley's pasture.

As the anchor read the news of Lucas and Katie's abduction, an eerie chill delivered the disquieting realization that they had been stalked—and probably still were being watched, even at that very moment.

How else could that photo be explained?

Chapter Thirty-Seven

"We have a bit of good news!" Lord Waverly announced to the weary group. Lottie, Lady Waverly, and Mrs. Albright put down their bridge game and joined the circle of men who'd gathered on various sofas and chairs to pass the anxious time by napping—or trying to.

"Someone has issued the photo to the press!" He snatched up the remote and turned on the television. The family grimaced as he kept clicking the remote and the photo flashed on half a dozen different channels.

"We hope the abductors have made a fatal error," Lord Waverly continued. "As far we're aware, other than the rebels themselves, we're the only ones with access to that photo. Every news station from here to the United States is being questioned for their source. Also, the forensics team was able to trace the envelopes and paper delivered to us by the terrorists back to a small paper mill outside London."

"But Denny, how can the paper mill be helpful?" Lady Waverly spoke everyone's confusion.

His face beamed with the excitement of progress. "The mill specializes in selling products to university and college bookstores in the greater London area. We now suspect the person who sent these letters is living as a student in London."

"With all due respect, it still seems as though we're searching for a needle in a haystack," Sidney proclaimed.

"Perhaps." Lord Waverly was undaunted. "But we've had people searching for that needle round the clock. A list has been compiled of Bosnian students registered within the greater London area. This—" he said, slicing an official-looking envelope through the air as though he were a knight wielding a powerful sword, "is a profile of the man from the hotel reception, Mensur. It has been nearly three months since he's been seen in London." Opening the envelope, he drew out the one-page profile on Mensur and laid it on the table.

"This is all they have?" Lady Waverly asked after skimming the two-paragraph summary on Mensur's life.

"Not quite everything. I believe the profile states that he lost both his parents in the Bosnian war and that he has no known family. The investigation has turned up the possible existence of a half brother, which Mensur failed to mention on his university registration."

The crowd halted their breath in unison, praying this would be the key piece of information in finding Lucas and Katie.

"If that is the case," Lord Waverly continued, "then it is probable the half brother could be acting as the accomplice keeping us and the media informed, and could lead us straight to Mensur."

"Even if it's not the brother, whoever sent those letters would still be able to give us that information," Andrew noted speculatively.

"So how do we find this person?" Mrs. Albright asked, growing a little taller as if preparing to knock on every door in London herself.

"DNA evidence has been gathered from the seals on the envelopes and tests are being run as we speak." Lord Waverly relished for a long moment in the glory of being the giver of optimism before delivering his next piece of information. "But it will take several days at best to receive the test results, and then we must hope that the either the U.K. or the American DNA database can come up with a match."

The buoy of optimism sprung a leak, hissing out a tangible frustration that weighted the room.

"Wait a minute, everybody," Charles interjected. "This could be good news. If the terrorists are responsible for getting the information to the media, that means they are desperate to gain attention for their cause. As long as Lucas and Katie don't do anything foolish, their lives are probably not in any immediate danger. It's obvious Mensur—or whoever this man turns out to be—he and the others have been waiting for the perfect opportunity to carry this out. They'll not want to end it too soon. That might allow time for the DNA results."

There was only one possible flaw in Charles's logic, which no one dared speak. As far as they knew, Katie—even Lucas—might already be dead.

"It's more hope than we had five minutes ago." Lottie gave the crowd a feeble smile and started toward the kitchen. "I'll make us something nice for tea. Thank you, Lord Waverly—we are truly grateful for all you're doing."

"Wait! I have another bit of good news that I was saving for last." Lord Waverly's eyes sparked with renewed excitement.

"Secretary of State Harriett Clayton will be here to hold a press conference in front of the hotel." Rewarded by the complete turn of Lottie's countenance and the astonished expressions of his other listeners, he held up his arm to look at his watch. "If she's running on time, she should be here at the house in just shy of two hours."

"Here? *Here,* here?" Lottie pointed to the ground beneath her.

Lord Waverly nodded. "She'd like to have a quick assembly with the family before going in front of the cameras."

Simultaneously, each woman self-consciously began patting at her hair, face, and outfit.

"For the love of Donald Trump's hairpiece!" Lottie exclaimed. "We've not much time to prepare! I've got to find something fabulous to wear!"

Everyone in the room turned to stare at her.

"Something that will also convey 'grieving, doting mother,'" she assured them.

***

"We are not safe here," Stanley announced after calling Lucas, Katie, and Janek downstairs for a private conference. "Janek, how many others are involved in this plot?"

Janek shrugged his shoulders, wincing at the pain the motion caused. "I don't know. I got known two other mans more in Croatia and maybe someone in London."

Stanley's heavy lids closed, as if he were too exhausted to go on. He slid his back down the wall until he was seated in a squat position. "Janek, my brother, what have you done? What have you done?" His voice was barely above a whisper.

Lucas crouched down and put a hand on Stanley's shoulder. "Stanley, we will go. We don't want to cause any more trouble for you."

The shattered man shook his head without looking up. "No, it is not safe. I'm sure they will be outside watching. I'm afraid it won't be long until they come to the house."

Lucas looked to Katie, who returned his unspoken question with a decided nod. "Then we must go. We won't put your family in any more danger."

"We are in danger whether you stay or go." He spoke into the hollow between his knees.

"Then we must all leave." Urgency rose in Lucas's voice. "I believe it's dark enough to make some distance across the back end of the pasture unnoticed."

Stanley looked at him, then at Katie. "We cannot. Indira is ill with leukemia." His face streamed with unchecked tears. "We have nowhere else to go. I sold everything when I came back from America to pay for her treatments. Soon, I will no longer be able to buy fuel to drive her to the big hospital."

Katie sat next to him and pulled the burly man against her shoulder and let him sob out his woes.

"Have you any family that could house you—just for a short while?" Lucas suggested.

"We are all that is left of our family," he sniffed. "Kata's husband along with Indira's father and mother were killed during the war. Janek's wife is dead, and his son, Marko's father, went to work on a cruise ship. He has not contacted us for over six years."

"What about Marko's mother?" Katie asked.

"She give him up and run away when he was baby," Janek supplied, catching the fever of Stanley's melancholy.

"Right then, we'll stay until we can all find a way out of this," Lucas replied, losing himself in thought.

Stanley wiped his eyes on Katie's nightshirt. "You were brought into this situation against your will—please do not feel obligated to stay."

"Marko…please…take the boy," Janek pleaded.

Lucas looked at Stanley. "You were also brought into this situation against your will." Stanley shot Janek an aggravated scowl. Lucas continued, "We owe you our lives. We'll stay with you."

"Thank you," Stanley choked, and renewed his sobs.

Katie wrapped her arms around her once-jolly neighbor, returning his head to her shoulder.

"We might..." Lucas hesitated, "...want to call in some authorities, but we can't be guaranteed what will happen to Janek. If the other terrorists..." He winced at his choice of words. "Sorry, um, if the other...the others...name him as an accomplice, he could face punishment—harsh punishment. Of course Katie and I can plead his case and try to lessen the penalty, but there's no guarantee." He lowered his head solemnly and motioned for Katie to follow him back upstairs. "We'll leave you two to discuss the options."

The BBC was still broadcasting the story of their disappearance when Katie and Lucas reentered the main room. A hostage negotiations expert was giving his opinion of the situation. Kata, engrossed at her sewing table, took no notice of them as they reclaimed their seats on the floor. Indira's dull eyes lit up as she made a silent inquiry by stroking her frail hand down Katie's hair. Upon receiving Katie's permissive smile, she gathered it up and resumed playing hairdresser.

Katie gave a disgusted grunt at the completely inaccurate yarn the hostage expert was spinning. She turned to Kata, who, like everyone else, looked tired. But her tiredness was a part of her being—aged into her soul. Katie wondered at the adversity this woman had known to look so worn. A shoebox full of horsehair and an overturned stool sat at Kata's feet. Continuously, the woman gathered a clump of strands, blunt-cut them to create even ends, then wove them several times through three strands of fishing line that were tied across the stool legs. Katie studied her process with interest as her nimble fingers rapidly pulled together the beginnings of a weft of hair.

"She's making a wig for Indira," Stanley announced from the entryway, answering the curiosity in Katie's face. "We hope she can return to her schooling this fall." He beamed with pride at his ailing young niece.

Both she and Lucas, startled by the sooner-than-expected sound of his voice, stared at him expectantly.

Stanley met their gaze with anxiety in his eyes. "It is as I suspected. We are under surveillance. Two men wait in their vehicle outside the gate. If there are any men on the grounds, I don't know. We have decided Janek must face his consequences."

Lucas nodded and raised himself to a stand, his natural, easygoing stride replaced by a serious, businesslike approach. "Is there a telephone I may use?"

"I keep a cell phone for emergencies. The reception is not good." Indicating the approximate location of the phone, Stanley jerked his head in the direction of the back bedrooms.

"We will now take you to Croatia, where United States Secretary of State Harriett Clayton is about to begin a press conference," the BBC broadcaster announced. In the blink of an eye, Harriett Clayton stood larger than life on the television screen, in front of a podium flanked by two American flags, with Lottie, Charles, and Lord and Lady Waverly seated off to the side.

Like two small children, Lucas and Stanley dropped to their knees in front of the television and stared slack-jawed at the screen.

356

"Katie, perhaps you should notify your government first," Lucas suggested in response to seeing the American government already in action.

"Oh right, let me just pull their hostage hotline number out of my pocket. Oh wait! Oh darn! I must have misplaced it when I put on this nightshirt," she retorted, feeling nervy at the realization of just how massive their situation had grown.

Lucas did not chuckle at her snarky remark. "Maybe Stanley has a phone directory."

"No need for a phonebook. I know the number for the U.S. Embassy here," Stanislaus supplied proudly.

They both turned to him with planet-sized eyes.

"Wha—?" Katie began.

"I was considering applying for citizenship…I had lots of questions," Stanislaus explained.

"So you called the embassy?" Katie replied.

"Shhh," Lucas silenced the exchange. "She's about to speak."

"Ladies and gentlemen, I am here on behalf of President Obama and the United States of America to rebuke the insupportable act that has been taken against one of our fellow citizens, Kathryn Sutherland, who was taken hostage, along with her British employer, Lucas Hayden, three days ago.

"Our hearts and our condolences go out to the families and friends of these two victims. I stand here today to give them my assurance that the American and British governments are working diligently to not only bring these hostages home safely, but also to locate and bring to justice the terrorists who have the audacity to capture, torture, and use our citizens as political pawns.

"To the Bosnian rebels who have claimed responsibility for this act of terror, I beseech you to release these two innocent people. We agonize over the horrific tragedies that have plagued your country…"

"Is that where we are? Bosnia?" Katie interrupted with inopportune giddiness.

Stanley nodded dismissively, trying to stay tuned on Harriett.

"Wow! I've always wanted to visit Bosnia. Stanley, how come you never told me you were from Bosnia? I would have had so many questions to ask you!"

"Shhh!" Lucas and Stanley ordered in unison.

"…want to have sustainable peace in your country, the American government—and, I am sure, the British government—will not tolerate being bullied into taking action for any cause."

There was an explosion of applause set in motion by Lord Waverly.

"I have an idea!" Katie broke in.

"Shhh!" was the commanding response from both men.

"I will not shhhh!" she rejoined, annoyed at being shushed for the third time in as many minutes. "I have something important to say!"

They turned to her, reluctant to peel their eyes from the red skirt-suited Harriett, absorbing her commendations.

"We should call your parents or the Waverlys, seeing how they're sitting right next to the Secretary of State!"

Lucas blinked a couple of times as if his mind staggered under the weight of the suggestion. Stanley's face registered his comprehension, and without another second's delay, he bolted down the hallway and retrieved the cell phone.

Lucas watched the service bars on the phone flip intermittently between zero and one-half. Thinking quickly, he punched out a text message, careful to repeat word for word Stanley's directions to the farmhouse, and sent a copy to Andrew, Sidney, Geoffrey, his parents, and Lady Waverly. Harriett Clayton was wrapping up her speech, and Lucas was anxious to make contact before she left the podium and, subsequently, the company of his parents.

"Come on, come on!" he urged the sporadic signal, wielding the phone in every direction.

Another thunder of applause burst from the television, and Harriett began moving from the platform. She paused, stopping to shake someone's hand as the phone chimed in Lucas's hand, flashing a "message sent" indicator.

They watched with baited breath, knowing their fates depended on the speed of Stanley's lousy service provider. The cameras followed Harriett's exit, also leaving the forms of Lottie, Charles, and Lord and Lady Waverly.

"We have just heard United States Secretary of State Harriett Clayton give a poignant speech on behalf of American hostage Kathryn Sutherland," the voiceover of the BBC announcer broke in as the camera cut back to the studio, leaving the group to fester in unfulfilled anticipation.

"We'll now take you live to our American correspondent, Nancy Wallace, who is in Colorado at the home of Kathryn Sutherland, where quite a crowd of friends and well-wishers have gathered together in support of the hostage victim."

The screen flipped from the news anchor to the front of Jim and Sheila's home.

Katie's mouth dropped wide open in disbelief.

Tents and sleeping bags populated the lawn, where people milled about holding candles and wearing concerned faces.

"Yes, it's nearly dawn here in Colorado, but as you can see behind me…" the reporter gestured to the home in the background, "people from all around the country have gathered here at the home of Kathryn Sutherland to express their love and support. We've seen quite a few notable figures here. Sheila Evans, who plays Eve St. Sebastian on the popular American daytime drama *Love's Lionesses,* is here and has agreed to grant us an exclusive interview. I just found out only moments ago that Sheila raised Katie along with her own son, Christopher. As you can imagine, she's deeply affected by this tragedy and has taken a temporary leave from filming."

Katie scooted closer to the screen. She couldn't believe Sheila would be caught on camera looking this horrible. *Unless she were truly distraught.* She took in Sheila's grieving voice offering money and autographed headshots in exchange for Katie's safe return. Katie's heart clenched. Sheila was not acting; she really was an anguished mother. Standing right beside her, united in grief as if they'd never had an argument, was Jim, pleading for his daughter's safe return.

His daughter…. The words played in her head, then moved down to fill a place in her heart. A place she hadn't really known was empty until just then. She knew Jim and Sheila loved her, but she'd always wondered if they'd agreed to raise her because they wanted her, or as a favor to her parents out of friendship. She'd never know if they had wanted her then, but they wanted her now. And that was enough—

enough to understand, that despite how they came together, she really did have a family of her own.

Katie couldn't hear the announcer over her sobs. She felt ashamed that in her fears of becoming old and all alone, she taken so many people for granted. But the passing of each familiar face struck her with a palpable humility. She had never realized how many caring people graced her life and, like it or not, would never leave her. She was surprised to see both her brothers had traveled to show their support. Janice and Beverly Martin gave tearful accounts of her as a child. Dylan's boss, Senator Hensen, and a handful of other congressman and senators were there—not that they cared for her beyond what her misfortune could do for them in the public opinion polls, but still. There were neighbors, work colleagues, teachers from elementary through high school, Professor Bell and his colleagues…all were among the hundreds who camped on her lawn out of concern for her well-being.

The reporter walked inside Katie's parents' house, which was wide open and lit up, and the camera panned across the living room sofa, where all five of her closest friends—Christopher, Anna, Dylan, Rob, and Heather—were sitting. Katie put her hand to the screen, desperate to hear their voices, when a shot blasted through the quiet night outside Stanley's picture window.

The terrifying sound rattled the broken nerves of the household as everyone dropped to the floor, Kata, Indira, and Marko screaming in horror. Outside, a man's raspy voice shouted over the commotion, calling out menacing foreign sentences.

"He wants to talk to Mensur. He wants to know what's happening," Stanley translated in a whisper.

361

Janek ran outside to answer the man's calls. His hard voice sent a chill down Katie's spine as she remembered how days ago he was an angry, militant, kidnapping terrorist.

"Janek is telling him that Mensur and the hostages have been seriously injured and are being treated by the doctor who lives in the house," Stanley whispered.

The man shouted another terrifying phrase before shooting off another booming round into the still sky.

Janek came running back into the room.

"He says he will return in one hour and he wants to see Mensur and the Duchess alive or everyone inside will be slaughtered like pigs."

Chapter Thirty-Eight

"Mensur is dead," Stanley announced as he reentered the sitting room, adding another layer of gloom to the somber atmosphere.

Lucas broke the silence, pointing at the door. "Is this the only entry?" he asked the brothers, his shoulders dipping with relief at their affirmative answer. Fresh blood was already creeping through his and Janek's bandages as they muscled pieces of large furniture in front of the door. He cast a scrutinizing gaze at each of the windows and sighed. "We should be safe from anyone entering through the windows as long as they don't have access to a ladder—let's pray that they don't."

Stanley's phone vibrated against the floor to the tune of "Yankee Doodle Dandy." Katie and the other women stared at it apprehensively; the men had gone down the hall to retrieve more furniture from the bedrooms.

"Hello?" Katie croaked, unsure if answering was the wisest idea.

"Hello. Is this Kathryn—Kathryn Sutherland?" a no-nonsense woman's voice asked in perfect American English.

"Yes. Yes, this is Katie." Something about the authoritative nature of the caller compelled her to use her "best manners" voice.

"Kathryn—Katie," the voice softened a little. "This is Secretary of State Harriett Clayton."

"Holy crap!" Katie gulped, forgetting about her best manners.

"Katie? Katie, are you okay?"

"Yes. Yes, Mrs. Clayton...ma'am...I mean Senator...I mean Secretary—"

There was a short chuckle on the other end, and the voice became almost maternal—not a tone Katie would have thought Harriett possessed. "Any of those will do just fine. What I need to know, Katie, is if you are safe."

Katie took in her surroundings—the men now dripping tracks of blood; the pale-faced, cancer-ridden Indira; the haggard-beyond-her-years Kata, huddled in a heap of frightened tears on the floor; and Marko curled up in the rickety armchair, who was somehow sleeping soundly through the commotion.

"No, we are not safe," Katie forced herself to speak evenly. "We have less than one hour to resurrect a dead man or they say we'll all be slaughtered like pigs."

"All? Who else is with you, Katie? And who is dead?" Harriett urged, her voice crackling through the broken cell phone reception.

"One of the kidnappers is dead. I'm with Lucas. We're in the home of a doctor and his family. They're good people." She fought to keep her thoughts and words succinct.

"Is that the location indicated in your text message?"

Katie nodded, then realizing Harriet couldn't see her, replied, "Yes. Yes it is."

"Hang in there, Katie," Harriett resumed her matter-of-fact Secretary of State voice. "We're going to try to get you out of there."

Try? Try? The word hummed through Katie's mind, offering very little comfort. If it weren't Harriett Clayton on the other line, Katie would have given her a piece of Yoda advice: *Do or do not. There is no try!*

"Katie, I'm going to turn the phone over—there's someone who wants to speak with you."

364

And her brief conversation with Harriett Clayton was at an end.

"Katie, love, is that you?" Lottie's little voice trilled down the line.

"Yes, I'm here," Katie squeaked, wiping away a tear.

"Oh thank the Lord you're not dead! Can you put my son on the phone?"

Katie called to Lucas, who halted his work to hobble as quickly as possible over to her, holding his pained side. His befuddled look was enhanced by the bruise around his eye.

She held the phone out to him. "It's your mom."

He took the phone eagerly. "Hello Mum!"

"Hello Chicken, I love you so much. And I'm so proud of you for not letting them run off with Katie alone—though if you ever do it again, I'll run you through with me dullest kitchen knife for giving me a heart attack."

"I love you, too, Mum." A tear trickled down his cheek.

"Can you put Katie on the line? There's something I want to tell the both of you."

Lucas pushed the speakerphone button. "Right, we're both here."

They heard her take in a deep inhale. "You two cheeky little monkeys!" she reprimanded in an unamused tone.

Lucas and Katie stared at each other, dumbfounded.

"If you make it out of there alive, so help me I'll skin both your hides for deceit."

"Mum, what are you running on about?" Lucas asked.

"Don't think for one second I didn't recognize the bra the forensics team found shoved in the bottom of your shopping bag, Chicken, *before* they were able to trace it back to Ms. Katie."

Katie bypassed red and turned purple. "Please tell me you didn't just say that in front of Harriett Clayton."

"Damn right, I said it front of Harriett Clayton, and the Waverlys, too. I'd say it in front of bloody Barack Obama if he were here. I want you two to admit you've been very naughty bunnies."

Lucas said sternly, "Mother, this really isn't the time."

"Bollocks! This may be the only time! You're not going to die thinking you've pulled the wool over me eyes."

"Mum, I think you've misunderstood the situation."

"Have I? I've heard an account from an old village fisherman describing the sunrise escapades of a couple matching just your description."

A mortified groan escaped Katie's lips. "People are going to think I'm a slut-bag!" she groaned, more to herself than anyone. "I could die today with Harriett Clayton thinking I'm a slut-bag. You might as well engrave 'slut-bag' on the headstone that will sit above my mangled body!"

"Oh Lordy! Have the terrorists been giving her drama lessons?" Lottie quipped.

"Katie, no one thinks you're a slut-bag," Harriett Clayton called solemnly through the phone.

"Listen Mum, we have to go," Lucas broke in. "Things are about to turn very serious here. And for the record, Katie has higher morals than you give her credit for. Nothing happened between us. Is that what you wanted to hear?"

Lottie sighed impatiently. "Of course that's not what I wanted to hear!" Her gloating tone vanished into aggravated disappointment. "I don't want to hear about Katie's high morals. High morals won't bring me grandbabies."

"Oh, wouldn't that be lovely!" Lady Waverly cooed in the background.

Regaining her composure, Katie grabbed the phone from Lucas. "Goodbye Lottie. I hope I live to make you regret this conversation," she said, and clicked the phone shut.

Another shot rang out—only this time, Janek and Stanley were waiting by the window to answer the gunman's calls. The men yelled at each other through the glass.

Katie was terrified again and desperate for a distraction. She watched Kata, who focused diligently on finishing her weft.

"May I help?" Katie dared approach the woman, hoping the desire to help was a universal language. The woman understood, and wordlessly turned over a stool and tied fishing line across the legs, preparing Katie for her lesson. Kata slowed her pace, making exaggerated movements for Katie to follow. It didn't take long for her catch on, and soon her troubled mind was absorbed in the task of looping tufts of horsehair.

Lucas paced the floor, raking his fingers through his hair. "I wish I could understand what they're saying out there!"

"Sit down and let me show you how to do this," Katie urged. "It'll help take your mind off things."

"I don't think it will," he protested.

"Then do it to help Indira."

He gave a reluctant nod and sat down across from Katie at the stool, allowing her to be his teacher.

Stanley approached quickly. "They are coming. We'll have to hide in the cellar."

"How much time do we have?" Lucas jumped to his feet, pulling Katie up with him.

"We have told him that Mensur is in bad condition."

"That's putting it mildly," Lucas replied.

"He has gone to get the others to see what should be done," Stanley continued. "Ten, fifteen minutes—maybe—plus the time it takes them to get through the barricade against the door."

While Stanley repeated the instructions in Bosnian, Janek rummaged through the house at top speed for supplies.

Indira rose to her feet too quickly for her feeble frame and swooned. Lucas lunged in and caught her before she hit the floor. He raised her to his chest and held her effortlessly across his arms without as much as a noticeable flex of his muscles. Katie felt a twinge of envy; Lucas had never picked *her* up with such ease. In fact, she knew for certain that there was definite muscle flexing happening the few times he had been her rescuer.

Indira blushed wildly. The color was a stark contrast to her usual pasty complexion, giving Katie a glimpse of the potential beauty the young woman held. She rested her head timidly against his shoulder, and he smiled that heart-stopping Prince Charming smile at her. Katie knew that like herself, Indira was experiencing a very serious crush.

Stanley scooped up the little bundle of sleeping Marko, and Kata began throwing her sewing materials into a box to take with her.

Katie grabbed the two stools, shoved a Styrofoam head under her arm, and followed the procession down the stairs and along the corridor.

At the very back of the house was a small room, more like a large pantry, that housed an antique desk set, a couple of filing cabinets, and some odds and ends like photo albums and plaques. Taking up the majority of the exterior wall was an old threadbare tapestry. Stanley pulled it aside, revealing an *Alice in Wonderland*-size door, and slowly, methodically, turned the antique combination wheel until the lock clicked.

He muscled open the door that squeaked its resistance, then ducked inside. Careful not to jostle Marko, he pulled the cord on a precarious swinging light. He led the way down a short flight of stairs and deposited the sleeping boy on a clumsy recliner, not dissimilar to the one from which the boy was initially scooped. The room must have been roughly eight by eight feet and six feet high, but only Lucas had to crouch down to keep from bumping his head. For a dank stone room, it was remarkably cozy, decorated much like the television room upstairs, minus the television. Populating the majority of the space was a worn loveseat that matched the sofa upstairs, an old recliner, a folding card table, and two matching chairs. In the darkest corner stood a dusty bookcase with a collection of old paperbacks, writing tablets, pens, and a pile of folded blankets. Water storage containers that could have been from the Second World War took up the last two shelves and ran along the perimeter of the wall.

Lucas set Indira gently on the loveseat and tucked a blanket around her. The original flush still staining her cheeks, she colored deeper. The effect was radiant. Katie became determined to enhance

Indira's lovely maiden look by helping Kata finish the long fall of mahogany hair.

"I must make sure the windows are secure," Stanley told the group, already ascending the stairs.

"And I must pee," Katie stated.

"Now?" Lucas interrogated incredulously.

"Yes, now," she defended. "It's been a while and who knows how long we'll be holed up down here." Turning to Stanley, she asked, "I've got enough time for that, don't I?"

Stanley issued her an indulgent smile and let her pass.

It felt good to be alone…even if it was on the toilet with the threat of maniacal terrorists beating down the door at any minute. Katie purposefully slowed the flow just to have a few extra seconds of contemplation. She must have contemplated too hard, because she was suddenly overcome with the undeniable urge to go number two.

"Oh no! Not now!" she hissed to her bowels.

"Katie, who are you talking to?" Lucas lightly tapped on the door, anxiety ringing in his voice.

"Just myself," she answered, trying to sound casual, her face flaming hot with embarrassment.

She gave a little push trying to move the process along, but three days' worth of number twos did not want to be rushed.

"Katie, hurry up, will you?" Lucas demanded, frantic.

"Lucas, go away! Who are you, the bathroom marauder? Why are you always interrupting my most private restroom moments?" She felt the added pressure of now having to do this chore silently as well as quickly.

"Katie, we don't have time for this, let's go!" he insisted, his voice commanding.

"Go back to the cellar! I'll take my chances with the terrorists," she snapped.

He grunted in frustration. "What are you doing in there?"

She decided the question was too stupid to merit an answer, but bit back a retort on the off chance he was replaying the scene of her twirling panties and figuring her to be doing something equally ridiculous.

"I'm coming in!"

"Noooo!" she shrieked. The sudden lurch in her abdomen pushed the bulls through the shoot.

The doorknob rattled, prompting her to begin a frenzied search through every cabinet within her reach for some matches.

"Stop! I'm going poop!" she confessed, feeling the very last of her pride joining her number two in the toilet.

"Now? Can't you hold it?"

"Do you think I'd be dropping the kids off at the pool right now if I had a choice? Go away! You're just making this more difficult."

"Hurry up then." He tried to sound stern, but she heard him sniggering as his footsteps retreated down the hallway.

Paydirt! She found a book of matches. Lighting every single one, she ensured the residual smoke gobbled up any lingering number-two vapors. Before she could close the cabinet, she spied an unopened triple pack of toothbrushes lying right next to a never-been-squished tube of toothpaste. The temptation was too great as she subconsciously ran her tongue across her filmy teeth. She listened carefully for a moment but heard no sound of either Lucas or vigilante gunmen. It wasn't hard convincing herself that brushing her teeth would be an act of community service. Besides, if she had time to wash her hands, she should have time for a quick brush. A stab of guilt stuck into her chest as she tore into the package and popped out a brush. Was she stealing a basic necessity from poor third world people? What had become of her? She scraped her front tooth contemplatively, then examined the creamy white tooth-gunk left behind on her fingernail. Grimy teeth—that's what had become of her. She shoved the toothbrush into her mouth, promising to replace the borrowed treasure with a dozen Walmart toothbrushes just like it if they ever got out of this mess.

Happily licking her minty tongue across her minty teeth, she was unperturbed by Lucas's rude entrance. "I heard the toilet flush ages ago. What are you doing?"

She shrugged sheepishly, unable to hide her toothbrush quickly enough.

"Katie, you stole a toothbrush?"

"*Borrowed* a toothbrush," she corrected defensively. "Sonja, I'll call it...and I'm going to replace it."

His eyes smoldered on the verge of anger. "Are you trying to get us all killed?"

"I couldn't help myself," she pouted. "It's been at least three days—that I can count—since I've had any sleep, a poo, or a toothbrush. I saw an opportunity to die with a spring in my step and a twinkle to my teeth, and I went for it." She held her ground and stared challengingly into his steely eyes. "For having been bound, gagged, thrown into the trunk of a crazy man's car, and knifed, I've been a pretty good sport so far. I think as long as the gunmen aren't kicking

372

down the door yet, we deserve a couple of small indulgences before we get locked up in a cellar for who knows how long."

In a moment of brazen desperation to make him understand, she stepped into him, lassoed an arm around his neck, and kissed him with all the passion deserving of her last mortal kiss.

He seemed to be contemplating the command of her lips, then broke away. His face was still set in severe irritation. She stepped away and dipped her head to hide behind her veil of hair. She wanted nothing more than to join her poo and her pride on the ride down the long sewer pipe.

He looked about to speak—then, shaking his head, changed his mind. Snatching the toothbrush from her hand, he stomped over to the sink, grumbling incoherent words. She ventured to look up at him.

He'd already loaded the toothbrush with paste. "May I?"

Smiling a little too readily, she replied, "Sonja would be honored."

After a quick brush, he wiped his mouth on the sleeve of his too-big-in-the-body and too-short-in-the-sleeves borrowed shirt, he dropped Sonja in the pocket of Katie's nightshirt. No longer feeling the bold seductress, she took several cowering steps away from him. His head tilted in amusement at her faltering confidence. He flashed a lecherous smile and heeded her advice to enjoy one last indulgence as he reached out and pulled her to him.

The front door nearly banged off its hinges, bringing Lucas and Katie to their senses. He grabbed her by the wrist and dragged her down the corridor. Still in a daze, she forced her good leg to run. She could still feel the residual tingle in her face from the scratch of his budding beard.

Stanley leaned out from the half-size door and motioned wildly for them to get inside. Pushing Katie through first, then himself, Lucas helped Stanley pull the reluctant steel door closed.

Chapter Thirty-Nine

The next time Katie Sutherland found herself trapped in a bomb shelter, she was going to make damn sure she had a watch. She didn't know what was making her craziest—the sounds of thunderous stomping and overturned furniture hitting the floorboards above them, the murderous shouts and occasional gunfire, or the inability to gauge how long they'd been silently listening to the marauding.

Katie laid a finished weft of horsehair on the rickety card table, then sucked the tip of her finger, hoping to ease the throb of a budding blister. She and Lucas had become so adept in their weaving skills that Kata had been able to concentrate on pinning the wefts to the wig cap secured to the Styrofoam head. Katie regarded how the wig was coming together, and because nobody had spoken one word for what could have easily been a decade, she nodded in satisfaction.

Giving herself an opportunity to stretch the aching muscles in her neck, she looked
around to see how the others were faring the quiet captivity. Stanley paced the floor, wringing his hands behind his back. Indira toyed at the stubby tufts of hair underneath her scarf and stole longing gazes at Lucas. Marko still slept in his recliner, and Janek sprawled on the floor in front of him, napping. Katie studied a fleck of ear granola that bobbled in sync with his heavy breathing before returning to her project.

She and Lucas had just handed over their final wefts when the heavy footsteps clunked directly overhead. It seemed as though everyone's breath caught in unison. A victorious scream pierced through the still room, causing Janek to pop up from his nap and perch, ninja-ready. Katie's heart raced—then raced even harder in response to the loud metallic clunk of someone attempting to kick in the hidden door. Angry, muffled words shouted in Bosnian seeped down to them. Stanley looked to Janek, then dropped his head—but not before Lucas and Katie caught the horror in his eyes.

Lucas crossed the room in two easy steps. "What is it, Stanley? What did they say?"

Katie caught sight of Marko trying to clear the sleep cobwebs from his head, his lower lip trembling. She stood just in time to catch the eight-year-old frame that came bounding into her arms. He was almost too big for her to hold.

"He is telling someone he's found us and he will waste no time in killing us. The only one who will live is Katie…for now. He says he will make her pay for Mensur's death."

Katie felt cold terror fill her veins. She forced herself not to fall into a state of hysterics by clinging to the tiny hope that she would be lucky enough to catch an errant bullet through the heart. In an instant, Lucas had her and Marko encircled in his arms. Putting his cheek next to hers, he held them both tight. "I'm not going to let anyone hurt you," he promised with conviction. His whisper was hot against her ear, and his warm tears spilled onto her face.

Kata was the only one not idly waiting for the attack. It seemed the promise of imminent death filled her with a determination not to kick the bucket before Indira could have a head of hair. She bent her head into her project with ferocity. The whir of her sewing was the only sound that occupied the tiny room.

Quaking from both fear and pain, Katie could no longer ignore her wounded leg. She pushed Marko into Lucas's chest and crumpled

376

into her chair just as a sequence of bullets was fired into the door. The blasting pinging sound charged against the metal but did not penetrate. Katie was too caught up in the dizzying pain to react, but she took in the terrified shrieks of her companions, and felt their relief when the door held. Then, she shut her eyes and blocked out everything around her.

When she opened them again, the looks on everyone's faces told her something was horribly wrong. She scanned the room to find Kata's broken form slumped across Indira's legs. For one petrifying moment Katie feared the door hadn't held and the woman had been shot. Then she heard the crying that shook Kata's entire body. Indira bent over and hugged her aunt's head, showering her with her own tears.

"Stanley, what's happened to Kata?" Katie whispered, noticing everyone but Lucas was crying.

Stanley sniffed. "There was not enough mane to finish the wig. Hair was the only gift she had to give to Indira."

"When we get out of here, can't we go to the stable and get more hair?" Katie offered.

Stanley shook his head. "It is impossible, the horse has been sold."

Katie's eyes also began to pool as her own hopes for Indira's beautiful head of hair were dashed. She regarded the wig dangling from the Styrofoam head. It was scant at best and pieces of the cap underneath peeked out between carefully positioned wefts. It would take a whole other horse's tail to draw out its full potential.

More loud turbulence and gunfire from above jolted them from their melancholy. A thunder of voices stormed as men screamed back

377

and forth. But they weren't Bosnian voices; they were lovely American and British voices, and German ones—which weren't so lovely, but welcome nonetheless. Katie's heart began to pound.

A loud knock rang through the cellar and a sturdy German-accented voice sounded in English: "United Nations Peacekeeping—is anyone down there?"

Stanley sprinted to the top of the stairs shouting, "We are here! We are here!"

"Can you open the door?"

"Yes," Stanley replied.

"Good. Do so only when I tell you it is safe," the rigid German voice commanded.

Katie smoothed her fingers along a section of wig while her stomach did loop de loops. Would she soon be freed from this nightmare?

Looking around at the state of her company, she didn't experience the elation she expected to feel. She observed her new friends: Kata, with strands of short, wild ponytail clinging to her tear-stained face, her only wish to give her niece a head of hair; the orphaned Indira, feeble and pale, with her most important possession, a scarf, covering her balding head; Stanley, who had abandoned his American dream to help his family, now watching his world literally crumble around him; and Marko—what would become of the tenderhearted little boy?

Katie stared down at the wig again, discovering that she had inadvertently tangled some of her own long strands into the horsehair. Her slightly lighter color complemented the mahogany horsehair, creating an effect of salon perfect-highlights. She ran her hand down the length of her own hair and suddenly realized she had the resources to not only complete the wig, but to make it even better than imagined. Before she could change her mind, she grabbed a piece of fishing wire, tied her hair into a low ponytail, and started cutting. It took several attempts for the scissors to chew through the thick stalk, but eventually fourteen inches of her most prized possession—in fact, her identity— fell limply to the table.

Without the weight of the heavy cascades, her head nearly floated away. Apprehensively, she ran her shaky fingers through the ends of her new haircut. When her fingertips hit just below the bottom of her chin, she realized what she had done, and cried—not for what she had lost, but for what she had given.

"It's safe to open the door!" the German hollered. "Do not come out—we're coming in!"

Stanley opened it wide, and two by two, camouflaged soldiers wearing blue helmets with a white UN logo above the ear pushed their way through, forcing Stanley backward down the stairs with the ends of their rifles. Each unison step the soldiers took was quick and strategic. The first two men landed at the bottom of the stairs and skimmed over the group.

"Is Kathryn Sutherland down here?" a harsh American voice with a Southern accent barked.

Katie stood, hands still shaking from her haircut. "Yes, I'm here."

The stocky American soldier looked perplexed as he took out a photo of Katie and compared it to the Katie standing in front of him. Just then, Kata wailed something in Bosnian, picked herself up from the floor, and dashed to the table, grabbing two handfuls of Katie's luscious fallen hair. Indira choked on a series of sobs that rendered her speechless. It only took a moment for the befuddled soldier to take in the gaunt, pallid girl on the loveseat, the Styrofoam head, the long tresses on the table, and the barely recognizable Katie to understand what had just taken place.

"Soldier, let's move!" the commanding German voice barked. Without another word, the American soldier moved to the table, grabbed Katie around the waist, and carried her off.

"Wait!" she demanded. "What are you doing? I need to say goodbye!"

"Sorry ma'am, just following orders. It's for your own safety," he said in a Southern drawl.

"Lady! Come back!" Marko wailed. Katie craned her neck to see him struggling against Lucas's hold, tears sliding down his cherub cheeks. She tried to run to him, but the vice grip around her waist was unbreakable.

Red-faced from crying, Stanley reached out and grabbed her hand as she passed. "Goodbye Katie, pretty lady."

Between the two soldiers who flanked the one who carried her, Katie caught glimpses of the shambles that remained of Stanley's house. Her heart wrenched as she wondered how the family would ever recover. She caught sight of Lucas, not far behind, surrounded by another three soldiers, and knew by the torn expression on his face he had the same thoughts.

"How come Lucas gets to walk and I don't?" Katie complained to her bulky soldier. She couldn't tell if he seemed annoyed, but he halted the brisk procession and set her on her feet. She smoothed the baggy nightshirt over her knees and tried to summon as much dignity as possible as she limped along, trying to keep stride with her camo-clad bodyguards.

She blinked, then blinked again, barely believing her eyes when she saw all the commotion outside. White UN vehicles, Jeeps, trucks, ambulances, Humvees, even a tank all waited on standby around the perimeter of Stanley's property. Three bound and bloodied men were being prodded into the back of a pickup by soldiers with rifles. Was she really the cause of all this hullabaloo?

The sight of Mensur's stiff, lifeless corpse, still wearing his sinister sneer, being carried away was more than Katie could endure. Having the United Nations called in was one thing, but having the death of a maniacal, justice-seeking fanatic on her hands was quite another. With the finesse of a proper Southern belle, she put the back of her hand to her forehead and collapsed against the body of one of her militiamen.

Chapter Forty

They sat…and they sat…in some military-type compound…somewhere. A general or corporal—maybe a prime minister, or even the chairman of the Federal Reserve, for all Katie knew—interrogated Lucas and her. She didn't know which was worse—living through the terrorist attack or the excruciating recounting of it. Eventually, Katie's stomach growled so long and so loudly that it could not be politely ignored.

"Why don't you two go and get some rest? I'll have someone drive you to your hotel," suggested the General Corporal Prime Minister of the Federal Reserve.

"Sir?" Katie ventured as he escorted them down the sterile corridor. "What happened to Stanley—Stanislaus—and his family?"

"They are also being questioned." For the first time he looked at her as a person instead of a fount of information. Slackening his shoulders, he dropped the military persona. "The girl has been taken to a local hospital and we have Janek in custody. But you should be able to see the others tomorrow—"

Though she worried for Indira and Janek, she couldn't stop the smile from springing to her face. At least she would get to say goodbye to the others.

"That is—before you leave for London and after we ask you a few more questions," he continued.

Her smile slid to the linoleum.

***

The Jeep pulled in front of the Vegas-style, glass high-rise hotel. Despite its off-putting name, The Radon Sarajevo, the hotel boasted a five star plaque next to the door. Katie gulped, very aware of her oversized man's nightshirt of an outfit. At least Lucas didn't look much better in his matching bottoms and baggy, bloodstained shirt.

The two soldiers in the front of the Jeep jumped out and opened the rear doors more like doormen than military men.

"Compliments of the Waverlys," one British soldier crooned, obviously impressed to be in the company of people who'd been in the company of the Waverlys.

"We've been instructed to pick you up at noon sharp tomorrow," the second British soldier informed them.

***

Wandering through the largest and most luxurious suite she had ever seen, Katie had to admit the loveliest sight was not the marble kitchen, the giant jetted bath, or the sauna. It was her backpack crammed full of clean clothes and toiletries resting neatly against the bed, along with Lucas's two shopping bags of newly purchased clothing. On the bed rested a note written in an elegant script. She grabbed it.

Lucas & Katie,
Thank the Lord you are safe! We can't tell you how delighted we will be to see you at Pellyn Hall as soon as you are returned to London.
Room service has been ordered and will be delivered within one hour after your arrival.
Please try to get some rest after your terrible ordeal.
Yours,

She handed the note to Lucas and headed into the bathroom to shower.

Swaddling herself in a plush robe, Katie wiped the steam from the mirror and pondered her new image. Even dripping wet, her unskillfully bobbed hair bounced with natural curls that used to hang taut from the heavy length. Days of fasting and worry had eaten away at her figure. Normally, that would have made her ecstatic, except the chapped lips and the dark half circles under her droopy eyes haunted her. The woman staring back at her was a stranger inside and out. She watched the steam gobble up her image, and then exited the bathroom, which Lucas entered without a word.

The lavish suite was big and empty, and Katie couldn't help drawing the comparison to how she felt inside. She should be happy; she was safe and relatively unharmed. But looking at all the opulence surrounding her, it seemed an undeserved and vulgar contrast from where she'd just been. Knowing the tribulations of not only the people who saved her life, but also those who tried to take it, Katie contemplated her moral responsibilities.

She picked at the selection of food in front of her, feeling guilty that her biggest worry was whether she was more hungry or more tired.

"What's wrong?" Lucas asked, fresh from the shower and also wearing a robe, watching a lone tear streak down Katie's cheek.

"It's not fair—that I have so much and they have so little."

"Shhh, I know, I know." He gathered her up in his arms and held her. "But you can't punish yourself...that won't help them."

She sniffed in response. "You're right, it won't. But I promise you, I won't forget about them. I'm going to help them—not just Stanley's, but all the broken families. Somehow, I'm going to find a way to bring them happiness. I guarantee you that." She was speaking more to herself than to him, but she knew if she made the promise aloud, she would keep it.

He held her tighter. She didn't want to move from the position, so she didn't. She held still in his arms until sleep came to claim her.

"Where are you going?" she asked drowsily when he tucked her into the sheets.

"To bed—in the other room. Go back to sleep."

She gripped his forearm. "Please stay."

Smiling down at her, he tucked a strand of short, jagged hair behind her ear. "You're beautiful," he whispered, and snuggled in behind her.

A good night's sleep did not come as easily as Katie would have hoped. Her dreams were vivid with images of Mensur's dead body, his haunting sneer etched in rigor mortis. She thrashed as she saw little Marko running in terror, getting nowhere, and she screamed when she saw the medics carry out Lucas's mangled, lifeless corpse. Three times she woke up, dripping sweat and screaming, and three times Lucas had to reassure her back to sleep.

She was only able to keep her eyes open on the following day because she was terrified of what she'd see if she closed them. Not that it mattered, since she was forced to sit on an overly hard chair in a too-air-conditioned room and dredge up every horrific image she was trying to forget. She studied the walnut wood paneling without really seeing it while a different General Corporal Prime Minister of the Federal Reserve, plucked every detail from her mind.

As the official thumbed through a file on the desk, Katie thought of Lucas, currently being questioned in another room. Before they were separated, he held her and whispered in her ear: "Stay strong. Janek needs us." She put her hand against her cheek and flushed, remembering how good his face felt against hers. It wasn't the time or the place for an epiphany, but nonetheless, she had one.

She had finally found a man she couldn't reject.

Not because he was faultless—she hadn't overlooked the stack of sweatpants on his bedroom shelf—but simply because she didn't want to. She smiled. There was hope for her after all.

Having hope suddenly made everything all right. No matter what, her future was still bright. She made a vow, right there, that somehow she was going to help others have their chance at a bright future—starting with Janek. His fate depended on how she depicted his life-saving change of behavior.

Katie straightened in her chair, looked the General Corporal Prime Minister of the Federal Reserve the Second straight in the eye, and accepted the onslaught of questions with a whole new fervor.

***

Katie blinked her eyes several times. The bright sunlight was a stark contrast to the fluorescent lights in the wood-paneled room where she'd spent the last several hours. The more she blinked, the more she could make out the figures standing in the distance. Lucas walked up to meet her, encircling her in his embrace before leading her toward Stanley, Marko, and Kata, who were waiting in front of the Jeep that would drive them to the airport.

Katie opened her arms as Marko ran to her—for what she refused to believe was the last time. She kissed the top of his head. "I'll never forget you, okay?" She gave him an encouraging smile as she wiped her tears with the back of her hand. It hadn't been thirty seconds and already she was a complete bawl-baby.

He wrapped his arms around her neck, nearly strangling her with his hold. "Will you come back?" He could barely get the words out through his sobs, and his tears were running hot down her neck.

She pulled back to look into his big, dark eyes. "Yes I will, Marko. I promise you someday I will come back."

Stanley gently pulled the boy away and Kata dropped her head against Katie's shoulder. Katie felt the outline of each and every bone in the woman's back as she ran a consoling hand over her. When Kata lifted her head, she held Katie's cheeks in her calloused hands before running all of her fingers through Katie's cropped hair.

"Thank you," Katie said, knowing Kata wouldn't understand anything else.

As Kata turned away, Stanley stepped forward.

"Thank you Stanley. Thank you for everything," Katie sobbed, wrapping her arms around the man who would never again be just Stanley Speedo to her. "There's so much to say—I...I...don't know where to start."

"Shhh." Stanley pressed her head against his shoulder. "I will miss you, neighbor. I'm sorry for the circumstances, but I'm glad fate brought you back into my life."

"Me too," Katie sniffed. She had to be satisfied with that because she was crying so hard she couldn't say more.

Lucas stepped up to clap one hand on Stanley's shoulder. "Please Stanley, I want you to have this." He pressed a slip of paper into Stanley's thick hands.

Releasing his hold on Katie, Stanley unfolded the paper. For a second, Katie feared his eyes would actually pop out of their sockets as he scanned the contents.

A tear, followed by another, crept down Stanley's cheek. He didn't bother to wipe them away. He put his hand to his heart as he shook his head. "I cannot. I cannot possibly accept. Thank you, Lucas."

"Of course you can," Lucas insisted. "Consider it repayment for saving two lives—plus a pair of pajamas, some Walmart shampoo, and a shirt. Oh, and Sonja."

Stanley looked at him quizzically. "Sonja?"

"Katie's Bosnian toothbrush." Lucas shot a glance at Katie to see the blush layering her cheeks, and chuckled.

"It is not necessary," Stanley protested. "Had it not been for my brother, your lives would not have been in jeopardy."

"This would have happened with or without Janek's help. It's fortunate for us that Janek *was* involved or we never would have ended up in your shed," Lucas countered.

Stanley opened his mouth to give another rebuttal, but before he could speak, Lucas closed Stanley's hand around the check. "Please accept—if not for everything you have done for Katie and me, then for Marko and Indira—use it to give them better lives."

Stanley dipped his head, fighting back a cry. "You are a good man, Lucas."

"So are you, Stanley—a very good man."

"Take good care of Katie pretty lady."

"You can count on it."

Stanley pulled Katie into another stronghold. As he did, she was able to snatch a peek at the check and nearly had a heart attack. Thinking she must have seen too many zeros, she peeked again. It was no mistake; the writing matched the numbers. She shuddered, but she didn't know if was out of relief for Stanley or fear of how she'd reimburse Lucas even a fraction of that sum.

"This doesn't count as my trip to Bosnia. I'm coming back to see you, Stanley," Katie promised.

"I'll hold you to that promise. My country is very beautiful—and I swear, despite your experience, peaceful."

"I know." She squeezed his hand.

***

Katie stopped short at the sight of the Waverlys' jet that had been sent to convey them back to England, and gasped. Lucas had to make a quick step around her to avoid stumbling. He grabbed her wrist and pulled her across the tarmac.

As the engines began to hum around her, Katie felt her heart race. She wanted to blame her surge of adrenaline on the thrill of having a jet all to herself, but with the way Lucas's eyes were watching her, she knew otherwise.

"Is that all my life is worth to you—half the amount of that check?" she teased, trying to cut the sizzle in the air.

"Of course not, Rabbit. You weren't even close to half the amount. Restitution on stolen toothbrushes isn't cheap."

She giggled, thinking how proud his mother would have been of his smart mouth. Then she turned serious. "Lucas, I don't know how

I'm going to be able to repay you half of that money. I mean, I'll find a way, but it might take a while."

He looked as though she'd stepped on his heart. "I wasn't expecting repayment."

She wanted to stab herself in the jugular for putting that look on his face. "Lucas, I'm sorry…I…I didn't mean…"

His mouth twitched into that heart-stopping grin and she almost did a retreating backbend onto the seat as he scooted into her. He smelled like soap and brand-new clothes.

"Maybe we could call it your signing bonus to a company that is no longer operating in the black?" His eyes glinted. He caressed a path along her neck and the curves of her jaw with the back of his two fingers.

Every speck of her rippled with delight at his touch. She had to make an effort to steady the exultant hum in her head, but she managed to put on her best professional front. "Despite that under your employ, I've been given a concussion, poisoned with alcohol, taken hostage, knifed, deprived of sleep, *and* pronounced a slut-bag in front of my government, I will accept the position."

"Thank you." He bowed his head ceremoniously. "And despite the fact that since employing you, I have been puked on, broken my engagement, shot, deprived of sleep, given away my life's savings, *and* have gained the reputation of a philanderer, I welcome you aboard."

He moved in even closer, eyes smoldering.

"Now that we've got that settled…you never did tell me what the status is with that boyfriend of yours."

She gave him her grandest smile and tried not to melt into the Waverlys' fancy-pants upholstery. "What boyfriend?"

"Brilliant," he breathed, smoothing his lips over hers.

"Wait!" she yelped, shimmying away from him. "Kissing cousins cause catastrophic confusion and create colossal consequences!"

"Sorry?" He blinked, his confusion morphing into laughter.

She wanted to jab a pitchfork into her head for her stupidity. Why didn't she think before expressing her imbecile proverbs? Ignoring the flames in her cheeks, she attempted to gather her composure. "What I mean is—are we still trying to be cousins? Because that just might be a little too creepy for me."

He studied her for a few intense moments. "No more cousins…but how you do feel about interoffice dating?" His lips twisted into a grin.

"It sounds like a big mistake to me." She raised a seductive eyebrow and pressed against him.

"Probably." His grin turned mischievous and he captured her mouth with his.

Chapter Forty-One

"Andrew!"

Katie saw his form jogging toward them and tore across the tarmac of the private terminal to meet him, her gimpy leg trying to keep up with the rest of her.

"How are you?" he wheezed in response to her long embrace, giving her a twirl as he gently lifted her from her feet.

Puddles welled in her eyes as she took in the faint bruises and cut still healing on his face. "It's good to see you, friend."

"It's good to have you back. I've missed you, Duchess."

Katie rolled her eyes and groaned. "That's a name I could go the rest of my life without hearing again."

"Too bad." He winced as she bit his shoulder.

Strolling behind, carrying her backpack and holding his bandaged side, Lucas nearly did a double take watching the pair's interaction. Andrew released Katie and turned his attention to Lucas. A strained moment of silent deliberation ensued as each man sized up the other. Then Andrew reached out and pulled Lucas into an emotional hug that expressed what he could not speak. Lucas returned the gesture. Katie felt her bottom lip tremble and marveled that it took near-death to dissipate years of animosity.

"They told me a family member would be waiting, but I'll admit, I didn't expect it to be you," Lucas stated.

Andrew dipped his head. "I begged for a second chance given that I buggered up my last airport pickup."

"And I came along just to make sure he didn't bugger it up again," a familiar brogue came from out of nowhere behind them.

Katie's impulse was to run and knock Mr. Scott down with a big bear hug, but then she saw how Lucas's eyes ignited into an explosion of chocolaty fireworks and knew this moment belonged to him. Lucas wiped the tears that drizzled down his rugged jaw line with the cuff of his sleeve, dropped the backpack, and sprinted into the waiting embrace of his uncle Avery.

Andrew picked up the backpack and slung it over his shoulder, then put an arm around Katie. "Love the new hairdo," he smirked, tugging at one of her short, untamed curls.

"Thanks." She nudged against him with her shoulder. "I did it myself."

The two walked along companionably, allowing the long-overdue reunion between uncle and nephew to take place.

"I never thought I'd see you back in England," Lucas's voice trembled with emotion.

"Neither did I, lad, neither did I," Mr. Scott agreed, resting a hand atop his nephew's shoulder. He beamed down the tarmac toward Katie. "A remarkable lass once told me, 'A home, if not left from time to time, can become a cage.'"

Lucas followed his uncle's gaze. "She is bloody remarkable, isn't she?"

"That she is. I'm chuffed to see you love her as much as I do. I have to admit, I had at one time hoped—"

"Is it that obvious?" Lucas interrupted.

"Lordy! I haven't seen a man so besotted since I first met your Auntie Jane."

Lucas blushed like a young schoolboy revealing his first crush.

They stood for a moment appreciating the animated exchange between Katie and Andrew before Mr. Scott, radiating with perfect happiness, broke the silence.

Patting his favorite nephew on the back, he teased, "I daresay you'll fit into her Amazing Plan quite nicely."

Acknowledgements

To everyone who helped and supported me through this endeavor, a big giant thank you. Especially to those of you who read the very first draft and are still around to pick up this final version—if that's not true friendship I don't know what is. Thanks to my family and Erik for your encouragement and support, and thanks to my Moab friends for not rolling your eyes (in front of me) during the past years when I talked incessantly about my book. I'm sure you thought this day would never come. From now on, I'll try to talk about something new—like maybe the sequel I'm working on.

Thanks to my little group in the Salt Lake City chapter of the League of Utah Writers, Marsha, Peggy, Mary, Nolan, Gordon and Margie. Thanks, Margie for becoming my writing buddy. I know I never would have finished this book without your encouragement.

Clint Johnson, the best thing I ever did was attend your workshop. Thanks for teaching me the difference between sucky writing and quality writing. And thanks for believing I had the talent to do something with my manuscript. Thanks Melissa at Media Chick for the advice and mad editing skills, and Thanks Nellie for the amazing cover art, and Annie for your "tweaks" (P.S. That wasn't meant to sound naughty).

I know that's a lot of thanks going around. I'm almost finished. To anyone who is reading this, THANK YOU!

Made in the USA
Charleston, SC
10 June 2012